SILENT SHE SLEEPS

Leaves slapped Josie's face as she ran. She was certain they meant to kill her. She heard the trooper following her, his heavy breath, the crunch of the leaves, the cracking of sticks. As they came to the creek, the man took Josie's arm. He lifted her into the air. "I'm not going to hurt you!" he shouted. Josie kicked at him savagely. He was still carrying his shotgun and his face was red from the effort of running. He set his gun down in the grass and knelt before her so she could see his face. "Now listen to me!" he said. He held her by her elbows, pinning them behind her back. She stopped struggling. They were both breathing heavily. She saw his shotgun. She kept staring at it as he said something Josie couldn't understand. When he had said the thing, she looked at him. His face was nearly against hers. She smelt the stink of tobacco on his breath and wrestled against his hold on her to be set free.

At the trailer she saw Jack cuffed and being pushed into one of the three sedans. Jack looked back toward her, his face bloody with a fine scarlet sheen; it was the only face of Jack Hazard she would ever remember. She shouted at him: "JAAACK!"

Jack looked down between his knees, ashamed.

The trooper holding her said in the calmest voice imaginable, "You don't want to talk to him, honey. That man there is the one that killed your mamma."

Craig S. Smith earned a doctorate of philosophy from Southern Illinois University at Carbondale. He lives with his wife Martha in Switzerland. *Silent She Sleeps* is his first

CRAIG SMITH

Silent
She
Sleeps

Mandarin

A Mandarin Paperback
SILENT SHE SLEEPS

First published in Great Britain 1997
by Mandarin Paperbacks
and William Heinemann
imprints of Reed International Books Ltd
Michelin House, 81 Fulham Road, London sw3 6rb
and Auckland, Melbourne, Singapore and Toronto

Copyright © Craig Smith 1997
The author has asserted his moral rights

A CIP catalogue record for this title
is available from the British Library
ISBN 0 7493 2330 2

Typeset in 10 on 12 point Bembo
by Intype London Ltd
Printed and bound in Great Britain
by BPC Paperbacks Ltd
a member of The British Printing Company Ltd

For Martha

... when a husband and wife have
a single heart, they bring ruin to
their enemies, joy to their friends ...

Odyssey Homer

Part One

Lues Creek

Lues Creek comes out of the wooded hill country of northern Lues County. Surrounding it is once prosperous mining country full of crossroads with names like Gallows Hill, Pilatesburg, Clems Hollow, Prophets Grove, Carbine Ridge, Codswallop, and Huree. The creek tunes up fast on its run to a place called Hazard Falls, then spews out over a polished stone ledge in the way that only wild things can. A thousand feet below, the water crashes into Lues Creek Canyon and breaks apart on the wet stones so that the lower canyon walls are hidden in mist. The creek gathers itself again a short way on and carves a crooked path through a silent woods. Six miles or so below the falls Lues Creek joins up with the town of Lues and its lonesome, crooked sister, West Lues Creek. From here to the Ohio River at Pauper Bluff, Lues Creek runs on through places with no names. The roads are unpaved and uncommon; it is a hill-locked land full of deer, timber rattlers, and folks who are solitary and cautious to a fault. There are no fences and no farms; what cabins you might see you know to avoid. The locals survive on pure stubbornness. It has always been this way and remains so today. It is a place where every turn affords a haunting vision of primeval time and every story, if someone bothers to tell it, comes down as legend . . .

Hazard Falls

It was a gray Thursday afternoon, and the students were skipping a class in General Science. They had been out for about an hour. They wore their fraternity and sorority sweatshirts and all had on jeans and either boots or tennis shoes; the two young men had blue nylon day packs slung across their backs. One of the packs was already empty, the other was mostly flattened; they all carried a beer can as they hiked. They were laughing. The woods about them was alive with springtime. The earth was black. The trees were close-set. There was a faint haze to the air, an old quiet to things. Last up the trail was Melody Mason, who was smoking a Lucky Strike filterless cigarette and shouting to the others that she needed to pee. She was a city girl and the thought of pulling her jeans down in the woods was more a fear of bugs and weeds than of mixed company. Still, Melody didn't really have a choice. She was a girl who liked her beer a lot. When her companions ignored her first complaints, she called out again, "I'm going behind this tree. Nobody look! You guys! Don't look!" Bob Tanner, who was in the lead, called back that he was going to look, even though he kept pushing forward up the trail. Tossing her beer can into a patch of wild flowers, Melody slipped her jeans over her hips and screamed back that he had better not. She heard their distant laughter, then nothing more.

Melody was a plump, pretty girl. She had dark hair and there was a certain sparkle in her eyes. She was a girl with a reputation, she knew, but it was mostly exaggerated. Melody had a bit of a problem with alcohol, that was all, and boys took advantage of it sometimes. Melody had been at Lues State almost a full year without indulging in these woods. There was plenty to do in her sorority house and in some of the dives in Slewville as everyone called Lues. She was only in the woods today because her suitemates, Cat and Susie, had talked her into it and because Bob Tanner was with them. They were all taking Melody to Hazard Falls. Still squatting beside her tree trunk, Melody rolled her eyes: Hazard Falls was some kind of slew-heaven and she had told them so, like that meant something. Melody took a drag on her Lucky, then keeping it in her lips, stood up.

2

She didn't recognize the poison sumac she had squatted in. She pulled her jeans over her hips with some effort and looked out across the greening forest. She sucked it in, causing comic little puffs of smoke from her Lucky, and bounced a couple of times as she snapped her jeans to, then stepped back into the path. For the first time, Melody was struck with a chill of fear. Her friends had ditched her. She looked at the trail ahead of her, then back the way they had come. A palpable threat, the silence of the woods went on for miles. Melody felt sure someone was back up the trail watching her. Nervously, she dropped her cigarette on the path, leaving it to burn out, and started running in the direction she had last seen the others taking. Repeatedly, she glanced back over her shoulder as she ran. Melody stopped herself almost immediately. She listened for her friends between her desperate gasps for breath. Ahead of her was the muffled roar of Hazard Falls, but that was all that she heard. Her voice squeaked, "You guys?" She repeated herself and looked behind her again. The trail was hazy and empty. She swore with a whisper and decided to start on. That was when the hand grabbed her. Melody screamed, and still screaming, she spun around into the face of Bob Tanner. He was shouting too.

It was a joke. The others came out from behind different trees, laughing at her. Melody knew it was because she was *city* and they were all from places like Raccoon Holler and Frog Pile Junction. "You guys scared the pee out of me!" she confessed, now laughing as hard as they were.

Mocking her, Jim Burkeshire squeaked, " . . . *scared the pee out of me.*" He was like that, really smart but not always nice. He was Bob Tanner's frat brother, and she didn't care if he took a flying leap into this frigging canyon they were hiking to. Melody let it go without responding to him. She usually did when guys treated her like that.

Bob Tanner gave her a smile, "Come on, you got to see the falls. This place is great." He hadn't let go of her yet.

His hand was hot. The touch of it was nice, and Melody wished he would get up the nerve to ask her out. He had only been trying since October.

Melody asked for a beer, and Cat Sommerville pulled the last can from Jim Burkeshire's pack. "You guys, we drank all twenty-four!" Cat announced. They all laughed and accused each other of being alcoholics.

As soon as they started up the rocks which guarded the falls, the footing grew treacherous. Melody downed her beer in two final gulps and threw her can back into the woods, belching prettily. The five of them scrambled across the rocks. Bob Tanner and Jim Burkeshire raced ahead of the others to the crest. Susie Hill and Melody found themselves last in line, staring up at Cat's tight little virgin butt.

"*You guys!*" whispered Susie Hill, "*we drank all twenty-four!*"

Melody smiled up at Cat evilly, whispering, "Slip, bitch!"

Cat's black glossy hair swung freely over her shoulders. She looked like Ali McGraw, or tried to anyway. Briefly, she looked back toward them, smiling.

As soon as she turned away, Susie Hill responded, "Fall, cunt!"

"So is this place like *safe*?" Melody asked.

Susie laughed, "Fuck no! That's why we're drunk." She scampered up the rock, then stepped over the crest. Like the others, she passed out of sight. Melody heard Susie screaming as if she had gone over the cliff, then listened to the faint reverberating echoes of Susie's voice coming back from the canyon walls. Once more Melody looked behind her. This time she wasn't disappointed. About a hundred feet below her, a man was standing beside a tree. Melody couldn't say exactly how old he was. She saw very little of him actually, since he pulled back out of sight immediately. He was probably in his twenties, she guessed. He was average height. He had dark features but at such a distance Melody could get no distinct impression of him, other than her certainty that

4

he was a slew. The denim jacket and feed-store hat were the giveaways. He looked like one of those Georgia hicks in *Deliverance*.

Squeal like a pig! Melody shivered and pulled herself quickly toward the crest of the boulder. She looked over her shoulder once as she did so and saw he was looking at her again. She fought the impulse to shout out something stupid. She just wanted to get with the others. At the top Melody saw her friends safely below, and her fright of the slew faded. When she looked back, he was gone, or hiding at least. She was safe; he wasn't coming after her. He knew better with Bob and Jim so close by. Melody focused on the canyon briefly. It was nearly a quarter of a mile long but only two hundred feet across at its widest point. On all four sides, blood-red sandstone walls, glistening with the mist of the falls, descended perpendicularly to the stream below. This had the effect of making the thousand-foot gorge seem even deeper, if that was possible, and despite Melody Mason's determination to be unimpressed with Lues Creek Canyon, she was excited by it, a little.

Okay, she thought, *the place is incredible.* She hadn't expected anything like this view. Even a confirmed city girl had to take a moment for this. This was great! She urged herself toward the edge of the rock where she could get a better look. On her end of the canyon the falls poured over a rock that was still above her. Thirty or forty feet below the top of the waterfall, a natural stone ledge, about the width of a country road, made it possible to walk out from her side of the canyon, cross behind the falls, then go onto the other side and climb out. Because it was so dangerous, a wooden guardrail ran along the rock ledge. Like a lot of things in Lues, it was slipshod workmanship; Melody could see that much even at a distance. The boards were warped and rotted looking.

As Melody took in the sight of the canyon, Bob and Jim were running back and forth behind the falls. They were soaked and laughing. Melody laughed too and had the impulse to join them. This side of the waterfall, Susie Hill and Cat Sommerville huddled in the niche of the wall twenty feet back from the guardrail. They too were soaked and laughing, and Melody decided they had already run under the falls once. It looked great, Melody thought. Beyond the falls, the ledge narrowed down to a couple of feet at one heart-stopping moment, then widened to about the width of a city sidewalk before it joined into the boulders on the other side. They were planning on crossing the canyon here and then going up where the falls actually began. There were no guardrails up there, and the rocks were slippery, or so Bob had told her. All afternoon Melody had heard about the height of the falls and the kids who had jumped to their death or fallen, but a thousand feet had been meaningless until she had seen it. Even from here, well back of any sort of precipice, the sight of such a descent made her knees quiver and her heart pound uncontrollably.

Melody looked down toward the bottom of the gorge. Thousands of boulders were strewn so thickly in the stream bed that the water trickled in various channels throughout the canyon floor. There was no ground visible. The water collected near the far end and seemed to disappear into the rock. The canyon was noticeably cooler than the air just behind her, and for a hypnotic moment, Melody considered the lure of falling. It was easier than she dared think about, as simple as the dream of flight. Nervously, she looked back to see if her slew was coming up over the rocks. He was still out of sight, and she was sure he couldn't have gotten closer without her seeing him, but then they were always disappearing in *Deliverance* too. They just never went away.

Bob Tanner came out from under the falls and waved for Melody to come down to the ledge and join them. He shouted something but his voice was lost in the thunder of the falls. Melody looked down into the gorge again, then shook herself out of her trance and stepped carefully into

6

the cut-rock stairway. She ducked under a hanging slab and breathed in the moisture of the stone. Fifteen feet below, Melody came out into the misty air at the very edge of the world. To her left, the canyon opened under her. To her right a vertical wall of red sandstone soared up toward the source of the falls. Directly before her, Melody saw Cat and Susie still standing close against the wall. Her suitemates were grinning as they watched Bob and Jim still running senselessly behind the waterfall, still howling like lunatics. Melody walked toward the two girls. "I think someone is following us," she said. By now the slew was simply a perverse curiosity she thought to share with them. A single slew was nothing to worry about as long as the five of them stayed together. Cat asked her what she meant. Melody pointed back toward the crest of the boulder and stepped out toward the edge of the canyon again. Gripping the wooden railing firmly, she looked down briefly; the mist rose up around the rocks a thousand feet under her. She backed away almost unconsciously, then gestured toward the rocks, "I don't think he came out of the woods, but there was a slew following us along the trail." Melody added with a wince, "I think he watched me pee."

Susie's lip curled, "He probably went up to sniff it after you left."

Cat gagged, "You guys! That's gross!"

Susie shouted up toward the rocks, "I hate slews!"

Melody joined her in chorus, "Go home, Slew!" Their voices echoed inside the canyon: *slews, slew, ew, ew.*

Cat tried to shush them. "You guys, what if he hears you?"

At their backs, there were screams. All three turned in time to see Bob Tanner and Jim Burkeshire coming at them with their arms flinging about crazily like a couple of lunatic slews. They ran together, Bob at the very lip of the rock. Bob was coming right for Melody. Jim grabbed Susie, pushing her back along the ledge, still screaming incoherently. Bob took

7

Melody by the shoulders and turned her out toward the canyon so she was leaning precariously into the old railing. Over her own screams, Bob was shouting maniacally, "Don't jump, Mel! Don't do it!" His damp hands held Melody tightly, but the force of her weight, coupled with his pushing and tugging against her, snapped the water-rotted board she was leaning against. Her weight pulled her out into space. Bob's grip wasn't as good as it should have been, and as he saw the board breaking free he had no chance to adjust his hold on her. Melody could feel her weight pulling out of his hands in the next instant. The sudden panic in Bob's broad face was obvious. Melody's arms slipped entirely out of his fingers. She felt herself stopped as Bob still held her sweatshirt, but that was all he held her by. He had lost control. The cotton sleeves stretched out slightly as they faced one another. They separated imperceptibly and her screams went mute in the next desperate second. His voice too went silent. The only sign of their struggle was written in their widened stunned eyes. Melody didn't even know if the others saw what was happening; she could see nothing but the face of Bob Tanner. She felt her body pulling back further. The sweatshirt pulled up gently over her soft belly; it inched up across her back.

Melody whispered calmly, "A little help, here." It was all the breath she had to offer.

She saw Bob's face glisten in a horrible sudden sweat. She saw the red stone wall, then the gray sky above. Vaguely, she heard both Susie and Cat scream something. In panic, she looked below. She heard herself whimpering. She looked once more at Bob Tanner. He was leaning toward her, his face white and wet now, his eyes focused on the canyon below. Melody's hands clawed at his forearms. It was her only chance. Her sweatshirt slipped up as high as her shoulders. Her fingers slipped over the wet cloth of his sweatshirt, then her fingernails caught through the thick cotton and tore into his flesh like talons. He was coming with her, she thought

8

wildly, and the panic froze her fingers so that she couldn't let go.

Jim Burkeshire stepped up beside Bob. His fingers slipped between Melody's bare belly and her jeans. He jerked her toward him easily, and as Melody caught her own balance, she pushed past both Bob and Jim. Bob windmilled suddenly at the edge and Jim knocked him back to keep him from falling.

Melody stumbled into the niche of the wall, gasping like someone who's come out from under water. She heard Susie and Cat still screaming. She heard Bob answer all of them loudly, "I had her!" He turned to Jim, "I had her! What were you doing?" He walked toward Melody, who shivered as he got closer, "I had you, I was teasing!" Melody curled away from him. When he came closer still, she staggered past him, making her way toward the broken railing. Sickly, she got on her hands and knees as she got closer to the precipice. She thought she was going to vomit. Irresistibly, Melody looked down into the gorge and heard the others telling Bob to leave her alone. Her gut somersaulted as she realized she would *still* be falling if Jim hadn't caught hold of her. She studied the mist as it shifted slightly amid the rocks below. *Still falling!* The thought almost caused her to pass out. She blinked, and sucked at the air, a long, deep gasp. She was glad she was on her hands and knees. Despite herself, she pulled back slightly and laid her forearms on the stone to get better balance. *Now!* she thought. At just that moment her thousand-foot freefall would have ended. Blackness edged around her vision, the center alone in focus.

That was when she saw something on the rocks below. Even as Melody stared, the mist covered it. Now it cleared again. Almost an illusion, it was utterly still, tiny, distant, the color of flesh: *a nude body,* she thought. She squinted; it was just a speck on the rocks. Melody felt a hand taking hold of her jeans just below the small of her back. "Are you okay?" It was Jim. The backs of his fingers were touching her bare flesh. The feeling bothered her. She looked down to the figure below. "There's someone down there!" she told him.

Letting go of her jeans, Jim Burkeshire knelt beside her. The others came closer and leaned over to look as well.

"I think it's a body," Melody whispered.

Susie was the first to respond, straightening up. "Oh, God."

"You see it?" Melody asked.

"Oh, God," Susie repeated.

Melody saw it clearly now and felt a cloying certainty that someone had fallen. It wasn't a hallucination. The imagined sensation of her own fall overcame her.

Bob came between them, "Where!" They all stared straight down into the abyss. "I don't see it," he said.

Melody shook herself out of her stupor. "There!" she cried irritably. "Right below us!"

"I see it!" Jim shouted, pointing. "It's just beside the waterfall."

Cat, standing over him, jumped excitedly, "There! There! I see it too!"

Melody screamed urgently, "You see it?"

"It's a body!" Jim cried. "Jesus! Someone jumped!"

Bob stared dumbly, "What is it? Where?" He was baffled.

"Someone jumped," Jim answered him. "That's got to be it."

Bob couldn't believe it. He stared, but he didn't see it. None of them did now. The mist seemed to swallow the image, so they were almost convinced it wasn't real. Finally, Cat said they had better check below to be sure. "I mean I don't want to call the police if it's like a sheet of plastic or something."

Susie giggled, "Maybe it's a blow-up doll. Some dork was up here poking his squeeze and pop! There she goes, folks!" Susie made a wavy line of flight with her hand and arm, indicating a swirling, drifting descent. They all laughed nervously; then almost in a single motion, they all looked back down into the canyon.

Lues Creek Canyon
They went back the way they had come. It was a long, circuitous descent off Hazard Falls back into the woods. Melody watched for the slew, but he was gone. It was nearly thirty minutes before they came to the trail along Lues Creek well below the canyon, and they had hurried to make it that fast. They followed the trail until they were forced into the creek, then waded upstream into the rocky vaults that closed off any view of the falls from underneath it. They swam a short way, and finally, waist deep in the cold water, they came inside the great red rock walls and saw the falls as few ever get to see them. From the floor of the canyon they couldn't see the ledge they had stood on, nor even the guardrail; it was simply too distant. The wall seemed a giant red monolithic slab over the center of which a thread of white water poured. The bulk of it fell in a long heavy stream that crashed over the rocks far in front of them with a terrible energy. Some of the stream at the top of the falls broke off from the main strand, spraying apart so that it seemed almost like rain falling over that end of the canyon. Even a quarter of a mile away, the air was thick with mist from the waterfall. All five of them pushed toward the falls, but because of the heavy rocks, they soon took separate routes. Melody found she was walking in water no more than knee deep, then suddenly she was into it as high as her chest. Slowly she worked her way into the canyon. It was cold work. Overhead, the sky was stone gray. The light of day seemed to be fading, although that was only an illusion; it was still mid-afternoon. Melody saw Cat moving ahead of her well to her left while Jim Burkeshire, close on Melody's right, emerged from behind a small group of boulders.

Momentarily she lost sight of Susie and Bob. "You guys okay?" she called.

Bob appeared suddenly as he came out of the water and stood on one of the boulders, looking at the falls. "This is crazy!" he said.

Without looking at him, Jim pushed forward seriously, "So go back," he said. Bob Tanner leaped into the water again and pushed on. If they were teasing him, at least they were all getting wet.

As they drew nearer to the waterfall, visibility was more difficult. Melody felt the water moving around her hips, then stepped up on a smooth boulder. She imagined seeing the slew waiting for her and shivered with the thought. He had just been out in the woods, she told herself. He wasn't *following* them. Then the thought crossed her mind that the slew had tossed someone off the ledge; that was why he had been out here in the first place. *And I'm the only one who saw him!* she told herself. The thought frightened her vaguely. She looked for the others. Cat was standing on one of the bigger rocks now. She was totally soaked. Her black hair was flat against her scalp and she was trembling. Despite her fears, Melody smiled, whispering, "Get pneumonia, whore!" Melody couldn't see the others. Maybe, she thought, the slew had heard them saying they had better check it out and had come into the canyon to wait for them. Maybe Cat and she were the only ones left. "You guys see anything?" Melody called. She knew they hadn't or they would have said something; she just wanted to hear their voices, something besides the roar of the falls.

Nobody answered.

Cat looked down at her sickly, then jumped back into the water. They were getting closer to the falls. Melody thought the guys were in front of her on her right, but then she saw a man's dark lean figure moving close to Cat. Tensely, Melody watched. The two figures glided beside each other now, and

12

Melody realized it was Jim. Susie came up beside Melody, her eyes locked on Cat as she whispered, "Drown, slut!"

Melody smiled. Together they watched Bob climb up on another stone. He looked directly into the falls.

"To your right!" Melody called.

He jumped down again and angled right. Melody saw that Susie was staring ahead vacantly.

"Come on!" Melody commanded. "We're almost there."

Susie answered, "Fuck it!" and plunged forward. They all wandered among the heavy stones just in front of the falls trying to find a way through. It was a labyrinth of narrow, watery passageways, the boulders sometimes as high as fifteen feet. Jim Burkeshire stood up on a rock and stared about. Melody had lost sight of the rest of them. The falls were almost directly overhead; she still needed to push to the right. A heavy mist poured over her face. "You guys?" she shouted.

Jim Burkeshire answered from his rock, "Still here!"

Bob's voice cut through the roar of the falls from well off to the right, "You guys really saw something?"

Up to her waist in the cold water, Melody waded around a rock that was twice as tall as she was. She found two more and climbed up into the crack between them, only to come face to face with more stones. Melody was soaked, discouraged, and convinced now that what they had seen was just some reflection or, like Cat had thought, a sheet of plastic.

Susie called to them from behind Melody, her voice shaking with cold, "Let's go home. It was nothing."

Jim Burkeshire answered from far to the right, "Another minute!"

Cat screamed.

Pat Bitts

Dressed in his waders and slicker, a plastic cap slipped over his felt stetson, Sheriff Pat Bitts splashed back into Lues

13

Creek Canyon along with two uniformed Lues city police officers and his own deputy, Jason Miller. Bitts, who had known Lues Creek Canyon since he was a boy and was now fifty-seven years old, picked his way carefully along the east edge of the creek to avoid the deep center with its occasional sink holes. Miller, without the aid of waders, followed Bitts less fastidiously. The policemen took the shortest route, straight up the center of the canyon. Bitts and his deputy got to the base of the falls first and saw the dimly reflected lights of the other two coming through the twilight. The police officers were still within the dark labyrinth of boulders which lay before the falls. Bitts cast the light of his Coleman about but didn't see the corpse. The campus security officer had described the location before he had gone on home, soaked and pretty much seven-eighths of the way to a jim-dandy cold. Bitts pointed his light in front of the falls, which was where he had said the corpse was. He saw nothing at all. Bitts had to shout to be heard, and called to Miller, who was standing beside him, "That boy said she was in *front* of the falls?" Miller nodded, and the two of them shone their lights fruitlessly into the flashing sheet of water, then into a couple of sink holes. Their lights searched again behind several boulders, then into the raging white water before them. Finally Miller's light fell on a particularly violent sink hole and he shouted that he saw something. Bitts aimed his light at it also. The hole was fully fifteen feet in diameter, rimmed partially in boulders. The water churned relentlessly. Something was in there all right. He saw what appeared to be hair, then the white lump of a human shoulder. He watched it spin then slam against the rock. The body was suddenly swallowed up while the two men watched in sick fascination.

Bitts studied one of the rock ledges behind the hole. The ledge afforded access to reach in and grab at the body. Seeing the opportunity, Bitts started forward; Miller followed. Miller was short, maybe five-seven in his *thick* socks, but he could dead-lift a big man with a single hand. Bitts had seen him do it in too many fights to count. Bitts himself was six and a half feet tall. Before he had got *sense*, Bitts had backed down from nothing but God. Bitts braced himself on the rock and holding Miller in an interlocking wrist grip, let the younger man lean out to snatch the corpse from the maelstrom. On his second try, Miller caught hold of the long hair. The two city policemen came next to Bitts and Miller. One of them caught the arm of the corpse. As he brought the body toward them, the second officer took the other arm. Slowly they lifted the bruised, split body up from the churning waters. Now the four of them waded back with the body caught between them to a huge flat rock and laid the victim across it. The torso had been ripped open beneath the ribs in a gaping wound that stretched from the kidneys past the navel, then down to the vagina, a savage evisceration. The action of the sink hole had made it worse. The corpse was wrapped in its own guts. Bitts slipped on his latex gloves, while his deputy got his camera unpacked. The cops stepped closer to watch Bitts and Miller, but they said nothing.

Bitts looked at his watch. It was 8:20. The flesh was still supple, no sign of rigor mortis, not even in the smaller muscles. While his deputy photographed the corpse, Bitts took mental notes. The skull had been struck repeatedly. Deep gashes lay under the long, thick ropes of bronze-colored hair. One of the eyelids was ripped open like a flap of cloth. The face was puffed up, the nose smashed flat. Bitts pushed the cracked lips apart and saw what was left of the teeth sheered off at the gums or broken partially and embedded in the cheeks. He had a pretty good idea she had lost her teeth while being swept about in the sink hole, but he held the mouth open while Miller photographed it with his Pentax. He saw a thin, deep ligature that encircled her neck, just under the jawbones. He saw bruises below the ligature, the marks of a strangler's hands. The wrists had deep

15

indentations and so too had the ankles. She had been bound for several hours. There was a good deal of swelling. He touched the ribs and found two broken. Across the ripped torso, Bitts's eyes came to rest on what looked to be the letter *h*, but he couldn't be sure, even in the direct glare of his Coleman. The mark was faint and thin, the work of a razor. The cuts were a day or two old and had begun to heal.

Bitts looked overhead. The falls sent a fine spray over his face. He had assumed, when the call first came in, that the victim had fallen. Bitts's theory had been that his anonymous callers had been with the woman on the ledge above; she had gone through the railing and dropped to her death. They had telephoned his office anonymously simply out of fear. That, he had decided, or it was a prank call. Good theories, until they got into a head-on with the facts. The woman hadn't fallen and this wasn't a prank. He pointed his Coleman through the gray light toward various rocks close by. He was looking for clothes. He found none. Bitts reached under his slicker to an interior pocket and pulled out a neatly folded body bag. He spread it out beside the corpse. With Miller helping, they slipped the shoulders of the woman's corpse into the bag. Next they brought the sack under her hips, and finally Miller put the legs in. They adjusted the bag and brought the zipper unceremoniously toward the head.

All four men took the east edge of the canyon on their return, the water consistently quiet on this side. At the end of the canyon, in absolute darkness now, Bitts managed to keep the water out of his waders, as he had going in, by walking along a submerged ledge. He had first found the footing when he was a boy. Back then, he had used the ledge to keep his nose out of the water, since in those days he couldn't yet swim. He let that memory, his first time into Lues Creek Canyon, wash over him as they waded out of the serpentine defile. The others were too wet to bother with where they stepped, and putting the body bag in the water between them, swam back out of the canyon to the trail. They hiked briefly through the dark path to the trailhead, the body carried now between Bitts's deputy and the senior of the two patrolmen.

At the trailhead, they came to three vehicles, two county sedans and a police van. The police offered to take the corpse back to the university medical center, and Bitts nodded. He was pretty sure they wanted to blow their siren through campus. Bitts stripped off his waders, his slicker and the plastic raincover for his Stetson. He was perfectly dry, right down to his thick silver hair, and Miller, his hair soaked, his uniform plastered against his body, his boots squishing with water, watched enviously. Bitts enjoyed the moment. Age has few rewards the equal of besting a man in his prime, even if it is only tending to the creature comforts with the superior forethought of a man practiced in the field. Bitts reached in the back of his sedan, grabbed a light county-issue jacket to keep the spring chill off, then looked at Miller's condition with an old man's sympathy: two parts worry and one part chuckle.

"Get home, get a shower and get something warm to eat."

"What are you going to do?" Miller asked brightly.

The police van's doors slammed, and the two officers waved as they headed out, their siren bleating.

Bitts's old leather face creased with flinty humor. His gray eyes glittered brightly as he peered out from under his sweated old stetson. "I'm going to tape up the area, then I figured since I'm on campus, I'd go looking for some *babes*."

Calls

At Greek Circle, Pat Bitts turned off the road and watched his deputy drive on through campus. Bitts used the pay phone in the parking lot. Polly answered on the second ring.

"How you doing?" he asked.

"My husband's out, why don't you come by?"

"That old bear is a mean one is the way I hear it. I don't think I want to risk it, even for a country-beauty like you."

"Was it a bad one, Two-Bit?"

"They're all bad, Pol."

"You come on home now. There's nothing there that can't wait until tomorrow."

"The call we got this afternoon was from some kids. I thought I might try to see if I could find who it was."

"And it can't wait till morning?"

"Well, they're all mostly home now." He looked at his watch. It was just nine o'clock and a Thursday night. They'd all be home inside three or four hours. "It's kind of important," he added.

"I'll be up."

"No, you get some sleep! I'm looking at midnight if I don't have any luck. If I find them, it'll be later."

"I'll be waiting," Polly answered.

Thirty-six years they had together, and he had never once come home late from one of these calls without her there to help him put the night behind him. "I'll call you when I'm leaving," he said.

When they broke off, Bitts checked the telephone directory in the dim light and found two Yeagers. Calvin Yeager was the new head of security at Lues State, and Bitts wanted permission before he started through the twenty-two houses on Greek Circle. Bitts had called Yeager that afternoon and asked him to send someone into the canyon to check out the report Jerri, his dispatcher, had just received.

Bitts had a hunch that Yeager coveted more than spending his golden years as some kind of glorified supervisor of parking lots, and expected Yeager would be coming after the position of sheriff in four years. The coming fall election was a foregone conclusion: Bitts was running unopposed, but if Yeager wanted his job next time, he was welcome to come fight for it. Win or lose, that was just fine with Bitts. Once his lawman days were finished, he was aiming for a

18

long tenure on the Ohio River with a fishing pole, plenty of cold beer, and Polly beside him.

"Cal?" he said into the phone. "Listen, I'm sorry to bother you at home, but we've brought out the body."

"Anything I can do?"

"I want to find the kids who called the report in," Bitts answered.

"That could be tough."

"I thought I could nose around Greek Circle here and find out something. You know they pretty much lay claim to the canyon."

"Yeah, we've had some problems with that. Listen, Two-Bit, it's fine with me if you break down every damn door on the circle and bust them all for marijuana, but if you want any cooperation from them, maybe I ought to come along. It'll keep them from getting so nervous. I've had a lot of contact with the frats. I might be able to help, I guess, is what I'm trying to say."

It was a nice speech, as far as it went, but Bitts knew the university was fiercely resistant to unescorted law enforcement agencies on campus. It was a policy that kept the reportable consumption of drugs and alcohol at zero, and that made the moms and pops of the great Midwest happy with Lues State. "I'm at the west end of Greek Circle," he answered.

"I'll find you," Yeager answered.

Ruminations

Hanging up, Bitts went back to his cruiser and began putting together a rough chronology for his own purposes. He scrunched back in his seat, called in his position to his second-shift dispatcher, and snapped on the lamp on his console. Taking a pen and a small notepad, he muttered fondly, the way his uncle had always done it when he had been the sheriff and Bitts was his deputy, "What are the *observable* facts here, Two-Bit?"

The call to the sheriff's office had been received by Jerri Harkness at 4:41. Jerri had said the caller was a male, calm, intelligent, cautious. That alone was a curious piece of information. Most people finding a dead body lost about twenty IQ points. Jerri had told Bitts there were voices in the background, two in fact, at least one of them female but she thought both. Bitts calculated thirty minutes from the base of the cataract to the first public telephone, the one he had just used. It was maybe five minutes quicker if you knew to use the east edge of the canyon, where the footing was level and the water rarely rose over your knees. With the call occurring at a nice round 4:40, that put the death as late as twenty-five minutes before the call, 4:15. Assuming the callers were *not* the murderers, there were other factors to consider, of course. Had the killer still been inside the canyon when the kids started in? Had they interrupted him or maybe walked right by him as he left? With the boulders scattered about, it was possible to conceal yourself. On the west wall of the canyon, the water was deep and still and the big boulders provided absolute concealment, even some underwater caves. The killer might have started out, heard them coming and taken shelter there.

Bitts had found the body at 8:20. Typically rigor mortis set up between two and six hours after the death. Assuming a typical situation, at least until he could get the autopsy from Waldis, the death could not have occurred earlier than 2:20. Neatly on the left side of the pad, he wrote TIME OF DEATH − 2:20–4:15. He drew a heavy line under the numbers, and whispered to himself, "Working hypothesis: kids go into the canyon, leaving the trailhead no later than 3:40."

His brow creased. He drew a rectangle, roughly duplicating the general shape of the canyon. By the falls he placed an X. At the entrance, he placed another. At the entrance he wrote 3:40. It was maybe too much to hope for that the kids had seen the killer, but it was possible. Certainly it would have been beyond the killer's control that he met someone as he left the canyon. It was a chance, anyway, and given the condition of the body, Bitts was inclined to put the death as close to 4:15 as reason and circumstance could afford. The killer had taken a big risk murdering the woman inside the canyon, simply because his exit would have forced him through the defile at the canyon's south end. Once into the slot, there was no hiding. Anyone coming in as he left was going to get a look at him, a close one.

He looked out at the parking lot at the flash of headlights, but saw it wasn't Cal Yeager. He looked at his numbers again. Too many variables to be certain, he decided, but it was possible to imagine the killer and victim left the trailhead and went into the canyon as late as 3:30, in other words, a few minutes before his witnesses had arrived at the entrance to the canyon. "They could have gone in anytime before that, but let's say as much as two hours earlier." Bitts wrote 1:30. "Far as you know, Two-Bit, it could have been last night." He shook his head and looked away. He had nothing but common sense to guide him, and common sense told him anyone standing around in that cold water for longer than an hour or so was going to end up about as sick as the dead woman.

Sheriff Bitts flipped to a new sheet. He looked at his watch. He looked around into the dark of the forest. The killer took the woman into the canyon alive? Have to. Lead her in bound? Not likely. Middle of the afternoon, nice warm spring day. Someone would be on the trails; have to figure that if you were planning a murder. It wouldn't be smart to force someone into the canyon with just about anyone happening along to witness it. "Found her inside?" He wrote the following in column form: walked in tog., led her in, follows. Bitts bounced the tip of his pen onto the pad several times, then wrote at the bottom of the page, clothes! He underlined the word. Her clothes were carried out or they were left somewhere in the canyon. Easy enough to find out tomorrow, he told himself. He tapped his pen on the pad again. "A man follows a woman into a canyon, a man leads a woman into a canyon, a man walks with a woman into a canyon. All possibilities exhausted?" His mouth twitched like a kid in a tough arithmetic test. "No. A man carries a dead woman into a canyon." To his list of possibilities he slipped in the phrase, carries body in. He liked none of his choices, but they represented the only logical ways the two people could enter the canyon, and at least two people had been there, the killer and the victim. He checked off each according to its likelihood, trying to eliminate his improbables. A dead body carried into the canyon was unreasonable. Too easy to get caught; the time of death too early. He placed an X beside the suggestion. Forced her into the canyon, either bound or held by the threat of some weapon? Again, the possibility was as likely as carrying a corpse in. The killer risked being seen forcing his victim into the canyon. That left two choices. He followed her into the canyon, or they went into the canyon together without threats or force.

Bitts tapped the pen vacantly against the notepad. "Only possibility: she goes in with the killer not expecting any trouble. Of course not. Nice day, interesting view of the canyon. Carry gear in, carry gear out, *a backpack*. Of course, he was planning it all along. Friend, boyfriend, or husband . . ." That had to be it. How else did the killer get her inside the canyon unnoticed? Bitts considered the problem briefly, then tapped his ballpoint to retract it. Then again, he told himself, maybe someone had noticed them. Be nice to find the witnesses. With any luck, they had seen something.

With any luck, this could all be wrapped up pretty quickly.

A Few Anomalies

There were a total of thirteen fraternities and nine sororities in the Greek complex. The houses were set to either side of a large circle, sororities on the inner circle, fraternities all butting their backends into the woods. The houses were large, three-tiered structures, sufficient for forty to sixty kids, all university owned, rented by the various chapters of national orders. Like the rest of campus, the houses were built of concrete, the complex marked by distinctive architectural design, the buildings within the complex pretty much interchangeable. When Cal Yeager showed up, Bitts and he started around the circle, fraternities first. They hit the first door at 9:45. Yeager did the talking, since, as he said, he knew most of the people. His son Vincent actually answered the door at their second stop. Yeager explained that they were looking for some kids who had found a body. The kids weren't suspects and they weren't in trouble. It was just important that Sheriff Bitts talk to them. As witnesses they could help clear up a few *anomalies* in the investigation – he actually said "anomalies." After the initial questions, which Yeager asked, Bitts would try them with a couple, "Did anyone see any hikers this afternoon? A young woman with long reddish blonde hair? Maybe between one o'clock and four o'clock?" To this some of the young men said they would ask around; others sent someone through the house while Yeager and Bitts waited. Vincent was no different from the rest; the law didn't cross the threshold without a warrant. A little smirk on his face, and his dad just took it, the way he took it from all of them, smiling, friendly: Good ol' Cal Yeager, the sap. After an hour and a half, the two men had nothing for their troubles but unspoken insult and, for Bitts at least, the mother lode of indigestion.

When they started on the sororities they found a different attitude immediately. Bitts reflected, maybe a bit too sarcastically, that they had already been notified of his presence and had had enough time to get their marijuana flushed. In each house, he and Yeager were able to enter the formal lounge and call the women into their presence. Bitts made his plea without Yeager's help this time. He was running out of chances, and he wanted those witnesses. Two women had been with his male caller. He needed them. He had a co-ed who had been raped and murdered, he told the women. He didn't know if she was a co-ed or not or if she had been raped. He wanted them scared and told them he needed to know a few things in order to find the girl's killer. The witnesses who had called his office could be of enormous help. Having said this, he turned the screws down a little, the way Yeager never would, and said he didn't want to leave someone like this loose to attack other college women. That got an uncomfortable movement in the crowd, as he had expected, then he tried to look at each woman in turn. He had their attention now, and stepped almost into their midst: "A man like this won't stop until he's caught. He waits until one of you gets alone, then he grabs you, like he grabbed that poor girl this afternoon." He let this settle over them, before he added. "The women I'm looking for hold the key to this, and they probably don't even know it . . ."

At the third house, as Bitts said these words, a lone hand went up. "I think we'd better talk," the girl announced. The girls to either side of her flushed and looked at her. She looked at them, and the three of them stood, all about nineteen or twenty, all pretty much worried. When the others had gone, Cal Yeager and Sheriff Pat Bitts faced them. The one who had first announced her involvement was a beautiful young woman, thin with dark glossy hair nearly to her waist. She dressed well and had the look of a totally conscientious student. She seemed tormented by the secret, a girl unused to deception. The other two were cut of a different stalk. They were nervous, but Bitts saw immediately they weren't at all relieved to have come forward. They had an edginess about them that Bitts couldn't entirely trust. They hadn't hardly a neighborly acquaintance with the truth.

"A young man called us this afternoon," Bitts said to them.

Conspirators, the three of them looked at one another. "There were two others with us," the pretty one answered. "They're both in Tau Lambda Kappa."

"Their names?"

She looked at the other two again, then answered him, "Jim Burkeshire and Bob Tanner. Jim made the call to you."

Bitts turned to Yeager: "Can you get them?"

Yeager nodded. "That's just across the street."

When the young men arrived, Bitts pointed toward two empty seats, then told Cal Yeager, "I want to talk to each one in turn, and I don't want these people comparing notes. They can study or they can sleep, but I don't want any talk among them." To the kids, he added, "If one of you wants to get some blankets and pillows or maybe some school books, that will be okay with me." Fiercely now, Bitts looked at them in turn, daring them to lie again.

The thin, intelligent one of the young men answered, "We're okay." He hadn't lied to Bitts. It was the other one, the big dumb one, but Bitts had seen this one, Jim Burkeshire, in the background at the Tau Lambda Kappa house while his buddy Bob Tanner was busy lying six ways to Sunday. He had almost called this Burkeshire kid out to ask him some questions, just a gut instinct. Well, he thought, trust the gut next time, Two-Bit. Cal had been handling them all with his kid gloves on, and Bitts had minded his manners. Enough of that!

Bitts pointed at Cat Sommerville, not entirely a friendly gesture. "I'll start with you."

When they had settled into a study room, Bitts asked the girl about the afternoon. As she started to explain where they had gone, he stopped her. "You went up to the falls?"

She nodded. Her look seemed to ask him what he had expected.

"And what time was that?"

"I don't know what time we started exactly. It was around 1:15 or 1:30, but I checked my watch when the last beer was gone. I was thinking we were drinking too fast, you know?"

"And what time was that?"

"Ten to three."

"How much had you drunk by then?"

"A case."

"You were right. You were drinking too fast. Where were you at that point?"

"We were on the trail just below the falls. I got to the falls about three o'clock, I guess, maybe a couple of minutes before that, not more."

Bitts looked at her watch. "Was that the watch?" Cat nodded. "Have you set it since you got back or wound it?" She shook her head, and he gestured with his fingers to see it. She took it off and handed it to him. The hands indicated it was 11:57, the same as his own. He gave her back the watch.

"We didn't actually go to the top of the falls. We went out on the ledge just under them." Bitts nodded to let her know he knew the area. "We were going to hike across, then go to the top."

"What caused you to change your mind?"

"Melody saw the body."

Bitts smiled angrily. "What are you saying? You mean to tell me you could see the body from there? That's a thousand feet!"

"We saw something."

Bitts shook his head. A thousand feet was simply too far to see a body in water. It was impossible. The human figure looked about the size of a bug from on top of the falls. He had been there plenty; he knew. "But what you saw wasn't the body?"

"We thought it was a body. That's why we went down to check. And that's what it was."

26

"You were on the ledge just under the falls at three o'clock, then went down into the canyon?"

"That's what I said." Cat Sommerville gave him a look of obvious resentment. Her expression seemed to say, she was telling the truth, and she couldn't understand why he wouldn't accept that.

"What then?" Bitts asked her.

"We were in the canyon, in the rocks in front of the falls, and we were trying to get up closer, to where we had seen the woman. It took a long time."

"You didn't know it was a woman at that point?"

"Well we had all seen her. Bob hadn't, but the rest of us had."

Bitts smiled despite himself. "Let's start over, and this time the truth, young lady."

Cat Sommerville answered coolly, like a woman whose virtue has just been doubted, "What do you mean?" It was a good act; that or they were talking at cross-purposes.

"I mean you didn't see that woman from the top of the falls. Now tell me what you did see."

"We saw her. I told you. Why would we go in the canyon if we hadn't?"

Bitts pretended resignation. "So you're in the canyon. Tell me what you saw."

"I was the first to find her. I'll never forget it."

Bitts nodded. He was pretty sure now they had all worked up the same story, and he was going to get five statements nearly identical in their details. He just couldn't figure out why, unless these kids had actually killed the woman.

"What time was this?"

"I don't know. I didn't look at my watch."

"How did you know it was a woman?"

"Excuse me?" The look Bitts got was something beyond astonishment. She thought he was crazy.

"Did you assume it was a woman because you saw long hair?"

27

Cat looked trapped, nervous, as though she imagined he was making some kind of come-on. Noticing the effect, Bitts walked entirely away from her. He looked out one of the windows into the dark night. "Tell me exactly what you saw."

"I saw the body of a woman lying on a rock. She didn't have any clothes on. I know what a woman looks like, you know!" This was supposed to be dripping with irony; instead the effect was shrill, odd, even panicked.

Bitts felt a warm rage boiling up in him at being lied to so crudely. First the boys, when Yeager had talked to them, now this one. What was going on? "Describe the body to me."

"It was almost like she was asleep, but her eyes were open. They were rolled back and her face was swollen, but she was beautiful. She was so beautiful and we just all stared at her for the longest time."

Bitts had an idea, the only logical explanation: "Was she close to the water's edge? Could the body have slipped into the water after you left?"

"No. She was on a large, flat rock maybe ten or fifteen feet to the side of the falls. Her head was almost at the water level, but that was all. Her hand was in the water, I guess."

"She couldn't have slipped into the water?" he repeated.

"I told you, I don't see how."

Bitts pushed at the soft spot, "Why didn't you people stick around after you called my office. Why didn't you identify yourselves?"

"We voted. The majority wanted to stay out of it. They were afraid."

"How did you vote?"

"I said we should call and identify ourselves. So did Jim."

"What time did you call my office?"

"I don't know. 4:30, 4:40. We came back, took showers, changed clothes. Dinner was at 5:15. We just made it. I did, anyway. Melody and Susie didn't show for dinner."

"Did you know the dead woman?"

"No. I'd never seen her."

Still at the window, Bitts studied her. "We'll have an ID tomorrow. I don't want to find out she was a friend of yours, maybe a classmate."

"What is your problem?" Cat Sommerville had become progressively angrier as they talked; this was pure aggressiveness, and it bothered him. It could have been an act, but if so, it was a good one.

"The woman I found wasn't beautiful, Cat; she wasn't lying out in the open either. I'll tell you what I found: I found a woman who had been gutted. You know how a hunter guts what he kills, Cat? That's what I saw!"

Cat Sommerville's face was expressionless but washed entirely of color.

"Is that what you saw too?"

"I told you what I saw."

The two of them stared at each other in a cold rage.

"Any marks on her?" Bitts asked, finally.

"Something on her stomach, some kind of letters, I don't remember what. I think there were marks on her wrists and ankles, I didn't really look, and something on her neck, like a band; I don't remember exactly."

Bitts's eyebrows raised slightly. "Anything else?"

She shook her head. "I was scared, confused. I don't remember."

"Bruises on her neck?"

"I don't know."

"Think, girl!"

"I am. I don't know. I can't remember. There was something here." She pointed just under the jawline. "I don't know about the bruises."

Bitts stayed with the young woman several more minutes, but he couldn't really push it; the harder he went at Cat Sommerville, the stiffer she got, so he played along with her. He let her hang herself with the details, and he milked out

29

as many as he could. Maybe one of the others would scare into the truth, especially if he could catch a contradiction. This one, not likely.

"Good enough," he said finally. "Is there anything else you can think of I ought to know?"

"Only about the man."

Bitts felt his pulse kicking in. Here it was, the thing falling into his lap. He hadn't even remembered to ask, he had been so upset about the lying.

"What man? Talk to me."

"I didn't see him. I don't know if anyone else did, either. I mean besides Melody. She thought he was following us."

"Into the canyon or out of it?"

"Above the falls. It was before we saw the body. She said she thought he had watched her . . . you know."

"I don't know."

"She had to pee, and she thought he watched her. Anyway, Susie said he probably sniffed it. Something like that. I said they were gross, and they started screaming and calling him . . . something."

"Calling him what?"

"A slew. That's what the kids call the locals." She gave Bitts a look as if to say, *You're a slew; you know all about slews.*

Over the next hour or so, Sheriff Bitts discovered essentially the same story. What he couldn't understand was why they were lying, if that was the case. There was simply no reason for it, and yet nothing they said made sense. He pushed, cajoled and even tried to trick them. There were minor discrepancies, obvious mistakes even, but none of them seemed to be working off a script. Bitts looked at the estimates he had made before he had talked to them. Nothing was impossible, just earlier than he had anticipated. So maybe they weren't lying. But if they weren't, Bitts had a whole new set of questions and still no answers. Had someone else come after the kids? Had the killer been waiting inside the canyon? Did he follow them back in? Had he been interrupted at three o'clock, then waited until past four before he returned to the body? Maybe the kids saw something he realized he didn't want them to. But what? Bitts ran his hand over his face in a gesture of frustration. He was just going to have to wait and see what Waldis could do with the post-mortem.

Walking back into the lounge to face the kids, Bitts saw that, like his own, their faces were drawn and exhausted. Cal Yeager's eyes were red and heavy. Bitts looked at his watch and saw it was a quarter-past two. The woman had been dead twelve hours, if he was to believe what these kids had told him. At first light, city homicide would take over the primary duties of the investigation. They would have the manpower to scour the woods and canyon and confirm or refute much of what the kids had told him. Beer cans, cigarette butts, footprints, a broken railing, and maybe something more, something that could put all the irreconcilables together.

"From here on out, the city police are going to conduct this investigation. That means a Lieutenant Colt Fellows is going to be in touch with you. He's probably going to have some more questions." A low groan came from them, nothing that he could place, just the exhaustion that is typical of people who have been through it the way Bitts had put them through it. He stared at each in turn, a dangerous scowl. "That's not even the end of it, folks. Detective Fellows will want depositions – "

"What's a deposition?" This from Tanner.

Bitts's face twisted wryly. "A statement under oath. You lie on a deposition, we'll have you in the Vienna Correctional Facility for perjury." Bitts let this settle over them, then finished, "Hopefully there'll be a trial and you can each testify. You may not realize it, but what you have to say is critical to this case. In the meantime, if you think of anything you didn't tell me, tell it to the detectives or call Mr Yeager. Mr Yeager is your director of security on campus." Cal nodded and met their inquiring glances. They were all too tired to show much emotion. They all still looked like kids, not murderers.

Josie Hazard

Sheriff Pat Bitts was at the trailhead to Lues Creek Canyon at 7:15 the next morning. A beat-up Ford Pinto that one of the reporters drove was there, and a half-dozen unmarked detective vehicles were parked in the small clearing as well. A WKTV van with Missouri plates was parked up at the beginning of Trail 6. Like the detectives and the reporter, none of the camera crew was in sight. As Bitts came out of his cruiser, he saw Colt Fellows walking around the WKTV van, apparently coming down from the top of the falls. Colt was still dry.

"Two-Bit! Glad you could make the party. I went ahead and started without you." In his mid-thirties Colt was a big man, overweight and generally flush. He had a thick, short neck, and a round, mean face that one or two ill-advised men had tried to adjust. Colt Fellows's eyes were deep-set and quick. Chief of homicide, Colt was a man with ambition, huge appetites, and modest intelligence. At a crime scene, by all accounts, he was a bulldozer. "How you doing, old man?" There was a touch of affection in this, if not sincerity, as he reached to take Bitts's hand.

"I've had longer nights. Where were you when we went swimming last night?"

"I let the politicians go swimming; I was down at the medical center on the receiving end: that's where the professionals start to work. *Forensics*, Two-Bit. That's the future! You get wet and couldn't join us or just wetting your whistle?"

"So what did you find out?"

"It's a simple case, Two-Bit. First, got a name. Josie Hazard. She's a stripper out at the Hurry On Up. One of our upstanding orderlies spotted her when Birts and O'Malloy brought her in."

"You say the name is Hazard?"

Colt grinned, "As in 'I married a lunatic.' The worst of them: John Christian. You remember Jack Hazard, don't you, Two-Bit?"

"I've arrested him a couple of times."

"After I got an ID last night, I got hold of Jack. He and this old gal's kid showed up and confirmed the ID. He wouldn't talk much after that. It was just like I was invisible." Oddly, this delighted Colt, and Bitts could see he had put together his conclusions before his investigation had properly started. Nothing new there.

There was the sound of a car coming up the trail, and Bitts turned back to see Jason Miller climbing out of his '73 Torino, two large, lidded cups of coffee in his hands. He juggled the cups briefly, closed the door with his foot, then started for Bitts and Fellows.

Colt Fellows laughed and shouted loud enough for Miller to hear him, "Damn! Two-Bit, how do you get your people trained like that? I don't get a cupcake on my birthday."

Miller came toward them and grinned at Fellows, not entirely unfriendly. "If you'd quit acting like a horse's ass, they'd bring you coffee! I'd bring you coffee if you did something about that bad breath." He handed a cup to the sheriff: "There you go, sir. Cream-to-Thursday, like you like it." To Fellows, "How's it going, fat-ass?"

"Keep grinning, Jason. You're the one going out to arrest Jack Hazard this morning."

Miller started to sip his coffee, but looked up at the name of Hazard. "What are you talking about?"

"Your body last night. It was Jack Hazard's wife. She's a stripper at the Hurry On Up. Blows half the town for drinks. And Jack don't give a damn."

"You some kind of expert on the strippers out there?" Jason asked him.

33

"All I know is the old whore flunked her swimming class last night. One frigging less Hazard, am I right?"

Jason grinned coldly. "No, but you're stupid."

"Did Waldis look at her?" Bitts asked.

Fellows shook his head, "You know better than that, Two-Bit. Waldis wouldn't come in for it. The good Herr-Professor-Doctor prefers his customers to die during his office hours." Colt shrugged, a what-are-you-going-to-do expression. "We looked for prints. Nothing. Waldis will do her first thing this morning. Knowing Waldis, that's about ten. That guy's colder than one of his stiffs. But hey, he's the best. Like I always say, takes a stiff to know a stiff. So anyway, Waldis finishes up, pronounces the old slut dead, and we go for the warrant on Jack: that's my autopsy. And you guys are taking him down."

Miller smiled easily, sipping his coffee. "Got any proof it was Jack?"

"A lawman's instincts, Jason."

"Gee, that's good enough for me." Miller turned to Bitts: "When are we going to get him?"

"When I say," Bitts answered. There was no humor in this, and Miller's face went blank. He turned on his heel and made a quick exit from the two men. At the car, he pulled out waders and a heavy raincoat. He was prepared this morning.

Bitts called to him, "We're going up the trail, Jason. You won't need that."

"What's up there?" Fellows interrupted.

Bitts smiled mystically, "Woods."

A Simple Case

Bitts and his deputy hadn't gone far when they began sighting empty beer cans. "What's this, a beer blast?" Miller asked.

"How fresh, Jason?"

Miller was twenty-four, a connoisseur of the hops when

34

his wife would let him out. He picked up one of the cans with a twig and smelt. "Day old, Two-Bit. Still some in the bottom."

"Take it into evidence."

Miller's eyebrow raised slightly, but he did as he was told. As they walked up the hill, Bitts laid out what he had. "I found our callers last night. They said our corpse was lying in one piece on a rock beside the falls."

"What?" Miller was incredulous.

Bitts shrugged philosophically; he hadn't any better idea than before what it all meant: "Five of them said our victim was lying there like Sleeping Beauty."

Miller thought about this for a while, then he asked, "What do you make of it, Two-Bit?"

"I need to confirm what the kids told me. One of them saw a man up here at the falls. Could have been the killer. Be nice to find something he left behind."

"Like a dozen beer cans?"

"Not this brand. We ought to find twenty-four of these. You find something other than your namesake on a beer can, we stop the presses."

Miller nodded and walked toward three more. "You want pictures?"

"Why not?" Bitts watched him photograph the cans then collect them into an evidence bag. "Footprints, cigarette butts, clothing, gum wrappers."

"Maybe we ought to get a warrant and go out to Jack Hazard's place if we want to find her clothes."

"Unlike Colt Fellows, I like to have a little evidence before I storm a man's castle."

Miller laughed. "You think it was someone else?"

"I thought last night it had to be a husband or a boyfriend. Someone she knew, anyway. I couldn't see how a woman would go into the canyon in broad daylight with anyone but someone she knew."

Miller shrugged. "If she's a hooker, that could be anyone, right?"

"A couple of problems. I was thinking last night on the way home. She was tied up for a while, a long while. You saw her wrists?"

"Her ankles too."

"You see any letters on her belly?"

"No. She was gutted too bad."

"I saw what looked like an *h*. One of the girls said it was an H-O-R."

"H-O-R?"

"Whore: girl called it slew-spelling for prostitute."

Miller, like Bitts, was a local, which is to say a slew. "Well, I like you too, bitch!" He bent to pick up a couple more cans without bothering to photograph them.

"Jason, I don't know what to do with the rope burns. She was tied up somewhere, I don't know how many hours. You tie a woman up and carve something in her flesh, she's not going to go into that canyon willingly. So how does she get there?"

"He takes her in."

"I don't like it. It's a busy trailhead. Greek Circle is not two hundred yards away. Someone could have seen them too easily, especially if she didn't want to go in there. There are better places to commit a murder. Almost anywhere would be better." In this Bitts was absolutely right. The forest stretched north and south well over a hundred miles, much of it pristine wilderness.

"Well she got there!"

Bitts smiled grimly. "That she did, young man, that she did."

"What's your theory, Two-Bit?"

"My theory is it's not a simple case, Colt Fellows notwithstanding. I'm going to ask you something, and I don't want you to get mad." Miller got a curious look on his face, but said okay. "What do you suppose you would do if Charli was playing around?"

"Who's she screwing around with?" The young man's humor was gone.

"Hypothetical."

"Hypothetically, who's she screwing." Jason looked ready to ignite. A vein in his neck throbbed angrily.

"What's it matter?"

"Well, I'm going to kill him!"

"What about Charli?"

"I'll see how I feel about her after I kill *him*!"

"You don't think you'd tie her up and carve *whore* on her belly, assuming you knew how to spell a word with that many letters?"

"No, that's not the first thing to cross my mind, Two-Bit."

Bitts shook his head. "I don't think Jack Hazard would do that either. Just a lawman's *instincts*."

"You just don't want to come to the same conclusion as Colt Fellows," Miller said finally.

"You might have something there, Jason. That thought keeps me up at night."

They walked on quietly until they came to a cigarette ash that lay perfectly in the middle of the path. Filterless, it had burned entirely, but the brand name, Lucky Strike, was clearly imprinted in the ash. Knowing the ash would break apart the moment they touched it, Bitts had Miller photograph it then bring up the dirt around it. Miller pulled out a long-bladed pocket knife and dug a thin divot out of the trail. Carefully he slipped the dirt and the ash into an evidence bag, using a twig to tent the plastic.

"You think Jack smokes Luckies?" Jason asked.

"We'll check the sleeve of his T-shirt when we talk to him."

When Bitts had confirmed that the railing along the ledge over the canyon was broken, he checked his watch. The hike up had taken just under fifty-five minutes. In the canyon, the investigators and news people were combing through the boulders. Colt typically let newsmen trample his evidence. It bought him their good will.

"We better call County Parks and Recreation and tell them to get out and fix this," Miller offered.

Bitts didn't respond. He stared out into the canyon for a long time, then without turning to his deputy he said, "I got a woman dead at three o'clock, Jason. They're looking straight down on her, and she's as clear as those two men just beside the falls."

"Not too clear."

"Four of my five witnesses could see her. Now here's the problem. I got the killer up here just back where we were looking for footprints."

"Okay."

"How does he kill her and appear up at the top at the same time?"

"He kills her at two or 2:15."

"Or the man back here isn't our killer." Bitts stared down into the rocks considering the vast distance, the weird trail of facts. "Either way," Bitts offered, "I don't like it. There's just something wrong with this whole thing." Bitts considered briefly. "Something *very* wrong."

Twenty-three minutes later, Bitts and his deputy arrived at the trailhead, Jason Miller with their sack of cans, Bitts carrying the second evidence bag, which contained a single sliver of dirt and the last half of the burnt ash of a Lucky Strike. Fellows, still dry, came toward them grinning. He was breathing like a spent mule in his excitement. "We got him!"

"What are you talking about?" Bitts asked.

Fellows held up a plastic evidence bag with a huge grin. Inside was a wristwatch. "It was lying right on top of one of the boulders. Jack Hazard's name is on it! Is that boy country-stupid or what?"

Colt Fellows was percolating with his own importance. "Come on Two-Bit, let's get a warrant!"

"I want the autopsy first. And I've got some other things I want to look at."

Less than six months before, the county council had developed a program they had dubbed the CRP, which stood for the Coordination of Resources and Personnel. The program, which both law enforcement agencies predictably retitled CRAP, was designed to eliminate the need for two homicide units at the city and county level. In theory it meant the sheriff became dependent upon the city for his investigations and the city was dependent on Bitts, beyond the city limits, for the arrest of homicide suspects. The design of a committee of politicians, the program was as useless as a wad of knotted-up fishing line.

"I already called Waldis's office," Colt answered. "They'll have a brief ready by eleven. We'll take it to Scott, and you can get Jack as soon as Scott gets us an arrest warrant."

"Did you get a time of death from Waldis?"

Colt grinned happily. "Six to seven o'clock. Officially, the call is six."

Bitts glanced at his deputy with a look to shut him up. The Lues police had been called at 7:05. As far as they knew, that was the first report, and Bitts wasn't tipping his hand, not just yet. "Give me till four. If I can't give you a good reason not to bring Jack in by then, I'll get him, assuming Avery issues Scott a warrant."

"If we get that son-of-a-buck now, we'll make evening news on WKTV. They're out here, Two-Bit; they'll cover the arrest! But they're not coming back for a bust an hour before they go on the air!"

"I'm not ready to go for a warrant yet."

"What do you need, Two-Bit! A written confession on the canyon wall? This is it." Colt shook the plastic bag with the watch at Bitts. "It doesn't get any easier. You got a man who's spent more than half his life in prison. You got an old whore-stripper who's been screwing around a little and got caught by her husband, you got a watch with the killer's name on it. Just what more do you want, Two-Bit!"

"I want to get a few loose ends straightened out in my own mind first."

Theatrically, Fellows looked at Miller. "Help me out, Jason. Tell me what I'm missing."

Jason answered laconically, "Brains, Colt."

A Hostage Situation

After Bitts had left, Miller made a hard run up the hill to the falls, then came down at full throttle. Carefully, he recorded the times, then, hardly recovered, threw himself into the creek and started back into the canyon. Forty minutes later he came back out, staggering in exhaustion.

It was at that point that Lieutenant Fellows chose to approach him, offering a cup of coffee from his thermos.

"The old drunk works you too hard, Jason," Colt announced pleasantly. "You come into the city, I'll make you a detective. Coffee and doughnuts till nine, guaranteed."

Taking a sip, Jason grinned at the big man. "Trouble is, Colt, I'd have to look at your ugly face every day."

Colt took the insult in his stride. He liked Miller, liked his style. "Offer's open anytime you want it, Jason. I'm not kidding. I could use you. I'm talking better money and no ceilings."

Miller looked at him curiously. "I like it where I am, Colt. Two-Bit's taught me a lot."

"Ah, Two-Bit's best days are past him, Jason. Besides, since the council took away your investigative work, what do you got to do besides break up fights? You want some action, you *got* to come to the city."

Colt knew he had scored with this, and saw the younger man considering. "I'll think about it," he said finally.

Fellows moved in closer, his voice dropping almost to a

whisper. "So tell me, what's the old fox up to? Two-Bit's holding something back on me, I know it."

"You talk to him about what he knows."

Miller walked away and went to his Torino. Colt watched him calling his dispatcher, then jotting down some kind of message. When he had finished the call, he got the look of a kid who's just put it over on his old man.

"What do you have?" Colt asked him.

Miller's pale eyes flashed as he came toward the detective. "Chalk your stick, Colt. You're miscuing. The woman was Jack Hazard's *ex*. Her name's Josie *Fortune*, not Hazard. Two-Bit's at her apartment on campus right now and wants me there five minutes ago. You want to come along?"

Colt looked around for another detective to send, but they were all still in the canyon. "Give me the address, and I'll send someone out in a few minutes."

Miller went back to his cruiser to get the address and copy it out for Colt. Colt waited for the information, leaning against Miller's driver-side back door.

"How about the kid," Colt asked him casually. "Is she Jack's daughter?"

Jason shrugged. "I doubt it. She's got her mother's name."

"Two-Bit's sure taking his time getting her, isn't he?"

"She's okay. *You* told us she's with Jack."

"If they're divorced, that little girl doesn't belong with Jack. Especially if he just killed her mother."

Miller didn't seem to get it. "We're going out there after lunch. She's been there all night, maybe longer; she's good for another few hours."

"Listen. You work for the old drunk. No one's blaming you, Jason. But I got a different boss. My boss don't like to see children in danger."

"Here's the address on that campus apartment. I've got to go, Colt."

Miller started to shut his door, but Colt reached out to

hold it open a moment, "I'm thinking about the kid, Jason. When's Two-Bit going to get around to remembering her?"

"What do you want me to do, Colt? We're going out there to talk to Jack later. She'll be okay."

"I just want you to remember what I'm saying."

Miller shrugged agreeably. "Sure. I hear you."

When he had driven off, Colt hurried to his unmarked, stripped-down '71 Chevy. The car sank under his weight as he dropped into the seat. He picked up his mike and called the city dispatcher. "Duey!" he said. "Get me the state police patched through. We've got a hostage situation!"

Part Two

Homecoming

Coming south into Lues, Josie Darling had strange flashes of recognition. Certain turns in the road, certain smells, set her heart pounding with a sense of nostalgia, a shadow smile on her heart. It was nothing she could place exactly; it was the spirit of the countryside, the unpaved roads now and then that twisted away into the hazy forest. Josie saw one of these gravel roads coming up at some distance, so had a chance to slow down and contemplate it. She was nearly to the town of Lues and tired from her second long day of driving, but this place held promise and she turned off the highway excitedly. She thought this was the way, but before she found home, the road ended like most of the roads in Lues County, coming up against Lues Creek.

There was a little parking area by the creek, but no one was in sight. She was now five miles off the highway, in deep country, and the stillness of the place gave her chills. The only sound was the rushing creek water and a faint stirring wind that moved in ghostly dance among the high branches. She got out of her car and walked up along the creek. This wasn't the place, but the sand beside the creek reminded her of her last and only real memory of Lues. A memory which would be twenty years old in April.

Josie had watched three dark sedans coming up the road to Jack Hazard's and her mother's trailer. They came fast and kicked up big tunnels of dust behind them. As the cars got closer she saw they belonged to the state police. Behind her, the door of the trailer creaked open. Jack stood next to

43

her. She knew it was Jack, but she couldn't remember his face. She remembered the road, the dust, the cars, the great bending curve, and how the cars pulled off the road and came across the field toward them. They parked broadside before Josie and her stepfather. More than a half-dozen state troopers took up positions behind the sedans, their shotguns visible like black pipes against the gray sky. One of them called out something. He had a ferocious voice. Their shotguns racked simultaneously while three troopers ran at them hard, their weapons silent in their hands. Two of them took Jack down to the ground. The third trooper took Josie's wrist. She twisted away under his grip and broke loose. Behind her, one of them shouted, "Get the kid, for Christ's sake!"

Leaves slapped Josie's face as she ran. She was certain they meant to kill her. She heard the trooper following her, his heavy breath, the crunch of leaves, the cracking of sticks. As they came to the creek, the man took Josie's arm. He lifted her into the air. "I'm not going to hurt you!" he shouted. Josie kicked at him savagely. He was still carrying his shotgun and his face was red from the effort of running. He set his gun down in the grass and knelt before her so she could see his face. "Now listen to me!" he said. He held her by her elbows, pinning them behind her back. She stopped struggling. They were both breathing heavily. She saw his shotgun. She kept staring at it as he said something Josie couldn't understand. When he had said the thing, she looked at him. His big face was nearly against hers. She smelt the stink of tobacco on his breath and wrestled against his hold on her to be set free.

At the trailer she saw Jack cuffed and being pushed into one of the three sedans. Jack looked back toward her, his face bloody with a fine scarlet sheen; it was the only face of Jack Hazard she would ever remember. She shouted to him: "JAAACK!"

Jack looked down between his knees, ashamed.

44

The trooper holding her said in the calmest voice imaginable, "You don't want to talk to him, honey. That man there is the one that killed your mamma."

Something moved, and Josie looked up into the woods to see a fat doe moving through the leaves. Josie watched it momentarily, then stared at the creek again. This wasn't the place. It didn't happen here. The familiarity was in the air and the sounds of the creek. She had no idea where home was; she only knew she was close. Somewhere along this creek. This creek. Lues Creek. They had lived close to Lues Creek; it was all she could remember. She listened and the sounds of the water were like indistinct voices calling to her out of the past. She asked herself how she could have ever lost such memory.

Eventually Josie got back into the car and drove another ten miles before the traffic turned to sludge. The city of Lues, these days maybe twenty-five thousand souls when the school is closed, nearer to fifty thousand when classes were in session, wasn't really familiar. What Josie remembered came to her as she was stopped in front of the city limits sign: the physical sensation of sitting inside a pickup truck between her mother and Jack. It was wintertime of all things. Josie imagined the smell of their leather coats and the faint stuffiness of the heater whirring. It seemed there was frost on the windows. The sensation was with her as long as she kept her eyes unfocused and cast just past the city limits sign into the refracted sunlight of her dirty windshield. When Josie realized it was a memory and not some fantasy, that if she turned slightly she could see her mother, she tried to look at her within the memory, her eyes still fixed on the sundogs in the glass of her windshield, but as she tried, the whole of the memory crashed. Josie was again in heavy traffic on a hot August day in a town she didn't remember. The cars were stretched out for about five miles, half of them trying to get into the mall just ahead of her, the other half trying to go on to the university. Josie was stuck in the

45

turn lane for the mall even though she wanted to go straight. She looked for an opening in the left lane, but the cars were rolling by at a steady pace and no one was letting the right lane break in. She looked again at the city limits sign, then past it into the sky. Her mother was beside her. Jack was driving. Josie didn't try to look at them now, but absorbed their odors and the sound of the truck. Some cast of light, some scent in the woodlands, some dark memory: these gave Josie her mother as clearly as the memory had ever been, and yet it was too little, too brief.

Josie was certain she would see her mother's and Jack's pictures the next day, when she went to the library. She knew young women usually get pictured when they are murdered. She thought Jack Hazard would be pictured as well, because he was the husband and killer and because we love to see the eyes of such monsters. She knew too that the pictures would be like seeing strangers. She would see her mother and Jack, and that is what she would remember, someone else's images of them; in the end, they would be only soulless specters on paper. Memory, even the faintest glimpse of it, is altogether different. Josie wanted one image, one smoky impression before she saw the newspaper photos.

For years after the state trooper had caught her beside Lues Creek, Josie told herself her mother wasn't really dead, that there had been a terrible mistake; she was alive and waiting for Josie to come back. Josie thought if she could get home she would find her. Eventually Josie had given up the idea and with it, gradually, whatever vestiges of memory she had carried out of Lues.

She knew why of course. Her new parents had always hated Lues and Josie's life in it. The Darlings had many virtues. They were fine, good people who took Josie out of the foster system shortly after her removal from Lues. They had loved her as their own, and all they ever asked in return, besides her natural affection for them, was that she forget the past, that she not talk about Lues or Jack Hazard or how

46

her mother lived and died. They told her that *that time* was over. She could be anything she wanted, they said. She could make any life she cared to, but first she had to leave *those things* from Lues behind her. They told her to forget the past in many ways. They were gentle and persuasive, and Josie learned to honor their fears as her own. She forgot her first childhood so long and so hard that it came back as something else, something unrecognizable and terrible. She let it get out of hand, and even then she kept her silence. She did not look back. As a teenager she told no one that Jack Hazard still came out from under her bed, his face bloody, his killing only half done. She never spoke of the woman's wailing voice that still sometimes called across the threshold of dawn, "Josie!", a haunting lament or summoning or warning. Josie had always been afraid to answer the voice, in case she would find out what it meant. Like the town of Lues, that voice held terrible secrets, and she had always found reason to resist its seductions.

There was a point in Josie's life when things made sense, and Josie's memories became like other people's: splotchy and embarrassing, random as a roulette wheel, neurotically normal, desperately ordinary. That was the childhood Josie claimed. She had made her revolutions and compromises. She did some of the things we all shouldn't have done but did. She missed some of the other things. She was a bright, fearless scholar, a fumbling young girl with a few mistakes under her belt. She was guilty of her share of events and innocent of most things. There were some poignant memories of this time, her second childhood, some things she would like to do over. Josie had long ago come to terms with that life, if we can ever really say we have made our peace with the child we were. She grew up in her adoptive home a perfectly middle-class, suburban girl. She had hated as much as the next teenager the prefabricated life of the Midwestern small town. Unlike most of her friends, Josie got out as soon as she could; she headed east to where the

47

ivy grows. Like most revolutionaries, she came back home because she missed it. A year later, Josie got her courage back and this time she left for good. She went off determined to make her own way and build her own home.

This was the life Josie could trace; there were records of her immodest achievements, official and otherwise. There were memories and stories and friendships and losses. That childhood was the one she had always known, the one she was always ready to face. That girl was Josie Darling. But there had always been the other childhood locked behind a row of shotguns across a gray sky, the yawning emptiness of losing what she could not remember, and the whispering of some far voice which told her that Josie Fortune was not entirely the same person as Josie Darling.

Josie blinked away the frustration and disorientation, and realized the cars in front of her were moving. She shifted to first just as several cars behind her blared their horns. The engine of her VW complained, and Josie jerked forward a few feet before stopping again. In the seat beside her and in the back, Josie carried the sum of her property: a computer and printer, six boxes of books, and two suitcases. She had left another thirty boxes of books in Boston. In a fit of disgust with her Eastern Look, most of the outfits bought for the sake of Dan Scholari, Josie had given away about half her clothes to Goodwill. Despite her best efforts, she had still lacked room for all her worldly possessions, so had boxed up most of her personal items and shipped them back home to the Darlings, treating them, she realized, like real folks and saving, for the price of their inconvenience, just a few dollars on a storage bin. At the same time Josie had promised them she would take a trip upstate from Lues County at Thanksgiving or Christmas, dates and times unspecified. Like real folks they tried hard and made sacrifices; like a real daughter Josie treated them unconsciously to second-class citizenship. The mother she was so desperate to find these days, Josie would have treated likewise; it's how love goes.

Just as Josie was leaving Boston and starting off for Lues State University, she had stopped at a garage sale on a whim and found a ten-speed she couldn't live without. It had been repainted white with no logo, but Josie was certain it was a high end road bike that wanted nothing but use. It was light, quick, and solid. The gears flopped one to the other like a habit; the frame and wheels were good. As she was still having some pain in her ankle, Josie knew biking was better for her than running, her sport of choice. She had shelled out the forty dollars the people had asked, tossed the bike onto the roof of her cracker-box VW Rabbit and, using some borrowed twine, tied it down on an army blanket with a history. It wasn't exactly the triumphant return to Lues that Josie had fantasized so many times when she was still a child, but it wasn't a bad return either. Josie liked coming home in secret. No one in all the town imagined Lues was her real home. She was a kind of Odysseus, gone twenty years and slipping back in another disguise. She wore the perfect disguise in fact. She was no longer seven years old!

Josie checked the passing lane again, which was moving steadily now, but there was still no chance to get into it. She tried to nose out into the traffic, but that about got her bumper ripped off and brought another chorus of horns. In Lues County there aren't many roads, and the ones they have are tight and mean, so you won't find the usual rural polite-ness that marks so much of the country. The cars in front of her began moving ahead quickly now, all turning into the mall. She looked back into the left lane again and saw there was still no opening. The traffic cop in front of her now was directing her to turn into the mall, and Josie mumbled that she didn't want to go to the mall. The cop was one of these middle-aged four-by-fours, three doughnuts from his first heart attack. His whistle shrieked. He pointed at her angrily. She was first in line suddenly and looking at a mall parking lot that was more congested than the highway. The cop pointed into the mall. Leaning out the driver-side window,

Josie edged toward him. He shook his head obnoxiously and gave his whistle several shrill blasts. His arms made large gestures toward the entrance of the mall. Josie used her turn signal to indicate that she didn't want to go into the mall, that she wanted help getting into the left lane. This infuriated him, and he blew his whistle so it gave one long screaming complaint. At the same time, he spread his arms like a blue Jesus.

All the lanes stopped. He walked toward her shouting, "Take a right, lady. And move it!" When Josie sat there, he repeated himself. "Take a right, I said!"

She smiled pleasantly as he came within range, close enough to read the name CROUCH on his name tag, "I'm going to the university. I need to get over to the other lane." It was easy enough to do, she thought. He had the traffic in the whole town and half the county stopped. All he needed to do was get out of her way.

"Should have thought of that about a half-mile back, baby. Now take a right!" He walked back a few steps and stood directly in front of her, signaling again for her to turn into the mall.

It was hot, and Officer Crouch had been out for a few hours, so Josie understood his temper, but no one called Josie *baby* – not without retribution. Josie put a scream in the engine and popped the clutch of her little Rabbit. *Baby* about took the fat man's knees out before he jumped aside. Traffic was still stopped both ways along the highway, the cars coming out of the mall waiting the command of Officer Crouch as well. Josie had a clear shot down the road, something she hadn't seen for the past half-hour, and she hit it like a true Bostonian. In the mirror she could see her cop waving his arms angrily. That was all. Soon enough Officer Crouch was a small speck in the panoramic distance.

Josie came into the downtown and saw a few grim blocks of depressed real estate, vaguely familiar. She pushed past some of the more lively businesses which catered to the university crowd, mostly the same places that sit on any small-town main street: a couple of convenience stores, the typical fast foods, KFC, Wendy's, Pizza Hut, Burger King, McDonald's, and then a couple of local-yokel-wannabe-burger-palaces. Finally, Josie came to the entrance of Lues State University, just under Presbyterian Hill, the site of the community's first college.

The hill Josie remembered, not the bridge over the creek nor the showy welcome sign before the university. Both the bridge and the sign looked new. It's odd in most of America if anything besides a bad joke lasts twenty years, so Josie knew she shouldn't have been disappointed that most of the place was unfamiliar, but she was. She wanted it to come back all at once. She wanted to know everything the way a movie gives us a setting on a slow pan or a book encases the history of a place in a paragraph. Lues State was eagerly modern; nothing looked twenty years old. Nothing of it came back.

Josie braked hard for several freshmen crossing Willow Avenue. They were like fawns stumbling into an empty highway, oblivious to their danger. They would be her students in a few short days, she realized. She had had students at Bandolier, but these were different. There was a kind of innocence here, the real essence of the term *freshman* that the urbane eastern student could never have. They looked to have only a fifty-fifty chance of making it through registration. Before they had crossed, Josie looked past the bunkers that comprised the administrative complexes and noticed a road sign nearly concealed by some branches. It directed her to University Housing. She checked her campus map and saw her X placed over the housing office.

Josie spent about an hour getting processed for her apartment, mostly standing in line, then climbed back into her VW with her new key and yet one more round of paperwork. Beyond the sports complexes, Willow Avenue turned into heavily shaded woods suddenly, and Josie told herself the place wasn't so bad. It was pretty, actually; there were stumps and logs enough for a thousand pedagogues and their disciples. It was a woodland with a library. To the right and left there were occasional clusters of buildings, all of them turned out in concrete, all of them sterile fortresses, but between the building groups were lush acres of forest. She passed the university medical center, an imposing structure, then she found a small sign that read FACULTY APARTMENTS, which directed her up a narrow road into a thick grove. Josie made several turns on a fairly busy one-and-a-half-lane pavement before coming to two units facing one another. Each building had twenty apartments all on a single level. The buildings were long and institutional and made her feel like she had joined some kind of aesthetic commune instead of a modern campus, and they were made of concrete, like everything at Lues State. From the outside, the place was about as appealing as the fat cop who had called her baby. The apartments faced out into a large, shared parking lot, which at the moment was filled with young unmarried professor types, all of them, like Josie, temps. Both buildings managed to butt back against the forest. Josie's was set up over a fairly substantial ravine with Lues Creek running through it. She would be paying twenty-five dollars extra a month to hear the stream off her back balcony.

Josie pulled the VW in tail-first so to unload it easily. She had the car cleared quickly except for two boxes of books she would take to her office on Monday, and toured the apartment with a quick once-over. It was better actually than she had hoped. It was relatively clean and spacious and, the reason she had picked it, fully equipped. As Josie had requested on the forms she had filled out in May, she had a master bedroom with a double bed. The mattress was firm, the sheets starched. The matching headboard and side table were done in some kind of macabre Spanish style. The second bedroom was set up as an office, everything done in scratched, gray steel: bookshelves, computer console, a writing table, and an office chair. These had seen too many wars, but they functioned. The kitchen was loaded with the essentials, everything except food, but Josie regretted not packing a few of her things. The pots and pans were beat and dented, the plates chipped and shabby, the glasses foggy.

The main room offered a six-foot couch and two chairs in a scotch plaid just this side of nausea. The lamps were rickety and complemented in a vague way the bedroom motif, something for the last son of a bankrupt Spanish hidalgo. There was a tiny fireplace, two prints of Picasso, one with a bullet hole in it, and a telephone out of another era, the sort that used to double as a murder weapon in Miss Marple mysteries. Josie inspected the thing with a pragmatist's irritation and antiquarian's fond humor. There was no jack for it, nor any method to attach an answering machine. You were supposed to be able to mute the ringer, but the dial was locked up with rust at full volume. The lady at Housing had told her she could have voice mail next year, if she renewed her lease. Josie shook her head, telling herself it was just something she was going to have to get used to, like life without cable TV. She looked at the television set miserably as she thought about life without CNN. It was as old as the telephone and had rabbit ears on top. Jenny McNeal's parents had had rabbit ears on their basement television set. That was the only time Josie had ever seen them in a functioning environment. Josie snapped the set on and waited. Finally a picture in black and white of an electrical snowstorm presented itself. She flipped the knob and found three stations, only one of which had good reception, the only thing good about it, as it turned out. She turned the set off, opened a sliding glass door and entered a small balcony. About four feet by ten, the balcony jutted out over the ravine, Lues Creek some fifty feet below. Despite the public feel of the balconies, pressed up against one another as they were, Josie liked the effect. The creek was tight and quick; the air over it was noticeably cooler. The forest just beyond had a consoling effect as well. Her balcony it seemed put her almost into the middle of some antique poem, if she looked straight ahead, anyway; it was a place to dream and remember.

She nodded happily at the place, and left the door open to air the apartment while she unpacked her boxes. For anyone accustomed to real life, the apartment would have been disappointing. For Josie, weaned on a decade of collegiate impoverishment, with a twenty-month hiatus as a faculty wife, the place was great, sprawling even. Josie had things the way she wanted soon enough. She needed to do some shopping, but she wanted to try her bike out first and see the rest of the campus. It was only about 4:30. She took a quick shower and put on some shorts and a blouse and tennis shoes.

As Josie started out the door and was digging around for her new key, the phone rang. Since she had requested the line be unlisted, it had to be a wrong number, but she parked the bike and went back inside to get it. "Hello?" she said tentatively. Someone was on the other end. There was a low, steady breathing. So it was a wrong number. But Josie hated the silence that comes over a line in use. It was the kind of silence that reminded her of Dan Scholari's silences. Josie looked around her new apartment. Her happiness and excitement with Lues had washed away suddenly. The place was hot and tight. The woods beyond were darkly oppressive. Setting the phone back in its cradle, Josie forced herself to the door and took the bike in hand without the enthusiasm she had had just moments before. Then, as she was shutting the door, the phone rang again. She parked the bike and went back inside angrily.

"Look!" Josie answered, "You have the wrong number!"

On the other end Dick Ferrington answered, "Josie?"

"Dick," she said, confused, hesitating, "I'm sorry. Did you just call?"

54

"No. No, I'm at school, and I thought I'd give you a call to see if you were in town yet."

"How did you get my number?"

"It's published." He said this as if it were the most natural thing in the world.

"What?"

"New faculty listing. We're a modern university, Josie, computer age and all that."

"I told them I didn't – " Josie broke off her complaint. She didn't need to sound like a scared little girl her first afternoon in a new town. " – Never mind."

"Listen," he said, "I know you're probably tired, but how about we get that drink you mentioned in your letter?"

Dick Ferrington

Her temper was cooling fast. Dick Ferrington's voice was working its old magic. Josie caught a profile of herself in the mirror as she still held the heavy telephone receiver. Six years before, when Josie had met Dr Richard Ferrington, she was working hard on becoming an anorexic. For the past three years, Josie had been changing all of that. She was still pale from her lost summer in the east, but otherwise not so bad. She checked the details: blonde shoulder-length hair pulled back loosely into a band. Green eyes that could get icy in an argument and liquidy for a sentimental story or a dopey, lopsided grin. She had a real weakness for both. Eyebrows needing to be plucked again, thick like a little girl's.

Lips and mouth and cheeks terminally wholesome: she looked like a woman who needed an affair. The nose at least had some character. The married months had given it that lived-in look. Legs, definitely her best feature. Pecs, abs, and biceps . . . improving. Yes, she thought, a quick blush, some mascara. Yes, she was ready for that drink. She couldn't exactly ask Dick to put off their meeting for six weeks.

"Sure," she said. "I was just going out for a bike ride, but I can do that tomorrow." She curled her leg back and checked out the hamstring and buttocks. *Oh, Dr Ferrington*, Josie thought, *have I got a surprise for you!* She knew he was still expecting the emaciated academic, and Josie was pretty proud of the changes.

"Take the bike down the hill," Dick said, "and turn right on Willow. Liberal Arts is out a half-mile or so from your apartment. I'll be out in the parking lot waiting."

"How do you know where I am?"

"It's published, Josie."

"Right." Silently Josie cursed modern bureaucracy and its damnable efficiency. "I look like I'm ready for a bicycle ride and not a drink. Nothing fancy."

"This is Lues, Josie. There's nothing fancy in the whole town. We're just simple country folks."

Josie knew how simple and country Dick Ferrington was. Three awards from the Modern Language Association, a member of the Board of Directors of the Joyce Foundation, author of four books, and not even forty. "Ten minutes," she said.

Their friendship was not as coincidental as it might seem. Still an undergraduate, Josie had gone to a conference devoted to James Joyce, an abiding passion for Josie since she had first read *Ulysses* at the age of thirteen. It had been a huge meeting and brought in all the major scholars of Joyce from around the world, Dick Ferrington among them. Josie had read Ferrington's first book on *Ulysses*, and she knew he was from Lues State. In fact, she had first approached Dick's book with trepidation, as if something of Lues itself might be embedded in the academic tome. What she found was a man both brilliant and lucid, a kindred spirit in the philosophy of literature too. Once Josie saw in the conference directory that Dick Ferrington was in attendance, she had made it a point to look him up. She was expecting to see a dotty old scholar without enough concern for his appearance to wipe the chalk dust off his hands. Coming face to face with the Dick Ferrington of flesh and bones, Josie had nearly swallowed what few academic credentials she had, reverting to a series of regrettable pubescent paroxysms.

Despite everything, they had begun a friendship and correspondence which had lasted until Madrid, three years later. A couple of weeks after she got home from Madrid, Josie found out through a mutual friend of theirs that Dick's wife had vanished while he was gone. Her body turned up a hundred or so miles south of Lues a couple months afterwards. Josie had sent a card of condolence. She didn't know what else to do. It was awful, too awful really for her to call him. Six months after her card, Josie got a note back from Dick. He said he was trying to adjust. He told her what Cathy had meant to him. The details were poignant but somehow left her outside of his grief. Josie was a close friend. His letter confirmed that and failed to hint at more. That was okay. She had plans by then that didn't include Dick Ferrington; cliffs to jump off, would be the more accurate description of the next two and a half years of her life.

Once Josie had secured her job at Lues State, she had written her old friend to tell him the news. In the letter she had suggested they meet for drinks as soon as she got to town and had mentioned the day she was coming. She had meant to call Dick that evening, but an afternoon together was fine. Some afternoons, after all, drifted into long evenings. Their first had, and several after that. The thought of these times – of reviving them, actually – excited Josie as much as her move to Lues. She came off the hill on her new bike, and rolled out toward Liberal Arts, picking up speed and feeling almost like the girl she had been six years ago in Venice.

Josie passed a thick grove of trees, dark and cool, then came upon a sudden spray of concrete, three bi-levels and one tower, all linked to a huge parking lot. Dick was standing at the entrance of the lot, watching her as she pedaled toward him. Three years had improved Dick's physical aspect, if that were possible, and Josie felt suddenly like the same anemic undergraduate he had known. Ferrington was wearing dark blue shorts and a white Lues State T-shirt, the Lancer logo figure tightly contained in one corner of the shirt. Most men past thirty have trouble not looking ridiculous when they dress down. Men almost forty save the shorts and T-shirts for their wives and kids and fishing buddies. Dick Ferrington, as usual, was the exception. Deeply tanned, the arms and legs fit for mountain climbing, the hair now with just little gray at the temples, Dick Ferrington could tempt even a woman with commitments. As it happened, Josie had no commitments at all.

"You look great!" he said, flashing a beautiful white smile. "Where did you get these muscles, Josie?"

Josie smiled at the compliment, her Midwestern accent coming back without her willing it so that she sounded something like a hayseed. "Hey, old man, you don't look too bad yourself." Without thinking Josie reached out to his belly and felt the ripple of muscles. The touch turned things around for a moment, and they both looked at each other intensely. She felt like telling him to forget the drink, let's just have sex right here, and he had the same look. Finally Josie calmed herself down a little and stammered something stupid, hoping to cool things a little. The mood was a bit too much like a flash fire. "It's been too long! I've missed you," she said.

A shadow of sadness crossed his expression. The shoulders slumped a little. "It's been a hard couple of years, Josie."

"It's been three years," she told him.

"Three years." His voice was a whisper. His eyes were distant. "You didn't know Cathy, did you?"

"No. I've never been to Lues." She didn't mean to lie, but once she had, it felt like he saw through her.

"I thought you had," he said. He searched her with a penetrating look.

58

"No." She looked down at the pavement, the coward in her lie.

"That's right," he said. "About five, six years ago, Annie came to campus. But you didn't come?"

Josie nodded. Annie Wilde was the director of Josie's dissertation at Bandolier and her best friend. "Annie came eleven years ago, Dick. Eleven years ago, I was in high school." She laughed at him, "You're turning into an absent-minded professor on me. That or you've been working those abs harder than your brain." She touched his belly again. She wanted that first glow between them back. She didn't like that he mixed her up with Annie or forgot the places they had shared together.

He smiled easily. "Listen, I'm going to put the past behind me. I want to know about *you*, the dissertation, your plans here, what you're going to teach, everything!"

Dick drove them off campus in his sleek black Mercedes, negotiating the snarling university traffic in perfect equanimity.

"How do you like our campus, Josie?"

"It's beautiful if you ignore the buildings."

Dick laughed, "With all the concrete we'll be safe if there's a nuclear war."

After they left campus, Dick took her past some small row houses, through a couple of twisting streets, then up into the hills west of Lues. The road climbed quickly, like a lot of the land around Lues, and soon they came to a restaurant on the crest of the ridge. Lues Creek and West Lues Creek joined just under the hill in a long stretch of rapids. The university seemed a gigantic serpent following Lues Creek back north into the primeval forest.

At that hour the Skyline was dying for business, and that was probably why Dick Ferrington liked it; the place was quiet. The hostess knew Dick as Dr Ferrington, and she knew that he didn't care for an early dinner. As they passed the restaurant and entered the lounge, Josie saw a couple of the waitresses watching her, and realized she was trespassing on their fantasy. Dick and Josie both ordered beers, and in the quiet that followed he leaned back with all the humored confidence of his breed and said, "So I want to hear about this dissertation. What's the word known to all men, Josie? That's it, isn't it, 'Ulysses and the word known to all men'?"

"That's the title, but it's a little more complicated than just answering Joyce's riddle, I think. How did you know about my dissertation?"

"I looked at your application. For knowing the *word* you sure talked your way around pronouncing it in your letter. You were like some miser who's got all the gold. You wanted everyone to know you had it and you weren't sharing a bit of it."

"Oh come on. You know the game. Everything's got to be bigger than life. Besides I'm not giving away my future books and articles to some hiring committee."

"So what is the word? The suspense is killing me."

He was teasing her. He had written three of his four books on *Ulysses*. He knew all the various answers to the riddle: that it was love, that it was *logos*, that it was death, that it was love *and* death (a scholar who couldn't count, apparently). There was even one theory that it was some word that we all knew but couldn't pronounce. In the end, Dick Ferrington had done some version of an academic screaming on paper and called any attempt at answering the riddle "fruitless." It was probably that pronouncement more than anything else that had ignited her search, though Josie wasn't about to admit that to Ferrington at this point.

"Blavatsky almost answers the riddle in another context," she said. "Joyce takes her mumbo-jumbo mysticism and turns it into the real word, the way we all have spoken it. The riddle, you see, isn't Joyce's at all; he just gives us the answer in practical terms."

"And nobody but Josie Darling has seen it?" Dick Ferrington was skeptical.

"Everyone who's read the book has seen it; they just didn't *recognize* it."

He laughed. "Come on, Josie! You have *a* word, a theory, nothing more."

"It's *the word*, Dick. I've solved the puzzle."

"What seventy-some years of intense scholarly scrutiny by the best minds in the business haven't answered, Josie Darling, scholar *extraordinaire*, has?"

"You got that right anyway."

Josie had finally intrigued him, and there was the look, too, that she had beaten him. His scholarly pride was ruffled.

"And what does Annie say? Does Annie know the word now, or aren't you even trusting your dissertation director?" Ferrington's face had a certain flushness Josie didn't like. He looked ready to ignite. It was a look Josie knew too well, but she had never seen it in Dick Ferrington's face.

"She's says I'm going to be a superstar."

He dismissed her casually. "What is it Freud says? Every man is a hero in his own dreams, something like that?"

"It was Herodotus, Dick. 'Every dog has its day.' "

Still amused, at least pretending to be, he told her, "I hope you do, Josie."

"I guess you don't think the word's very important?"

"The truth our friend Mr Joyce teaches is that there is no final answer, no word, no meaning, just riddle upon riddle into infinity. You remember Oedipus, don't you?" She nodded irritably. Dick was indulging in a teacherly streak of condescension that Josie didn't care for. "Oedipus was a solver of riddles. He was a man with the answer, like Josie Darling. He thought his riddle-solving was going to do some good."

"He saved his city from the Sphinx, Dick."

"Oedipus saved them from the Sphinx only to bring a plague! There's a truth for you riddle-solvers!"

"Oedipus saved the city from the plague too, Dick."

Coldly, as if both of them were talking about something

61

else, Ferrington answered her, "It cost him everything, Josie. Solving *that* riddle destroyed him. He looked at the face of truth and it destroyed him."

Josie stopped herself from answering. Dick Ferrington was hardly concerned with riddles. He was talking about his own terrible truth, his own destruction, perhaps. He raised his glass and the bartender nodded, limping as he went to find Dick's brand. The waitress snuffed her cigarette and went to the bar. Josie saw in the actions of all three a familiar routine, old habit if you will, and saw as well a Richard Ferrington who was a bit less Olympian than her younger eyes had admitted to, a man too intimate with lonely places like the Skyline.

After the dissertation, they talked about some of the Joyce Foundation members that they both knew. Dick told her he had been to several meetings during the last two years and remarked that Josie had been conspicuously absent. "You can't keep this great genius of yours under a bushel basket, Josie. Like old Christians on a hilltop," he suggested with something of a metaphoric conflation, "our modern brotherhood wants that bright smile and energy in the flesh. That's what feeds the literature of Joyce, a living, breathing audience of elite minds, talking and sharing, not just essays and the occasional answer to riddles."

She nodded preemptively, "I've had some troubles."

"Your divorce?"

Josie had actually sent Ferrington two letters. The letter she had sent him before she had applied for a job at Lues State – on the chance he might throw his weight around on this end – had mentioned her divorce, nothing of the problems there had been because of it.

"Listen, I don't want you to say anything about it. Promise?"

He raised one eyebrow, as good as an oath.

"My husband . . . my ex-husband was an extremely violent man."

62

"Josie, I'm sorry."

Josie was too embarrassed to notice if there was much sincerity in Dick's sympathy. Without thinking, she confessed more than she intended: "We were married twenty months. I can't tell you how many times he hit me or knocked me against the wall, and worse. He always had some excuse later, some apology; he was the master at making up afterwards, and I just kept buying it until one day I found myself waiting to get hit, and I realized what he was doing to me. I filed for divorce the next day."

Dick nodded approvingly, but he was already a thousand miles away. She knew it and couldn't stop herself from going on.

"That's when things got really bad. Look," she said, bringing her story to a close hurriedly, "it makes me uncomfortable to talk about it. I know I'm supposed to be the victim here and it's not my fault, but I don't think that way. It feels like it's all my fault. I feel like I could have done something to stop it. I mean I had to fall in love with the jerk in the first place. That puts some of the blame on me."

"Josie, we never know what's in the heart of another person. We can't. You aren't responsible for other people's crimes. You can't know what kind of person someone is until it's too late."

She nodded, but she didn't believe it. Josie was certain she was living her mother's nightmare. Somewhere long ago she believed she had learned what love is through her mother's example: her mother had been killed by the man she loved. Josie had come close twice. She wasn't a victim, she was an active participant. She had chosen a man who was capable of terrible violence. She was certain that somewhere deep inside her she had been trying to find her own Jack Hazard, everything forgotten but the essentials: how to get yourself killed.

"I believe we do know," Josie said with sudden defiance. "I think we're drawn to violent natures or to kind ones

63

because we know what's in their soul, and whatever it is they have, it's what we think we need. I don't know how we know, but I think there's a signal, and when we find what we want or think we want, we fall in love. It's why we marry the same people over and over. It's why victims are always victims, at least until they learn what's going on in their own heads and change it. Annie calls it 'revising the soul.' "

"I think you and Annie have gone a little too New Age on this for me, Josie. I read Annie's last book. The old girl's gone to the moon, in my opinion."

Josie flared but couldn't quite answer.

"We're just lucky, or we're unlucky. That's all it is," he said. "Some maniac sees us and that's it. Our world turns upside down and there's nothing we can do to change it. There's no karma for violence or whatever Annie wants to call it."

Dick was talking about his wife, Josie realized, and it wouldn't do any good to get in a fight about Annie. It wasn't Annie's book that bothered him; it was some faceless man's violence against his wife he was raging against.

For a moment, both of them were quiet, their thoughts diverging toward their separate agonies.

Finally, with that kind of social desperation we feel around bankrupts, ex-convicts, and the recently unemployed, Josie asked him, "So how are the kids?"

Years ago Ferrington had showed Josie a wallet snapshot of his family, two girls and a boy, the family dog and the gorgeous wife. Seriously gorgeous. It was an image that had stayed with her as a reminder of Dr Ferrington's status. Josie had always reinforced the image at some point in their conversation with a question about the family. Suburban dad as well as world-renowned scholar, Dick Ferrington had always obliged and generally threw in a good story about the dog, too.

"Kids are good, Josie. Expensive but good. I've got one

off in college, Chapel Hill, like old dad, and the two girls are at prep schools in New Hampshire." He talked about the girls for a moment, then described his son's academic intentions at the University of North Carolina.

"You're not old enough for a kid in college."

"I'm ancient, Josie. I'll be forty in November. No, Cathy and I got started early. It made it tough in the beginning, but I'm glad we did it that way. Cathy got to see them grow up; most of the way, anyhow. I keep thinking I ought to sell the house now that I'm alone, for most of the year anyway, get a little apartment and travel more, but I don't know, it's kind of nice to have the woods at my back. It's why I chose Lues in the first place, and the older I get, the more I feel the wisdom of Thoreau. There's a lot of truth in that Yankee Puritanism." There was a slight dampness in his eye. "I just – " he smiled at himself and ducked his head. "It's three years September they found Cathy's remains."

"They never identified the killer?"

Ferrington studied her intensely, the eyes still glistening. "After they ruled me out, they tried to link Cathy's death to some kind of serial killer. That got the FBI involved in it, so naturally I never saw a report and even the rumors dried up. Those people are very private about what they know. The truth is I don't think they know anything; according to our local people, there was never any hard evidence. They have no idea why it happened or who possibly could have done it." He shook his head, and Josie realized only then the pain he had gone through.

"They really thought it was you?"

"Everyone loved Cathy, so I was the only one the police could think of who might have a motive. You know, 'We always kill the one we love.' So they're trained to look close to home first; when that lead fails, they generally fail, sophisticated methods or not. Of course I was in Madrid reading a paper when Cathy vanished, so they had a little trouble figuring how I could have done it, try as they did."

65

"That's terrible," Josie answered.

"I think they gave up on me as a suspect after a couple of weeks, but of course they didn't extend any apologies." There was a lament in this that surprised Josie. His voice carried the bitterness of a man who's known more than his share of troubles. Josie supposed there was the guilt by accusation that clung to any kind of inquiry like that, too. It was a hard taint to scrub off, as much internal as public.

"It's bad enough to deal with grief, Josie. You're crying your eyes out, your kids are lost, people are coming by and you talk and talk about . . . what you can't have back. The last thing in the world you need is some second-rate detective trying to fit you into his scheme of things with his specious reasoning and inevitably confused chronology of events. I tell you, I thought for a while it wasn't worth living. The kids kept me going. They needed me. If it hadn't been for them . . ."

Josie felt the ache of recognition and nodded. When her mother had died, there had been no one at all for her. "They needed you more than ever after something like that," she said.

"And I needed them. Of course, I hardly see them now. They're away at school nine months and the grandparents want time with them . . ." He shrugged cavalierly, a man alone and living with it.

"So are you going to remarry?"

He smiled, looking down into his pretty lap. "Nothing on the horizon, Josie. How about you?"

He was fast on the return, and Josie was left with her own bald intentions hanging out like a sagging slip. "My divorce was final this spring," she said finally, "so I guess my horizons are pretty clear too."

"Well, it's too soon. I wouldn't worry."

Ferrington's smile was patently obtuse, but she knew him well enough to see this was a dismissal. He wasn't interested. It was the confession of her abuse. Ferrington could have any woman he wanted. Why bother with a used punching bag?

When the bill came, Josie reached for her purse, but Ferrington stopped her. "Not this time, Josie. You get a paycheck in two and a half weeks, first of September, just like the poem. You buy then."

Josie nodded good-naturedly. "It's a date, Dr Ferrington, and I mean to hold you to it."

Ferrington's eyebrows rose wickedly. "I'm looking forward to it." So maybe he just wanted to take it slow. Okay. Slow was good. Slow she could live with.

On the drive back, Ferrington's expression had a sudden mischief about it, a prank or joke. "Oh, by the way, they're giving you an office across from Henry Valentine."

The name meant nothing. "Is that good or bad?"

"Val's been here . . . I came, let's see, thirteen years ago. He was a full professor then. I think it was about the dawn of time that Val showed up at Lues State."

"Oh, God, one of those."

"No, no! He's not *that* old. He's just been here forever. You'll like him, Josie."

"But?" Just something in the man's tone.

"The kids love him. I mean crazy for him! When this guy walks into his classroom, the kids all stand up and applaud him."

"No!" Josie had never even heard of such a thing and assumed this was just so much Ferrington hyperbole.

"It's the truth! It's a Lues State tradition; every year, every class, every time. They stand and applaud. The man's a legend."

"Not so bad of a neighbor then. I think I can handle a legend."

"The downside is he's always got kids in his office. I mean they tell him things they wouldn't tell a shrink. I don't know how he handles it. I wouldn't want that kind of responsibility, but Val loves it. He's there for his kids, and they use him.

67

Of course, that's the problem. His door is always open – literally; so you're going to hear it all." Dick's eyebrows lifted in ironic condolence. "There's a reason they give the office across from him to a lecturer. None of the regular faculty would take that slot if it came with a promotion."

"Nobody ever said a lecturer has it easy," Josie answered.

As they came to Josie's bicycle, Ferrington announced pleasantly that he wouldn't see her Monday at the faculty meeting. "I'm flying out tomorrow morning for Zurich – the Foundation's workshop on *Ulysses*. I'll be gone all week."

"I thought about going, myself," Josie answered, "but I didn't think I ought to miss the first week of classes, not as the new kid on the block, anyway."

For a moment Josie considered the man. She had thought there might be more, that she might lean over and kiss him – a friendly kiss – but he had already dismissed her. He was thinking about Zurich.

"Say hi to Fritz and the gang," she told him, and pushed her way out of his car.

As he drove off, Josie had the feeling that a lot had changed between them. And why not? Time hadn't stood still for either of them. She'd been a fool to think that because she had shown up in Lues Dick was going to want some kind of romance. He probably had all the romance he wanted. Of course he did. Two and a half weeks until a drink: a man like Ferrington was just booked up! *Get in line, girl.*

Tiredly, Josie pedaled back to her new apartment. The place was shabby after all.

She checked herself in the mirror. Pretty resistible stuff.

Footnotes in the Nightmare

Josie arrived at the Liberal Arts complex at just past noon the next day, intent on finding her past in a capsule. The pavement of the parking lot was already steamy with the August heat. She took her bike through a plaza between

Varner and Brand Halls and rolled by a thin ribbon of concrete back to Worley. Inside the building Josie shivered. Her back was wet from the brief ride, and she was suddenly a part of a giant refrigeration system. She sneezed several times and thought about going back for some sweats but decided she would get used to the cold. She didn't. The entry of Worley Hall was a long narrow vault, almost fifty feet high and twenty feet across. It was constructed of raw concrete forms, giving it a monolithic effect. Along both sides of the entryway, several past presidents and honor-laden professors were screwed to the walls like so many ill-starred moths. Not long ago, these would have been white men, but times are rife with revisionists: digging deep, Lues State had found the colors of its past. There was a racial and gender balance sufficient to convince anyone of the university's long tradition of multiculturalism. Josie studied the faces with a perverse curiosity. For one thing, with a single exception, they all looked like they belonged to the same fraternity. Men and women, caucasians, negroes, and orientals: they were old, ostentatious, and strained ever so slightly to smile fondly. Their eyes told you, like all the teachers everywhere, I *know* the answer. The exception to the gallery was the centerpiece, an American Indian who had been a student, not at Lues State as it turned out, but at its forerunner, Southeastern Presbyterian College. In 1917, this full-blooded Shawnee – his name inadvertently omitted from the plaque – had left his freshman class with two other Native Americans to join the United States Army. This one made the wall by dying.

At the security desk, Josie checked a plan of the building. Her search for Jack Hazard and her mother began on the sixth floor, which was devoted to Journalism. She had some help with the procedures, which turned out to be a bit easier than she was used to, and soon enough was sitting in a long, narrow room, a window to the stacks behind her, her head bent into one of the big metal bins which allow you to crank

69

through time with a handle set at ear level. Josie spent several minutes rolling through the local and national cataclysms twenty years ago, holding out high hopes that she could understand her life through a simple newspaper account. Her optimism lasted about five minutes.

Josie had expected her life and her mother's and Jack Hazard's to be scripted on long columns which would describe the violence Jack had done to both of them and finally the culminating act against her mother, but that wasn't the way of it. Josie started in January and rolled into August without success. She knew that by August she had been taken to the upstate flatlands to live with the Darlings, so, dejectedly, she cranked back to the beginning of the year and started reading again, this time peeking into the corners. Josie had been scanning headlines the first trip through. She thought all murder was a sensation. She hadn't quite come to terms with the fact that her mother's death was a back-page affair, even in the chronicles of a back-page town. Her eye fell invariably to the same headlines she had seen before. She was still missing the little things: the honor society students at Rensselaer Junior High School, the salesman of the month at Dempsey's Auto Fair, the centennial birthdays of lives too stubborn to quit. She found herself constantly drifting, a student of a world that had no interest for her, except in a particular fact that remained elusive. If there were no splashy headlines, at least, she thought, she ought to find a single story, a narrative of her mother's death. She really didn't care about the other lives and bodies. She had been too long in her specialties; she had forgotten the vast interconnectedness of even the most insignificant of lives.

She found a "Police Bulletin" that was usually on page six but sometimes stuck back on page ten. It came out once a week but not always on the same day. Sometimes it was apparently not included. She skimmed these bulletins. In January alone Josie found six Hazards on the honor roll:

70

drunk, drunk and disorderly, drunk driving, assault (at a tavern), drunk, and drunk again. Finally! She was on the road to Jack Hazard. Josie began looking at these bulletins systematically, and shortly the name John Christian Hazard appeared. Age thirty-three, he was taken into custody for assaulting four members of the Lues State Football team at a tavern called the Hurry On Up. The Hurry On Up featured topless dancers.

Josie made a detailed note of the proud moment and rolled on. Shortly, she found this weird title and article, dated February 10:

Mysterious Dearth

A nude female was found dead at the side of Stop 16 Road by passing motorists late yesterday afternoon. Sheriff Pat Bitts reports the woman was struck by a passing automobile sometime in early hours this morning. No identification has been made of the nude woman struck by a passing automobile.

Josie looked up from the prose and took a deep breath. Welcome to Lues, she told herself. In vain she looked for a follow-up article about the woman; it might well have been her mother, she realized with a strange sense of nausea. There was nothing to tell her if it was so. She read the next two city arrest reports, but there was no mention of a vehicular homicide, although another Hazard was arrested for drunk and disorderly. His name was Virgil. She read the obituaries for several days, but there was nothing to finish the report of the mysterious *dearth*. She went back to the article and copied it, *sics* and all (found yesterday, killed this morning, nice trick). Beyond the inaccuracies and first-grader grammar, Josie was frustrated with the report's utter emptiness. There were hardly enough facts to notice what hadn't been included. Were her clothes found close by or did they vanish? Who reported finding her? Had she come out into the road unexpectedly or was she walking along the side when she was hit? What did her blood show – alcohol, drugs, diabetes? Was her car found? She looked back two days. The high temperature between February eight and ten was 53 degrees. The low was 38 degrees: a cold night for streaking in rural Lues. Josie cranked the handle of her machine and searched everything again for the next few days. She was worried now that it might be her mother; the utter anonymity was the worst of it.

When she could find nothing more on the nude at the side of the road, Josie screwed down her concentration and pushed on. There were more Hazards drunk in March, their names like some kind of alcoholic's epic catalog. Then she found it. The article was placed beside an advertisement for ballet classes to begin in May, classes for all ages. She saw at once why she had missed it the first time through; it looked like part of the advertisement. Her mother, she learned, had been a dancer, of sorts.

Dated April 4, the first notice of her mother's murder read in full:

Dancer Discovered

Colt Fellows announced this morning that an unanimous trip sent local investigators into Lues Creek Canyon late last last evening where they discovered the nude body of Josephine Fortune, 27. A dancer at the Hurry On Up, which features topless dancers, Fellows, Chief of Homicide Detectives, said his division and the sheriff's department are working in concert on the investigation as a part of the new county and city Coordination of Resources and Personnel (CRP). Longtime sheriff Pat Bitts was unavailable for comment.

Josie looked up from the article in a perfect daze. Something like ice formed in the pit of her stomach. Her name was Josephine. *Josie*. Josie Fortune. Josie's own name, once upon a time. And Josie Fortune had taken her clothes off for a living. Anyone could look for the price of a drink. Josie understood now why they had taken her upstate, why the Darlings had done her the service of burying her past. *And buried it should have stayed*, she told herself sickly.

Josie rolled the plastic scroll to the next day. This time the mention of a bar owner in the title alerted her, and she looked at the text closely:

Bar Owner Changed

State Police arrested John Christian Hazard, 33, of rural Lues early yesterday afternoon for the murder of Josie Fortune, 27. The arrest was ordered shortly after City Homicide investigators discovered Hazard's broken wristwatch near the site of the murder in Lues Creek Canyon. The murder occurred sometime after six o'clock, Thursday, the result of strangulation according to the coroner's office. Colt Fellows, spearheading the investigation, sought state police assistance after Sheriff Pat Bitts was unable to be located. "We were looking at a hostage situation with the victim's daughter, and we moved fast," Fellows explained. Hazard was turned over to city authorities for interrogation after state troopers apprehended him. Hazard's stepdaughter, Deborah Josephine Fortune, 7, was taken into custody by sheriff and is expected to be turned over to state welfare workers. Hazard is being held pending a bail hearing.

Josie copied out the story and cranked the handle searching for her mother's obituary, but there was none.

On April 8, not a week after Josie Fortune's murder, there was a final installment in the saga:

Scott OKays Plea

County Prosecutor Don Scott announced early this morning that John Christian Hazard, 33, has agreed to plead guilty to charges of accidental homicide in the death of Josie Fortune, 27. Under the agreement, Hazard will not be sentenced to more than twenty years in a state correctional facility yet to be determined. Fortune's body was discovered last Thursday in Lues Creek Canyon. Authorities report that she was stranged.

Stranged? Josie cranked the film through for several more minutes, but there was nothing else to find. It seemed she had all she could gather. She rewound the film finally and boxed it. She left the room and returned the material to the librarian. Outside, the heat drained what little energy she had, and she went home. The great project she had set for herself had turned out to be something she didn't care to pursue. The death of the woman who had given her life had nothing to do with her. It was simply the story of a murdered prostitute.

There were still things to do before school started, and Josie drove out to the mall to pick up the odds and ends she would need to make life a bit more comfortable. Miserably, she wandered through the stores, listening to the grating twang which was neither Midwestern nor quite fully southern, a kind of whining cross of the two that exited through the nose. It was considerably different from the midstate dialect she had spoken as a child, and she hated it passionately. The people seemed friendly enough, but there was a slowness she couldn't stand. It was enough to fill her with regret at coming here. What had she expected, though?

She had always hated home. None of it was much different from what she had left years ago, except that this was just a deeper, more lonesome brand of country. Down here misery added an extra twist; that was all.

And it seemed to her she was doomed to run fast and far until she had landed no more than a few inches on a map from where she had started. Josie heard her own voice slip into the cadences of the clerks who waited on her. She felt her metabolism changing even as she waited for them to punch in the price of her purchases. Five different clerks asked her, "Is it hot enough for you?"

Annie Wilde

Josie phoned Annie in Boston and got her answering machine on the third ring. Annie's voice was a foghorn in minor key, "I'm at the firing range with my Uzi so I can't answer this call in person, but if you leave a message, I'll call you after my karate lesson." After the tone, Josie started talking. Annie picked up as soon as she recognized Josie's voice. "You want to come home. You've made a terrible mistake and you're flying back to Boston first thing tomorrow, am I right?" Josie told her she was right, and she wished it were true.

"I'm teaching that 'Magnificent Metaphors' course. I saw the class roster on that thing, Josie. Four hundred. I can use another grader if you want to come back."

Josie was under contract; she didn't really have a choice and said so.

Apparently catching the weariness in Josie's voice, Annie answered, "My first teaching job, Josie, I had a herd of cows just at the window of the classroom, see, and sometimes I'd get so frustrated I'd talk to the cows instead of the kids. They were far more attentive, chewing their cuds, staring at me. One of them actually went onto college – "

"Classes haven't started yet, Annie, but I have some things I want to talk about."

"And you don't want to hear about my cows?" Annie sounded mildly disappointed. "So, how's Dick Ferrington? Did you kiss him on the mouth like I told you?"

Annie was a being a sport. They'd already had their fight about Josie's decision to teach at Lues. The place was an academic swamp, according to Annie.

"Dick didn't seem very interested," Josie answered.

"Count yourself lucky, Josie. The man's a bore. All good looks and footnotes."

"Listen, Annie," she announced, "I found some things in the library today."

"I hear that happens sometimes."

"My mother's name was Josephine, Josie like yours truly."

"Josie Hazard?"

"Josie Fortune. She kept her name when she married Jack, I take it. She was twenty-seven when Jack killed her."

"How did it happen, Josie?"

"The murder? I don't have much. The paper is terrible. No. It's so bad it's funny. These goobers must get drunk before they write. You wouldn't believe it! All I know is she was strangled to death." Josie shuddered as she admitted this to Annie. She hadn't really registered the meaning of such a death when she had read about it. She had been thinking about coincidences and what her mother *was*. Jack Hazard, John Christian Hazard, thirty-three, had looked right into her face while he killed her. They had touched, struggled; then she had died in his hands. "Jack strangled her in some canyon. He confessed to it all a few days later, part of a plea bargain. They called it an *accidental homicide*, Annie, and gave him twenty years."

"Accidental? For strangling someone?"

"That's what the paper reported."

"Twenty years? So, is he back by now, paroled, good behavior, early release?"

76

"I guess I need to find that out." Josie had no intention of finding Jack Hazard. She wasn't sure if she had ever planned to find Jack and talk to him.

"You need to talk to him, Josie. He can tell you about your mother. And look for the name Fortune in the phone book; do a search of the whole region. You might have some family – "

"I think I already know more than I care to."

"What are you talking about?" With the instinct of a great teacher, Annie smelt a quitter.

"Are you ready for this?" Josie asked her.

"I'm sitting down, if that's what you mean."

Annie's wheelchair humor never failed to jolt Josie's composure, but at present it hardly registered with her; she was thinking about her mother's shame.

"She was an exotic dancer . . . a stripper, Annie!"

"I knew you came from good blood!"

"Annie, it's not a joke! Jack owned this bar called the Hurry On Up, and she *danced* for him."

With acidity, "So you've got her whole life figured out?"

Josie told herself it wasn't *Annie's* mother they were talking about.

"I figured out some of it, yes. For starters, he manipulated her, degraded her, probably beat her. It was all foreplay to the last act, if you know what I mean."

Annie cut in, "Listen, did I ever tell you about my night in jail?"

"Once or twice."

"I'm a *jailbird*! Do you have the story of my life from that little piece of information?" Josie didn't answer. "It means nothing, Josie. So I attacked a United States Senator! Big deal! The man said the handicapped weren't his problem. I changed that! I was the biggest problem he ever had!"

"It's not the same thing, Annie."

"People found out he pressed assault charges against me, and he was *done*! I went around Vermont in my wheelchair

77

and got on every television station in the state. He couldn't get elected dog catcher after that!"

"You went to jail for principles, Annie! This is just sordid; a woman who strips for men for a living is – " Josie couldn't finish her thought. The only words to answer were too violent to contemplate of one's mother. "It's humiliating."

"You need to find out why she did it. You need everything you can find. We always have reasons for what we do, even if we don't understand them ourselves. Find your stepfather. You can start with him."

"I don't think I can talk to the man," Josie answered. "I mean do you really think I'll get the truth from a man like that?"

"So help me with this, Josie. Are you afraid of his truth or his lies?"

"What's he going to tell me, that his Josie was sure one humdinger of a wage-earner? The guys all loved it when Josie came on stage? What do I want to hear from the guy?"

"You took a year of your life to go find out what happened, Josie. You didn't know what it was going to bring you, and you still don't. I'll tell you something else: if that woman you read about today was anyone but your mother you wouldn't jump to conclusions. If she were just some woman you decided to do a biography of, you would research her completely, you'd see the world as she saw it, and write about it without a lot of *stupid* prejudices." She hesitated. "I'm sorry, Josie, but it's the truth."

"Maybe."

"No maybe to it, sister. What did you think, your mother was a saint, maybe a virgin?" Her voice had its lilt again. "You started something here; now finish it!"

"I get the point. I'll try to find out more."

Josie felt weary with the responsibility Annie wouldn't let her shrug away. She remembered that we needn't always love our best teachers, that sometimes we loathe them for what they make us do for ourselves.

"Go find where she was killed. Stand where it happened!"

"I don't know. That's . . ."

"You thought about doing that?"

She hadn't, but she knew she should have. She realized the truth about her mother had scared her, and that she had put her mother's life away as quickly and easily as the microfilm she had boxed. She had left the library fully intending to do anything but continue looking for her mother's life, or even her own. "It scares me. The whole thing scares me, and I don't know why."

"Did you see her picture?" Josie answered that she hadn't. "Did you remember her yet?"

She told Annie about the memory of sitting between her mother and Jack: " . . . but that's all."

"Any names? Any people quoted?"

"In the article about her murder? A few. Lawyers and cops. I like the sheriff, he was always unavailable for comment, probably a drunk."

"Find them. Talk to them. Systematically, like a real researcher, Josie. You remember research don't you?" Josie said she wasn't sure. Annie let the joke go unacknowledged. "The newspapers always get something mixed up, Josie. Remember our campus rag? The profile on me? I'm a marathon runner. Did you know I get out of this chair at nights and run?"

"You told that boy that's what you were."

"He was looking at me, staring right at my wheelchair, Josie, and he said, 'So do you have any hobbies, Dr Wilde?' and I said, 'I run the Boston Marathon every day', only he thought I said 'year.' Talk about dumb, he didn't even blink. The next thing I know, it's published and people are sending me entry blanks for their races."

"I'll keep looking," Josie answered. She didn't mean it. Her training in research extended only to esoteric matters; she had no confidence in her abilities to understand life, no touch with reality, no intention now to learn about it.

Colleagues

At about 8:15 Monday morning, Josie drove to Liberal Arts. Once at the faculty lot, she carried one of her two boxes to the department's general office in Brand Hall and borrowed a master key for her office. The secretary told Josie she would need to go to Building and Grounds for her office keys. She gave her a small blue slip of paper. On it were scribbled the letters "Br-outside," for the outside doors of Brand, she assumed, followed by "Br105," kindergarten code for Josie's office door. On a line at the bottom of the slip the secretary scratched her initials. "Give them this and a dollar for each key and they'll set you up." Josie opened her office and dropped off the books. On the way back she returned the master key, then went out for the second box. The parking lot was busy with a few students and several faculty. The lot seemed huge as Josie walked across it with the heavy box in her arms. She turned around a few times to check behind her, an old habit, and she felt anger that even now, a thousand miles from Boston, she still checked her back, she still worried. How was it, she asked herself, that Dick Ferrington had put it? *We're just lucky, or we're unlucky. That's all it is. Some maniac sees us and that's it. Our world turns upside down and there's nothing we can do to change it.* Maybe he was right. Well, Josie had married her lunatic. Even geography couldn't quite erase his presence entirely.

Across from her office, Josie noticed Henry Valentine's name on the door. Lues State's own legend was apparently running late. Down the hall, in the opposite direction to the main office, she found Dick Ferrington's office. Like Valentine's, it was dark. Several of the faculty introduced themselves as Josie tried to make her way to the main office to meet the chair and the other two lecturers she had been hired with. They came out of doorways and blocked her in the hall, all of them appearing suddenly, giving her the same look people give the lobster in its tank. At the department office, Josie found Dr Smith in a small conference room.

She was a few minutes late, and the orientation had already started. Smith was a flappable and sloppy man with long greasy hair and dusty reading glasses that he let perch on his nose just under the line of his vision. He had a sharpened, weasel expression and might once have been energized with a scholar's pursuits and a schoolteacher's worries, but he had long ago given over to the Lues pace of things: slow, and nothing very urgent except getting to happy hour. He called Josie Dr Darling, and when she corrected him, he became uncomfortable with the whole matter and forgot to introduce her to the other two lecturers. One was a thin Korean woman, who was dressed nicely and kept a leather briefcase on her lap that cost more than Josie's monthly stipend at Bandolier University. The second new hire was a Nigerian man. He was nearly seven feet tall but couldn't have weighed more than 160 pounds. He had a habit of clicking his tongue randomly as Smith talked to them, and during the meeting he held his Nigerian passport in prominent view. After Josie settled into a seat, Smith picked up mid-thought with his 'department procedures' and ran a fast-forward that still managed to get hung up on the department's difficulties three years ago requisitioning its own copy machine and other historical trivia. He slapped his knees suddenly, a little cloud of chalk dust emanating from his trousers, then gave them something of a snarl: "We need to get over to Varner Hall for the meeting."

As Smith had no talent for small talk, the four of them walked in an executioner's silence through the hot air. At the lecture hall, Smith pushed ahead, leaving the new people alone to face two hundred bored and testy professors. All faces seemed to turn as the three new lecturers entered the hall. The professors had coffee and doughnuts in their hands and time to kill.

The Korean was the first casualty; she was peeled off from the group by several men in suits, administrative types who circled around her, their noses wet, their tails wagging eagerly. She was a two-pointer, in Affirmative Action scoring, and Josie heard her telling them what they needed to do to get her a green card. A dotty old woman in blue sweats took the Nigerian aside, trying to get him to pronounce his name slowly enough for her to repeat it. Josie saw him open his passport and show her his name, but the woman still couldn't get it. Josie stood by herself for only a moment before she was hit by three smiling faces. Over the next half-hour, she drank rank coffee and resisted a second stale sugar doughnut while what seemed like a hundred academics introduced themselves. She wished Dick Ferrington were here to run some interference. Dick could have told them she was really a scholar; right now, she was feeling more like shark bait.

When a tall, very bald man entered the room, the woman talking to Josie about her grading techniques gasped and nodded toward the fellow. "Henry Valentine."

Another woman came toward them, whispering the name as well, and Josie found herself fascinated.

"Val's looking *healthy*, I see," the first woman commented.

"They say heart attack victims always look flush and healthy before it hits," the other woman offered.

Josie looked at them curiously, "Has he had problems?"

"No. No. But we keep hoping."

Inexplicably, Henry Valentine was the college's bad boy, even though he looked to be not a day under sixty. Josie thought he was kind of cute in an ugly old man's bad-boy way, and she found herself drawn to him with an outsider's affection for the local maverick. When yet another professor had mentioned him, Josie answered with pretended naivety, "I hear Dr Valentine's students applaud when he walks into the classroom." This brought a studied pause from the woman, before the chilling exit line, "I'm not at all confident what Val is doing would be called *real* teaching."

The next to discuss Dr Valentine mentioned Val's inevitable retirement; there was a wistful look in his expression as he said this. In fact with everyone who happened to mention Dr Valentine, and once he had arrived, everyone seemed to, Josie discovered something between deep envy for his popularity and a near-supernatural fear of his displeasure, though whatever fear they evinced hardly restrained their talk behind his back. Envy Josie understood. She felt it herself. Who wouldn't want to face the applause of one's admirers? The fear of him, Josie found unaccountable.

People talked about other things, of course. They had more cooking on their grill than Henry Valentine. They were professors after all, and so passed their time in a complex and meaningless game of trench warfare, tossing canisters of mustard gas to fall as they might. Their alliances were quick and shifting, their smiles like daggers. Josie had seen all this before but not actually from her own trench.

After doughnuts there was a long meeting, then a greasy buffet of meatballs with beer and wine for chasers. On her second time through for the meatballs, Josie turned out of line and squarely into Henry Valentine. Valentine had big hulking bony shoulders. His eyes were hooded and fearsome and keenly bright, oddly disenfranchised from the smile he offered. The face was tanned to a deep brown, weathered almost to the point of ruin. The hands were huge and slow moving, though with a young man's power. He wore a soft, shapeless long-sleeved cotton shirt that he buttoned to the top and slightly baggy, faded jeans, the look of a tramp in his Sunday best. "I read a wonderful line in Henry Miller last night," he announced with odd familiarity. His voice was deep, faintly southern, fully grand in a way that was entirely his own. "Let me see if I can recall it *precisely*, yes: 'There are no ready-made infernos for misfortune.' " He studied her reaction expectantly, but Josie had no response other than letting her mouth gape open in confusion. "I'm Henry Valentine; my friends call me Val." He said this as if it were a magnificent fact which bore repeating often.

83

"Josie Darling," she answered. "I'm new. I don't have any friends."

"Oh, I know who you are, Miss Darling. I chaired the hiring committee for your position. I had a Herculean task convincing these . . . these *colleagues* that it is not a racist act to hire an American citizen."

"Thanks, I guess. What were you reading of Miller's? I don't know that line." Josie had read all of Miller, and had even stomached some of it, a fact she was not willing to admit in most academic circles.

Val stared heavily into her eyes, only now letting go of her hand. There was a faint, goatish scent about him; it was an intoxicating odor, Pan-ish. "It's wonderful, isn't it?" Val responded.

"It's a bit out of context for me." Josie had no idea what he meant by "no ready-made infernos."

Valentine's smile widened. He couldn't give a damn what Josie understood, so long as she was awed. "*The Tropic of Cancer.* I think it a lovely image, that a personalized hell is created for each misfortune. The idea of everyone in a burning lake of fire has always bored me stiff. For me, hell would be – " he looked about, choosing his image carefully – "school lessons from the likes of our *colleagues*." He seemed conspiratorial; at least he acted as if he thought Josie and he were old friends. His hircine odor cloyed in the back of her throat, and Josie staggered slightly. The man exuded not open lust so much as the expectation that Josie should find him irresistibly exciting. The notion was both comic and true. "And what would be your hell, Josie?"

Josie didn't miss a beat here. "Riddles without answers."

"Spoken as a true Joycean."

Josie took the compliment as a chance to excuse herself, and seeing a crowd starting out of the lecture hall, followed. She wanted to spend some time in her office. Classes, after all, were starting Wednesday, ready or not. At Brand Hall Josie checked the department office for messages. She found a slip in her mailbox with the date and time. The message was: *D.S.M.I.A.A.W.* She looked at the letters, frowning dumbly.

"I took that," the girl at the desk said. Obviously a student helper, the red-haired girl had *The Pre-Socratics* propped up in front of her, getting a head start on the semester. "Does it make any sense?"

Josie read the message again, shaking her head.

"She made me write it like that, then read it back to her. Strange lady!"

It came to Josie at once; it was Annie's message: *Dan Scholari Missing In Action, Annie Wilde.* "Got it," Josie answered. "Thanks."

"What's it mean?" the girl asked.

Josie looked back at the note, understanding perfectly now what it meant. "It means there are no ready-made infernos for Miss Fortune."

"You got that from those initials?"

"Ten years of college ought to be good for something, don't you think?"

In her office, Josie tried to call Annie, but she had no luck getting through. *Missing in action?* Dan hadn't shown up for the Bandolier's kick-off faculty meeting, and he hadn't called in to get excused, apparently. Annie thought it was important enough to leave a message, and Josie wondered if there was any way he might know she had come to Lues. She had been careful. She had kept her plans utterly secret. Her parents knew what she was doing. Annie knew. The director of graduate studies, and no friend of Dan Scholari, knew, and that was it. She had told no one else where she was moving. Of course, M.I.A. didn't mean Dan had followed Josie out of Boston or anticipated her move somehow. That just wasn't possible. But it wasn't possible either that Dan Scholari would miss a required faculty meeting without calling his dean. At Bandolier they were brutal about the details. Dan had been there long enough to know they would make his life hell if he missed such a meeting.

So what was she supposed to think? He was here? Is that what Annie was saying? Good God! When was the man going to give it up? Josie had told Dick Ferrington things had been rough, but that was hardly the extent of it. The marriage had been rough; the divorce had nearly killed her – twice. The first time, she had just moved out and gotten a lawyer. Things had gone well for a couple of weeks. Then one evening Dan had come by her new place to talk about the property division her lawyer had presented his lawyer. She hadn't wanted to let him in, but he was sober and seemingly in good temper and the questions he had were seemingly legitimate. The moment Josie undid the chain on her door, he had come after her. He had hit her and had kept hitting her, apparently, until he heard the police sirens. At her first opportunity, Josie had pressed charges. This hadn't been a domestic quarrel or a husband's sudden temper. This was an open assault, a cold-blooded attack, and she made that clear to the police. That's what you're supposed to do. Everyone told her to do it. She had told herself to do it. Josie thought of herself as a fighter. She didn't crawl into holes and hide. She didn't run away. She had put up with too much in the marriage, but the marriage was over, and she was forgiving nothing anymore. She got tough and she stayed tough, and she stood up in court and described what Dan Scholari had done with dry-eyed detail. She stared the man down in court, the way Annie said we must stare down our nightmares, and she told the judge the threats Dan had been making since the arrest, which he had hoped would keep her from testifying. For her courage, Dan got three months in jail, suspended. The conviction didn't cost him his tenure at the university of course, not even a semester's leave without pay. It simply angered him, and the day after his last meeting with the judge, Dan started calling Josie at all hours with his dead silences, dropping off unsigned letters at her apartment and at school with cryptic death threats as only a professor of literature can do. She still recalled having to look up citations in order to find vile descriptions of women's deaths.

Josie had let the threats go because she thought Dan would tire of it. Dan hadn't done these things before; he had simply shown up at her door, pleaded his way in, and beat her into a coma. She convinced herself that the harassment and threats were a form of goodbye. It is one thing to threaten violence, quite another to know you will go to jail if you indulge in it; Josie had shown him she wasn't afraid to stand up in court and denounce him, so she was sure he was done with her except for the barking.

And finally he did stop. The silence lasted two months, but then one night, as Josie was coming out of the library, Dan caught her. She didn't see him until it was too late. He was crouching in the shadows beside her driver-side door and appeared before her just as she was fumbling with her keys. She looked up in time to see his fist coming at her face. She went down hard but still conscious. Dan was good at leaving her conscious as long as possible. He liked to talk while he beat her. He called her *baby*. It was his pet name for her. When Josie tried to scream for help, Dan kicked her in the face, breaking her nose for the third time since they had met. After that, he broke four of her ribs and fractured her ankle. He punched her in the shoulders and arms and back and stomach. He pounded on her thighs, then struck her several glancing blows across the face. It was all over pretty quickly considering the damage he did. It took a minute or two, about as long as his record performance in bed, or so Josie had cracked to Annie later.

Someone found Josie lying almost under her own car. Josie heard his voice, but she couldn't respond. The man screamed at someone to call an ambulance, then knelt beside her until the ambulance came. Josie didn't remember any of the things the stranger said, but it helped to try to focus

87

on the sound of his voice. She slipped in and out of consciousness. She felt nausea and thought she was going to die. She even heard someone ask if she was dead. Josie thought about her mother lying on the cold ground somewhere about to die. Even then her mother had no face or form; she had no name. She was only the great abstract Mother that she had always been. For the next hour it was the sole thought that held Josie to life: that she had to find her.

The same policeman Josie had interviewed that fall came to the hospital to take her statement. He told her she couldn't let her ex-husband get away with this. Josie told him she didn't know who her attacker was; she didn't recognize the man. Description? She really didn't see anything at all. Annie had raged that she *must* charge him, but Josie couldn't. She had reasons, hours of self-justification, but the truth was, she knew that next time Dan would kill her. After she got out of the hospital, she had hidden in and around Boston and even spent a few weeks with friends in Provincetown on Cape Cod. In August, she had slipped out of town on tiptoe, and Dan Scholari was left to wonder where his punching bag had gone.

That, at least, had been the operating hypothesis. Now Josie had to decide if Dan *could* have found out. He wasn't a stupid man. He knew about Lues. Could he have possibly guessed she was coming to the one place in the world which really frightened her? Could he see that she must find her past to keep herself from repeating the same mistakes over and over? It wasn't possible! And yet it was all she could imagine. One moment, she was living her new life and chasing around a new campus; the next her own private madman was sneering at her out of the shadows of her mind.

The knock at her door caused Josie to jump and gasp. Beside the door was a large bare pane of glass and she saw it was Henry Valentine, but the adrenalin was already coursing through her.

Josie open the door mumbling a curse that she let rest somewhere between Henry Valentine and Dan Scholari.

"I met him, you know?" The brown face, the bald head, the curious grin. What in hell was he talking about?

She shook her head in confusion. "Who?"

"Henry Miller. It was the year before *Tropic of Cancer* was published in the States, a year before his . . . his *moment*, Josie. I went out to find him at Big Sur. I was just a kid, a would-be writer, and he was . . . GOD! The world thought of him as this obscure writer of dirty books, but I knew, Josie, and I *found* him, and he was everything I knew him to be."

None of this seemed important. Josie's life was at risk, maybe; and this man was talking best literary experiences. Josie checked her watch. It was almost two o'clock, late enough to get off campus — maybe with some company — and lose herself for a few hours. With a big man. Yes, Val had some size about him. She looked him over carefully. It was a runner's body, a man with powerful hands, and oddly cold eyes. He looked to be a man who had never been scared. She wanted him to be that man, at any rate.

"I'd love to hear about it," she answered. Her look was second cousin to full-throttle flirtation. "Miller's a favorite of mine. He's so . . ."

" . . . right! He's so damn right!" Val answered, glowing, juvenile, academic. If Dan showed up, maybe they could have a literary debate before the murder.

"Do you suppose we could get a drink and talk about it?" Josie asked.

Henry Valentine thought it the most natural thing in the world that Josie should want to spend the afternoon with him. His big, loose lips unfolded and from deep in his chest Josie heard him say, "That's the best idea I've heard this semester!"

In the bright sunlight of the parking lot, Josie volunteered to drive, if Val would show her how to get to Building and

89

Grounds before they left campus. At Building and Grounds, Josie was glad she wasn't alone. The parking lot was filled with service vans and trucks. There was hardly anyone stirring, and the woods were close by. It was a dangerous, solitary place. Val waited outside while she presented her blue slip of paper and got two keys. She thought it curious that she didn't need to show her identification and a bit second-class that she needed to give them a dollar on deposit for each key she took. She asked the boy working behind the counter if the president of the university had to put a dollar down for his key, and he looked at her, snuffed slightly and answered, "I don't know, he probably just sends somebody over here to get it for him." He handed her the keys and took her money. "That's it," he told her.

"Why didn't the department just give me these keys? They did at Housing."

He shrugged, pushing his hornrims up along his nose, "You sent money to Housing, and they sent us the deposit. The departments don't do it that way."

Outside, Val was leaning against Josie's VW. "Have you seen our canyon?" he asked.

"Lues Creek Canyon?" Josie responded. It was where her mother's body had been found. "I read something about it."

Val's hesitation seemed intentional. Without really answering her, he pointed up the road. "It's past Greek Circle. You can't really go inside the canyon unless you're ready to take a swim, but there's a trail that runs up into the woods and takes you to the falls. I'll show it to you if you want."

"Some other time," Josie answered, hardly wanting to get out into the woods, with or without company. "Right now, I'd rather have a drink. Those welcome-to-Lues speeches parched me."

"I know the perfect place, Josie."

It was Josie's second trip to the Skyline. "I came up here with Dick Ferrington on Saturday," she said as they got out of the car at the restaurant. "He told me it's a good place to eat, but all we did was drink." She hadn't really liked the place, and she had less taste for it the second time around.

"Yes, Dick," Val answered. "He had some business out of town, I hear."

"A workshop in Zurich, the lucky bastard. So is this the Liberal Arts bar, or something?"

Val considered the shabby façade for a moment, then answered, "No one from Liberal Arts comes up here."

"Except you and Dick Ferrington?" she answered.

"Ferrington is a scholar. I let Ferrington drink here." Val barely smiled as he said this.

Somewhere into their third round of whiskey sours, the department gossip and Henry Miller wearing them both out, the afternoon washing away, Val looked about the empty lounge and signaled for another drink. It was a gesture like Dick Ferrington's: the raised glass, the cocked eyebrow, the waitress catching the gesture and going to the bar, the bartender already mixing the drink. "This place used to be a scandal," Val announced. He smacked his lips, the old local with the juicy stuff for the new kid.

"Why is that?" she asked. Josie thought scandal a perfectly delicious idea. She was thinking Val was perfectly delicious, too.

"It was called the Hurry On Up. They had topless dancers and quite a ring of prostitution as well."

Josie stared at the man dumbly. She was sick to her stomach, felt as though she'd just been stomped in the gut, in fact. She tried to show nothing, tried to blink innocently.

"One of the owners burned it down about eight years ago and sold the lot. The next owners built this place, but people still remember what it was. The Skyline is the third restaurant to try to make a go of it up here. Great ambience, great view of the town, but it's dead."

Jack Hazard's place with his featured dancer, my mother. Here.

" . . . But I don't think they're going to make it . . ."

91

Josie struggled to focus politely on the man's words.

"The owners would be better off giving up and going back to the old venue; I understand the whores used to pack them in." A fine, southern genteel grin at this.

Josie took her drink in a gulp, waving at the waitress for another. *The whores.*

"Did you ever come up here when there were dancers?" The question was hard for Josie to ask, but here it was, her first opportunity to find out first-hand about Josie Fortune. She was trying to imagine Val, twenty years younger, staring at her mother as she danced. She imagined doing it in her mother's place, a solo performance for the old man.

"About half the trade went on out in the parking lot. Not exactly my style, Josie."

Josie felt a jolt of confirmation. Her mother did more than take off her clothes. *Well, why not?*

Their drinks arrived, and Josie took a reckless gulp. Then another.

"So you never came up here?" Josie asked. Just how had her drink gotten empty again?

"I leave the slews to their entertainment, and they leave me to mine."

"What's a slew?"

"Slews and losers. A slew is a local, mud wasp mean and country stupid. A loser, aptly, is anyone connected with the college."

Josie felt woozy with intoxication, curiously affectionate for this old maverick professor. The sort of thing handed down from mother to daughter, no doubt. The only question, what to charge?

"I take it you don't really respect Lues State as an institution?"

Henry Valentine's big loose lips wrinkled in pleasant contemplation. "We have a nice library, Josie."

They had dinner before they left. Despite Val's rather solemn promise that it really was a good place to eat, the food wasn't good at all, what she could taste of it, anyway. Afterwards they had coffee and brandy chasers so that by the time they got to Josie's car, the dusk drawing down over the hills, the narrow road off the ridge seemed dangerously unstable.

"I'll take you home," she said, feeling the slurring of her words, and wondering if she dared go back to her apartment afterwards. She glanced at the old man wickedly. Ask him if she could use his couch?

One way of putting it. She had put off the issue all afternoon in stupid denial of her situation. She had gotten drunk and now she had to make a series of decisions which might mean her life. Dan was . . . *anywhere.*

"If you don't mind, I need to get back to campus. My van's there."

"Great, I live on campus."

Val told her she could let him off at her apartment and he would walk. He preferred it, actually. A lovely night. And it would be safer for her.

"Safer?" Josie kept it slow, blinking away the drunkenness.

"We've had our troubles here," Val answered vaguely.

"What kind of troubles?" A chill of sobriety hit Josie, and the feeling reminded her of the reason she had gotten drunk.

Val shook his head as if he were sorry to have brought it up. "Usual things – rapes on campus, even a few murders. Dick Ferrington's wife, for example."

There was almost a lilt to Valentine's warnings, a peculiar pleasure in the chill he sent down her spine. The monsters were multiplying. Josie turned onto the road to her apartment complex, downshifting as she did.

"There were others?" Her voice cracked.

"Mostly domestic things. Slews kill each other the way we swat flies. But the campus isn't safe, Josie. It's never been safe. It has quite a history, but they keep it covered up. If the truth got out, it might hurt enrollments. I don't suppose you read about the precise number of rapes we have each

93

year in the brochures we send out about Lues State, but every once in a while someone does a feature in the campus paper. The numbers are staggering. You want to be careful, especially after dark."

Josie pulled her VW into the parking space before door 27. By now, she had lost all notion of courage and pride, and looked down the walk in both directions. She checked behind them, staring into the darkened lot. Shutting off the engine when she was sure the way was clear, she asked with pretended casualness, "Come in for a drink?"

Her hands were shaking as she turned the key. Inside, the air was tight and hot. She said something about not leaving the air conditioning on and felt Val at her back. Too close. He was thinking something was going to happen. She turned the light on and shut the door, locking it behind them, then attaching the chain. She looked about the room, then down the hall. The doors to her office, the bedroom and the bathroom were all shut. Josie was sure she hadn't closed them. Was Dan waiting?

Get it together! she told herself. Dan was in Boston. Dan had overslept, missed a meeting. Trying to smile, Josie looked at Val. "Have you seen these apartments?" she asked.

"Not for years."

"Come on, I'll show you." She opened the office door and walked in, remarking some absurdity about the scholar's study. The room was grim, hot, ugly. It was also empty. She checked in the closet to be sure and made a joke about the bogeyman; then looked at the window. It hadn't been tampered with. She was still trying to remember if she had shut the doors. Val was watching her with drunken amusement, a patient man. She was accustomed by now to his ugliness, even drawn to it. It was a magnificent ugliness, the face like some scarred cliff.

"And here's the bedroom," Josie said, crossing the hall and walking into the room purposefully. She went to the closet, then checked the slender window that looked out over her

94

balcony to the forest. Under the bed she saw her shower shoes but Dan Scholari was missing. She looked back at Val when he closed the door. They were alone in her bedroom, her bed between them. The bogeyman grinning hopefully.

"I'll mix us some drinks," she offered, walking toward him. Josie reached past Val, dancing around him a little to take the doorknob. She felt him sliding behind her, his body almost touching her back. "I know how this must look, taking you right to my bedroom, but it's not . . ." Josie turned into him as she tried to finish explaining that nothing was going to happen. Her back to the door, she looked up at him and couldn't finish her thought: " . . . it's not . . ." But of course she realized something was going to happen. It was what it seemed. It was what she wanted suddenly. Val reached up and put both hands on her breasts, his face austerely distant, the eyes even more so. She stared at him, confused, angry, scared, and feeling wickedly secretive. Neither of them moved as he held her, but a small voice in her head started screaming the old warnings. She sighed. No one had touched her like this for too long. His hands slipped the buttons of her blouse open, then took her flesh. Josie's warning voice was still screaming to get it under control, but all she could do was lay her shoulders back and close her eyes. When his hand slipped under her skirt, she made no protest. For several minutes they stayed like this, until finally Josie stirred, murmuring that she needed to get something from the bathroom, before things went any further.

Dizzily she left the room to get the unopened box of condoms that she had been carrying around since the beginning of the AIDS epidemic. Or so it seemed. In the hallway, Josie wondered about Val, what something like this would mean. If it got out, it would ruin her credibility at Lues State. Would she see the men smirking? Would she get the looks of her female colleagues, the silent appraisal that left no doubt of their opinion? Would Dick Ferrington be jealous or write her off? Josie swore cavalierly. Didn't she have a right to do damn well what she pleased? And to hell with all of them!

Josie pushed the bathroom door open unsuspectingly, then came to a full, startled halt. Before her, she saw bright red markings on the mirror over the sink. Still not in the room, she couldn't read the words, but she was sure they were written in blood. The shower curtain was pulled shut as well. Josie was sure she hadn't pulled it to. For a moment, the certainty that Dan was beyond that sheet of plastic nearly undid her.

She looked back toward her bedroom. She thought to say something to Val, but stopped herself. It was the old shame of abuse, the embarrassment of an ex-husband who can't let it go. He wasn't waiting, she told herself. He had been here; that was all. *He's gone*, she whispered to herself, as if to make it real by wishing it so. What had he written? A combination of anger and courage and old-fashioned curiosity sent Josie into the room one cautious step. She knew that what was printed was something terrible and personal, that it promised her death, and she had to know at once what it said. She was ready to bolt as she stepped into the room, ready to fight, ready to scream, ready for anything but the words on the mirror:

WilcuM
HoM
jOsie

But not blood. The letters were written in the lipstick Josie had left out on the sink that morning. They were oddly shaped, written with the crooked uncertainty of a desperately stupid or psychotic man. Dan Scholari? *Missing in Action*. Had he guessed or found out? And now what did he mean to do? Kill her? Drive her mad?

She ripped the shower curtain back and saw she was alone. She looked again in the mirror. She saw her blouse undone. She fastened the buttons in a sudden fit of sober

96

morality, all the while staring past the letters into the face of a doomed woman, the daughter of a murdered whore. She looked back toward the bedroom. She had shut the door on Val, and thought of him now with saving objectivity. *My God!* she thought. She started back toward the room without the condoms, then turned back. She wet one corner of a towel and wiped the mirror. The red markings smudged over the glass. She pressed harder and the wax began gathering toward the edges. She picked out most of it, cleaned the glass with a second dampened corner of the towel, then dried it. When she finished, she went back to open the bedroom door. Val was standing at the far side of the room by the slender window, the curtain pulled back so he could stare into the dark woods. Thank God he was still dressed! His body, at the distance of the room, was that of a young man's. Josie forgave herself her attraction to him; Val was curiously handsome at this distance; he was fascinatingly intense. Not so foolish, she thought, but she just didn't want to sleep with him now. She wanted . . .

She didn't know what she wanted, but not this.

"You're going to hate me," Josie announced.

Val looked back into the dusky room to where Josie stood beside the door. "I'll leave," he answered.

She walked back toward the front of the apartment, leading the way. Val rapped on the bathroom door, so that Josie turned back in surprise. "May I?" he asked. She nodded and went to the balcony door. Absently, she checked it to see that the latch was turned to lock. It was, but when she tugged at the handle, it slid open. Startled, she shut the door, feeling it catch and lock this time. She had locked it, but it hadn't caught on the latch. He had come in from the ravine sometime during the day. But that was crazy! How would anyone know it was unlocked? Josie looked out into the darkness. How did he know anything?

WilcuM HoM jOsie. What was Dan doing? More to the point, she thought, what was he planning? Why not just finish it? He could have easily, she realized. He could have just waited.

Val came out of the bathroom. "You're okay?" he asked.

Val was the one Josie wasn't safe with, she decided. This was going to get back to the department. *We've hired a regular slut!* First day, first man.

These are the wildfires of office gossip. Scandal had seemed such a juicy thing a few drunken hours before. Not now, suddenly. Henry Valentine disturbed people. People gossiped about him whether they knew anything or not. If the two of them were linked, Dan might as well show up and finish her quickly. Better to be done with it that way, than go for the slow death of department gossip. Besides, with Dan she would have had a fighting chance.

Ruined, she decided, *and the semester hasn't even started.*

"Can we keep this just between us, Val?"

"What's that, Josie?"

That was his answer, coy, humored, and almost enough to stir Josie back to the feelings she had had in her bedroom, enough to finish what they had started. "Thanks. I'm just . . . I had a little too much to drink, and I'm . . ." Val seemed to have gotten older, the old-man gestures coming with an odd kind of impotence, " . . . excited. I really am. I just don't want to move too fast; I'm too new to campus, you know?" From across the room his eyes met hers. Josie could see nothing clearly change in his expression, but the old-man act dropped dead. He popped the chain, flipped the deadbolt, and stepped into the dark, closing the door behind him. Josie followed quickly to watch him through the peep-hole. She couldn't see him, and opened the door so she could look after him into the darkness. When she did, Josie saw nothing but the night.

Confession

Even though it was after midnight in Boston, Josie called Annie, thinking to leave a message. After Annie's spiel about her Uzi and karate lesson, Josie told the answering machine, "This is Josie, *the slut*; I just almost slept with a man who repulses me, kind of, and I needed to talk – "

"What, what, what?" There was breathlessness.

"You're up?"

"Who? How? When?" Annie demanded. "Whew, those country boys move fast. Have they got another position? I'll give notice tomorrow! I can be there by sundown."

"Hi, Annie."

"All of it, sister! I want details!"

"In a minute. No sign of Dan?"

"Nada, ney, nothing. You got my message?"

"I got it."

"I didn't want to scare you but it bothered me that he didn't show for our meeting this morning. I asked the dean about it. Not a happy dean, Josie. He said *Doctor* Scholari is walking a tightrope. He didn't call in sick, and he isn't answering the phone. It would be funny if he lost his job over this. I mean a conviction for assault didn't blemish his wonderful record, but missing a meeting could end it all. Well, that's the academy. Now what's going on in Lues? Who's this man you almost slept with?"

"I think Dan's here, Annie."

"Oh, God."

"I think he broke into my apartment while I was out today. I just got back, a half-hour ago. He left a note on the bathroom mirror."

Annie swore angrily and wanted to know what the note had said.

"It said 'Welcome home, Josie.' Everything was misspelled."

"Call the police."

"I've seen how the police handle these things."

"Call them, Josie."

"No way! It's what he wants. He wants me to make a fool out of myself. If he really wanted to hurt me, he would have stayed and finished it."

"You don't know that, Josie. Dan's a sick man."

"No police. I've had it with police. The last time I went to the police it almost killed me."

"How did he get in?"

"I left the balcony door unlocked."

"Josie!"

"Listen, I locked it, but it wasn't shut tight, so the lock didn't catch. I won't make that mistake again." Josie looked at the balcony door. She had already pulled the curtain.

"So now what do you do?"

"I don't know. You'll call me if he shows up?"

"Sure, I'll keep checking, but what if it's not Dan?"

"My God, Annie, who else could it be? I mean how many raging lunatics do I know?"

"Counting me?"

Josie laughed. It was all the emotion she had left.

"Take a couple sick days, Josie; go see your parents. Go somewhere, anyway. If he can't find you, he'll come back for classes with some wild story, and that will be the end of it."

"I'm tired of running, Annie. I'm sick to death of it."

"Then call the police."

"I can't. It's like admitting this whole thing is starting all over again!"

"It *is* starting all over again, Josie."

"Okay, but this time I handle it differently. This time I'll be ready."

"You mean you'll get a gun?"

"No guns." They had had this conversation before.

"You need a gun, Josie!"

"I've never touched a gun in my life. And I don't want to start now."

100

"Get a gun. Police or a gun. I mean it. Can you buy a gun there without a thirty-day waiting period?"

"This is Lues, Annie. God, Guns, and Guts. I think it's part of the residence requirement that you keep a gun. But I don't – "

"Great, get one in the morning. Get a .357 magnum with a four-inch snubnose barrel. It will fit in your purse. Get the hollow-point bullets and carry it with you *everywhere*. Bed, bath, and class – loaded! And make sure you get hollow points! More punch! Do they deliver?"

Josie laughed, the tensions breaking apart. "I don't think they deliver. They're not quite like pizzas."

"It's a business idea. If you make it through this, think about it. *Just in time handguns . . . Pistols in thirty minutes or less . . . Buy a gun, get your bullets free.* That sort of thing. You'll never get rich teaching, Josie."

"I'll think about it."

"I'm serious about the gun, Josie. I've been to Lues; it's not a nice place. Too many trees!"

Josie thought about what Henry Valentine had told her; she thought about the message on her mirror and the balcony door. She could run; she could call the police; or she could get some protection.

"I'll get a gun tomorrow. First thing. I promise."

"And learn how to use it."

"Promise."

"That's the way, Josie! And don't be afraid to use it, just shoot him on sight. We'll get you a good lawyer once he's a corpse."

"I won't even blink," Josie told her, meaning it.

"So how did you avoid him today, besides almost have sex with the first man you saw?"

"I spent the day in a restaurant with this . . . this guy. Oh! Turns out this restaurant used to be where my mother worked! You believe it? Dick takes me there Saturday, and Val today."

"Are the strippers still working there?"

"The Hurry On Up burned down eight years ago. Val says they had prostitution up there too. Real nice place. I can't wait to find out more." This with utter sarcasm.

"Who's Val?"

"Henry Valentine."

"Never heard of him."

"Quotes Henry Miller. Got nice hands, but I think he's about thirty years older than I am."

"Now this sounds like *real* trouble."

It was, Josie told her, and started at the beginning.

The Nickel

The parking lot in front of her apartment was full of life and movement when Josie went outside the next morning. Southeast of Presbyterian Hill, about a mile on from the city limits, Josie found the place she was looking for, Bower's Guns and Ammo. The building was an old structure with a fairly large addition off the back of it. The paint-peeled sign at the edge of the highway had been used for target practice. The whole place needed a whitewash. Close by there was a bait and tackle shop. Down the road a couple of hundred yards, Josie saw a small, broken-down house set just inside the heavy forest. The owner of Bower's Guns and Ammo was a bleached-skinned, big-bellied man in his sixties. He was somewhat shorter than Josie, who had to stretch to get to five feet two inches. Bowers had gun oil under his nails and long oily yellow-white hair.

When Josie said she needed a gun, he told her in a slow, Lues-nasal twang he couldn't help her, that she needed a license even to buy ammunition or use his range.

Josie bit her lip to keep back the tears of frustration and anger and fear. She looked out into the parking lot, certain Dan Scholari was waiting, laughing at her.

"Tell you what," Bowers said, "if you really need a gun

today, I've got a couple used pieces that might work for you – as long as we deal in cash."

Cash, Josie had. They talked briefly about the kind of money Bowers needed, and then Josie paid a range fee and bought a box of fifty hollow-point magnums. Mr Bowers took her back to his indoor firing range with two used .357 snubnoses. He loaded both guns for her, showing her how to eject the casings and how to set the thumbset safety. They both put on ear protection, and Josie fired the steel blue Colt at the fresh silhouette Bowers had sent down the wires. When Josie finished six shots, Bowers handed her the other gun. Josie liked the second gun better. A double-action Smith and Wesson, it had a nice nickel sheen to it and thick rubber grips: "a handful," Bowers called it. When Josie finished firing six rounds through it, Bowers took off his ear protection and motioned for her to do the same. He had Josie load the nickel-plated gun, this time on her own. As she did, he said he wouldn't recommend this big of a gun for most girls, but Josie seemed plenty strong enough to handle it. He was right about that, at least from a physical standpoint. What Josie didn't know was whether or not she could really point it at Dan Scholari and kill him, much as she hated him. Josie lifted the gun and felt Bowers's hand on her shoulder. "Ears." Josie put the little green cups over her ears and pointed the gun toward the silhouette again.

As Dan's big fist seemed to roll toward her face, Josie dumped six charges, the shock waves recoiling through her hands and wrists. It was a feeling like grain alcohol poured directly over adolescent hormones. Josie hit two dry-fires before she realized the chambers were empty, then let the gun down in an orgasmic daze. Mr Bowers apparently knew the feeling and laughed, signaling her to take the ear protection off. He suggested Josie fire in groups of two, and showed her a stance he called the Weaver Stance; then he placed her arms so that her wrists and elbows were locked, and had her dry-fire it a few times. He had her bring the sight into the target instead of holding steady on the bead, and squeeze the trigger. "Squeeze him dead," he whispered. He held the first gun up for her to load, and Josie shook her head. She popped the six spent shells with a single flick of the chamber's lever, and loaded her "nickel" again. The smell of the powder wafted up to her nostrils, a sweet burning oddly nostalgic stink to it, and Josie's hands still tingled. Her fears waned. She wanted only Dan Scholari in front of her. She snapped the cylinder shut, pulled the ear-cups in place, and ripped the silhouette this time, three sets of twos, all somewhere on the target. Bowers nodded happily. Removing his ear protection, he went back up to the front of the store.

"You're a quick-study! You sure you never handled a gun?"

"Never."

"Well, work with it, and see what you think."

When Josie finished the box of shells, with one cautious bullet left in the chamber, she brought the silhouette up along the wire and counted her marks, nearly thirty of her forty-nine rounds. She went back into the store and said she would take the gun. Bowers wanted to clean it for her, and Josie told him there was one bullet left. He looked at her curiously, then smiling as gunsmiths do, which is to say with all the confidence in the world, Bowers reached back to the counter and moved a box with a flip of his fingers in order to show her a fearsome semi-automatic Python nine-millimeter pistol with a barrel at least ten inches in length and a handle grip that was big enough for a minor arsenal of firepower. "No one's coming in here we don't want to come in," he said, and suddenly Josie liked Lues a little better than before; country does have its charm. Bowers broke her gun down and showed her how to clean it. The process was fairly easy, really; it required only patience, oil, cloth, and a stiff-bristled ramrod. When he finished, Bowers put the kit back together in its box and sacked it for her in a plain brown bag. Josie took two boxes of shells and loaded six in the chambers of her nickel, then set the safety.

Paying the man nearly all the money she had, just under three hundred dollars, Josie dumped the contents of her purse into the sack with the gun-cleaning kit and bullets, then set the revolver into her purse. Mr Bowers suggested that when she got home she unload the revolver and dry-fire it. "You might want to work with that purse too. They're lousy, but it's all you've got unless you strap that snubnose under a suit jacket like a detective; you want to get quick at flipping that latch with your left hand while you reach across and draw the gun out business end ready." Josie saw what he meant, and adjusted the carrying strap of the purse so it hung lower, then moved the gun within the purse, so the handle was the first thing she touched. At the door she checked the lot before she went outside. The smell of gun-powder on her hands intoxicating her, she prayed only that Dan Scholari would come soon.

Vigilance

But Dan Scholari did not come. On Wednesday, in fact, he appeared on the Bandolier campus in time for classes. According to Annie, nothing at all was said about his missing the college-wide meeting or his assignment to work registration.

On the phone that night, Josie asked, "Where was he, Annie? Did he say?"

"I cornered him and asked, Josie. He said his car broke down, that he had driven all night to make it for classes."

"His car broke down – *where?*"

"He didn't say."

"Did you ask him why he didn't call the dean?"

"He was lying, Josie. I didn't have to ask."

"So it was him. He knows where I am."

"Well, we don't *know* that."

"We know Dan."

In the days following, Josie continued to carry her purse with the .357. The nickel. She had no idea when Dan might decide to steal a day from classes and fly out for "a little business" with the ex. She couldn't very well ask Annie to call her every morning to let her know he was on campus. Day followed day, the first week and weekend passed, and every hour of it Josie knew the fear that only imagination can sustain. A thousand miles could be covered in a handful of hours. That thought kept her vigilant.

Josie tried to set up a new pattern for her life, to think about the unexpected, to look even when she knew no one would be there. She went twice to the range, firing the gun until her hands trembled. She carried her purse everywhere and kept it empty except for her nickel and a pack of fifty bullets. She had one organizing principle in all that she did: stay alert to stay alive. Each night Josie unloaded the gun and practiced drawing it from the purse and dry-firing it in the same motion. She practiced doing it while she was sitting in a chair. She practiced it standing or walking across the room. She worked on it until she could do it smoothly, and each time she drew the gun out, she tried to imagine Dan coming at her at close range. Josie would kill him without a word and do it without hesitation. There would be lawyers to cry for the man later.

By the beginning of the second week of classes, Josie saw the world differently. She looked for dead ends, shadows; she found even the walk to a rest room a gauntlet. Could he be waiting in that corner? Would he be inside the rest room, maybe on a seat inside a stall, his legs pulled up, waiting? He waited in a thousand fantasies; and maybe he watched her from somewhere real. Sometimes she wondered if it was really Dan Scholari who had broken into her apartment. It was a curiosity only, but the idea nearly maddened her. Who but Dan Scholari had such hate in him? She looked into the crowds for Dan's face; she would see *him* coming, but if it were someone else? How would she know him in time?

And then came the temptation to believe he was gone forever, that he had come once into Lues to let her know he could have struck and chose not too, and then he had gone away, with only the shadows of big trees left to scare her. It was a fabulous temptation and urged the sort of laxness he needed for a perfect surprise. She set routines to help her remember she was under siege. She stopped herself several times each day and thought about her movements, thought about the times she did things; she looked at her vulnerabilities and did something about it if she could; if she couldn't, she stayed extra alert – though always for no apparent purpose. Day following day, Dan Scholari met his classes at Bandolier, seducing new conquests, no doubt. All the time knowing he could come for Josie at his leisure.

Josie didn't turn a corner or step through a door without thinking of Dan Scholari's fist. Sometimes at night she heard footsteps in the parking lot in front of her apartment building. She thought, *It's now, he's here now!* But it wasn't. Dan Scholari slept peacefully in Boston; Josie exhausted herself with anticipation.

On Josie's second Friday in Lues, she spent the day at her office. She spent most of an hour talking to Dick Ferrington about Zurich and their mutual friends. Josie told Ferrington about her classes, what she was doing and planning, and for a moment was almost tempted to confide to him about the macabre message on her mirror, but then she let it go. It was over, history. Besides, Dick Ferrington inspired no confidence in her. He was a man uninterested, these days, in other people's troubles.

Josie was invited out for drinks "with the girls" late that afternoon, and welcomed the chance to get acquainted with her new colleagues socially. They went to a place called Cokey's. It was a big splashy campus tavern. Seven of them from all over the campus drank and talked, and for a while

Josie imagined everything was fine: she had started real life and it was going to work out.

That night, the moment she got home, Josie saw on the balcony door:

LEt MeE IN, pleEs!!!

It was printed on the outside of the glass with lipstick, written backwards so Josie could read it, and somehow the care taken to do that was worse than the rest.

When her breath came, finally, she called Annie, but Annie wasn't home. She got hold of her on Sunday, and Annie had no idea if Dan Scholari had been on campus Friday. She had been in Vermont, plugging her new book on a couple of local television stations. They loved her in Vermont, criminal record or not.

"I'll check, though," Annie told her. "I'll ask around tomorrow."

Annie called her Monday night. Dan's last class on Friday finished at eleven. He had apparently taught the class and left campus. " . . . But the guy leaves campus early every Friday, Josie."

"He could have made it here, Annie. I wasn't home until ten. That's eleven hours."

"Josie, did you call the police?"

No, she answered. The police weren't going to be able to handle this. The first thing they would do, Josie announced with bitter confidence, "is check *me* out! *Lonely woman just trying to get some attention*. No way, Annie! If he wants me he can show his damn face! I'm tired of it. I'm not going to let him get to me with this by turning me into some kind of laughing stock with the local cops!"

But of course Dan was getting to her anyway. Every night, every shadow, every footstep she heard.

The First of September

On the first of September, like the poem, Josie went out for a drink with Dick Ferrington. They had seen each other almost every day since his return, but other than their one long conversation about the workshop, their talk had been limited to hallway meetings and professor chatter about papers to grade and books to read. On the morning of the first, Dick stopped at Josie's office and made a simple gesture of getting a drink. Eyebrows flashing villainously, Ferrington made a joke about meeting her at four and said that he might be late. Four o'clock was the hour of Molly Bloom's adulterous meeting with Blazes Boylan in *Ulysses*, and Blazes had been late. The insinuations were quite clear. And about damn time!

The fantasy stopped when Ferrington showed up at the Skyline quite late, nearly five, in fact. But that was fine; what wasn't was the man's attitude. He was distracted about something that had happened at school. He was talking about it, and even made it sound, in what she imagined was a slip, that their drink together was an *appointment* which he could have easily done without. Something had him going, some committee or another. As she didn't know the players, she couldn't follow. Worse, he didn't seem to care whether or not she understood. Finally, he changed the subject with a great show of attention for her – and what she was doing, by God! Hardly finished with saying that, he slipped back for one more Promethean rant against *administrators*. The poetry of the man was all wrung out. He was caught up in the steel jaws of fruitless committee work, a fox a chewing his own leg off, and Josie found herself thinking how much more interesting Henry Valentine would be sitting across from her, tall and ugly, intensely energized, wonderfully primal. And very nice hands. Yes, Josie decided with utter finality, someone else was welcome to the leftovers of Dick Ferrington's bankrupt soul; she wanted none of it.

Before they had finished their first round of drinks, the

phone rang at the bar. Entirely alone in the lounge except for the bartender and the waitress, they stopped talking and watched the old man limp toward the phone. After the bartender had picked up the receiver, he listened, then barked out, "JOSIE FORTUNE?"

Josie had just turned back to her drink when the barman answered the phone, but she looked around stupidly at the sound of her childhood name. The bartender called the name out again as if the room were crowded. Dick smiled and leaned forward slightly to whisper mockingly, "You appear to be the only *Josie* in the room." Josie looked up toward the bartender and answered that her name was Josie. He held the phone up apparently to indicate she should come take it from him, and Josie walked to the bar, uncertain but curious. He told her to keep it quick, and Josie nodded, as she pulled her earring off.

"Josie here," she answered.

Silence was all that waited, and Josie handed the receiver back to the bartender, her anger on a short fuse. As he hung it up, Josie asked, "Did you recognize the voice?"

"What are you talking about?"

"It was an obscene call. Did you know the caller's voice?"

The bartender studied her, then sucking his teeth thoughtfully, he answered, "It was a guy, a man's voice, that's all I know."

"Was it long distance?"

"Who knows, lady?"

"A Boston accent – eastern sounding?" Josie pressed.

A thin man in his fifties with a history of alcoholism, if his skin and eyes were any indication, the bartender had been fidgeting with his glasses and bottles, but now he stopped and placed both hands on the bar. "You tell me, lady. It was your obscene phone call."

"I need to know," Josie said. "What did it sound like? Where was he from?"

"Lady, I wasn't paying attention, okay? I work back here.

I know you're out there drinking, having fun, that's great; I'm working. See, this is what I do for my living. Someone calls me up, I answer it. I don't pay attention where he's from. What do you want? Boston? Okay, it was Boston. Long distance? Sure. A Chinese operator jabbered at me for half an hour!"

"Is that line listed?"

"Yeah, right on the phone."

"I mean is it listed in the book?"

"They don't need to list it in the book; that costs extra. They list the restaurant in the book. What do you think, we're rolling in green? See the crowds?" He gestured to his empty lounge.

"So how does anyone know this number?"

"How do I know how they know this number? They drink here, they look over the bar and read the frigging number!"

Josie felt something behind her and spun around, grabbing for her purse. She had her hand in the purse when she realized it was Dick. "What's the matter?" he asked. As he spoke, Ferrington looked down and saw Josie's revolver. His eyes squinted tightly as he stared at her, but he said nothing. Josie snapped her purse closed and breathed heavily. She was out of control, again.

"It was an obscene call," Josie answered. "I was trying to find out – listen, let's drop it." Josie saw the bartender shaking his head as if he were amused, but he wasn't. He was angry. He was angry with anything that ruffled his quiet routine. Well she was angry too. She didn't like being called to the phone by her childhood name; she was especially sick of the silence. The silence was the worst of it. Why didn't he just come find her, the coward? Josie caught herself. This was what he wanted. She composed herself. She walked back to the table like a woman who had just been the butt of an embarrassing joke; no one was laughing, but that only made it worse.

Dick followed her, and still standing as she took her seat, he asked, "Are you okay? Do you want to go?" He couldn't quite keep from looking at Josie's purse.

"No. I'm fine. Sit down. Everyone's looking." In surprise Dick looked around the lounge. Then realizing she was joking, Dick smiled uneasily and sat down. "Did anyone know we were coming here?" Josie asked, the pretense of humor gone.

Dick's brow knitted, "No. Who's Josie Fortune?"

Josie did a long pause, too long. "That's what I was trying to get out of the bartender."

"Jimmy."

"That's what I was trying to get Jimmy to tell me. What a jerk."

"And?"

"And what?"

Dick hesitated, confused. "What did the caller say? Can you repeat it?"

Josie studied Dick. "Nothing," she answered. "He didn't say anything at all."

Maybe an hour later, Josie paid the bill and they left, still in their separate cars. After the call, they had never really gotten their footing, even enough to play out the old routine of prophet and disciple. Josie asked about the kids, and heard a pretty mundane story about the dog; Ferrington talked about the seminar he was teaching on *Ulysses*. He had set the class to find the word known to all men. It was still something of a joke to him, and Josie's last fantasy of the day involved the good doctor and her .357 shoved right through his pretty teeth. They talked some about the department, and Josie lamented her failure to get anything started on her dissertation research – realizing as she said it that she had dropped the true research she had come to Lues for. She chided herself for the failure. She knew she ought to make an effort to pick up the search and learn something about her mother. Old ma, the dancing hooker, and steppa, who *stranged* her.

Dick took a fatherly concern about her research troubles, having no idea what real troubles she had. It was all damnably professional and polite, much cooler than old times, and when it was over there was no talk about another drink, and quite frankly that was fine with Josie.

Annie's Call

"Annie, something happened," Josie announced.

When she had described the call at the Skyline, Annie asked her if Dan even knew the name *Fortune*.

"I told him everything about me years ago. It's how he's found me here."

Annie's silence bothered her, and Josie asked what she was thinking.

"I don't like it, Josie."

"You're not alone, Annie."

"I mean I don't think it's Dan. How did he get the number? How did he know you were going to be there?"

Josie had no answer and said as much. It wasn't reasonable to assume Dan could know she would be at the Skyline. The *Fortune* had made some sense, but how would he know her appointments?

"He's hired someone to watch me. He's just scaring me."

"He's scaring both of us, kiddo, but that doesn't mean it's Dan."

"He knows Lues scares me, that I've always been afraid of coming here, that I can't remember any of it — "

"That's what I'm thinking, Josie. You can't just assume this is Dan. The first note mentions *home*; now you hear about *Fortune*. That's not Dan's *hook*, Josie. Last time it was literary citations!"

"He did some other things too. He just doesn't want me to know it's him."

"Listen to yourself, Josie."

Josie stopped. She *was* listening. She was arguing from conclusions. It was Dan because she knew it was Dan. Dan, because the alternative was unbearable.

"You think it's Jack Hazard?" she asked.

"I think you better start finding out some things, Josie, that's what I think. Have you been into the canyon where they found your mother? Have you gone out to where you lived? Have you talked to anyone who happened to know your mother?"

Annie knew the answers; she had been making a few subtle nudges lately, but this was a full-throttle shove.

"I've been kind of busy."

"A great epitaph."

"I'm dealing with it, Annie! Look, I still think it's Dan. Lues has nothing to do with what's going on."

"You're *living* with it, Josie; that's not *dealing* with it."

"I don't know what to do, Annie. I mean, I'm trying. What do you want me to do?"

"Look, I can't do it for you, Josie; you're going to have to do it on your own or just quit your job and come back east. We can get you back in classes in January. One or the other."

"I'm not going to run away, Annie. That's what he wants."

"You *are* running, Josie. You've been running since you got there."

There was resignation in the old woman's voice, the disappointment of a woman who expects more of her friends, and Josie made a hurried excuse to break off the conversation.

Annie sounded relieved to be rid of her.

Running in Place

Josie was trying, she told herself. She was facing up to her troubles. She was trying as hard as anyone could. She had set her life around new routines; she had even gone back to the range to shoot her .357 a couple of times. She meant to join a weight training program as soon as she had some time, and she was already registered for a self-defense class that was starting in November.

What did Annie want her to do, anyway? What good would seeing the place of her mother's death do her, or seeing the little trailer they'd lived in? It was probably gone anyway. Josie had found out about her mother, about Jack. What else was there? That was history! It had nothing to do with *this*.

She spent that weekend in her apartment, trying to remember she wasn't scared. She graded papers, then read a couple of books on the writings of James Joyce. She was thoroughly comfortable hidden away. She had survived two days more and had stayed busy with her desperately mundane life. The following week was no different. She left for the office when the parking lot was alive with activity. She got to Brand and kept her door locked. She opened it for each student. In the halls she moved alertly; she carried her purse everywhere, the revolver inside. What more could she do? She had no choice but to play the part for which she had trained all of her life. That meant long hours preparing for her lectures and grading papers meticulously. There were always fresh stacks; there was always something she needed to read. Assuming it could reveal anything, what chance did she have to look into her past? Her office was always busy with her students. She was a regular Henry Valentine. There were graduate students who wanted to talk about the admission standards at the better universities; there was an eighteen-year-old poet who needed eyes for his epic about his almost-state champion Huree football team, and a forty-eight-year-old grandmother named Harriet who was trying to write sonnets, her first efforts at any sort of poetry; they were crude but touching poems about her divorce and the devastation of starting over so late in life. She had set for herself the pace of one sonnet a day and wanted Josie to read them all. Josie gave the woman all the energy she could muster, as she did all of her students. Her students came into her life, odd, insistent, and all the more poignant for their intensity, and Josie turned none of them away. For all of them she was there. She listened and advised and spoke as honestly as tender egos could bear. In stolen hours, she raced into her paperwork; she read hundreds of pages at a sitting.

Part of the life, Josie knew, was social, so she went out for drinks with small groups of faculty. She went to houses and the faculty bars and lounges and listened to the gossip and politics, to pet theories and foundationless dreams. She listened politely about the books that were planned and would never be written, about the moral dimensions of a misspelled word; she listened to the stories of the typical absurdities into which freshmen stumbled; she heard the feminists rage and watched the white men strangle on their suppressed impulses to be cute. Josie joined a couple of reading circles and watched full professors fumbling like undergraduates with the works that had no blueprints. Josie drank tall glasses of academic chatter and because it was in the job description, she even remembered sometimes to laugh at their cruel wit. She felt foreign to all of it, but the isolation didn't come from any feeling of superiority. It came because she realized that none of this much mattered. It had nothing to do with reality or staying alive.

Staying alive was what Annie had been talking about. Chasing instead of being chased. Josie kept telling herself that she needed to go find out something more about her mother, or at least check to see if Jack Hazard was a free man, and maybe had a history of leaving his future victims notes. It was a sensible precaution. She knew Annie was right, that none of this was quite Dan's style, and yet that first-step, that first look at the truth of her childhood, had terrified her more than words scrawled on glass. The terror came from the certain ugliness of her first childhood, and that was a terror that lived so deeply in her, a memory so distant and haunting, that she preferred death to knowledge.

Val

Henry Valentine was almost always in his office, and there was always someone with him. It started sometimes before eight and lasted usually until well past five; his only break seemed to be class. He kept the door to his office open, and when Josie passed she heard the confessions of his students, by turns marked by silliness, eroticism, or tragedy. A boy had just lost his father. A girl had been raped by her boyfriend. Another wanted to go home; she hated Lues. There were boys who had conquests to brag about or nothing at all to be proud of, mature women who worried about their teenage children and what was to become of them in a world such as this, men past thirty who were back in school and uncertain about their futures, desperate with the fear that life was passing them by while they studied. There were intimate things, terrible things, voices that droned on and on, laughter and agonized moans. Val let them say what wore upon their hearts, and their honesty was startling. Sometimes the kids were loud, almost shouting or laughing. Sometimes there were whispers. The whispers were the worst. Once, Josie heard a female voice telling him in a bedroom whisper, "I didn't want them to, I mean the three of us were just friends, but they took their penises out and started slapping the back of my head . . ." Josie pushed into her office and closed the door quickly, never knowing the rest of what had happened, sick with knowing what little she'd heard. Another time Josie heard a woman tell him, "I didn't care after that; it just didn't matter. I stabbed him again. The blood came, and I kept stabbing him. I didn't care." That one, Josie never even saw; she knew only the disembodied voice of murder – or maybe a fiction writer reading her story. When Josie did look into the office, she saw Val invariably facing the speaker, staring

117

intently with those large, quick eyes of his, a sympathy like an old dog's or maybe God's.

When Josie and Val passed in the hall, the two of them didn't speak for some reason, but there was always a look, a hot silence, something left undone. Twice Josie met him as they came out of their respective offices together. No one was coming in either direction. For a moment each time, they stared at one another with peculiar intensity. Josie knew that she had only to step back into her office and he would follow, and they would close the door. She had almost wanted to, and only the thought of departmental gossip stopped her.

One day, Josie saw Val heading into Varner Hall. She knew he was going there to teach a class. A pile of books braced against his hip, Val was late but sauntered like a man who knew the party would never start without him. Curious about something, Josie followed him into the building. As he stepped from the hallway into his classroom, Josie hurried forward, then stopped in front of the door. Some fifty kids rose as if on cue, their sudden cheers startling her. She even saw two of her own students in the crowd. They were quiet kids who sat patiently – all right, miserably – through her lectures but they were wildly different, she realized, in Henry Valentine's class. They loved him. They grinned and stomped and clapped as loudly as the rest. Josie understood the feeling of failure Val inspired in all of the other faculty: this couldn't be real teaching. Val stood before the class perfectly at ease, his heels together, giving a slight, appreciative bow like a long-experienced actor on an old and familiar stage. As the cheering faded, he turned to close the door and saw Josie. His face registered no surprise; he seemed to know she had been following him. He even understood her envy, his expression a kind of abashed amusement, a good-humored apology for success. The conspiratorial friend, Val winked, then shut the door.

Virgil Hazard

Her phone never rang, so the night that it did, Josie felt a cold certainty that it was *him* again. Dan Scholari or Jack Hazard or the Devil in Hell who meant to drive her mad. It was late, and Josie had been grading papers for hours, and she was groggy from the work, but the moment the phone began ringing she was alert, a kind of cold anger coming over her. As she picked up the phone, she was ready for the silence that would come. She wasn't ready for Annie Wilde.

"Amazing things these computers," Annie announced.

They hadn't talked for over a week, and Annie's breezy enthusiasm was strange even to Josie, who knew the woman well.

"Computers?" she asked. Annie still wrote with a quill.

"I have a grader for my 'Magnificent Metaphors' course, Josie. I told you about that?" She had, Josie told her. "Turns out she's combining women's studies with computer programming. Great idea! Fabulous! If you don't finish your dissertation and the handgun delivery thing doesn't work out, you might try it. Anyway, I asked her to do a little work for me, a project I've started about this exotic dancer . . ."

Josie groaned.

"I'm thinking about a biography of a common woman, see. I call it *Pawn of the Patriarchy*. How do like you like it? Good title, huh?"

"Great title. So what kind of work did your grader do for you?" This was Annie at her best or worst, according to your perspective. After the pep talks had failed, she did your work for you until your utter shame kicked you into gear. Annie had started reading Blavatsky at the beginning of Josie's dissertation research. "Eight hundred pages of metaphysical agonies," Annie had called it. She gave Josie daily reports until Josie had finally taken the book from her and done the work she should have from the start. The worst of it, of course, was that Annie had been right. Blavatsky, who was

119

little more than a passing jest in the human comedy of *Ulysses*, was the key to the whole riddle of the word known to all men. It was Blavatsky who had called the word known to all men *MAH*. Turning the word into *maaaaaa*, the newborn's cry, Joyce had both mocked the mystic and revealed the true word known to all men – and spoken by each, no matter what his language. Such was Annie's genius to find the true center of a thing somewhere out in the periphery, her passion to nag her best students until they fulfilled their own highest expectations.

"Turns out she can access the county records of Lues."

"How can she do that?" Josie was genuinely intrigued.

"Computers, Josie! I tell you it's the future of scholarship! Now, do you want to hear something really interesting?" Annie asked.

"Okay."

"John Christian Hazard and Josie Fortune bought county lot 771 with the building and all furnishings, including a liquor license from a Louis Bonner Hazard, the Fourth, for thirty-eight thousand dollars. This is three years before your mother was murdered, Josie. The business address was the Hurry On Up, Rural Route 6, but it's city property. Nine months before her death, they sold the tavern, *et al.*, to Virgil B. Hazard for fifty thousand dollars. Virgil *B.* is Jack's brother, by the way."

Josie recalled a Virgil Hazard who had been arrested for D and D or some kind of alcoholic crime or another, and decided it must be the same fellow. "How do you know they're brothers?" she asked.

"I got that from county records too. Do you want me to fax you a copy of their birth certificates?"

"Not necessary! Besides, the only fax machine we have is in Harrison Hall over in Administration. I'll take your word for it, Annie." Josie was smiling into the receiver, shaking her head and wondering how she could ever imagine Annie had given up on her.

"So Josie, what I want to know is how your mother managed to dance for Jack Hazard, when Virgil had already bought the place?"

"Excuse me?"

"I'm not talking loud enough?"

"You're saying Jack Hazard didn't own the bar when my mother was killed? Annie, the paper said – "

"They'd already sold it, Josie. County records prove it."

"But she was a dancer?"

"I'm afraid they don't put that kind of information in the county record of deeds; I don't know what she was doing, and I don't think you do either."

"This could be like your marathon thing, couldn't it?"

"No promises, Josie; just some contradictions. You don't dance for a man if he's already sold the bar. As far as that goes, I never heard of a former owner dancing for the man who bought the bar from her, but then I don't know Lues that well!"

"That doesn't make much sense, does it?"

"I've got more."

"You're incredible."

"Incredible, okay. Perfect? Not yet. I can't find out where Jack Hazard is right now, but I know he was released May 17 this year from the state correctional facility in Vienna; sounds like a wonderful place."

"I don't believe you!" Josie laughed. "You got all that from Boston? You're the greatest!"

"It's just research, kiddo. Someday, if your dissertation director *lets* you, you'll be a doctor, too. Then it will happen for you, too, just like magic."

"Annie, I'm sorry I was such a coward about this. *I* should have done it."

"Well, since you're volunteering, I do need you to check on something for me. I'll pay you your standard research fee."

"What's my standard research fee?"

"A shoulder to cry on. Now write this down." Annie read off a telephone number.

"What do you want me to do with it?"

"Call it, and keep calling until you get something. I've tried, but I can't get an answer. I thought I was a night owl!"

"Whose number is it?" Josie asked.

"Virgil Hazard, Codswallop. I guess Codswallop's a place or a town or something; it sounds like a brand name for a jockstrap."

"It's a place," Josie giggled. "What do I say when I get him?"

"He's Jack's brother, so ask him if his sister-in-law was ever a dancer at his bar, after she sold the place to him."

Josie wanted to know that one too, as Annie had undoubtedly expected she would. "How did you get the number, Annie?"

"My grader is amazing. She found it through the Lues County directory assistance! Can you believe it? What are these high-tech wizards going to think of next?"

When she got off the phone with Annie, Josie tried the number even though it was late. There was no answer, but around seven o'clock the next morning she got Virgil Hazard on the line. She could hear the sleep still in his voice. Josie identified herself as DJ Darling from the university, her voice bright and professional, her purpose a bit vague even in her own mind. He was cross about the call and assumed she wanted work. Why hadn't she called him at the club? he asked. Josie answered that she had only his home number, and said she wanted to talk to him about the Hurry On Up. He got quiet. She heard him lighting a cigarette, the scratching of flint, the breathy exhale of smoke. Finally he answered, "What did you say your name is?" Josie repeated herself, "DJ Darling." It was the truth; rather, it was a truth. "I'm working at Lues State University on a research project about Lues County, and I wanted to know about the Hurry On Up. You were the owner of it, weren't you?"

Virgil Hazard hung up.

Codswallop

Codswallop was almost an hour north of the university. The countryside hilly and wooded, here and there a pig farm or small-change cattle operation struggled to make it. There was an old grocery with a rusted-out sign and a sagging wooden porch, two gas stations, only one operable, and five bars. One of the bars was called the Bust of Country. Just a guess, but when Josie saw the sign, she pulled into the lot. The place was stacked with pickups even at 4:45. As Josie came through the door, a 300-pound doorman stood at the end of the long entry hall checking the IDs of a couple of men. All three men looked at her.

The two customers went on, and the fat man rocked slightly from one foot to the other as Josie approached him. The hand-printed sign on the wall beside him said it was two dollars to get in after six, free otherwise. The man's eyes took Josie in with a quick appraisal. She was wearing a dark blue business dress and matching jacket, a white silk blouse underneath and white pantyhose. The skirt was short, but that hadn't seemed a problem on campus. This was different. He was looking at her as if she were dressed up in a costume, the overworked executive out for a hot afternoon of fun in the country – with real live country boys. Josie leveled her gaze on the man, not a bit of fun in her.

"You want work?" the fat man asked.

Flustered at the assumption, all the more so since she had anticipated it, Josie answered sharply, "I want to see Virgil Hazard."

"Mr Hazard's busy."

So it *was* Virgil's club. Josie congratulated herself and pushed on wryly, as if the man could comprehend her irony.

"So who do I see if I want work?"

"Mr Hazard."

Josie smiled, "I guess we're not communicating; work is what I wanted to see Mr Hazard about." The man smiled as if this were funny, checked *the goods* once more and called

123

to the bartender. The bartender, muscular and young, picked up the bar phone, and a moment later, through a set of black curtains, a short, bulky man came out toward Josie. He had on an open black shirt with thick gray hair sprouting out of the top, and wore a grungy fake-gold necklace. In costume and attitude, Virgil Hazard seemed unconscious that twenty years had passed since his youth.

As he was Jack's brother, Josie had been expecting the reflection of Jack Hazard in the man's face and figure, still not knowing what that was, but she saw nothing here besides a middle-aged man who still did too many drugs. But the eyes, around the eyes, there was something familiar. "Come on!" he said automatically, and turned to lead her around the bar. In the main room, which Josie could see only after she had passed the doorman, were three stages placed so that a number of tables and chairs could be set between them. Around each stage there were more seats, for front row viewing. Each stage was about twenty by fifteen feet and included brass poles and spot lights. At the moment only one stage was lit up, a single dancer moving across it. The air was smoky. The track lights flashed on the dancer, and a sea of feed-store caps below her tilted up reverently. The girl was thin and pretty with dark red hair and a prominent nose. She was entirely naked except for a G-string and lone dollar-stuffed-garter on her left leg. Her breasts were small and pointed. Garth Brooks sang "Papa Loved Mamma" and she executed a perfect back flip, walking over with her hands. Several of the men shouted as the girl did this and presented their dollars like neat green penises all around the edge of the stage. Josie realized she had stopped to watch, and hurried to catch up with Virgil. She pushed through the dark curtains and bumped into him as he opened his office. Virgil entered the room with Josie following still too closely. The office was small and cluttered. On one of the walls there were several unframed posters of superstar exotic dancers. On the opposite wall, there was only a large framed poster of Bogart from *Casablanca*. Josie shifted her attention from the glossy smiles and mournful Bogart to Virgil Hazard's cluttered desk. He had a huge ashtray filled with butts. The office stank of it. Next to the ashtray, she saw a stack of beer and liquor distributors' invoices with a couple of "*overdue*" notices stamped in red. Beside these he had an album-size ledger unfolded, the company's checks. Virgil took a seat behind the little black wooden desk and gestured for Josie to sit in front of the desk where a lone straight-backed chair waited. He was almost treating this like a real interview, she thought with some humor. As she sat down, he reached for a folder marked *Applications*. The word was written in a large, round script and done in green ink.

He tossed a single sheet toward her, a generic application. "Where have you worked, honey?" His tone was all business, but his eyes fixed on Josie's legs as she crossed them.

"Have you ever heard of the Hurry On Up?" Josie asked. Her tone insinuated she had worked there, but of course the name of the place stopped him cold.

Not exactly happy, Virgil Hazard answered her smile with a tight, twisted grin. "Let me guess. You're the college chick with the local history project, right?" He stood up as he finished his question, Josie's signal to exit.

But Josie held her ground; the hard part had been getting here. A little temper from a pudgy coke addict was not as difficult to face as walking into this place had been. "I want to know about the Hurry On Up, before you owned it."

This stopped him for some reason, and he stood considering her from behind his desk, his smile creasing his gray, flabby cheeks. Josie took the expression as permission to continue. "Did they have dancing there?"

"What was your name again?"

"DJ."

"You're talking girls, right? Strippers?" Josie nodded. "No, they didn't have strippers. I started that."

125

"What about Josie Fortune? She was one of the owners you bought it from."

"I know who I bought it from."

"Did she dance for you?"

The man laughed. "Listen, DJ, I don't know where this is going, and I don't care. They told me you said you wanted to work. Were they lying or were you?"

"I guess I was."

His eyebrows rose expressively, his intent a kind of mutual larceny. "I got an empty stage out there and a full house. I've seen 'auditions' pull a hundred dollars inside five minutes. It's easier than a trick if you have the stuff." His eyes settled on Josie's thighs again. He made no attempt to disguise the attention. Josie was confused, then faintly irritated that she had been misread so entirely. What did he mean *trick*? Did he think she was a – ? Couldn't he see? Couldn't anybody see, she wasn't that sort of woman? Virgil became positively genial: "Those boys out there will give their last dollar to see what's under that skirt of yours, DJ."

"Did Josie Fortune ever dance for anyone? Was she a dancer?" Josie struggled to keep her voice level and her temper in control. It was a losing battle.

Virgil tipped his head slightly. It was a look of curiosity, hardly more than a casual reflection. Was it the thought that he had seen her somewhere before? Josie couldn't remember the man at all, except the eyes, and, too, there was something in his voice, especially in his whining drawl that was both sour and familiar.

"What do you care about Josie for?" he asked. He was good-natured but suspicious.

"Can I be honest with you?"

The man's expression broke apart into a wild, cruel smile. "Naw, hell, just keep on lying. I don't want you to rupture anything."

"I'm doing research for a woman who's writing a book

126

on exotic dancers; it's kind of a feminist-perspective thing. Anyway, I read that Josie Fortune was this dancer – "

"You read it wrong. She never danced. She was the bartender at the Hurry On Up, but that was before she and Jack sold the place."

"She was your sister-in-law?"

Warily: "Look, honey, there's not going to be an interview here. You want to know if Josie Fortune was a dancer. The answer's no. She owned the Hurry On Up with my brother Jack; she worked it. They both worked it. That's it. They had it a couple, three years, and I bought it. End of story."

"I don't think so."

A dawning of recognition. "I get it. This is about the murder, right?"

Josie nodded.

Virgil Hazard's face tightened down angrily. "There's a door right behind you, *D.J.* If you're smart you won't let it hit you on that pretty little ass of yours on the way out."

"Why did they sell the place?"

"I got things to do, bills to write. Now do you want to take your clothes off and go to work or do you just want to waste my time?" He came around the desk, his mood darkening, his manner aggressive and deliberate. When Josie didn't move, Virgil sat down on the edge of the desk directly before her. He looked down at Josie's legs with obvious lust now. "Maybe you just want to show *me* what you got under that dress. Hmm? Is that what you want, honey?" He coaxed her meanly, the cooing of a man intent on driving her out in a hurry or getting his fondest wish, one or the other and he didn't seem to care which. "Show it to me. I want to see it. Show me what you got, baby."

Josie hit the latch of her purse as she let her legs slowly separate for him. She brought her hand across her waist and into the purse in a single unhurried motion, her legs splaying open for him inexorably. Transfixed, Virgil watched her, his nostrils flaring, his grin frozen. At the last moment he looked away from her legs to see what she was doing with her purse. He didn't do anything else. He didn't have time. In a single motion, Josie flipped the safety, laid the hammer back and put the snubnose between his spread legs, snug up against his crotch.

"Holy Jesus!"

Still seated, Josie held the gun with both hands now, straight before her face, her arms extended, her voice tight. "Seen enough?"

Croaking, his words breaking through the phlegm in his throat, Virgil Hazard answered, "Yeah, I've seen all I want. Now can you point that somewhere else, somewhere not so important, like my brain, just not there?"

Josie stood up, rising directly in front of him, the gun still nestled into his crotch.

"Just one more thing, okay?"

"Name it." A strained, pale smile with this.

"Do you know where I can find Jack?"

"At this moment I got no idea. Five minutes from now, he comes on shift to tend bar. Jack's the night bartender."

Uncle Virgil

"I'm going to back away a couple of steps, and when I do, I want you to go back behind the desk. I don't want you to do anything but sit back down. Okay?"

Josie and Virgil Hazard effected their tenuous treaty with care. Josie had no problem with the idea of shooting the man. She was certain her mother had been manipulated by Jack and apparently the manipulation included Virgil. She had owned her own place, and then they had changed things on her. The sale had only been a ruse, probably to get the ownership out of her hands. Josie could almost imagine their blandishments, then the arguments among the three of them that followed. There would have been the promise of higher profits; dignity always takes the back seat for that, then the

128

double-cross. Well, she didn't like it! Keeping her aim on Virgil's crotch, she decided she was just damn tired of all of it!

As far as Josie could see, Virgil Hazard was the epitome of corruption; he was nothing more than a pimp, and she didn't really care if she had to stand trial for castrating him or killing him if she had to. Virgil moved behind his desk, his hands raised to about the level of his chest. He was trying to smile, but he looked more like a man who had just wet himself. Josie could see he wasn't at all sure he was going to live through the next minute; he read people pretty well, she thought. Finally, a spark of sense pulling at her, Josie shifted the sights off him and lowered the hammer on her nickel. She snapped the thumbset safety on, keeping both hands on the gun and pointing it to the floor directly in front of her, her arms forming a V. "I want to know why the paper said Josie Fortune was an exotic dancer if she never danced."

"I can't help you there. All I know is she was my sister-in-law, right? So I knew her, okay? She didn't dance. Ever."

Believe him?

Virgil Hazard read Josie's expression; he saw it mattered, that emotionally she wanted his words to be true. "What's with you, doll? What the hell does it matter to you if Josie . . ." Something happened and his expression brightened into a sort of amazement, then he laughed suddenly. "I'll be damned! You're Josie's kid, aren't you?"

"I'm just trying to find out – "

"Jesus! I can't believe it! DJ, Deborah Josephine, you're Josie!" He dropped his hands, and he flopped casually into his chair. Little Josie Fortune wasn't going to shoot her Uncle Virgil, or at least that was what Josie read in the gesture. And maybe he was right.

Josie shifted her weight awkwardly, feeling like a kid, and let the gun slip to her side. She wasn't entirely taken in. "So do I know you?" she asked. "Are we like best friends or something?"

129

"I'm your Uncle Virgil!" He kicked his legs up on the desk and leaned back benignly in his chair, folding his hands over his ample belly. "Where have you been, Josie? Hell, Jack and I went looking for you about five, six months ago! No one would tell us where you were! Have you been here all along?"

Josie kept it simple and vague. "I've been growing up."

"I can see that. You look good. Don't shoot my nuts off or anything but you look damn good. Oh, and hey! sorry about the come-on; I get some of these girls in here looking for work; they get scared and need that kind of thing, they're kind of – "

Josie didn't want to hear it, what the girls *need*. "So why were you looking for me?" she asked preemptively.

"Jack got out of prison, and he wanted to find you."

"Unfinished business?" Irony without humor.

"Hey, that guy loved you. I mean you and your mom were his whole world."

Josie took this for what it was: a probable, ugly truth. After all, men like Dan Scholari and Jack Hazard loved women to death. She opened her purse and set the gun back inside. Virgil seemed about as threatening as a trout. "So you never told me why they sold you the bar."

"Long story."

"I really am trying to find out about my mother. It's what I came to Lues for."

"It's complicated. Running a bar's long hours, hard work, and the truth is, Josie wanted to go to school. So I mean there were a lot of reasons, but I guess school was the big reason. She wanted to make something of her life." He broke off suddenly, not saying the rest of what he meant to say, whatever it was. He shrugged fatalistically, a look to suggest school had killed her.

"She went to school? To the university?" To that point, Josie had discredited everything Virgil had told her about her mother. This she believed; this she could verify. More than that, she wanted to believe it. It was important to her that her mother had gone to college. It had a tangible worth in her own hierarchy of values.

Virgil grinned, "Loser State. You didn't know that?"

Josie shook her head numbly. "I remember Jack getting arrested. They beat him; they bloodied his face so I couldn't even recognize him — " She broke off, unwilling to say the rest, that it was the only thing she remembered.

"Well that there was all bullshit." Virgil's puffy face composed itself into an expression of old anger and resolute sincerity. Josie read it at once as the liar's protocol.

"He confessed to killing her, or do you mean the newspaper got that wrong too?" Unconsciously, Josie's left hand slipped back to the latch of her purse.

"He confessed all right, but he didn't have any choice."

"Look, it was a long time ago. It doesn't really matter if he did it or not. I just need to see him. I don't remember much about life here or my mother. Okay, I don't remember a thing. My whole life here is a blank. Do you think he'd talk to me?"

Virgil stared at Josie in dumb amazement. "Jesus, I've heard about things like that, but I never . . ." Virgil had no concept of what Josie had gone through. To Virgil, trauma was running out of coke at the orgy.

"Things are coming back a little," Josie answered. "I remember some things but I can't always fit them into place. It's helped to come back and see things, but I thought maybe more would make sense if I could talk to Jack. Maybe if I just see him . . ."

Virgil checked his watch. "Just go on out to the bar; his shift's started by now, he'll talk to you."

Josie laughed nervously, "I wasn't ready to meet Jack today. I'm kind of nervous about it." She took a couple of deep breaths. "Do you think he wants to see me?"

"He's dying to." He reached for his cigarettes and pulled

one out. "It's about the only thing he talks about – finding you, I mean, and seeing how you grew up."

"I'd prefer you didn't smoke," Josie told him. Cigarette in his mouth, Virgil considered this a moment, his eyes reverting to Josie's purse. Then he threw the cigarette on the desk.

"I'm sorry about the gun. I just don't like to be called *baby*. It's got real bad associations for me."

Virgil Hazard shrugged, "Don't worry about it. It's in the blood. Your mother kept a sawed-off twelve-gauge under the bar. I saw her pull it out a couple of times; no one ever doubted she'd use it either."

Josie had the impulse to confess what had been happening to her since she had gotten to Lues. Maybe it would make sense what she had done, if he knew, she thought, but then she stopped herself at once. This man was not her friend. She had no friends here. "So you and Jack really came looking for me?" she asked lamely, Lues creeping into her speech like a virus.

"Jack asked around. He talked to a couple of lawyers. They told him to leave well enough alone." Virgil shrugged. "We're just a couple a country hicks, what do we know? They said you wouldn't want to see him."

"What's he like?"

"What you said about your mother?" Josie nodding without knowing what he meant. "About it not mattering because it was a long time ago?" She blinked. Had she said that? "It matters to Jack. He did nineteen years for a murder he never committed. He don't shrug it off that easy. It left a scar on him. He's different than before. I never thought, well, he'll come back; he's already better, but he loved Josie, he really did, and then to be accused of killing her . . ." Virgil shook his head sadly. Josie could almost believe his sincerity.

"You said Jack didn't have any choice but to confess. What does that mean?"

"What they did was this. They got an old watch that nobody ever saw, I mean everybody knows Jack and nobody ever saw this watch, and they put his name on it and they dropped it close by where they found Josie. The cops found it and they gave him a choice – life if he wants it to go to trial or twenty years if he'll cop a plea. Jack figured twenty years, he'd be out in eight, nine years. If he fought it, they promised him it was all or nothing, no bargains down the road. Plus all the expense of a trial. Look, he's a Hazard, and there hasn't been a one of us born in six generations, maybe a hundred, that ever had any luck with the law, so I mean he thought about it and took the twenty, only they put the fix in and he didn't get his parole. He did the full time. Almost nineteen years exactly." Virgil shook his head. "All that time you were growing up, Jack was sitting in a cage. He didn't do shit, he didn't do anything wrong but love you and your mamma and they locked him away for it."

Josie pulled herself back emotionally. Just words, that's all they were. "Who planted the watch?" she asked. She thought she expressed enough sympathy in her tone to keep Virgil going, but the question itself was skeptical, even cruel.

Virgil gave a worldly shrug, though he was anything but worldly. "Maybe they just found it or maybe the cops put it there. Jack's trying to find out, but he's not having much luck. No one's talking. I don't know who put it there; all I know is the cops never gave it a second thought once they had that watch. They were waving it at him and saying it proved he done it. Jack and I went into Lues a couple of weeks ago, trying to get the police records on the case, and they said they'd all been destroyed. They were lying, but what the hell could we do? We got about as far with looking into Josie's murder as looking for you. I mean nobody's stupid enough to threaten Jack, not anyone who knows him anyway, but he's heard some things. I don't know, like Jack could get in some more trouble if he started putting his nose where it didn't belong. Jack hasn't given up, but it's for damn sure if he's ever going to find out what happened he's going to have to do it without the help of the law."

"Can't he just get a court order to look at the records?"

Virgil laughed. "Christ! they did send you away, didn't they? See a court order means a judge gets involved. That's a nice theory, but it don't work in Lues like that. Judges hear the name *Hazard* and they automatically get a number in their head. That's the number of years they're going to sentence the poor bastard to."

Josie was outside of this, this casual humor about unfounded persecution, the general paranoia about anything concerning the law. They were facing each other in a crumby little room inside a building that offered for fun an act which was itself nothing short of criminal, and here was the owner crying about injustices. Jack was going to be more of the same, she was sure of it. Virgil's story fit the profile on this type; it fit with everything she had expected. Family. *Uncle Virgil.* In Lues a virgin is a girl who can outrun family. Virgil might have been her family, but he wasn't blood; neither he nor Jack was blood. They were just a couple of men who had mixed her mother up in their own perverted fantasies and then, Jack by himself or with Virgil's help, ended up killing her. And now they had a story about it. Men like Virgil always had a story, always made everything reasonable and the law's version unreasonable; they were always persecuted by authority.

"I know some lawyers in Boston, Harvard graduates. If there's anything in what you're saying, they can find it out. I make one phone call," she told him with more bravado than veracity, "they'll turn this county upside down and find out where the records are."

Virgil rubbed finger to thumb. "I bet they can."

Josie let it go. He didn't want the truth. He knew the truth; it was all some kind of fantasy, this story about Jack's innocence.

"So do you want me to call Jack and tell him who's in here?"

She shook her head. She looked away. Nervous. *Twenty years* . . .

Virgil reached for his phone, hit a single digit.

"No!"

Virgil continued to hold the receiver but winked at Josie. "Yeah, Jack, I got a girl in here wants to audition. I want you to talk to her before she goes out. Yeah, she's fine; great legs, just talk to her. I know, we're *all* busy; talk to her, okay? Right."

He looked at Josie as he set the receiver back in place. His gray face wrinkled in some kind of affection and understanding: "You're *expected*, Josie. Just go talk to the guy."

Josie looked back at the door nervously. This must be what it felt like to chase monsters.

Jack Hazard

Josie caught sight of Jack Hazard immediately. He was busy pulling several draws. The other bartender was gone. Jack wasn't a big man. She had expected more of him, somehow. He wasn't even *average* height, and physically he was wiry, hardly enough man to assault four football players. Of course, Jack was past fifty now, and Virgil had said he had changed. Twenty years can alter everything. The face was hard and solemn, but at least it wasn't especially lined or baggy. Prison had probably saved him from his brother's drug habits. Still, there was a certain numbness about his look, at least as he pulled drinks. Josie's first impression, before he even saw her, was that she had liked the man when she was a kid; she didn't especially care for what she saw now. He had that prison air about him: the well-behaved, empty-souled con. He was a man with low horizons who'd steal a dollar from his only friend.

Josie thought about a woman in one of her classes. She

was Josie's age, and had a hick — a slew — for a husband; the woman was a slew herself, and it was all the more pathetic because she wanted something more, but as long as she lived in Lues with the man she thought she loved, she was never going to be anything other than a slew. That was probably what Josie's mother had faced. She had gone to school, and it was some kind of big dream for a hick girl, but then she had to go back home each night to a man like this, with his brother and their inevitable partnership in prostitution.

Small wonder the thing ended in murder.

Jack looked toward Josie as she thought about his hands taking her own neck and strangling her, as he had her mother. The look on his face was little more than a variation of his bartender's mask, feigned politeness, then seeing a pretty face, he flashed a cocky smile, "You're the new girl?" he asked. Twenty years with the boys, but he hadn't forgotten the charm. This was how a man came onto you if he wasn't sure about things. He was careful and friendly, not taking Josie in too overtly with his eyes, but letting her see what a *nice* guy he was. Like his brother, Jack Hazard reeked of insincerity. Josie saw nothing of the man that she could remember, but the voice somehow reminded her of her childhood. It had a small-town arrogance about it. It was country-shallow. Jack Hazard looked and sounded like the kind of guy who could talk forever, the ultimate authority about trucks, guns, beer, and pussy. Especially pussy.

"I'm Josie Fortune," Josie announced, reaching out to shake the man's hand.

The politeness vanished, and Jack's eyes locked into Josie's. He didn't shake her hand. In fact, he had the look of wanting to kill.

"Say it again?"

"Don't you know me? I'm Josie! I'm your stepdaughter. Virgil said you'd be glad to see me." Josie tried to smile.

"Josie?" She nodded at his confusion. "Josie Fortune?"

Josie almost laughed now at the man's look; he was totally stunned. Nor did he act especially glad to see her.

"Well you're not dancing here, kid!" Frowning, he looked past Josie's shoulder toward Virgil's office. A smoky rage. He was a killer, no doubt about it.

Josie looked out at the stages, the women dancing. The music was loud. All three stages were filled now. The girls were writhing variously for the small change at their feet. One of them had one of the men's feed caps and was fitting her breasts into it. Another did a backbend to bring up a dollar off the stage floor with her tongue. The third hung upside down, her naked legs wrapped about a brass pole.

Now she stared at her mother's killer. "Sorry, Virgil already hired me. I'm working, whether you want it or not!"

Jack ducked under the bar and started past her toward Virgil's office.

"I'm kidding! It's a joke."

The man's rage was obvious, and he seemed to struggle to understand what she was saying. He really was small, she thought. Next to her, they were almost perfectly at eye level with each other.

She was sorry to have baited him suddenly. He didn't seem an especially smart man, nor even very happy. "I'm a professor, Jack. I teach down at the college, at Lues State."

Slowly a dull grin broke over his face. Such a simple man, so perfectly simple: "Well, that's better! A professor? Damn!"

Some pride is pathetic to watch. This was especially so. What did Jack Hazard know of life other than taverns and prison walls? He probably couldn't even read! Hearing his wife's little girl had grown up to be a professor was beyond his enfeebled imagination.

"I just started teaching at Lues State this fall," she told him. "Officially, I'm still a lecturer."

"Everyone's talking about the new girl's audition, then Virgil tells me – " He broke off, smiling suddenly like a man who'd never known a prison door. "Josie, you look just like

137

your mom! I can't believe I didn't see it right away! You look great, kid!" He shook his head, and as he did this, his hapless, silly look triggered Josie's memory.

The handsomest man in the world. It was something the three of them had joked about, a long-standing by-play in the family. Josie had forgotten it, the half-serious, half-teasing praise her mother and she had always had for him. Josie remembered suddenly crawling across their couch in the trailer, the cheap fabric scratching her skin and shiny mobile home paneling part of the memory, her mother – the face of her mother clearly part of the image – reaching toward her so that she came in under the woman's arm. Her mother had had a beautiful face. Fine featured, finer than Josie's, the skin unblemished, a sort of glow about it. The hair was long and thick, a rich bronze color, a reddish gold. The memory gave Josie her mother's laughter too, wonderful laughter, and Josie heard the voice within her memory too, as the laughter faded and the child she had been slipped against her mother, *ah . . . Josie!* It had happened that way. Something had triggered their laughter, something about the handsomest man in the world, something about Jack Hazard. Her mother was sighing, laughing, happy, holding her daughter and the bright brief happiness that comes with love. They had all been happy once. Laughing and country proud . . .

What had happened to all that? Josie remembered nothing else. Probably nothing had *happened*; her memory was probably only a moment between a couple of violent episodes, a break when two adults tried hard to pretend nothing was wrong and a kid too hopeful to know the truth tried to laugh along with the adults. Even as she thought as much, Josie decided she had loved Jack, the way only a child can. Maybe their fights had been private, late at night after a lot of drinking. She didn't know if her mother had loved Jack as she had. Probably once, anyway. It just seemed like Josie had kept loving him even when her mother quit, had loved him to the moment she learned the truth.

That man there is the one that killed your mamma.

Still the grin, still the man she thought she had loved once, Jack told her, "Well, let me get your Uncle Virgil out here to take over the bar so we can go outside."

Jack was through the curtains before she could tell him she didn't want to go outside. Not here, anyway. *I don't know who you are!* she thought. *I'm not going outside with you!* Dumbly, she waited for him to return. She needed to explain a couple of things. Like that twenty years had passed, and that he had killed her mother and she wasn't especially ready to forgive what she didn't even understand! What did he think? What could possibly be going on in his head that he would imagine she might want to be alone with him?

The waitress came to the bar to drop off her empty glasses and pick up the drinks Jack had pulled for her. She said something to Josie, and Josie stepped toward her, asking what she had said. "I said, 'What's your name?' " Josie could barely hear the woman even though she shouted. The music was too loud.

"Josie!"

"You going up like that?"

"No!"

"You better change. Back there!" She pointed toward a room where the dancers came and went. "At least ditch the pantyhose, if that's what you're wearing. You wear pantyhose, you'll wilt their dicks!" The woman cut back across the floor toward the far corner, Josie calling after her, thinking to correct the misunderstanding. Then, in a conversational tone that no one could hear, she added, "My pantyhose are just fine, bitch."

Josie looked back toward the curtains where Jack had vanished. What was he doing in there? She would just tell him when he came back, not here, not now. She'd make a date to meet him in Lues; someplace real public. She swore at the sight of the dancers as the song came to an end; they were giving the men pretty kisses for their dollars. *Making*

139

dates for a parking lot blowjob? Sure they were. That was what Val had said they did at the Hurry On Up. Nothing changed but the girls.

Then came the disc jockey's rumblings, a sleazy carnival voice, the obscene huzzahs of a man among men and pussy in the air: "GIVE A HANDJOB FOR THOSE THREE LOVELIES, AND NOW, GENTLEMEN, AS ADVERTISED, WE HAVE *THE BUST OF COUNTRY'S* LATEST DREAM MACHINE STRUTTING HER STUFF TO SEE IF SHE'S GOT THE STUFF . . . FOR YOUR VIEWING PLEASURE THE UNSAMPLED PARADISE OF *THE BUST OF COUNTRY'S* LATEST AND FROM WHERE I'M SITTING COULD BE THE GREATEST ACQUISITION . . . JOSIE!!!"

Josie looked out from the bar and saw all heads turned toward her as she stood alone, a starlet before the roaring applause of her admirers. There was nothing to do but turn her back on them, looking as she did toward the dark curtains and Virgil Hazard's office. "DON'T BE BASHFUL," the voice cajoled. "WE MIGHT WANT TO LICK YOU PLENTY, BUT WE DON'T BITE . . . MUCH!"

A man from one of the closest tables approached Josie, still clapping his hands, like the rest of them, and he said something to her. When Josie smelt his breath, she decided he had been here from the opening bell. He tried to take her hand.

"I don't work here!" Josie shouted angrily, still trying to keep her back to the crowd.

"They said you were going to do an *audition!*"

"Let go of me!" Past the man, she saw the crowd waiting good-naturedly. Their good nature seemed to extend so long as she *eventually* gave in to them.

"Hell, everyone's waiting for it!"

The waitress slipped by her now, smiling coyly and offering another piece of hard-won wisdom: "Tell 'em you need fifty dollars before you do it. They'll pay it!"

Josie thought to explain, thought to shout her denial, thought to pull her revolver. The man, who had her wrist now and was suddenly a little more insistent, started pulling her toward the large room in the direction of the nearest stage. The song started. The other dancers were watching, clapping like the men.

Josie started to brace herself and fight the man off when she felt something at her shoulder and saw Jack reaching between her and the man who had her wrist. He was easily a head taller than Jack, but when Jack nudged the man, he faded away without protest, stumbling back to his table and his equally drunk companions. Jack took Josie's arm and turned her toward the exit. "Come on." The cheers at their back mixed with good-natured boos. Josie looked around and saw Virgil slipping under the counter to take over the bar. He made a gesture of a drink, then another sign that Josie didn't understand. As she passed the doorman and started down the hall, Jack was still holding her. Josie heard the disc jockey: "I THINK JACK'S GOING TO KEEP HER FOR HIS-SELF, BUT RIGHT NOW WE'VE GOT TWO-FOR-ONES! TWO DRINKS FOR THE PRICE OF ONE . . ." The song returned, a soft, crooning country ballad about friends in low places.

The bar faded from Josie's worries, and she thought about going outside with Jack. She balked suddenly. The parking lot, though still bright, was vaguely menacing. "Where are we going?" she demanded. It was all the protest she could summon at the moment.

"To get a cup of coffee or a drink. We need to talk."

Through the glass doors, Josie saw two men coming toward them across the lot. They were bearded, lanky workmen types; they were all workmen types at the Bust of Country. Through the glass door, they were studying Josie with interest, like the eighty or so voyeurs inside. Jack seemed irritated with their grins and happy nudges.

"Look," Josie explained, "I don't feel comfortable just

running out like this. I don't know you. It's been twenty years, I have no idea – "

As the workmen walked through the door, one of them said Jack's name and clucked his tongue with grudging envy. "This is my stepdaughter," Jack growled at him. Jack had a temper; she could see that.

The other one laughed, "Keep it in the family, Jack!"

Both of them went on, but they turned back to look at Josie when the big doorman said something and pointed toward Jack and Josie. Josie hated the feeling of their greasy eyes on her, and she blamed Jack. With all her heart she blamed him.

"I want to talk," Josie answered, "but I've got an appointment back at the university. A department meeting. I can't miss it. Can you meet me tomorrow?"

"What time?"

"I can be free after two."

Jack hesitated. "Sure. Where?"

"The McDonald's in Lues." He rolled his eyes. "What?" she asked.

The old grin, the one Josie recognized. "Nothing. McDonald's is great. We don't have to eat that stuff, do we?"

"I want to talk about things, Jack. I don't care if you eat or not."

"Two o'clock," Jack answered, smiling now and looking something like a stepfather, maybe even a proud one. "You really a professor, Josie?"

Josie tried not to be taken in by the act. She stared him down without answering, thinking of the murder, and then she pushed the door open and started away.

"Hey!" he called. Josie looked back. "Virgil says you got a .357 in that purse." A silly lopsided grin.

Josie's gut tightened and twisted. *With his bare hands he strangled her.* She blinked slowly, finding the proper distance in her voice: "Do you want to see it?"

The Parking Lot

Josie had parked close to the front of the tavern but well away from the door, almost to the woods at the north end of the parking lot. As she came outside, she scanned the trucks in her habitual manner and stayed off the line a bit as she walked toward her VW. Some kind of monster truck was parked beside her VW, so she couldn't see it. Josie looked out to her right to the next line of vehicles, then drifted a step or two wider, in case there was some kind of surprise waiting for just this moment. Dan Scholari liked parking lots. Josie looked behind her and thumbed the latch of her purse so that it opened slightly. She brought her right hand to the opening as she stepped out four steps wide of the truck and looked expectantly at the VW. In the next instant she had the gun out, the safety flipped off and the barrel pointing first toward the VW, then in a wide arc back around her, her arms and wrists locked, her legs flexed and ready for the attack. No one was there, but all the glass in her car had been smashed. The back panel of glass and both windows in the front doors were broken out completely. The windshield was spidery with cracks and in two spots the glass was bowed in, completely ruined. She saw two men moving parallel to her, two lanes over, some sixty feet away. They didn't see her. There was no one else in the lot, at least that Josie could see. Josie stepped beyond her car to check beside the passenger door, then went on past two more cars, almost to the woods. She slipped toward the front of the line to be sure no one was hiding in front of the VW. She kept both hands on the gun, her arms locked, her shoulders moving with the gun, and walked back the way she had gone in, approaching the car now from behind. Two men came out of the bar and started toward Josie without seeming to notice her. She reached into her jacket pocket and pulled her keys out. As she unlocked the door, she saw that the glass was all over the driver's seat. She turned back and rose to her tiptoes to look over the pickup truck bed to see the two men. They were coming closer, still apparently oblivious to her presence. Josie hurried into the car, sitting down on the shards of glass. She felt it cutting her as she moved her legs. She turned the key and thankfully the car started. She let the hammer down gently on the .357, and set it on the rubble of glass in the passenger seat. Then she shifted to reverse and backed out almost directly in front of the two men. At the sight of her or the broken windows, she didn't know which, one of the men called out drunkenly, "What happened?" The other hollered out something about a show, and Josie pushed the gearshift to first. The car leaped forward, and once on the street, Josie drove a little over two hundred feet before pulling into an empty lot. Painfully, she slipped out of the car. Setting her revolver on the floor of the driver side, she began picking the glass from the back of her dress and her ruined pantyhose. Occasionally, she looked around to be sure she was alone, and finally satisfied that she had the glass off her, she started removing it from her seat.

That was when she saw the sheet of paper on the floor of the passenger side. Nothing was written on it, but it wasn't hers. For one thing, it lay on top of the glass, not buried under it. Carefully, Josie leaned across and pick it up. On the back side were the words:

stil tHinkING Of u, hoR

She dropped the sheet and stood up to look around again. She was still alone, but it felt like she was being watched. She finished picking the glass out of the driver seat, and only when most of it was gone did Josie cut herself with the dust of it as she tried to sweep it out with her fingertips. Swearing bitterly, she hissed for no one but herself to hear, "Come on, Dan! Just once, show your lousy face! What are you waiting for?" The streets of Codswallop were empty.

In this great solitude, Josie's whispers sounded like a lunatic's prayer.

Problems in the Space-Time Continuum

Josie called Annie at her office, but she wasn't in. On her home answering machine, she left the message that Annie should call her immediately. Big news, she announced. Afterwards, Josie went to strip her business suit off and discovered the blood across the seat and back panel of the skirt as well as the bloodied stains on her hose and the backs of her legs. She went to the bathroom and set the dark blue skirt to soak. The white pantyhose (*wilt their dicks!*) Josie threw into the wastebasket. She took a quick shower to be sure the glass and blood was completely washed off her legs. It had been stupid to jump in on the glass, but at the time she had just wanted to leave.

Josie shut off the flow of water and stepped out of the shower. She looked steadily now into the mirror. Like one of the dancers, her breasts unfettered, visible; her eyes proud and angry. She was fully naked but no eyes to see her, not even a lover's eyes. She was alone, in other words. Her only friend in the world was a thousand miles away. *stil tHinkING Of u, hoR*. Another flight out here just to *tease* her? Maybe Annie was right. Maybe she had just better quit her job. Only she wouldn't go back to Boston. She would just disappear. Disappear and change her name.

No! She hadn't done anything wrong. She wasn't going to run like a fugitive; she wasn't going to keep running and hiding, and carrying this gun, and wondering if he had caught up with her again. It was here and now. *Fight* him! she told herself. Then she tried to put it behind her. She tried to think of nothing at all. All he wanted was to upset her. The man was sick! And she had the power to ignore him or at least to put it in perspective. She didn't need to be a part of his sickness. He could be out there all he wanted, but if he thought he could get close . . .

She patted the wounds on the back of her thighs even as her mind seethed with a mix of fear and anger. The cuts stung her, so that she opened the cabinet and put some first

145

aid cream on the back of her thighs. Then still naked, she stomped across the hall to her bedroom. She finished drying herself in front of her large, foggy mirror.

To distract herself, she studied her reflection. She tried to see herself critically, the way those men had seen her or wanted to. She threw the towel over a chair and posed stupidly like one of *them*. What was the point? she wondered. She saw nothing but the absurdity of the human form. She shook her head and went to the beat chest where she kept her underwear and dress-downs. She put on some jeans and a T-shirt. She was feeling better. Something to eat and then some reading in bed, just her and her one-thousandth book on James Joyce, and her nickel-plated .357 snubnose.

In the morning she would take care of the car. After her first two classes, she could drop it off and take her bike from the auto shop back to school. She thought about her insurance. She didn't know if they would pay if she didn't report it to the police, and that she definitely didn't want to do. She needed more humiliation like she needed a job working for Virgil Hazard! At the thought of that place again, Josie stripped her T-shirt off like a dancer, an exotic motion, and making a coy, silly face in imitation of their performance of facile lust, she thought of the men with their drunken gazes. She pulled herself away from the fantasy. Josie smiled at the woman in the mirror as she combed out her hair. She combed it back flat and wet; she looked like she was ready to dance in that old Robert Palmer video, except she was topless. Mean and topless. She thought about Jack's and Virgil's bar and threw the brush down angrily. She put her shirt back on and studied her face. Just like her mother. It seemed to her the wholesomeness was suddenly gone. Hardly a month in Lues, and she was a different woman. She was talking like a hick and thinking like a whore. Just like good ol' ma?

"I need to get out of Lues," she told her reflection.

In the kitchen Josie opened the refrigerator and looked at

her choices. The thing was full and nothing looked good. She tried to focus her thoughts on something, on anything besides Jack and Virgil Hazard, and Dan Scholari with his plane flights out of Boston.

The guy needed to get a life. Or at least show up in front of her gun sights.

Her stomach turned. The very thought of Dan Scholari plotting these little *incidents* started a series of thoughts and images. She hadn't seen the bastard since April, *the cruelest month*, and he was still —

"Why does Eliot say that April is the cruelest month, Josie? . . . Because taxes are due!" Her mother laughs at her own joke, and Josie laughs too, because her mother is laughing. Not so funny now. The cruelest because she died in April . . .

The image of her mother and the memory of her silly joke edged up in Josie's throat like nausea. They were in some apartment; the place clean and bare, something wrong or missing.

The telephone rang, and Josie jumped in surprise. She walked into the living room and heard Annie's deep, raspy voice as soon as she picked up: "Things are crazy here, but I had to call."

"Hi, Annie. Did you get my message?"

"No. I'm still at school. Your ex-husband went off the deep end this afternoon, Josie."

"He what?"

"Sometime after lunch, he just appeared in the dean's office with a gun."

"A gun!"

"He said he didn't like his spring assignment and wanted to *talk!*"

"Annie! Today? This afternoon? He was in Boston this afternoon?"

"And jail this evening."

"Annie!"

The old woman stopped.

"Annie, someone broke out all the glass in my car *this afternoon*. I thought it was Dan."

"Oh, God, Josie." Annie's voice was no more than a whisper.

"Whoever it was, he left a note, telling me he was still thinking about me. And he called me a whore."

Annie was quiet. Josie didn't even hear breathing.

Finally Josie offered the frightened, tentative question that begged to be asked:

"Annie, who's doing this to me?"

Part Three

Tobias Crouch

Desk-bound, his ankle wrapped tight in an Ace bandage, a cane leaning against the wall behind him, traffic patrol officer Tobias Crouch of the Lues City Police looked out across the office to which he was assigned for the next three days. He was thinking he wouldn't mind staying at a desk. At forty-three, he deserved a desk of his own. Across the room, Sanders and Jones were filling out reports, their shoulders hunched. Loser State graduates, like Crouch, they were detectives. Their careers were going places. Toby Crouch wasn't going to be a detective at this late date in his career, but he thought he deserved to stay at a desk until he retired, or Watch Command would be nice. That was going to open up next month. There was plenty of speculation about the new watch commander, but Tobias Crouch's name never came up. Crouch looked at his swollen foot longingly. He could milk his war wound only so long before Colt sent him back out. He knew if he asked Colt Fellows for a permanent position here Colt would laugh at him. If you wanted something from Colt you gave him something he wanted. The last time Crouch had done that was almost twenty years ago, a really big favor, and that was how he got on the force. He just hadn't been able to provide the man with anything else, no fortuitous saves, no secrets he had unearthed, no special favors. Because of it, Colt had left him to drift.

Ruby Collins, standing over Jones's desk, picked up a stack of papers and left the office, her ass a handful and a half.

Third year officer already bucking for sergeant. Wonder what she gives the boss? Crouch looked at the clock. It was early, just ten after seven. He wanted another cup of coffee and maybe a couple of doughnuts, but he didn't want to walk out and get them.

Sanders's voice. Toby came out of his reveries. "Take line three, we're busy." *We're busy.* Crouch looked down and saw the light flashing. He hadn't even heard the phone ringing. He picked up. Woman . . . complaint. Right. Yeah. Send her back. Crouch watched the glass until the woman passed. *Blonde.* She kept going. *One, two, three.* She opened the door. *Hello.* Even Jones looked up for this one, and he was dead below the waist. Sanders gave Crouch a you-lucky-bastard look. *Yeah, well, you were busy, fuck-head.*

Start with the legs: wrap those around your hips, big boy. Just think about that ass, Tobias. Turn around and smile, baby. Breasts high and dry. Freckles. God-damn! She walked toward Crouch, her step catching. *Know me, baby?*

Toby remained seated, watching her check out Sanders and Jones hopefully, "They sent me back – " Up tight, fake eastern accent. *Brassy bitch.*

Both men pointed to Crouch.

Her face flushed.

"Name?" Toby asked her.

She hesitated, then came forward, taking the chair in front of Crouch's desk.

"Josie Darling. I teach at the university."

Of course you do. "Address?" Toby wrote the name and address down on his planner. "Telephone?" And what was the problem? It was kind of complicated. *Maybe as complicated as trying to run down a traffic cop? Oh yes, you don't think I remember you, but I remember everything: and I pay everything back with interest. Cross your legs, baby. Holy Hannah, what color? Let's see . . . name, address, telephone, color of panties?*

The woman had a briefcase and a purse. The briefcase was a beat-up old leather thing with a broken zipper and
150

two big loops for the handle, someone's hand-me-down. The purse was expensive but worn looking. Her better days behind her. *Here comes the letter.*

"You'll get the idea from this."

Look interested. Crouch scanned the words quickly. *hoR? Where had he seen that?*

Professionally now. *Lieutenant Crouch, thoroughly professional, college graduate . . . Captain Tobias Crouch, City of Lues, chief of police with his boner lifting his desk off the floor.* He looked up impassively, the traffic cop with a twisted ankle pulling office time. Five-eight-two-eighty these days, 280 because the scales don't go any higher. *Do you like to fuck a fat man now and then, Miss Josie?*

"This is it?"

"There have been some other things."

"I have to know about them." Crouch took notes as she explained.

Baby, that nose is crooked! Stick it where it didn't belong? I can cure lesbianism. "I see. Did you report that?" *A visitor with you at the time? And were you fucking him at the time?* "And what was your visitor's name?"

Doctor Valentine. Be my Valentine. Playing doctor, playing with Doctor Valentine.

"You were embarrassed someone had broken into your apartment?"

Sure, yeah, start at the beginning.

Crouch adjusted his seat, his pants restricting him. *Hope we don't have a fire drill; hate to have to stand up. Might put out someone's eye.* "Arrested yesterday? Spell that name for me." She spelled the name of her husband for Crouch. "Do you know which precinct?" Of course not. "Go on."

Blah, blah, blah. Shut up and show me your tits. I see. Uh-huh. Okay.

"Who?"

"Jack Hazard." The woman started chattering on.

151

Heart hammering but with a bureaucrat's mask, Crouch reached for the letter again, and now he smiled to himself.

stil tHinkING Of u, hoR

Jack Hazard. That was where he'd seen it! *They got you on that one, you dumb slew; couldn't even spell whore!*

Colt tells that story once a year, Crouch recalled pleasantly, *Colt's favorite story, when he got in his cups. Who the hell knew if it was true? Dead stripper in the canyon; she's carved up with the letters h-o-R on her belly, and Jack Hazard in the hot seat, looking like what the cat drug in. "Okay, Jack. I believe you; you're an innocent man! The watch ain't yours; both my witnesses are lying. Just tell me how to spell* whore *and I'll let you go." Lawyer screaming; and Jack as dumb as the rock he crawled out from under, "I can spell* whore, h-o-R! . . . No! . . . h-o-R-E!" *"Book this sorry sack of — Boy! you are cunt-ry-stupid!"*

Crouch looked up in surprise, "Where was this you saw Jack?"

"It's not what you think."

Nervously she uncrossed her legs. *Blue! Blue panties.* "How do you know what I'm thinking?"

"I was doing some research."

The Bust of Country is where I go for my research, too, Mrs Darling.

"Okay, I have to be honest . . ."

Jack's stepdaughter . . . real name is Fortune . . .

Patrolman Crouch looked back at the words on the paper again. *Watch Commander Tobias Crouch.* He listened absently. *Spell* whore *for me, Jack, and I'll let you go.*

Crouch took one last peek under her little skirt. *Gone but not forgot. We shan't see the likes of them blue panties again, Matthew!* "Are you prepared to bring charges against the man doing this?"

Absently, in giant letters, Crouch wrote JACK HAZARD.

"What will you do if I press charges?"

Get my fat ass on a desk job. Serious, now, Tobias. Steady, boy;

152

this is the way, brother! Ol' Colt would love nothing so much as sending Jack back to Vienna . . . Jack-home-again-in-Vienna. That's a good one, tell Colt when the time's right. He does hate that boy.

Slowly, deliberately, and with great solemnity, Patrolman Tobias Crouch explained. This letter constituted a crime. Was she aware of the law against *stalking*? *Oh, I bet you are; all you feminist babes know about that one.*

"But I don't know who's doing it. I mean I'd love to find out; you find the man who's doing it, I'll press charges."

Crouch reached for the phone and hit Colt Fellows's extension. "I have a woman here who's received a threatening letter, only she doesn't know who the harasser is."

Colt Fellows answering, "Crouch, what the fuck are you talking about? Take care of it or give it to Sanders. I'm busy."

"You'll want to see this, Colt."

Keep your tongue in your head Colt, I'm giving you Jack Hazard.

Nervous. Thinks I called him to look at her. Kuntry Kute, the way ol' Jack would spell it; Kunt, you are going to make my career.

Toby cut into Colt's diatribe, "You'll know the author, Colt. Get down here; it's important."

It better be important . . .

Huge, fat, gray, Colt Fellows waddled into Domestic about two minutes later. A man in his mid-fifties, Colt was playing out his time to retirement, king of the small time, hero to fat men everywhere. Colt's way was rough as a country road. Say anything, do anything, Colt was the sort of guy to bend the world round to his view, and if it didn't bend, he'd break it in half. The guy was a walking, farting war zone, and nobody ever crossed him and lived to smile about it. As far as Toby Crouch was concerned, there wasn't a better cop anywhere in the world.

"Chief Colt Fellows, Josie Darling . . ."

He's pissed. Looking at me. Latrine duty! Trust me, Colt; I got your fondest wish, and I'll take Watch Command in exchange.

"Colt, I want to show you a letter Mrs Darling received yesterday. She doesn't think she can prove who's harassing her, and I think it's obvious who's doing it."

A hard look. I'm done if this doesn't ring his bell.

Crouch uncovered the paper dramatically. "Does that spelling remind you of anyone?"

Frowning, Colt slipped his reading glasses on and came around to stand next to Toby. Silently he read the message:

stil tHinkING Of u, hoR

Colt breathing like a foundered horse. He doesn't see it? FUCK!

Twenty years ago! You tell the story every Christmas! Look at my note! JACK HAZARD with stars and stripes! Goddamn, man!

Standing straight again, taking his glasses off in the gesture, Colt answered, "Jack Hazard."

Colt Fellows

Colt Fellows led, as Crotch-sniff followed him into his office. Ms Josie Darling waited in his outer office with Peggy. *Crouch on his cane; anything for a little desk time. Closer to the doughnuts. Broke it racing for the doughnuts.* "So what the hell is Jack Hazard up to?" Colt asked. "What's going on, Tobias?"

"That's his stepdaughter out there. Her name was Josie Fortune when she lived here; the county sent her upstate years ago when Jack killed her mother."

Standing behind his desk, Colt shuffled a stack of reports absently. He remembered the case, but he wasn't quite following Crotch-sniff's angle. Who could? "So Jack's writing her love letters now?" he asked.

Crouch shrugged and took a seat in front of Colt's desk, a nobody suddenly at home in the big man's office. "She shows up this fall teaching at Loser State, but ever since she's been in town she's been getting threats. First day in town, she gets an illegal entry at her apartment." Crouch read

154

Fellows's frown. "Didn't report it. The guy wrote something on her bathroom mirror. 'I want to fuck you in the mouth.' Something like that. Then yesterday, she's out at the Bust of Country and someone smashes her car windows in and leaves the love letter you just looked at. Turns out Jack showed up at the bar while she was inside. Doesn't take an Einstein to put it together, Colt. She didn't see him do it, of course, but – "

"What was she doing out there? She whoring on the side for Jack and Virgil?"

"She says she went out there for *research*." Crouch had an ugly grin as he said this.

"Research? What the hell does that mean, Tobias?"

"I don't know what it means, Colt. She's a professor. Maybe she was trying to find out where a hard dick goes."

"She ready to press charges on that slimy little son-of-a-bitch?"

Crouch explained about the ex-husband, a quick review of Miss Darling's history with the man and her misperceptions since arriving in Lues. Colt nodded, taking this in like so much ammunition. " . . . She was sure it was the ex-husband, this Volari-guy," Crouch concluded.

"Flying out and drawing pictures on her bathroom mirror?"

Crotch-sniff shrugged knowingly. "What can I say? She's a professor."

"But the old boy was in Boston getting arrested yesterday?"

"Pulled a gun on a student."

"Jesus." Colt shook his head tiredly. "This girl as fucked up as she sounds, Tobias?"

"And then some."

"She think it's Jack did this?"

"I don't know what she thinks. But you got her attention with that lightning-quick ID."

Read your notes, Crotch-ity. "Pretty good, huh?" Colt smiled

155

for Crouch's benefit and considered the woman's situation coolly. She was probably afraid she was jumping to conclusions after being wrong about the ex-husband. *Scared out of her mind. Comes to us but ain't going to let us do our job. Typical.*

"We got any evidence, besides my extraordinary photographic memory for a crime that's, what? fifteen, eighteen years ago?"

"Twenty years this April, Colt."

Colt Fellows was sure Crotch-sniff would know the day and hour of Josie Fortune's murder. *Always remember your first.* Crouch showed a sliver of a smile with the memory. *Slimy bastard.*

Colt looked away from Crouch as he recalled the case. The damnedest thing he'd ever run into. It had been a miracle of police work for Colt to get anything at all out of it. But then Colt was the magic man when it came to getting confessions. *Something from nothing, the secret of life.*

"You didn't answer my question, Tobias."

"Got nothing hard on him. But you've got that stalker law," Crouch ventured.

The stalker law was no good. Don Scott would want to look at everything for a while and then think about it twice before he went to Avery for a warrant. Colt wanted something he could push *today. Strike while it's hot,* he told himself. Long years had taught Colt that if he got a man like Scott to act quickly he wouldn't turn back, no matter how bad things got. It was God's caution for the rest of us that he gave the best minds intractability. Once committed, men like Scott would do everything in their power to avoid changing course, and they would never admit they had been wrong. Never. That was a fact as certain as springtime. *Catch Jack in the act,* he muttered to himself, *or make it seem that way.* If Colt could get Jack into custody, he could clear up the rest of his problems and put the whole thing to bed.

"Tell me exactly what's been going on with our Miss Darling out there."

Crouch fumbled through it a second time, the story changing somewhat. At the end of the narrative Colt rapped his knuckles against on his desk in frustration and paced briefly. "I want a real live crime committed, preferably something under our jurisdiction. I don't want her telling the prosecutor's office next week it was maybe someone else who was writing her this love letter."

"Who else could it be?"

"Half the guys in this county can't spell *whore*, Tobias. Half the cops on this force. A damn letter ain't no crime! I need her to say Jack did something to her, swear it out and let us take him down. That way there won't be any questions about our behavior after the fact." Crouch nodded dumbly. He had no idea what *fact*, after or otherwise, Colt meant.

"I don't think she knows what Jack did to her mother after he killed her," Crouch offered.

Colt Fellows studied Crouch in undisguised wonder. They both knew the truth, and they both knew they knew it. "*I can pass a lie detector. We did them in crim. class all the time: I can say anything you want . . .*" So Toby Crotch-sniff toppled the sheriff of the county and made Colt a very happy man.

Colt smiled at the memory. Tobias Crouch *was* a wonder.

Crouch answered with his own slender smile and shrugged philosophically. "If she knows what Jack did to her mother's body, she might be more agreeable to pressing charges. You convinced her it's Jack who wrote that letter. She just needs a little push from the master."

Fondly, Colt considered: he *did* have a way of presenting things. It was a gift, really. Maybe old Crotch-sniff was onto something. Colt found himself nodding his head. *Give her the full treatment, everything but an autopsy photograph.* Colt's eyes darted thoughtfully from one unfocused point to another. *Show her the kind of man's she's dealing with . . .*

"Send her in, Tobias. I'll see what I can get out of her."

As Crouch was leaving, Colt asked him as an afterthought, "What the hell happened to your ankle?" *As if anyone cared.*

Crouch was by Fellows's office door, just getting ready to leave. "She was a wild one, Colt!"

"That-a-way, boy!" Colt laughed until the door shut, then he turned sourly toward the window again. The fall rains had set in. The weather and the thought of Jack Hazard had darkened his mood. Colt didn't like people digging around in his old garbage, and when he had heard that Jack was asking about ancient history — asking about old case files — he had had Jack warned off. That had been a mistake. A bad one. He should have just let it go. Jack wasn't smart enough to work out what had happened to him. A warning just screamed guilty. And Jack Hazard had his own ideas about justice.

Getting soft in the brain, old timer. The thing about Jack Hazard, he never rushed to judgment, but if he knew a thing, really god-damn knew . . . then he'd kill you and not a word of warning, not a threat, just show up in your face and finish it. Damn little slew!

Well, this could be put to rest right here. Just finish things and sleep better at night. *All you need is an accuser . . .*

Ancient History

Josie Darling, AKA Josie Fortune, entered. *A little bit pushed around here. Afraid we're rushing her. Don't want to turn Jack in just because some word is misspelled. Well, let me fill you in on something, Ms Josie.*

"Have a seat," Colt said. Still by the window, hardly looking at the woman more than a couple of times as he started, Colt Fellows described the body of Josie Fortune as he had seen it in the medical center the night they pulled her out of Lues Creek Canyon. He had never seen a corpse as ravaged, he said. It was nearly the truth. Owl-eyed Eddy Elms had taken an ax to his wife and four kids about ten years back. That had been worse. When the quiet ones break, it's always a mess. Colt had also seen a couple traffic accidents that threw head and feet in opposite directions, and of course anytime someone went over Hazard Falls there wasn't much left but guts and bones for about a quarter of a mile, but Josie Fortune *had* been a bad one. A sadistic killing, he told Josie's daughter. "Your mother," he said, "was beaten, bound, raped, strangled, and finally – after she had died – eviscerated: cut open!" Crouch had been right; she had had no idea about any of it. "Your mother suffered," Colt told her. "But even that wasn't enough for Jack. He had to mutilate her corpse."

"He said he didn't do it." Her voice was weak, skeptical.

"He did it. He confessed to me, personally. Now I'm going to tell you something else. This is something that we didn't let out to the papers, but it's in the records and it's the truth. Before she was even dead," he announced, walking toward her and leaning back on his desk directly before her chair, "Jack cut something into her flesh, right across the belly: the letters *h-o-r*." Josie Darling blinked in confusion. "He was trying to spell *whore*, Ms Darling."

"I didn't know any of this." A terrible whisper.

"That piece of paper, where he calls you the same thing?" She nodded, coming around. "To me that's proof enough he means to treat you to the same thing he gave your mother, for whatever twisted reason."

"I don't even know the man!"

Colt was getting to her. She believed him. He could feel that much in her sudden resentment and that crazed tone of denial. "I ran that case. Back then I was chief of homicide. Jack and your mother had been divorced, I don't know, six, eight months, and he up and pulls her off the streets – "

Josie Darling looked at him. She was scared. Pale, shivering, certain. "They were divorced?" she asked.

Fellows smiled grimly. "You didn't know that?"

"No, sir."

"We worked through the night once we got your mother's body out of the canyon, and the next morning I got some people out to find out what background we could get. In the process, I found out Jack had pulled you out of your school and taken you up to his trailer. You weren't living with him at the time, but he grabbed you up – and no legal right to do it! It didn't take an Einstein to see what he was doing, so I moved quick. I had to. Do you remember any of that?"

"I remember being at Jack's trailer and the state police . . ."

Fellows nodded. "Just as well to forget some things," he told her with pointed innuendo. "I tried to get Sheriff Bitts to serve the warrant so we could save you, but ol' Two-Bit was drunk in the middle of the morning and whoring it on up, as usual. We didn't have the jurisdiction to make an arrest in the county, so I had to call in the state police. I told them Jack had a little girl held hostage. Let me tell you something, Ms Darling – "

"Josie, please."

"Josie. You get a lot of disappointments in this business, but every once in a while you win one. I won one that day. And I'm looking at what I won." Josie saw what he meant; she was softening up fast. "I've no doubt Jack meant to kill you, after a time, same as he did your mother. It's what he took you to his trailer for, probably why you can't remember it. When I got hold of him, he was crazy; he was absolutely out of his mind."

"When I met him yesterday, he took my arm and was leading me outside. It scared me. His eyes scared me, too. I saw his temper."

Fellows nodded sagely. "Did he say where he was taking you?"

"For a drink or something."

Colt's face creased into an ironic smile. "You were at a bar and he was taking you to another bar for a drink?"

"Yes, sir."

"You don't want to get alone with Jack. He's a dangerous man. All the tests they gave him over the years, he's a perfect psychopath, absolutely fearless and brutal. He doesn't understand things the way normal people like you and me do. He kills without even worrying about getting caught."

"His brother said he was innocent, something about the police finding a wristwatch that had his name on it, but it didn't belong to him."

"Virgil?" Josie nodded. "Virgil tell you about the eye-witnesses that picked Jack out of a line-up?" She shook her head. *That got her attention,* Colt told himself. "The kids that found the body: one of them saw Jack out there in the woods. Made a positive ID in a line-up. Then I got another, independent confirmation from a law enforcement individual."

"Do you remember the names of the witnesses? I'd like to talk to anyone who was involved."

Fellows considered for a moment, then straightened up and went behind his desk. He punched the numbers at Crouch's desk. He waited fifteen seconds, twenty. *Crotch-sniff raiding the doughnuts.* While he waited, Colt told Josie, "Officer Crouch was our other witness. He was working for campus security back then; he was the one who went into the canyon and found the body after the kids called us. He saw Jack staring down at him from the rim of the canyon." Crouch's voice came over the line and Fellows told him, "Get that case file on Josie Fortune. I want the name of the girl that eyewitnessed Jack."

He hung up and studied Josie Darling. *Scared, confused. But not ready to press charges.* "You want to talk to someone who knows, you ask Officer Crouch what he saw when he found your mother. He was the first lawman on the scene."

"I will."

"You know about the other people Jack's killed?"

Josie Darling shook her head. "I didn't know — "

"When Jack was ten years old, he shot his uncle with a hunting rifle, right in his uncle's kitchen."

The woman swore quietly.

Nodding, Colt told her, "After Jack's father passed away, Jack's mother moved in with her sister and of course the sister's husband. Jack and his three brothers came along. This fellow had his own family and he took another. Jack repaid him for his kindness one morning, maybe four or five months after they moved in. Not a word said, just walked into the man's kitchen while he was eating his breakfast, leveled that gun on him and fired. It was an old bolt action .22, see, so Jack, he had to take the gun off his shoulder after the first shot and cock that rifle again, bring it back to his shoulder and fire a second time. Put the first two in his face. The man was crawling across the floor and bawling when Jack put the third shot in his brain, point blank through the back of his skull."

"My God."

Colt shook his head. "I was a kid then myself. Everyone heard about it. Lot of older people know that story. That was big news back forty-some years ago. Kids didn't do that kind of thing every day the way they do now." Colt smiled grimly. "Virgil was there. Virgil saw it. Virgil forget to tell you about that?" Josie looked down at her folded hands. *Getting the message, lady?* "Jack wasn't six months out of the juvenile center, eighteen years old and a free man, because our legal system coddles its juveniles, and what's he do but shoot himself a . . . a black man up in Pilatesburg. I had nothing to do with that case. I was a rookie cop in Peoria at the time, but I heard plenty about it later," Colt smiled. "People talked about it for years. Four slugs down the poor bastard's throat. Stuck the gun in his mouth, Josie, and popped off four thirty-eights, all the while screaming something about that man being a *nigger*. Virgil didn't tell you about that, either?" Colt let this settle. This girl was turning to ice. "Jack did a short stretch for that: five, six years. He got out, and he married your mother, and, hell, he seemed to straighten up for a while. A good woman will do that to a man, even a man like Jack. But it always come back, what a man is and what he's got in his heart."

"Did you know my mother?"

Colt had always denied knowing Josie Fortune, but the truth was another matter. He shook his head forlornly. "In my business we just get to know the creeps like Jack. First I ever laid eyes on your mother, Jack had done killed her. All I know of your mother is she and Jack bought a bar, and they ran it together."

"The Hurry On Up."

"Did good business, I guess. I never drank there. I kept my distance from Jack; I mean when I go out for drinks, I don't feel comfortable with a *psychopath* serving the liquor; that kind of mind don't ever reform, he just holds it in until something breaks. Some college girls started coming in, you know, and Jack was a handsome man. Meaner than a snake and about half as smart, but he was a ladies' man, I'll give him that. Had one of those smiles, it just got to women. It wasn't long before Jack got mixed up with some of them and your mother divorced him. After that, Jack went downhill fast. Him and his brother turned the bar into a whorehouse and Jack got his girlfriends dancing for them, same show as they got up in Codswallop now; they make half their money in the bar and half in the parking lot with 'trade.' All the while your mother was trying to get a fresh start with a new life and Jack not able to let it go."

"Was she in school? Virgil said she was in college."

"I don't remember what she was doing. I just know I was watching Jack and thinking something was wrong. I knew something bad was coming. He was coming apart, getting more violent every day. Just a lawman's instincts, but I was helpless to do anything."

"I know he was arrested for assaulting some football players a couple of months before the murder. I read about it."

163

Colt Fellows nodded, moving for the decision. "Officer Crouch tells me you haven't actually seen Jack do anything, but he had the opportunity yesterday. Is that true?"

"He could have done it."

"I wouldn't mess around with this, Josie. He made a grab for you yesterday. He's been harassing you, how long?"

"Since I got here in August. I mean someone has, and it wasn't my ex-husband."

"You had an illegal entry?"

"First day of work. I was out all day. I must have left my balcony door unlocked. He wrote on my mirror, 'Welcome home, Josie'. Everything misspelled – like that note yesterday."

"Jack never had any education. I mean to say he's illiterate or next to it. Anyone will tell you that."

"He seemed kind of happy to see me, I think." The woman almost whined. She was afraid to do it, afraid not to.

"Sure he was, same as a spider when he sees a fly coming into his web. We need to get him in custody, Josie. He never should have been let out of prison for what he did to your mother, but that's water over the dam. The only way to fix it is to look at what he's doing to you right now."

"I read it was some kind of a plea bargain. Doesn't that mean there wasn't enough evidence to go to trial?"

"Truth is, our sheriff back then screwed up some of the evidence at the crime scene. We would have had to throw out everything concerning the condition of the body. I don't know what you know about the law, Josie, but without a body, it's real hard to convict someone of murder."

"I don't understand."

"This old sheriff we had, Pat Bitts, he was an old-style politician. He knew how to get himself re-elected; he just didn't know law enforcement. Well, anyway, he got crosswise with the medical examiner over the time of death, and that was just the half of it. Before it was over, I could see we were going to lose the case if it ever went to trial. We had our killer, Josie. We had the man who murdered your mother and mutilated her corpse, and it looked like we might lose him on a couple of technicalities, so we did what we could: we traded a confession for a reduced sentence. Jack and his lawyer was real eager back then to take my offer. Don't you doubt it." Colt let this settle, then added: "I'll tell you one thing more: I made sure the sheriff's goofs made the paper, and we got ourselves a new man in the sheriff's office next election. He's been there, ever since."

"If I press charges against Jack for this thing that happened yesterday, he'll just get out again."

"Don't be so sure about that. When Judge Avery sees Jack's history and finds out about these threats, he'll set a bail Jack can't make. And I'll see to it personally the judge knows everything Jack's been doing."

"Last fall, I did something like this to my husband – we were getting divorced at the time. He got a suspended sentence and I ended up in the hospital. He almost killed me."

"Where was this?"

"In Boston."

"Officer Crouch said you just found out about your husband being arrested again?"

"He pulled a gun on his dean; it was over some kind of class scheduling."

"How long were you two married?"

"Twenty months, but things turned bad after the separation. I was attacked twice. Both times I ended up in the hospital, so I thought all of this was just more of the same. I mean a rational person wouldn't fly out here and break into my apartment and write something on my mirror, but Dan's not rational. So I thought – "

"You thought it wasn't possible to know two lunatics?"

The woman smiled, ducking her head. "I seem to be living out some kind of childhood trauma. It's all I can figure. The lunatics aren't finding me; I'm finding them."

"Well, I can't help you with your ex unless he comes to

town, but Jack Hazard I can do something about if you let me."

Pretty girl, but a real weak sister.

"I just don't know how Jack could find out I was coming to Lues. It was like he knew I was coming, and that doesn't make sense."

"He's got a lot of family, Josie. If any of them found out about your coming, he'd know about it."

"I just don't know . . ."

"Why didn't you come to us sooner? Your first problem was a month ago."

Josie Darling looked at the carpet. "I thought I could handle it. I wanted to handle it." Her gaze lifted as she finished. *Wants to be a tough girl! Okay, tough girl, let's make the move.*

"This ain't Boston, Josie. You make a charge against Jack Hazard, we all stand behind you. When Judge Avery, that's who we'll get on this, when he hears what's going on, Jack won't see the light of day for two or three years. This is very serious stuff."

"That's the thing. He isn't really threatening me, not directly. What can I really charge him with? Writing a letter? Calling me a name? The word's not even in the dictionary." She laughed nervously, "Maybe we ought to arrest him for bad spelling?"

"He ruined your car."

"Nobody saw it. I can't swear it was him."

"But you know it was?"

She nodded. "I guess. It pretty much had to be."

"He touch you yesterday? You said he grabbed you."

She nodded: "He was taking me outside. I don't think he meant any harm."

"Anybody see him do it?"

"A lot of people saw it. We were in Virgil's bar. There must have been eighty people who saw it. They thought I was going to audition. To work there." Looking at Colt, shrugging, "It was totally confused, okay? Everyone was looking at me, waiting for me to dance, and Jack took me by the arm and got me out of it."

"I want you to go back to Officer Crouch's desk and sign a complaint for assault. When you get with Prosecutor Scott later you can add the other things formally, if he thinks it will help the case. He might want to go the whole nine yards: unlawful entry, criminal mischief, sexual harassment, all of it. But right now let's concentrate on what we can prove. A roomful of witnesses ought to seal this thing up. I can get an arrest warrant on that. Soon as you swear it out, I'll have the sheriff bring Jack in to us for questioning about these other issues and see if I can't get a confession out of him." Colt fought off a happy thought . . . *and when I take him back to Yeager* . . .

"He's meeting me at two o'clock this afternoon, at the McDonald's here in town."

"Then I'll arrest him myself and call you afterwards to let you know he's off the street."

"I don't know . . ."

"You look something like your mother, you know."

A long pause. *That was the right button. Josie with that fucking shotgun she kept under the bar. Matching bookends with her slew-brained husband.*

"If I thought I could be safe . . ."

Quickly: "Do you feel safe now?"

She shook her head. Colt said nothing more. He simply stared into the woman's eyes. *Weak. Not at all like her mother.*

"Do you want me there, at the McDonald's?"

Colt shook his head. "Definitely not."

She closed her eyes. *Let her fret it out.*

The phone rang. *Crouch.* "Got it." Fellows looked up at Josie as he set the receiver back. "That eyewitness was Melody Mason, age nineteen at the time, a sophomore at Lues State, parents Brian and Theresa Mason, Oak Park, that's the north end of the state."

167

"I know where it is. It's where Ernest Hemingway was born. It's pretty upscale."

Ernest Hemingway. Give it a rest, baby. I ain't one of your students. Colt shrugged pleasantly, "Could be Melody-anybody by now, but that's as good as I can do."

Josie nodded. "And Officer Crouch? You said he was a witness too?"

Fellows nodded. *Officer Cluster-fuck: I cannot tell the truth.*

"What about this sheriff who screwed things up? Bitts? Is he still around?"

"Pat Bitts. He's old as God now, Josie. Next thing to an Alzheimer's case. He was a drunk back then and what I hear he ain't let up even a little."

Josie shuffled in her briefcase for a pencil and a slip of paper and wrote out the information. Then she seemed to collect herself and come to a decision. "I'm leaving after this semester. In December. I just want Jack out of circulation until then; I don't care after that. Can you get me that much? Can you *promise* it?"

Colt Fellows was nothing if not a man of his word, and when he gave a promise, he always meant to keep it. It was, in his cosmos, the organizing principle of civilization. "You have my guarantee on that, Josie. You give me cause to arrest him, and Jack Hazard won't ever bother you again."

Memories of a Lawman

When Josie Darling shut the door to Colt's office, he turned again to study the gray sky. Something in the way Miss Darling moved reminded Colt of her mother. He hadn't seen it when she had come into his office, but it was there as she left, that same cocky walk-away.

It hadn't been long after Jack got out of Vienna that he'd met himself the prettiest girl anyone ever saw in Lues County, and married her just to get her panties off. They bought their own bar as a wedding present to themselves and paid

168

cash. Since Josie Fortune had had no money and Jack Hazard shouldn't have had much, Colt had kicked around the idea that the bar was bought with money from some upstate banks, without the usual loan papers signed. When one of his snitches, Alfred Moore, confirmed the notion, Colt decided it was best to simply watch and see how Jack's and Josie's business went. Business was plenty good, so one evening Colt went out to try to get some interest on the bank loan, as it were. He laid it out pretty plain with the names of banks, the dates, and the amounts that were stolen. Alfred was a damn good snitch, yes sir. They were all old jobs dating back to Jack's association with Hazy Mundy, but Colt had been certain he could get some kind of conviction if he let out what he knew. When he sat down with them, it was just Jack and Josie and Colt, about three in the morning, each of them with a shot glass, a half-full bottle of JD between them. There was an ashtray on the table and a pack of Lucky Strikes next to it. The place had only a couple of lights left on. Colt had caught the two of them cleaning up after closing, and after some little bit of small talk, Colt made his speech. It was one of his best; it was plain and simple and, in honor of Jack's reputation, marked with a respectfully conservative request for payment. Jack didn't say one way or the other if any of Colt's suspicions was true. Colt told him he would take two hundred dollars on the first of each month or he would turn what he had over to the state police. If Jack were innocent, he had nothing to fear; if maybe he knew something about those jobs, maybe he ought to pay Colt a "security consultant fee." Jack had Colt's word as a gentleman it would always stay the same price and would always stay just between the three of them, Jack, Josie, and Colt.

When he had finished, the three of them were silent. Pretty soon Josie Fortune reached for Jack's cigarettes and said something about not taking his last one. She swung herself up and went over behind the bar to get change for the machine. Not a good idea to study a jealous man's wife as she did a walk-away, Colt didn't really pay attention to her. Besides, he was on a tightrope with Jack Hazard, for God's sake. Jack was staring off somewhere between the middle of that table and murder. The next thing Colt knew, Josie Fortune had come around the end of the bar, a sawed-off double-barrelled twelve-gauge shotgun in her hand. She hitched the butt of it against her thigh, laid both hammers back, and leveled its hollow pipes at Colt's face, about three feet distant.

Josie Fortune was a beautiful woman. She was built with more curves and softness than her kid, and she was prettier too. Her face was a perfect oval, the features regular and delicate, her expression placid and thoughtful. The most striking thing about the woman was her hair. Josie Fortune's hair was long, heavy, and natural. As pretty as glistening bronze, as exciting as gold. Men groaned when she walked by, but she could make them laugh, too. She could be one of the boys with the ease that some rare women have. None of that had quite mattered at the moment, nor did anything ever again quite seem the same about her, from Colt's point of view. With her little sawed-off double-barrelled twelve-gauge pointed into Colt's eyes, Josie Fortune had looked to him like a damn Hazard, nothing more. And Hazards don't blink when there's killing to be done.

"I listened to what you had to say," Josie Fortune told him, "and I didn't interrupt you, so I expect you'll do me the same courtesy."

Colt had allowed as how that was only fair. He flicked his glance to Jack, who was just sitting there, still staring at the table, smoking a Lucky now, like nothing at all was unusual. Jack didn't give a fuck about anything, and was probably trying to remember where he kept the shovel. Since it was closing time, the mop and bucket were already set out.

"There's no one going to arrest me for those bank robberies," Josie Fortune had explained. "I didn't live here in

170

those days, and I'd never heard of Jack or Hazy Mundy or any of them back then, so I want you to know if anyone comes around even asking Jack *questions* about those days, I'll vanish from the face of this earth and when I come back, and I will, mister, I'll be carrying this shotgun and it will be the last thing you see before you turn into a piss-storm of blood. Are we clear on that?"

There were no tears shed when that old whore died.

The Cabbie

As Josie stepped out of the Lues Civic Center and into a steady drizzle of rain, her thoughts were all behind her. The charge of assault settled, she had asked Officer Crouch about his finding her mother in the canyon. What he told her was awful, worse than Colt Fellows's description. Jack had raped her repeatedly, he said. And no one was sure when he had eviscerated her, whether that was after she had died or while she was still conscious and able to watch the knife cut her. It was painfully clear to Josie that Officer Crouch was as violent as the criminals he allegedly pursued. He did everything but lick his lips when he described the effects of the brutality he had seen. He told Josie he had found the body in a sink hole directly in front of the falls, nearly ripped apart. They were right. Jack was a monster. *Pick him up and put an end to it*, she thought.

Josie's cab headed toward Presbyterian Hill. It was 9:43. Josie had a ten o'clock class. Her eight o'clock she had cancelled. She hated to charge Jack, but she was certain now that it was the right thing to do. Jack was too dangerous to leave unchecked. She had disliked both of the policemen. Nurtured for years on the lowest common denominator of humanity, they were both slobs who saw themselves as the unappreciated *good guys*. They saw everything in terms of black and white, good and bad, as if there were some line which divided actions into neat categories.

Her own actions, for instance. Was her lie to the doorman at the Bust of Country something she ought to be ashamed of? Was that lie bad? What about her "truth" that Jack Hazard had taken her arm and tried to rush her out of the bar? They were all agreeing now to call that assault. It was going to be a lawyer's field day if this stupid thing ever got to court, which it wouldn't. Words, only words. Was it wrong of her? It was the truth: did that make the accusation somehow less loathsome? Not really, but it remained, as Captain Fellows had pointed out, the only thing Josie could prove. Right now those words were her defense against further attacks. If she didn't use them, Jack would be free to come after her as he had been coming after her from the beginning. As he had come after her mother.

The cab turned left into campus and followed Willow Avenue past the administration complex, past the hill where her apartment sat, and finally into the thick grove of trees at the bottom of the hill. Jack had lied to her. Virgil had anyway. He had lied about a lot of things, lies of omission. Colt Fellows had set Josie straight on the facts. And it made sense, the way the state troopers had come for Jack. Jack had killed her mother and had taken Josie back to his trailer. *Had* he hurt her? Maybe that was the reason for her memory loss. Fellows had insinuated that pretty clearly. *Just as well to forget some things.* Josie shivered at the memory of his words. He knew what had happened. It was probably all in the police report, if she had the courage to demand it from them.

Josie saw the buildings of Liberal Arts through the trees now. A moment later, they were in the open, coming to the entrance. "This is it," Josie told the driver. He pulled into the parking lot and drove toward the central plaza before the buildings.

When he stopped, he announced in a perfunctory manner, "Six dollars."

172

The meter showed that she owed four dollars, fifty cents. "The meter says four-fifty."

"I had to come get you." The driver was a big man, with greasy, yellowed flesh, and greasy long hair and a pathetically long, thin greasy beard. He was boorish and he stank, and now he was robbing her of a few pennies, just because she was a woman and he knew he could get away with it.

Josie shook her head with resignation. She hated Lues. She hated the way men treated her here, the hick arrogance of them. Slews. Even Val called them that. *Well, it's what they are. Slews. Jack and Virgil, Colt Fellows, that Toby Crouch-creep, this . . . fat-ass! All of them!*

Reaching into the outside pocket of her briefcase, where she kept her cash, driver's license, and one of her credit cards, Josie found three twenties, and brought one of them out.

"Have you got something smaller?" the cabbie asked.

"No."

She waited the man out. Rolling his body over like some kind of over-wrought sea lion, he pulled his money from his pocket with a terrible huff. Now turning painfully about in the seat, he reach back and gave her a five, five ones, then eight quarters, counted out with dim-witted care. He had smaller coins in his hand and another five dollar bill flapping loosely between his fingers, but he wasn't letting go of any more money.

"That's eight dollars for the ride," Josie complained. "You said it was six."

"I don't got no change." He rolled back, so that his back was turned to her now, dismissing the argument, and with it his passenger.

"You don't have *any* change."

He didn't answer at first. His eyes burned into his rearview mirror. Josie met the gaze. She was sick to death of this place!

"That's what I said," he told her finally.

"Here!" Josie snarled, handing the man his quarters back.

"I don't want your small change." Turning partially to get the quarters, the cabbie still held the five-dollar bill in his fingers. Josie hadn't intended to grab the bill; she had meant only to show the man up for what he was, a piece of scum, scrounging up coins. But the five-dollar bill was there, flapping loosely in his fingers as she dumped the quarters into his cupped hands, and she grabbed it out of spite.

"Hey bitch," the man shouted, "you owe me a dollar!"

"You made me wait," she snapped. Josie pushed the door open and got out of the back of the car on the driver side.

He rolled his window down halfway, shouting as he did, "Hey fuck you, I want my dollar!"

Josie reached in with the hand that still held the five-dollar bill and took the man's scraggly beard and pulled it until his head came up against the window and doorpost. He screeched and swore in surprise and tried futilely to get hold of Josie's wrist. "Do you want to apologize for that?" Josie asked him coolly.

"Fuck you!" he hissed.

Keeping her fingers in his beard, Josie eased off the pressure so that his head pulled back slightly; then she jerked his big head back toward her, listening to the hard crack of it against glass and metal. Immediately she let him go, some of his beard still in her fingers, and started to walk away, wiping her hand clean and slipping her five-dollar bill into the side pocket of her briefcase. When she heard him getting out of the cab, Josie stopped and turned toward him. They were standing in the rain facing each other, both furious, both insanely intent upon taking this utter absurdity to some kind of showdown. *Is this how people crack up?* she wondered. Her brain buzzed with odd, old voices, primeval shouts of pain. She didn't know yet that she meant to kill this man. She thought, consciously, only that she was stepping over some line of reasonable behavior, not good and bad, but sane and insane. Something was risen up in her, and she liked the feeling of it even as it terrified her.

The cabbie was huge and fat, a blubbering, threatening slew. He was mad and maybe a little uncertain. This was campus, foreign turf for him. Contemplating him, Josie waited with an emotion that until then she had reserved solely for Dan Scholari.

"Come on!" she said.

That put him off somehow. "You owe me a dollar, bitch." He wasn't coming toward her. His voice plaintive suddenly, he seemed almost to back off.

A boy walking across the plaza peeled off from his group and came next to Josie. The kid was one of her students, Josie realized. *Great!* she thought, *a witness*. Her next image was of her own breakdown and this boy describing it to her dean; her imagination occupied at the moment, the highest authority she could imagine was her dean, but of course it would go beyond his small door. This wasn't going to be about small-change tears. It was part of the whole fabric of her life, the collapsing defenses that came when there was just too much to bear.

Too much, she thought miserably. It was all too much. This especially, a quarrel over the matter of a single dollar. Josie told herself this was how it went. Something of no conse-quence tips the scales. She realized suddenly that she meant to shoot the man, that she had meant it from the moment he had started with the name-calling. She wanted him to come at her, because she was going to pull her revolver and unload into his face, the way Jack Hazard had with the men he had killed. What terrified her was the fact that she didn't just turn and run away; she didn't care about survival here; she wanted to kill him. She begged him to come toward her with the insults of her gaze, and some instinct in the cabbie kept him at bay. It was as if he knew this wasn't a bluff, that she meant to destroy him. The boy next to Josie was going to be a part of this, she decided. He didn't understand any of it. He imagined himself her savior and hero, some kind of undernourished white knight, but he was here to be a witness, and he would see it in his dreams for the rest of his life and never understand that Josie had had a choice, that, in the beginning, they had all had a choice and chose badly.

The boy wasn't that much taller than Josie and he was a good deal thinner. He was meek, polite, and well groomed, doubtless his mother's pride. If he had ever had a fight, it was in elementary school, and he had probably lost it. Josie was his composition teacher, but she couldn't remember his name. She knew where he sat and to which class he belonged. She couldn't remember the papers he had written, but she knew the kinds of mistakes he made. One thing was certain: this was the worst mistake he had ever made. "Are you okay, Miss Darling?" he asked. These were the first words he had spoken. The innocence of the voice surprised Josie. What had he ever seen of the violence Josie knew?

Josie saw the whole thing as it was going to happen. The cabbie would hit him and push him out of the way, and then when he came at her, the way she wanted him to come, the cabbie would see the gun and stop, but Josie would fire before anyone realized that he had stopped. It would be self-defense if she fired quickly enough.

Did she really want this? Was she ready to lose everything over this minute or two of anger? A voice deep inside, a vicious whisper told her, Yes!

The cabbie took a step toward them now, pointing his big finger, "Butt out of it, sonny!" It was a high, tight voice. He was more scared than Josie.

The boy answered his step, but he had nothing to say.

Josie held her briefcase in her left hand. Her purse was slung over her left shoulder and hung to about the level of her left wrist. She would drop the briefcase on the next step the cabbie took, then lift her hand to her purse and snap the clasp open as her right hand crossed fluidly and reached in for the nickel, a well-practiced habit, unhurried, unruffled, deadly. She felt a moment of nervousness, but it wasn't the fear of this moment, it was the fear of what would happen afterwards, the veritable certainty that she would end her own life with this action, though it would be years coming to her what these few seconds had bought her. "It's okay," Josie told the boy. "I'll handle this. Just go. Get out of the way."

"If you want to help," the cabbie shouted, "why don't you give me my damn dollar! The bitch ripped me off!" Soaked from the rain, dancing from foot to foot, fighting for his dollar, the cabbie looked like a ridiculous oaf. Maybe, Josie decided, they all looked ridiculous. And oafish.

The boy still didn't answer him. The rain poured over all three of them so that they all scrunched their faces up, miserable and angry. The boy was quivering, Josie realized, but he wasn't backing down. None of them were. The cabbie was going to be on the concrete, his face shot off, his blood steaming, the rain pouring over him, while the living waited for the inevitable sirens, while this boy described what he had heard of the quarrel, while Josie let the gun be taken from her hands and was taken . . .

Behind Josie there was a voice, deep, faintly southern, blessedly familiar.

It was Henry Valentine. Val walked past Josie and the boy calmly and went directly to the man, his tall, lean figure standing so close that he almost touched the cabbie and blocked Josie's view. Val said something, and the cabbie turned and got back into his cab. A moment later, he was driving off, his middle finger giving them all the slew-salute. Val came up to Josie and the boy. He looked at the boy and extended his hand. "Henry Valentine. My friends call me Val."

The boy took his hand, "I know. I'm Nelson Rush, Dr Valentine."

"Val. And listen, Nelson, you need help with anything, anything at all, you find me. I like what you did. There were a hundred kids out here and no one else stood up to that

177

filthy slew." Val looked at the kids passing hurriedly through the rain, a surprising expression of contempt for all of them.

Josie looked at them too. She had hardly been conscious of so many witnesses. She had sensed movement around her, but she hadn't imagined the numbers which in fact had scurried past them as her confrontation had unraveled into a potential tragedy.

"What did you say to that guy?" Nelson asked Val. Val had taken over as the hero in all this, and that irked Josie to an unreasonable degree.

Val's wrinkled face hinted at a smile. Water splashed over his bald head and hung from the craggy edges of his face. "Nelson, all of life is about knowing the right thing to say at the right time."

"And you're not telling me what it was?" Nelson was utterly in awe of Dr Henry Valentine, having forgotten, it seemed, that it was Josie who had actually stood up to "the filthy slew."

Val shook his head, a magician with his trade secrets. "I'll tell you this much: it was a single word." He held a lone finger up dramatically.

Touching his arm and meaning to send him on his way, Josie told the boy, "Thanks, Nelson. I'll see you in class." The boy turned to leave, dissolving from Josie's consciousness. She looked at Val with neither awe nor gratitude. They were both soaked in the cold drizzle. Their eyes met in a brief testing of fortitude, then Josie looked away. She saw Nelson slipping into a crowd of students. *A sweet kid and no idea what he almost stepped into. Neither did Val.*

"So what was the magic word, Val?"

"I said, 'Here!' and gave him the dollar."

Josie flushed, "He was stiffing me, Val. I wish you hadn't done that!"

Val grinned. "Would you risk your life for a dollar, Josie?"

There was in this the proper dosage of chastisement, but
178

Josie resisted all temptation to explain: "You're damn right I would!"

These were magic words for Val, and he smiled with nearly as much respect as amusement. "A woman after my own heart. What do you say we get out of this rain?" Josie looked up at the sky angrily. She was totally soaked and still ready for a fight — with God himself if no one else showed up for the honors. She felt like a savage denied her birthright; she still had a knot in her stomach and a gun full of bullets.

Together they walked past Varner toward Brand Hall in an uncomfortable silence. There were hundreds of kids moving in the direction of the buildings, but Josie felt that she and Val were by themselves. "You know, I could have handled that," Josie said finally.

Val glanced at her with an inscrutable expression of amusement, respect, and solemnity. Finally, deadpan, he answered her, "Josie, I only meant to save the poor cabbie."

Words

If she didn't hurry, Josie was about to miss her ten o'clock. Her meeting with Toby Crouch and Colt Fellows had lasted longer than she had anticipated; then there had been the fingerprinting and finally a twenty-minute wait for the taxi, not to mention the brief interlude which followed the end of the ride. By the time she got to her office, she had only a minute to get upstairs to her classroom. She picked up a thick folder with 10:00 T-R written on its cover and headed back into the halls of Brand. She had to pass the main office, so stepped in quickly to check the mail. There were several memos and the department newsletter, with a picture of Henry Valentine prominently displayed on the front page. Val was receiving a plaque from the university president. She read the caption: TEACHER OF THE YEAR AWARD. Josie slipped it to the back of the stack, to be examined later, and whispered as she did, "Way to go, Val." Before she had come to the end of the stack, Josie saw a small red envelope with a mailing label attached. It looked like a greeting card company's envelope, but the label was university-issue. JOSIE FORTUNE was typed on it, nothing else. She looked about. The student helper at the secretary's desk was reading Plato's *Republic*. "Did you see anyone drop this off, Marilyn?"

The girl looked up, blinking. "What?"

"Did anyone unusual come in this morning and put this in my box?"

"What do you mean unusual?"

"An older man, in his fifties, kind of short and skinny?" *A filthy little slew named Jack Hazard.*

The girl shook her head, "I don't think so."

Josie opened the envelope. A card was inside. It was a sympathy card, tall silver letters in a fancy script. Inside, printed professionally in the same muted silver tones were the words:

Thinking of you in your time of trouble.

There was no signature, no mark of any kind. Josie swore silently, and turned to go.

. . . *time of trouble. His time of trouble!*

Josie was six minutes late for her class. She was feeling the prickles of her damp dress against her skin. She was wet and miserable. She hadn't had time, or hadn't taken the time, to look in the mirror and only belatedly thought how she must appear as she entered the classroom. The kids had the faces they always wore. *Can't be too bad*, she assured herself. Nelson – whatever his last name was – sat placidly in the front watching Josie with that private look kids get when they know something personal about their teacher. She met his gaze briefly; only now did she realize the courage he had had to stand next to her. She gave him a flickering smile, and he understood. She set her briefcase and purse on the table where the lectern sat, then reached in to get her class folder, intending to call roll. When she opened the folder,

180

Josie saw another message. Across her class roster in large red letters, she found these words printed with a crayon:

sooon, JOsIe, promiss

Josie read the message twice. She felt her strength going; she tried to breathe and nothing happened. She swayed and almost collapsed, but then something happened. It was a saving rage, and knowing he was *done*! Today, two o'clock, and then it was over. She shut the folder quickly and looked up at her class. A gentle, contented movement somewhere at the edges of her vision. They were not part of this. They were waiting for class to start. "Forget the roll," she announced with a strained effort at humor. She took a long deep breath, and stepped around the table feeling drunk or tired, thinking, *knowing*, it was behind her. "I think everyone's here," she said softly. "Speak up if you're absent." She heard a couple of giggles. Stepping away from her lectern and Jack Hazard's latest *composition*, Josie struggled to talk about revision. "The *second* look," she announced, "is often the *first* time we see a thing!" Straight from Annie that was, as all her best ideas were. She went on, she preached the dogma with passion; it was old-time Boston religion, but every once in a while Josie's eyes would fall to the folder and she would think about the message inside.

She prayed to God Colt Fellows could stop the man.

Hazards

Josie looked up from a stack of papers she was grading and checked her watch. She felt like Judas, but she knew it had to be done. At 2:15 she looked again, and she realized that it must be over. She set aside her grading and contented herself now with copying out a new class roster for her ten o'clock class, along with their grades and absences, all the while bravely staring into Jack's "promiss." Finished with that, Josie dropped the old class roster into her briefcase, out of sight, and turned back to her grading. A set of essays on the literature of the Puritans. The essays were miserable, of course. The literature was miserable: it was all the cod-liver approach to education: if it stinks it must be good for you. She laid on the failures remorselessly, her own version of an angry God suspending sinners over hell's fire and brimstone.

The phone rang at 3:30, startling her. She looked at the receiver. *It's over*, she told herself, taking the thing in her hand. "Josie, here."

"This is Colt Fellows. We got him. I've talked with Judge Avery about it and Don Scott, our county prosecutor. They're setting bail at a quarter of a mil, if and when Jack and his lawyer can get a court date to ask for it. Jack has to come up with 10 percent of that to get bond, and that's too much money, even if Virgil mortgages their tavern. Jack'll sit it out till the court arranges a hearing, which I promise will be after December. Is that good enough?"

"He's in jail now?"

Colt laughed, "In jail and screaming like a ex-con for his lawyer. They're all the same, Josie."

"Ex-cons?"

"Hazards."

He pronounced the word with utter contempt, the way Val pronounced the phrase "filthy slew." The room seemed to circle about her as Josie recalled Virgil's pathetic complaint of persecution. She shut her eyes to get back her balance. She managed to thank Fellows before she hung up, but she lost the last things he said. For a minute, she thought she might pass out, but several, slow deep breaths helped. She opened her briefcase to look again at Jack's message. She had forgotten to tell Colt about it. She looked at the phone, thinking she should call him, then let it go. She dropped the message in her briefcase again, then shuffled through the papers for the red envelope with its bogus sympathy card. It was still in the stack of mail she had carried away from the main office. Picking it out as someone might retrieve a piece of trash from a wet pile of refuse, Josie placed it neatly against the ruined class roster. She would need to drop them off with the police sometime. Obviously, there was no rush. That was Fellows's point; there wasn't going to be a court date until Josie was gone, which meant no one expected anything to come of the assault charge or any other complaints she might make. They meant only to put Jack away until she was gone, no hearing and no bail. It was the way Colt Fellows could guarantee her safety. It was hardly the way the law was intended to work, but at least there was justice in it, if there was justice in survival. A kind of twisted justice, at any rate.

Staunchly and filled with self-contempt, Josie whispered to the empty room, "Whatever it takes, kiddo." That was the Annie Wilde approach to things. And every morning that small, frail sixty-year-old woman dragged herself from her bed to her chair, from her chair to her bathroom, from her bathroom to her closet, from the closet to the kitchen, then into the streets and finally to campus where the *battle royal* took place – every girl for herself and damn the deans! – for a grinding fourteen-hour day seven days a week: Annie's own daily Boston marathon. Ninety-two pounds of grit, that one. In Annie's world nothing came easy. *Whatever it takes. And never a word of complaint.* That thought alone kept Josie sane.

Clarissa Holt

Josie had two long-standing engagements to honor that evening: drinks at five with her Women's Studies group and her reading circle at nine, Atwood this time around. At five o'clock, Josie caught a ride with one of the older women, Mrs Fischer, who taught geography. An apologetic creature, overweight and with a tepid spirit, Mrs Fischer was a part-timer, like a lot of the faculty wives. Her whole view of the world focused on her more substantial husband, but she was trying to change, or professed as much. She was in the Women's Studies group, after all, a meek revolutionary but revolutionary no less. She was just too sweet for confrontation. They talked about a recipe for lasagna on the way out to Cokey's, their regular meeting place. The key to it, Mrs Fischer explained, in her monologue, was the cottage cheese . . .

Josie loathed cottage cheese on principle.

With fifteen other women and plenty of alcohol to stir the revolution, they conspired against the patriarchy, Lues style. Following a tangent about sexual harassment, Josie struggled not to tell them about pulling a revolver on Virgil Hazard during her "job interview." She drank thirstily and smiled vacantly around the table. She was pretty sure Virgil Hazard would be a bit more considerate of the women he interviewed after his experience with Josie. Josie looked around at the women. They were isolated from the real thing; they couldn't imagine the genuine article, so they confused embarrassment with real threat, discomfort with loss, foul words with foul deeds. They were all certain that a problem existed but could not quite have defined it. Sexual harassment was simply the latest fad, and all of them were eager to have had something happen to them, a sort of rite of passage, so they related their experiences, the themes of which invariably proved men to be pigs, not criminals. They weren't visiting the police or calling a garage to get the broken glass in their car taken care of. They didn't have to strip for country boys in order to feed their children. They were all happily employed and promoted beyond their abilities. One of them started in on some creep in another department asking her for a date, and she had half a mind "to turn him in." The silliness of it disrupted the real issues, and gave to them the debilitating excuse to hide behind clumsy bureaucratic procedures instead of the courage to confront on their own what they did not like in language and action. Maybe not a gun to the balls or a standoff with a taxi driver, but something: courage for God's sake! They wanted off the pedestal, but they weren't quite ready to accept that the world is mean and unfair, contemptibly incompetent and even downright brutal. If you wanted to be in it and not insulated from it, you needed the courage of a fighter. Here they were, whispering about actions they ought to take, and action invariably meant to send it through Affirmative Action, to start something moving that left them the victim instead of a person taking charge. Josie drank deeply and kept her mouth shut, as the new kid is supposed to do, though she had been a woman for long enough to know garbage when she heard it.

Josie hitched a ride home with a quietly aggressive lesbian named Clarissa Holt. Clarissa was a professor in Communications, a thin woman with flat, dark eyes, a bumpy blade of a nose and tight thin lips. She was tall but seemed taller than she was because of her thinness and the curving, angular way she carried herself. Politically, Josie found herself on the opposite side of Clarissa on most issues, but she liked the woman's temper and spirit. Clarissa did not countenance stupidity in either gender. She had been in Lues thirteen years and was already a full professor – because she had earned it and not just put in her time. She knew the business and she was by all accounts a fighter. As the arguments at Cokey's had degenerated into the anecdotal embarrassments – the inane remarks of their male colleagues, usually – Josie had watched Clarissa's jaw grinding. When the conversation had turned to the matter of Henry Valentine, Clarissa had borne the general assaults on Val as long as she could, then had announced, to their general astonishment, "If Val bothers you, press charges against him." That was the standard cure for anyone else, but oddly, in the case of Val, such a suggestion seemed mortally dangerous.

The silence was long and nervous. Finally one of the women had answered, "It's just Val; it's the way he is."

Another of them had mumbled, "What good would it do, anyway?"

Clarissa had them on the run, and she knew it. She had called their bluff. "It would bring the rest of them in line."

Mrs Fischer, making love to her third gin and tonic, edged forward from a long wall of flesh: "Make an example of Val?"

At that point, Clarissa Holt had written them off and lit a cigarette, changing the subject. They all had breathed easier afterwards. It had been as if they had been challenged to confront Henry Valentine physically. The talk hadn't really surprised Josie. They were always talking about Val, always complaining. What she hadn't expected was the fear in their eyes. With three or four drinks to knock over resistance, there was generally a savage glee in the idea of giving one of the old bulls what-for. Routinely, they were prepared to hang them by their balls, if any of them still had 'em, chortle, giggle. Val was a different matter, and Josie found it curious. She revolted at the idea of charging a man for the way he looked at you, but she still liked Clarissa's courage, the put-up or shut-up attitude she had offered, and with Clarissa it wasn't just the booze. Clarissa got nicer with booze. Sober, she was a hell-cat, a hard-liner, a terror to the patriarchy, neither giving quarter nor asking it.

"Attending this circle," Clarissa remarked, as they came toward Presbyterian Hill, "is a little like watching your own arm being cut off. I mean they're trying to be feminists but they're ruining it." She looked at Josie to see how this was settling with her. "It's just so much talk to them. Not one of those women would stand up to a man, let alone Henry Valentine. They're afraid. And it's not just men they're afraid of; they're in this circle because they're afraid they're going to miss out." With disgust: "It's not political anymore; it's pop culture. It's enough to make me a heterosexual."

Clarissa turned into campus, accelerating into a group of three students as they cut diagonally across the street in front of her. She hit the horn, then her brakes with a dramatic squeal before they looked up with lazy drugged gazes.

Clarissa acted as if she always did this sort of thing, and carried on her discussion. "I've always hated men; after thirteen years in Lues, I don't like women either. This is just a new age sewing circle, Josie. I can't stand it!"

Josie thought she ought to say something, so offered the relatively neutral curiosity, "I haven't figured out what we're trying to do in this group."

"Originally, the plan was . . ." Clarissa stopped her explanation. She shook her head, "We're giving ourselves a damn good reason to get drunk twice a month."

Josie smiled. "Just so I understand the goal."

Clarissa slowed at Willow Circle, the road which led to Josie's apartment, and turning her little Civic onto the road, she let the car roar up the hill. "You seemed a little tense tonight," Clarissa remarked. "Is everything okay?"

Josie answered vaguely that it was Lues. "Too close to what I grew up with and too far from what I need."

Clarissa understood, she said. Her degree was from Berkeley but she had grown up in the hill country of Ashland, Kentucky. She parked behind Josie's ruined VW, checking out the damage to the car as Josie thanked her for the ride.

"Do you know who did it?"

"Not a clue," Josie lied.

Clarissa stopped her as she started out the door. "Let me know if I can help."

Josie considered the offer. She certainly needed someone, she thought. Things were spinning out of control, but like most people who most need it, Josie couldn't imagine how anyone could help. She was just going to have to muddle through on her own. She thanked Clarissa for the offer and said she would if things got bad.

At her apartment, Josie realized she would never make it to the reading circle at nine; she was exhausted and a bit drunk. She called Gerty Dowell to say her car had been vandalized and was sitting, in fact, in front of her apartment with the windows broken out, filling up with rain. Gerty was a simple woman who wore the same exercise sweats to school every day, baby blue with lime-green stains as old as Josie. She hurried through the halls, hunched and nervous, passing the gossip like so much flatulence without so much as breaking stride. Her one achievement at Lues State was to have been on the faculty the first year the school had opened, but most people believed she had been a charter faculty member of Southeastern Presbyterian College, *circa* 1895. Gerty was scandalized that Josie's car was damaged and offered to send someone out to pick her up – Gerty didn't own a car, which was the reason Josie had called her. Josie declined the offer with apologies for missing the group; she was upset and tired, she said. As an afterthought she mentioned that she had been in the Women's Studies group earlier. She didn't want to be found out later, but in retrospect she decided her remark was tantamount to confessing alcoholism with communist leanings, and she was sorry to have let that drop to Gerty; it would be everywhere by first light. "I'll make the next meeting," Josie promised.

Josie set the receiver back into its cradle, and realized suddenly that she was safe. It hadn't quite seemed real until now, but Jack Hazard was in jail until the new year – and she would be gone by then; she had only to write her letter of resignation, and this nightmare was behind her.

Bandolier

The day was over, and Josie still had a hundred pages to read in James Fenimore Cooper before her nine o'clock class in the morning. She gave over to it half-heartedly, and at ten set down the book without the slightest notion of what she had read. It was midnight in Boston, but maybe Annie was still up.

Annie was up and roaring. The whole place was abuzz
188

with rumor and speculation. Annie caught herself. That was the typical condition of Bandolier; this was worse than usual. All the talk had been about Dan Scholari: whether he would lose his tenure, and if not, why didn't they all go see the dean about their spring schedules, and what caliber *pistole* should one use? Annie shared the reactions of faculty members Josie knew only too well, and told her no one really knew anything of substance about the affair, though theories were rampant. Josie's name had come up a few times, even the thought that maybe she *hadn't* asked for it.

There was something hypnotic and nostalgic in listening to Annie, and Josie encouraged her to tell her everything. It was all the encouragement Annie needed. For the first time that day, Josie put aside her own doubts and fears and that nagging sense of dirtiness and guilt that had dogged her since she had left Colt Fellows and Tobias Crouch. She saw the familiar halls of Bandolier. She remembered Annie's office, the books stacked weirdly, even dangerously high, thousands of them and the pictures, some cut out of newsprint, others from the glossy pages of fashion magazines, some neatly framed, others fresh-cut from the pages like wild flowers, the *hero-women*, Annie called them. She thought of Annie rolling in her chair back and forth between her bookshelves calling for some book on high or digging into a stack of newsprint, and ranting against . . . everything. She thought of the wild mid-afternoon gossips, the late-night bottle of rye she would pull out of her desk, "Irish-till-I-die, Josie!", the endless arguments over poetry and psychology, myth and symbols, that whole world where dream and reality become one, the essential human cosmos that universities alone can offer but more likely try to stamp out as one would a grass fire. Even the sudden violence that occasionally disrupted it was never enough for Bandolier University to enter fully into the plane of the real world. Lues State didn't give Josie that same feeling. She wasn't sure if it was Lues or the change of position. She wasn't a student anymore. She was

189

an authority figure without the authority. She hadn't the freedom to shout her convictions or the punch to stick it to the old bulls. She hadn't even the guts to drop a hand grenade or two in the sewing circle. And she missed that. She was swept out of the wild and safe world of study into the calm and dangerous world of work. She wanted to go back, and yet she knew it couldn't ever be the same. Even Annie was changing, because Annie wouldn't stand still for any woman. As for men, she was always trying to get their toes when she rolled through a crowd.

"The only certainty at this point," Annie told her, somehow anchoring Josie's thoughts again on pragmatic concerns, "is that he'll undergo a week of psychiatric evaluation. If he's sane, he's in trouble; if they decide he didn't know what he was doing, he'll keep his tenure and be back in class the following week."

It was good to listen to Annie's raspy voice, possible for Josie to believe she was back in Boston with the faces she knew and the familiar academic wars, even Dan's troubles. It wasn't his first psychiatric stay, after all, just his first dean-at-gunpoint. Josie sipped at a cup of mint tea, encouraging Annie's rambles and listening with the dream sensation that Lues was far away, Boston close by. When Annie wore down, she pushed Josie for news. What had happened? Had she gone to the police? What had they said?

Ready finally to dip into it, Josie talked extensively about what she had learned, that Jack was divorced from her mother, that he had kidnapped her and tortured her before he killed her. She said there were witnesses who had seen Jack at the canyon, and there was a wristwatch that had been found with Jack's name on it. "Can you believe it? He left his name at the scene!" She told Annie about Jack's other two killings: his uncle, when he was ten, and the bizarre racial killing of a man in Pilatesburg.

" . . . I don't know what my mother saw in him, but

Colt said he was a ladies' man. I take it she wasn't very sophisticated . . ."

There was more, plenty to tell, and yet as she finished Josie realized she hadn't confessed the substance of her day. She left unspoken Colt Fellows's implied revelation that she had probably been molested by Jack and that was the reason she had no memory of her time in Lues. As for the delicate matter of getting Jack Hazard put in jail without having to prove he had done anything or for that matter giving him a chance to answer the charges, she hadn't elaborated on that point either. In fact, technically, she lied to Annie about it. She said she was going to have to wait and see about the charges but for now Jack had been arrested for harassing her. Touching her arm was a kind of harassment, wasn't it? The more she thought about it, the dirtier it made her feel. She wasn't sure if it was getting her wish that bothered her or the nagging thought that something just wasn't right about the whole thing. And the proof of its wrongness was she couldn't tell Annie what she had done.

Then there was the comparably minor incident in which Josie had fully intended to shoot a man down over a dollar. They talked nearly an hour, and none of these matters surfaced. The talk was all about Josie's safety, that her troubles were past her, and Annie was happy about that. She was happy that that bastard Jack Hazard had finally gotten what he deserved, and glad that Josie was finding out about her childhood, "and chasing monsters." Her own words got her going, and Annie repeated much sage and familiar advice, though she forgot to mention one of her favorite themes, the good medicine of truth.

Josie hung up with a feeling akin to nausea. She was the woman she hated: hiding behind bureaucracy. She was a coward. And she was a liar. She was lying about Jack Hazard and lying to her best friend because the truth made her queasy. She was looking at her Medusa but blinking in terror, *like a boy*, as Annie would say. She was free at last and had never felt more pursued. She tried to sleep, but her dreams were as bad as her waking fears. She knew that Jack Hazard waited under her bed. She felt the hand finally. It was slippery with the blood of her mother. She heard her mother calling her, and she woke gasping in near suffocation. What the woman said, Josie had no idea.

Re-Vision

The next morning, as she was leaving, Josie realized she was still packing her nickel in her purse. She took the gun out and, returning to her bedroom, placed it in the drawer of her bedside table. Then considering the purse, she tossed it in the drawer next to the revolver. *History*, she told herself. Outside it was still raining, misting really, and she peeked into her car to assess the damage. The upholstery was going to be ruined. Angrily, Josie walked toward Liberal Arts. At least today she was dressed for the rain with a raincoat and hat, but of course her feet got wet. Once she was off the hill and walking along Willow Avenue several cars splashed her, and Josie found herself revolving back to the rather continuous low-grade fever of disgust for Lues, longing to have her nickel along and forgetting to laugh at herself when she thought about shooting the driver of the next car that splashed her. At her office Josie called a garage to pick up her VW and fix the glass and see if they couldn't save the upholstery. It was going to take a month at the very least, she was told. That meant a couple of months, certainly. Maybe more.

It was almost nine when she got off the phone. She opened her briefcase, double-checking on the Cooper novel, then leaned across her desk to grab up the folder marked 9:00 MWF. She stopped suddenly as she did. How had Jack gotten into her office yesterday to write the note inside her ten o'clock folder? She had been so distracted in front of her class, so full of the promise his words gave her and so happy about the prospect of the man being arrested, that she hadn't remarked anything peculiar about what she had only assumed was Jack's latest and, as it happened, his last message. But it had been different, hadn't it?

He had to have used a key. Josie reflected for a moment on the lax security about keys. For an insider it was easy. You got a slip and forged the secretary's initials, then went to Building and Grounds. Or you stole the office's master key, but Jack wouldn't know about that. Once she thought about it, the other note was even more perplexing. It had been left sometime after the office had opened at eight and before Josie checked the box at ten. It hadn't been mailed on campus, nor come through the post. Someone had delivered it by hand that morning – using university-issue labels.

She sat down at her desk and called Colt Fellows. Fellows wasn't in, so she asked for Officer Crouch, looking at her watch impatiently. She explained to Crouch, when he answered in his lazy Lues accent, that she had found two more notes, " . . . but I have a problem." She explained the situation, that Jack wasn't likely to know his way around the university. She found it nearly incredible that he could have walked into her department office without being noticed.

Crouch didn't seem to pick up on what she was saying, and she interrupted him irritably, checking her watch again. "I don't care *why* he did it," she snapped. "I want to know *how.*"

"I think you probably need to talk to Colt."

"Will you tell him I called? I want to know about this, and I have these two notes that need to be checked for fingerprints. Have you checked the paper I gave you for fingerprints?"

Crouch's answer was half-apology, half-stall. She hadn't expected any different.

"Can you check this envelope and card I got yesterday? Jack probably delivered it himself."

"He could have worn gloves. It wouldn't prove anything if there are no prints," Officer Crouch offered.

"It would prove something, though, if there *were* prints. I want it fingerprinted!"

"Colt's handling this. He'd have to approve it."

"He's not in," Josie answered. "And I have to get to class. Will you tell him?"

Silence. *Maybe he is in*, she told herself.

"I need to talk to Colt about this myself, don't I?" Josie asked finally.

"I can't do anything until Colt tells me to."

"What if it's not Jack?" Josie asked him.

"What do you mean?"

Josie looked at her watch. Six after. She was talking to an idiot, and her class was about to get up and leave. Ten minutes was all they gave you; it was the universal and unwritten code of every college she had ever known or heard about. Ten minutes and not a second longer.

"Look, forget it! I'll call him myself when I get back from class."

Josie hung up in frustration. What was she doing? One day she was sure Dan Scholari was flying in from Boston, the next it was this hapless old ex-con who had looked genuinely happy to see her, and now she was starting to think the evidence pointed elsewhere, somewhere, nowhere. *My God*, she thought, *I'm losing my mind!*

Once outside, she broke into a run. Well, she told herself, she would talk to Colt Fellows about it later. Maybe she should talk to Jack, too. *Face him with it and see how he reacts . . .*

Josie made it to class just as her students were rising and shuffling toward the door. "Not through the Iron Duke, you don't!" she cried, herding them back to their seats. They gave the obligatory groans, most of them good-natured. Today the lecture was about the dying frontier, she announced, discarding her worries with the sudden excitement of knowing what she was doing: " . . . the evils of civilization – read *matriarchy*, ladies and gentlemen, as in mamma rules – and America's hero-male on the run: as in I don't want to grow up!"

Sixteen hands hit the air at once. *God bless Annie Wilde!*

When class finished, Josie went back to her office and made several calls to Colt Fellows throughout the afternoon. Out. Out. Busy. He's on the other line. Can I have him return your call? I'll see he gets the message.

Waiting for his call. A long silence, hour after hour. She tried again: "Colt Fellows's office? I'm afraid he's busy. Certainly. Maybe you had better give me that number again . . ."

Josie set her phone down, and looked tiredly at her watch. It was after two. Maybe she had better just get a taxi and go down there, she decided.

Her office door rumbled, and she started at the sound, then looking out from behind her curtain, she saw Dick Ferrington, tweed and penny loafers, a touch of gray in the temples, the square jaw set, blue eyes to die for. *If he just didn't look so handsome!* she told herself.

She unlocked the door and opened it. "Dick," she said, "come in."

As he walked in, he asked that she keep the door open, then he remained standing close to it. He was scowling.

"What's the matter?"

"That's what I want to know." Dick was agitated, his flesh an unattractive pink.

"What are you talking about?" Josie asked him.

"I think you know, Josie."

"Not a clue, Dick. What's this about?"

"I've got to tell you, when you wrote and asked me to help you get on here – "

"I didn't ask you to help me! I said I was applying for a position. I never asked for help!"

"I did you a favor, okay?"

"No, it's not okay. You weren't on my list of references. I didn't ask you to help me get a job."

A faint smile played cruelly around Dick Ferrington's lips. "Play it any way you want, Josie; all I'm saying is right now everyone's asking *me* what's going on."

"Damn it, what are you talking about!"

Through the entire conversation, Dick had been tapping a newspaper against his hand. It was a nervous gesture, but Josie hadn't quite connected the presence of the newspaper with Dick's visit. When he tossed the paper on her desk, Josie saw at once what he was talking about.

On the front page, in the lower right quadrant, was the headline, LOCAL PROFESSOR ASSAULTED IN TOPLESS BAR. What followed was a rather extensive and complete, if not entirely accurate, narrative of Josie's complaint against Jack Hazard, identified as her stepfather. If twenty years ago they couldn't get people connected to each other correctly, that didn't appear to be the problem now. They had Josie's name and employer prominently displayed and the reporter had even contacted the Bust of Country, so had information about Josie's "audition."

"Bastards!"

"What were you thinking, Josie? You think the university condones this kind of behavior?"

Josie's anger with Crouch and Fellows and the nameless author of the article faded briefly as she tried to absorb what Dick was saying. "What behavior? Being assaulted?"

"That bar is nothing but a whorehouse! What were you doing out there?"

What was going on? Why did Dick Ferrington care where she went? "I don't think I quite understand what your role is in this, Dick."

"I'm trying to find out what's going on with these charges and this 'audition.' What's it mean? What are you doing? Are you stripping?" He asked this with an incredulous bit

196

of a laugh tagged on, as if he thought there might be some better explanation but he couldn't imagine what it was.

"Is this an official visit, Dick?"

"If I don't get some answers, I imagine the dean will want some. You don't have tenure here, Josie. You're on thin ice."

"I've got a contract, Dick, and I don't remember any passages in it about having to ask your permission before I go to a bar!"

"We *do* have a morality clause. You think about that."

"I think I'd like for you to leave, that's what I think."

"Fine." He looked around the office. "Oh, by the way, if I were you, I wouldn't carry that gun on campus again. Permit or not, and I doubt you have one, there's a weapons ban on campus. The way you're going, someone might just say something about it."

"I don't know what you're talking about."

Dick shook his head. "You're messing up big-time, Josie. This stuff will follow you through your whole career."

He was out in the hall as he finished this observation, and Josie followed him. She caught herself before she hurled a string of profanities at the man. Instead, she slammed her door as she walked back into her office. Dick had left the paper. She picked it up and tried to read it. It took several attempts before she could get all the way through, her fury igniting at every statement, her eyes swimming out of focus. Finally, she shook off the confusion and steeled herself to read what lay on the page:

Local Professor Assaulted in Topless Bar

Lues State University's Liberal Arts Visiting Lecturer Josie Darling filed charges of assault against John Christian Hazard, a bartender at the Bust of Country in Codswallop, early Thursday morning with Lues City Police, officials report. According to Darling's complaint, Hazard, who is her stepfather, grabbed her and dragged her toward the door of the tavern with malicious intent. Patrons who witnessed the event said the trouble began when Darling, 27, attempted to audition in the nude and Hazard, 53, dragged her bodily from the dance stage and expelled her from the club, still partially clothed. Police Captain Colt Fellows commented that his department became involved because Hazard appeared at the local McDonald's with the intent of finding Darling, whom, he believed, was going to be at the McDonald's. "We hope this sends a loud and clearly message," Fellows announced, "that this city will tolerate violence against women." Fewllows is being held at the Civic Center Jail pending a bail bond hearing next week.

Josie threw the paper down. She checked her watch and stepped out into the hallway. Val was listening to a woman telling him about her abortion. Josie sighed and looked for a friendly face. Clarissa? She rejected the idea. Lesbianism. Josie didn't need any more misunderstandings! She knocked on Val's door, and the girl sitting before him turned to look at Josie, her face red, streaming with tears.

"Can we talk when you're free, Val?" Josie asked. She was sick at interrupting.

"I'll leave," the girl announced.

"No! I didn't mean – !"

The girl ducked her head and left the office. Josie watched her guiltily until Val told her to come in. Like one of the penitents, Josie took the seat before his chair, which was quite hot, and looked at Val for a long time before she spoke. Val looked not at a woman's breasts as one of the faculty women had complained but at a woman's heart. He stared into the source, a dismantling and penetrating gaze she had never noticed until this moment.

198

Finally, feeling her world crumbling and unable to stop it, Josie announced, "I need your help."

Short Skirts

Josie spent nearly an hour talking to Henry Valentine about what had happened to her since she had arrived in Lues and even some of the things that had gone before. She told him everything: her fears about Dan when she had arrived, the threats she had received, the fact that Dan hadn't been involved, her visit to Codswallop, the broken glass in her car, the note she'd found, the visit to the police and the subsequent assault charges against Jack Hazard. She went even further. She said she wasn't sure it was Jack, after all. She rambled incoherently about her memories connected to the man, about remembering her mother laughing, and finally she talked about the murder, how Virgil Hazard had claimed Jack was set up. There were no more secrets, no more shades of truth. She finished her narrative with the latest bump in the road, the unfortunate article in the Lues *Rapids* and of course her run-in with Dick Ferrington. She was out of ideas, certain that anything she did now was going to turn out ruinously, and she needed someone she could trust, someone close to things in Lues who could tell her what she ought to do.

The more she talked, the more certain she was that Val was the very person to help her. Val listened with a kind of genius. He caught the nuances of an event at once; he grew excited as she became excited, full of pity or outrage or gentleness according to the story's turns. He didn't intrude on her telling, never stopped the flow, never gave the look that so many can effect without seeming to: *What do you want* me *to do about it?* Val listened as we imagine, in our weaker moments, God must listen. His patience was beyond measure. She realized that he didn't force her to eclipse the details. When he spoke, his observations were incisive or

199

informative but always in full sympathy with her situation. His perspective and passions were her own. It was almost as if his voice were inside her head, as if he were the secret sharer of all her pain and fear.

When she had finished her story, and he had asked a certain number of questions and seemed to understand all that had happened, Val raised his eyebrows with the resignation of a man who knows the shallowness of human emotion, and announced: "This Captain Fellows set you up, Josie. He's the one who called the newspaper."

"But why?" Josie revolted at the naivety of her own protest, but could hardly help herself. She had trusted Colt! They had had an understanding; they had made a deal.

"You're *college*. He's a slew. Slews hate anything to do with the college. It wasn't even personal. It was just a cheap shot and he took it. He did it because he could."

"Like a drive-by shooting," Josie announced sardonically. The image was extreme, she realized, but there was a kind of ruin in her future that felt more like death than job troubles.

Val's big loose lips answered, the expression approving, condoling, full of an old, tired rage.

"He seemed so sincere!"

Josie felt the air running out of her. She was beat up again; only this time the bruises wouldn't show for a while. Josie hadn't quite connected the story in the paper to Colt Fellows; she had been too embarrassed with the details to see the relationship, but she knew Val was right. The reporter hadn't bothered with checking his facts, as she had automatically assumed. That notion had only been another uncontrollable impulse of naivety. Fellows had given the details in such a way as to discredit Josie at the university. At the same time the story had created a convincing charge of "assault," something to justify Fellows's actions.

"I'll sue the bastards," Josie murmured, meaning Fellows as well as the newspaper.

Val studied Josie calmly. "You could sue," he offered, "but from what you say, you might not get any satisfaction."

"But it's a lie!" There was that kid screaming again. Josie fought to get a handle on it. She hadn't the luxury any longer of idealism; she was in the middle of a dirty fight, and she needed to think like a survivor, like a mean fighter herself.

"From what you tell me, it's an interpretation, a matter of perspective," Val speculated. "Eighty men, as you say, saw the thing one way, you saw it another."

Josie thought about the men and the voice of the disc jockey. She thought about what she had done to Jack. She saw how others would perceive her actions. An objective view of the facts would not include the necessary subtleties in this case. Objectivity, like every other perspective, has its limitations. Objectively, Josie Darling had entered the Bust of Country for the purpose of getting work. She had had her job interview, then faced the crowd and lost her courage. The bartender had thrown her out, and, in a pique, she was calling that assault.

"Even if you prove maliciousness on the part of the paper or Captain Fellows," Val told her, "you won't get sympathy from the slews, and they're the ones sitting on juries, not the professors or students. The hard truth is," he went on, "everyone who reads about the incident – and everyone will – is going to believe it, or at least talk about it and make jokes. What you may want to think about," Val offered, "is how you want to handle our fine dean if he approaches you on this."

"The dean?" To Josie it was one more absurdity tossed into the stew, but Val was more serious than she realized.

"Here's the fix," he said. "If he comes after you for this, you're vulnerable to an investigation."

"Why? I don't understand." Josie felt a mild pressure screwing down into the middle of her chest.

"He could use the morality clause in your contract, as

201

Dick mentioned, or he could be particularly devious and invoke the 'no moonlighting' clause." Val had a faint, perverse glee at this thought. And why not? Universities are merely asylums without warders.

Josie swore loudly, "He wouldn't do that!"

Val considered for a moment. "I doubt he's smart enough to try the moonlighting issue – that might even work. If he does anything, he'll jump into the morality mess. Eventually, of course, you'll win your case in court, assuming you fight it long enough, but the point is, professionally you'll be washed up."

Pistoles in thirty minutes or less? Not so funny anymore.

"If you refuse to take legal action, they work you over, humiliate you for a while and leave you wearing the stigmata of scandal, even after they discover you did nothing wrong. You'll get work, maybe. But the recommendations will always have a shadow.

Maybe a career in computer programming. Or a fitness instructor? "Breathe deep, now!" Josie barely managed to stifle a groan. Her professional life was over. *What is that word known to all men? Who cares?*

"So how do I stop it? I mean I don't like either of my choices, here, Val." Josie was smiling, but the look was all teeth and grit.

"Dick Ferrington has Dean Meyers's confidence."

"I think I blew that angle." Josie's smile stayed locked in place. She was having trouble breathing and the pain in her chest had sharpened. She kept thinking this was all absurdly funny, and no one was laughing. Why weren't they laughing?

Val considered for a long moment, then announced, "Mend the fence, Josie. Tell Dick what you told me. Throw yourself on his mercy. He'll come through for you. Deep down, he still has a lot of respect for you."

Deep down?

"If Dick goes to the dean for you, nothing will happen. The whole thing will die down in a few days. People will whisper and laugh, and next week they'll be chasing something else. Dick's excellent at putting out brush fires like this."

"I don't think he wants to hear anything I have to say."

Val considered this briefly. "Dick's problem with you," he explained, "is that he supported your candidacy; he told everyone on my committee what a great scholar you are, and then you arrived and you weren't what people expected. You weren't what Dick expected."

"What do you mean?" Josie was genuinely confused.

Val had the look of letting something out that he shouldn't have. He was faintly embarrassed, but pushed on, now that it was started. "I've heard several things, from Dick indirectly and from others."

"Like what?"

"First of all, Dick did not talk to *me* about your candidacy. He knew better. I don't take instruction very well. I know he told you how he campaigned to get you on here – "

"He didn't mention you directly."

"He just implied it?" Val's expression seemed to ask Josie if she understood his distaste for Ferrington, or at least his tactics. "Everyone got excited about you after Dick pushed them around a little, and then we got this application from a Colombian woman. Affirmative Action kudos and all that, so they all went running to her camp and your friend Dr Ferrington shut up. Remember that. You got this position because I don't bend to fads. As far as I'm concerned, Affirmative Action can go fuck itself."

"What are they saying about me, Val?"

Val gave Josie a look so she would understand he was not one of *them*. Somehow that made it worse, as if the opinion of the college were universal, except for the local bad boy. "Provocative outfits, aggressive language in the classroom – "

"That's bullshit!"

He shrugged, "You're popular. That makes you suspect." Val let this settle. No one knew the dangers of popularity like Henry Valentine. "The latest is something about what's her name in Communications?"

"Clarissa Holt?"

"You caught a ride home with her last night? Tongues are clucking, Josie."

Josie swore savagely at this and stood up. Then she sat down again. She didn't care what anyone thought! Then, conformity coursing through her like a mickey, she counted the number of slacks she owned. "This just sucks!" she announced finally. She wanted to pack her bags and go back to Boston. In Boston there was some sympathy for originality or at least the illusion of it. Of course no one really cared what students said or did or thought; they were dartboards, as Annie had put it so succinctly in a similar context.

Val smiled benignly. "People have to have something to talk about; you just happen to be the flavor of the month. I'll try to say something scandalous next week and take the pressure off of you."

This was a joke, but Josie was still struggling with the issues of conformity and freedom. "What if I *were* a lesbian? *You* know I'm not. But what if I were? What does that matter? We're past all that nonsense, aren't we?"

Josie heard herself. If her IQ were a body temperature she would be dead of hypothermia.

Val shrugged sympathetically, "Morality clause . . ."

Josie had the urge to go fire her gun. It was the slew in her, no doubt. Short skirts, bad attitude, and hot guns.

"So I have to suck up to Dick Ferrington or this whole thing trails after me for the rest of my life. That's about it, isn't it?"

It seemed almost to hurt him, but Val nodded. That was about it.

Margaret Bennet

Colt Fellows dodged people so routinely that he hardly ever returned calls without at least four or five messages. He had been seasoned under the old system of message taking and had fired three secretaries who had urged him toward the new technology of voice mail. If he wanted to hear the bastards talking, he would answer the damn phone! Or so he said. Margaret Bennet was perfectly comfortable with Colt's methods and idiosyncrasies, all of them, thank you. She took phone messages so routinely that, as a rule, she didn't even bother calling in to see if Colt might be interested in talking to his caller. She said things like he wasn't in or wasn't available or he was in conference or he was on patrol, and she didn't mind doing it because that was the job. Colt was an important person and everyone wanted to talk to important people. His wife Betty got through. Two of Colt's three kids got through. Department *players* calling from outside got through, and that was it. Inside, of course, the policemen could ring him directly, at their peril. The mayor left messages, the prosecutor needed six or seven calls, the sheriff had to explain to Margaret his business before Colt would return his call, and if the governor ever called, Colt's very words, "I ain't in, and I ain't coming back."

It was, in a managerial sense, a very insulated administration. Josie Darling — with the legs and aren't I proud of them — made several attempts to get Colt that Friday, the day after Jack Hazard's arrest. Margaret Bennet had written "important, something about fingerprints." The next half-dozen she took down what the woman told her, and that was it. She left Colt alone. She had no expectation of moving Colt to return his calls. She understood that her job was to be passionately ignorant, eagerly concerned, and forthrightly protective of the boss. For that service she received good ratings on her quarter-annual reviews, regular pay increases each of her three years as an administrative secretary, and a sweet little bonus of one hundred dollars *every now and then,* directly from Colt's pocket to her purse and not even her kids knew about that money, let alone the IRS. The money wasn't that important. Margaret was hopelessly poor, and it mattered, but what mattered more was that Colt appreciated her. Colt Fellows had a number of shortcomings, among them an inability to speak without profanity, but one thing which he possessed to the point of genius was the ability to create private alliances. He had stepped in for instance when Margaret's ex-husband two years back was making noise about getting custody of their four children; Bertrand had never wanted to be around them when they were married! It was nonsense, purely a nuisance because the man was a hopeless drunk and hated the kids, but he did it because he had the money to do it and because Margaret couldn't afford an attorney, and without one she was bullied and scared and could hardly sleep for the worry of it all. Margaret had gone to Colt finally, and within a matter of days her ex-husband had ended up in the hospital. When he got out, he left town, the way he should have before he got his limp.

There were other alliances as well. Margaret hadn't gotten to be the boss's secretary by being ignorant. Every player in the department had some private history with Colt. It wasn't that kind of sloppy allegiance that usually happens between administrators and their subordinates, poker players and beer-drinking buddies evolving into professional allies. With Colt there was always a service and a debt. Everyone knew if you wanted something taken care of, you had but to ask Colt Fellows for the favor, no promises made and none asked; but when Colt asked a favor in return, you did it without being asked twice. If you wanted some kind of change or pro-motion among your peers, likewise, you had to execute some kind of favor for it, before you even asked. Colt Fellows had a sublimely simple notion of justice in law and fairness in the workplace: everything went his way or everything went to hell in a hurry.

At 4:30 Friday, Margaret Bennet patched through to

Sheriff Cal Yeager according to instructions, connecting her boss to the sheriff. The two men spoke amiably, Colt's big voice booming, Yeager's voice equally affable but never possessing the raw rough and tumble of a man like Colt Fellows. The truth was Yeager was a rather malleable sort who stiffened up only when he sensed weakness. In the presence of Colt, he was all suck, at least that was what Colt said. Of course that was the way of the world, wasn't it?

As Colt spoke it became clear that he wanted Yeager's cooperation, and following the lead, Yeager had answered as Colt obviously expected him to. Yes, an assault outside of city limits ought to be county business no matter where the arrest was made. Cal would gladly take the prisoner. There were no hard feelings of course, and certainly anytime they got the prisoner into county custody would be fine. Fellows rumbled about proprieties, a phenomenon as common as Halley's Comet. He wanted to straighten this out as soon as possible, and wanted to come down to Pauper Bluff himself in order to apologize for overstepping his bounds. It was just that he had needed to act quickly to save the woman from a possible second attack.

Yeager thought that was fine. Yeager thought anything Colt Fellows wanted was fine. Colt Fellows was the man who had handed him the office of sheriff on a platter, so to speak, the platter which also included Sheriff Pat Bitts's head when some of us were still worried about pimples. She had the whole story from Jason Miller who knew a lot more than he ever said and had the kindest eyes, with a bit of devil deep down.

"We'll leave with the prisoner at 9:15 tonight, Cal. I'll be there at 10:30. You'll be there, Cal?"

"I'll be there."

"You'll want a deputy or two on hand. The old boy I'm bringing in is none other than John Christian Hazard. You remember Jack Hazard, don't you, Cal?"

"I certainly do, Colt."

207

"Jack was slapping around a little whore at that stripper bar his brother owns up in Codswallop, but he's killed three people we know of, a hardened criminal, not someone you want to play around with."

"Ten-thirty, I'll be there and have my deputies on hand to receive him."

There was a light exchange about dinner sometime; they had been promising each other a social evening for as long as Margaret had been recording their calls and probably the whole twenty years they knew each other. Then Yeager clicked off, and Colt Fellows punched Margaret Bennet's extension. "You get that, Peg?"

"I got it recorded, Colt."

"It's a keeper. Get a fax out over my signature to Cal and copies to Scott upstairs. Keep it simple. Make sure you warn Cal that John Christian Hazard is 'an extremely dangerous prisoner' and apologize for our overstepping, blah blah, tell him Hazard will be delivered at first convenience, 10:30 tonight, time and date-stamp on all copies, a copy in our files too."

"Do you want to see it before I send it?"

"I got to go get drunk with Scott's two new deputy assistant prosecutors in twenty minutes; am I going to have time to see it?"

"I'll try, Colt."

"You're the greatest, Peg."

Well of course she was.

Five minutes later Tobias Crouch walked into Margaret's office. Margaret was busy preparing Colt's letter, but immediately intercepted him. Gun at his side and badge on his fat chest or not, Toby Crouch was most definitely not a player. Colt had gotten him a job on the force sometime in the last century and that was the end of it. Crotch-sniff was "somebody's dead cousin's orphaned pet rock," that was Colt's description, and his position in Colt's hierarchy had never changed.

"Do you have an appointment, Officer Crouch?"

"He just called me."

Yesterday he gets in and now today . . . called. Well, that's interesting, isn't it? Margaret looked askance at Crouch's ankle and cane. She didn't like the man. He never called her by name; he never looked at her, unless Margaret wasn't looking, then of course he looked plenty. Margaret was thirty-nine and holding (on for dear life), but she was still built pretty well, real well, thank you. She watched herself; she didn't let herself go the way some women did. You never knew what you might catch, as long as you kept a worm on the hook.

Margaret slid back to her desk, resting her fingers on the keyboard of her new Compaq. The thick mahogany door that led to Colt's big office opened as Patrolman Crotchsniff pushed through.

"Key-rye-st!" Colt screamed, "you're still on that ankle?"

Tobias Crouch stood with the door still open, cane in hand. He mumbled something. He was just inside the room but Margaret couldn't hear him.

She heard Colt Fellows fine, however. "I forgot about that fucking ankle!"

The door closed. Colt had something dirty going on. Something between Yeager and Crouch; now that was an odd pair. Colt couldn't stand either one of them. Yeager as sheriff of course was a necessary evil. But Crouch? Crotchsniff gave Colt the *willies*; he said it himself. What would Colt want with Crotch-sniff? Now that was a mystery . . .

Margaret finished Colt's memo to Cal Yeager, short but sweet. Colt's first apology ever, Margaret had found it difficult to achieve a credible tone. Well, no one was going to complain about not getting to arrest Jack Hazard, so it didn't really matter. Colt had done everyone a favor and this was just so much pro forma, as Mr Philip St Claire, her shorthand teacher at Southeast Academy of Business, had always called the things that didn't matter but did.

There had been five plainclothes waiting for Jack Hazard at the McDonald's, and a six-man SWAT team in reserve, all needed as it turned out. Colt had watched it from a van across the street. When the badges flashed, Jack Hazard had put three officers down with his bare hands before he was out of his chair. Jason Miller, who had been in the van with Colt, was laughing about it this morning. He said it was a miracle no one got hurt worse. Margaret had seen some of the results herself. The department had looked like a hospital waiting room this morning: broken fingers and noses, black eyes and stitches. Colt could apologize all he wanted; nobody envied this collar. Jack Hazard was probably the biggest man in the whole world.

Margaret hit the print button, brought the copies out, date-stamped them, and scribbled a perfect likeness of Colt Fellows's signature, perfect because Colt's signature was always done in Margaret's hand.

The door opened. Colt's voice, " . . . tell your mother it's Watch Commander Crouch she's talking to. See how she likes that!"

Crouch came into Margaret's domain, a curdled smile slopping over his fat cheeks. *Mr Watch Commander. Well, that's real interesting, isn't it?*

Reservations

Having scanned his eyes over Peg and her memo to Yeager, Colt Fellows left his office at five to five. He was in a good mood. He was always in a good mood when a problem that had been gnawing at him for weeks was finally settled and he knew exactly what he was going to do. In the Civic Center parking lot, the rain still falling, Colt climbed into his LTD. It was a nice car, none of that stripped-down to the basics for Colt Fellows anymore. He was Captain Fellows, by God! and he had gotten his wheels custom ordered from

Dempsey's Auto Fair, west of town. Dempsey was a champ, and the big eight he sold Colt purred like a well-fed lap cat.

Colt was running about fifteen minutes late, but he didn't care. He was in a dreamy mood, remembering old times and old debts. Keep the lawyers waiting. Let them know who was boss and who was the public servant. They didn't know it yet, but they would be running the investigation on Jack Hazard's and Tobias Crouch's deaths tonight. Scott would shuffle it off on them because they were the new guys, "outsiders" and so therefore objective, and because it would give them a taste of the fast lane, Lues style, so they might stick around for more than a year or two, which nobody from the outside ever seemed to do, and because Scott didn't fucking dare touch anything Colt was involved in! These boys would be plenty eager and thorough and predictably gullible. The aftermath was nothing to worry about. Colt just wanted them to see him this afternoon, before they got involved in the investigation. It was to be their first social meeting and he wanted them to know what a great guy he was and to remind them what a big one he was too – in every sense of the word.

They weren't the problem. The problem was Jack Hazard. Colt wasn't going to toss a drink down and laugh his way through that. Colt Fellows considered himself a brave man. More to the point, he was strong and quick and seasoned. He had fought men and he had killed men, and he knew his abilities and even, yes, his limitations. Frankly speaking, Jack Hazard bothered him; even in chains Jack scared the hell out of him, to be honest. He had watched Jack at the McDonald's. Past fifty and still able to fight five men down without breaking a sweat. Man! was he quick. As Miller had predicted, it took the SWAT to nail him, even though he had been unarmed. And afterwards, bound and shackled, he had broken an ankle, three fingers on two different hands, and one more nose, just for good measure.

God-damn little slew.

Colt admired the fight in Jack, but he knew there was more than fight. There was real danger in what he planned to do, though no one would believe it. That was all right. Colt believed it. He knew enough to be ready. He remembered the story about Hazy Mundy. It was instructive. Basically, Colt had told Josie Darling the truth about that killing. Basically.

Hazy Mundy was a big ol' colored boy from Paducah who got out of Kentucky just ahead of the law and found himself a comfortable little operation up in Pilatesburg, back in the days when Pilatesburg had something to recommend itself. From about 1947 to his death, Hazy ran six or seven whores at any given time, all out-of-town girls, and if you wanted to make a bet on a horse or a game or a fight Hazy was your man. As long as Hazy laid down his protection money, he was allowed to operate and was something of a local celebrity. Hazy was a straight shooter; he never cheated his customers and he kept his girls clean for the local farmers who wanted something besides old ma.

Hazy had started life as a card dealer, and he spent as much time as he could with a deck of cards in his hand. He could stack a deck for draw poker as easily as some old pro spreading her legs. Despite his other interests, Hazy never lost the urges of a great dealer, and when he played among his own people, Hazy took his turn at the deal like one of the boys. His people politely set in their ante, looked at the aces and kings and flushes he dealt them . . . and folded. Hazy could deal a wet dream of a hand and always deal himself one card better. His men were known to cry when they folded without a bet on one of Hazy's deals, and no one ever said a word about the ante they lost. It was payment for the pleasure of seeing a master at work.

Jack had drifted up to Hazy's club shortly after he got out of the Juvenile Center on Presbyterian Hill. Hazy put Jack to running some errands, collecting a few debts, and covering his back when there was a serious need. It wasn't long before

Hazy started sending Jack up north on some bank jobs, since Jack had skills that were wasted as a bodyguard to a man who terrified everyone anyway. Jack worked most of the year before he got invited to one of the inner circle Sunday evening poker games. Colt had this from Alfred Moore. Alfred had worked for Hazy several years and happened to be at the card game that Sunday night when Jack sat down to join them. Hazy took a pass the first chance he had to deal, but come the second turn, with Jack fresh off of winning a nice pot, Hazy took it upon himself to teach the boy humility. He dealt Jack a straight flush, rather a hand that was just one card from being perfect. Everyone else made a nominal bet, drew to their own flushes or straights or plugged together four eights, whatever Hazy felt like, and quietly folded. This was Hazy's show and Jack was the magician's guest from the audience, though he didn't know it yet. Of course Jack was nineteen, and nineteen draws to the inside straight flush. He must have seen heaven open up when he pulled the one card that could make him a winner. According to Alfred, who wasn't the most honest white man who had ever lived, it was a straight flush to the king of hearts. Jack pushed out about fifty dollars into the pot, and Hazy came up, of course, with a straight flush to the ace. Everyone guffawed; none of them ever saw anything like it, by God! "What was the odds!" "You could live a whole lifetime and never see nothing to equal it!" That kind of thing. They played another round, and pretty soon Hazy took up the deal. The first card didn't hit the table before Jack's finger was on it. Hazy stopped his deal and looked up at Jack in genuine astonishment. With only some coins on the table for an ante, there wasn't any reason to get excited, but everyone suddenly felt the tension in Jack's face. Here he was, nineteen years old, a tiny man really, and staring down not only the biggest man in Lues County but the closest thing to a crime boss anyone ever saw.

Hazy finally smiled at him and asked what was the matter. Jack answered, "You cheat me again, I'll kill you."

Hazy liked Jack; as far as anyone knew, Jack thought Hazy was next to God, but Jack had never been taught to back down. He hadn't had a good parental authority figure who had shown him how.

Hazy's smile faded. "Are you saying I cheated you?"

Hazy's astonishment had passed, and presently there was a real threat rising up out of that black man's soul. Jack didn't notice or didn't care, and answered with a hard edge that he wouldn't be cheated by no man. Hazy kept a little .38 just off his right hip under a big, ill-fitting suit jacket, and everyone knew Jack carried nothing but his mother-wit and two hard-knuckled fists. The moment he saw Jack was a little too proud to be useful, Hazy slipped the piece out and settled it "about twelve inches off Jack's nose." That was the way Alfred always told it.

"I don't think I quite heard you right, Jack."

This was Jack's last chance as far as Hazy was concerned, and of course he was sure Jack would take it, but Jack told him, "Put the gun down, Hazy, or I'll make you eat what's in it." Jack finished his speech with the word *nigger*, at least that's what Alfred Moore said, and the old giant positively smiled when he pulled the trigger.

Maybe that was his mistake. Maybe Jack just knew. Whatever the signal, Jack saw it and was able to slip off the end of the gun so quickly and smoothly, no one really saw him do it. Alfred and the others heard the shot and looked for Jack's face to kick back and rip apart; they flinched at the sound and they were sure Jack's blood would spray across them. Somehow during the millisecond of their reflex they missed how Jack got on top of the table. They heard a weird snapping noise as Jack broke one of Hazy's fingers, then heard a second shot out of Hazy's .38. No one even noticed this shot, because Jack took it straight on in the gut and didn't react to it. When the second finger snapped, Jack took

214

the gun from Hazy. Grabbing Hazy by the shirt with one hand, Jack fired from about six inches into his mouth. Hazy kicked back, dead in his chair, and before the blood had even begun to roll out, Jack put the last three slugs into him. When Jack finished, Hazy was still in his seat, his head perfectly erect, the front of his chin bloody, his lips shot off, his frame locked tight, absolutely rigid, the eyes wide open. To finish the portrait, Hazy still held the deck of cards in his left hand, the image of a man ready to continue his deal. Alfred swore to it that later, when Pat Bitts walked in, Hazy was still sitting like that, and Two-Bit had called out to him, before he understood what had happened.

After the shooting, Jack was on his knees in the middle of the table, his arms and face covered in Hazy's blood, his shirt turning a soppy pink from his own wound. The three other men sat transfixed, their faces covered in scarlet droplets. No one knew what to do, so they just stared at Hazy, like they expected him to deal, and then at Jack, wondering if he was going to snuff them or tell them to get rid of the body. Finally, Jack threw the gun down in front of Hazy, and crawled off the table. Jack stood for a good minute or so, his eyes casting around as he tried to figure what to do, then he told one of them to bring a car around and get him to a doctor. He told the other two they should tell what they saw, just as they saw it; he'd tell the law the same thing. They all nodded dumbly, and Jack walked back to the end of the room, went out the door, and as far as Alfred ever knew, walked in for his own surgery about a half-hour later.

Police Procedural

Colt slipped into Cokey's shaking hands, shouting and buying a couple of drinks on his way to see Scott's new men. He met them with a hearty god-damn! and bought the first couple rounds. He told some tall tales, and then each of them laid out what it was he wanted for the town and county of Lues. They were good guys, young and handsome, their future all before them, and they wanted what was best for Lues. *Don't we all!* They talked a good deal about drugs, that being a favorite these days, and Colt gave them every assurance that he would make it his number-one priority.

About 7:30, mellow with his drinks and satisfied the young men he had just talked to were bought and paid for, Colt went home for his supper. There were a couple of phone calls, which Betty intercepted, then after dinner, Colt asked for some coffee. Betty was afraid he was going to be up half the night. She started in on the coffee until he told her he was planning on being up half the night anyway, because he had work to do, a prisoner transfer.

About two years before, Colt had gotten something going with Peg Bennet. Peg just loved her boss, that was a blessed fact. It was nothing to break up a marriage about, just a little hardcore sex a couple, three times a month and the occasional office blowjob. Peg was a good girl and built like a brick shit-house. She appreciated Colt and she knew about Betty, who for all her faults was his wife, and Peg wasn't stepping into that kind of game. All's well when you don't get caught. Right? Well, Betty knew. How she knew, he didn't know. But she knew. She knew the first time it happened, and she'd given him a look damn near every time it happened since. So now when he said he was working late, it was written all over her face: *it's Peg Bennet, isn't it?*

"I got business tonight," Colt told her, and then he tried out something he thought might convince her it wasn't Peg, this time. "You know Jason Miller was telling me that when ol' Two-Bit was working the county, his old gal Polly used to wait up for him, no matter how late he come home and give him a roll if it was a dead one he'd fished up. He'd give her a call from the site and tell her what it was, living or dead, and if it was a dead one, she'd be waiting for him, oiled up and ready."

Betty looked at him with wide, soulful eyes, almost crying,

and then plenty mad, she answered, "I'll tell you what, Colt; you fish up a dead body somewhere tonight, you call me, and I'll oil up and go do Two-Bit. Will that make you feel any better?"

Betty had never really adjusted to Peg.

Shooting a Dog

At 8:30 Colt Fellows arrived at the Civic Center, and ordered the prisoner's hands and feet cuffed, the hands behind his back and a chain shackling his wrist and ankle cuffs. Since his incarceration, Jack Hazard had been an agreeable prisoner, but for this occasion, at Colt's instruction, three men showed up, one with a shotgun. The chain between the cuffs Fellows ordered to be pulled taut so that Jack could not lift his arms, nor move more than an inch or two on any given step. He would be able to hop a little, but he wouldn't be good for much more than that.

After Colt's call to the cell block, he ordered his Ford LTD gassed and vacuumed. He said he wanted his Remington pump shotgun, fully loaded, and he wanted a box of shells in the trunk. When he finished with his orders, Colt went to one of his cabinets and pulled out his Colt .44, a flat black piece, with a six-inch barrel and an ugly bore that spit a slug big enough to take out a fist-sized chunk of flesh. It was an old gun and Colt never carried it anymore unless there was serious business waiting. After loading it, Colt tucked the big gun in the small of his back. He still wore his shoulder holster with his .38 snubnose in it as a back-up. As an afterthought, he cached a box of .38 hollow-points in his sportscoat pocket. At nine o'clock Colt heard someone stepping into Peg's office. He called out Crouch's name, and the old boy limped into Colt's office. He was in uniform, but he still had his foot wrapped and he was on that frigging cane. Colt considered him a moment, then told him to get the ankle unwrapped and to ditch the cane.

He watched the fat man bending over to take off his shoe, then went on out. "You aren't down to lock up in six minutes," Colt announced, "I'll consider it your resignation from the force." Leaving Crouch, Fellows skipped on down the stairs, stopping twice to adjust his .44, the second time tightening his belt so it would stay in place. At lock-up, Colt entered the holding cell to check his jailer's work. Jack Hazard's face was blue and puffy, with several abrasions. There were still some open cuts on his cheeks and his lips were torn up some. Colt had had to let the boys have their fun. Jack looked up when Colt entered the holding area. Officer Newton came in behind Colt, locking the door as he did. Fig Newton was a ten-year man, straight arrow, respectful, not a player but not a problem either. He was a little like Jason Miller. You needed men like that, otherwise everyone was going crazy. If they knew some of their own would turn them in, they all moved more circumspectly. They took orders better and they kept their mouths shut.

"Any trouble with the prisoner?" Colt asked.

"No sir. I think he learned his lesson."

"You learn your lesson, Jack?"

Jack answered with his eyes, a blank, contented animal look. Thirty-three years of lock-up, Colt reflected. That was a long time, but he knew Jack hadn't learned a damn thing, except to wait his chances. Jack was wearing city colors, a bright orange one-piece jumpsuit. He had plain black city issue shoes, no strings, a couple of sizes too big. They were soled with thick black rubber and looked like what the clown wears. Jack was sitting on a bench, uncomfortably twisted off to the side with his weight on one haunch. He was forced to sit like this since his hands were pulled tightly down to his ass and the chain running behind his legs to his ankle cuffs cut into the seat of the bench.

"You don't look so comfortable, Jack. Let me know if them chains are a little too tight."

Fig Newton finished studying Jack and handed Colt a small ring with two keys. "Here's the keys to unlock him."

The locked door jarred behind them, and Colt turned to see Crouch through the bars. Newton pulled his keys out, and opened the steel door. With some show of irritation Colt looked at his watch. He slipped the ring of keys into his right front pants pocket. With amusement Colt noticed Jack watching. *Keep dreaming, Jack.*

"Fig, you take the prisoner out the back; Crouch and I will cover you from behind." Fig looked purposefully at Crouch. He obviously thought Crouch should help him, but Colt didn't want to say anything about Crotch-sniff's ankle. *Raise no suspicions.* Fig would be an important witness later. "Do as I say!" Colt commanded. They moved slowly because Jack could only step a few inches at a time. He rattled plenty, but he wasn't going anywhere.

From behind, Colt hollered, "Your choice Jack, hop like a pogo stick or I'll let Officer Newton drag you like an old steamer trunk!"

Jack didn't hop.

"Do it, Fig!"

Newton took Jack by the chain just under his hands and pushed him until Jack stumbled forward, got caught in his ankle cuffs and fell face forward to the concrete floor. Not a sound from the little son-of-a-bitch. Hazard didn't weigh more than 140 pounds on a good day, and Newt picked him up like a piece of heavy luggage, and, like luggage, bumped and dragged him about half the way to the car. When he got Jack to the LTD, Fig let Jack flop over the back fender. "Get up!" Fig ordered.

Jack bounced lithely into a standing position.

"In the back!"

Jack stepped forward with inching steps, his chains rattling. Colt was standing back, but Crouch was by the opened back door of the big Ford, and let Jack come too close to him. Colt pulled his .38 and hollered to Crouch to back away.

219

Crouch was slow to respond. Newton, who was unarmed, studied Colt for a minute, then helped Jack toward the opening to the back of the car. As Newt turned Jack and put his back to the door, Crouch stepped forward and shoved him, telling Jack as he did, "Watch your head!"

Jack hit his head and back as he slammed into the car, then rolled so that he fell across the seat. He dropped face-first onto the floor, and there remained trapped, his legs hanging out the car, his hips pinched between the seat and the back door. He was stretched forward, his arms caught up slightly so he couldn't lower his feet to touch the pavement. He lay helplessly, his face in the carpet. Colt holstered his .38 and called Crouch off. "Help him up, Newt." To Crouch he growled, "Get in." As Crouch walked around the car, Jack came up in the seat and noticed Crouch limping, his right foot the problem. Colt Fellows smiled. He had already decided Jack read this whole scenario even if no one else did. He was grabbing for straws, but not a bit of sweat to this point, not even when Colt had pulled his gun. He wondered if Jack would cry and beg at the end. There were plenty of tough guys who did. You never knew about the way a man died until you saw him facing it, his chances all behind him.

In Colt's Ford LTD there was a screen between the back seat and the front. Through the cage, Colt studied Jack's bruised face. A thin string of blood ran out from his nose and curled into his broken lips. To Crouch he announced, "You want to play, buy yourself a damn dog. Cut out the shit, you hear me?" To himself he added, *Jack's my dog.*

The rain hadn't let up, not for two days, but it hadn't gotten worse either, just a Lues mist, the kind of stuff that could settle in for weeks. As Colt drove, he used the wiper for a while, then got tired of hearing it and turned it off for a half-minute at a time. The radio crackled for a while, but once they were south of Presbyterian Hill and beyond the city limits, Colt reached down and shut it off. The highway cut back west after a couple of miles, and Pauper Bluff was southeast. There was no way to get there except on gravel roads. Soon enough they were rolling through the dark woods. There was really no reason to wait any longer to kill Jack. They were alone after only a mile or two, but Colt wanted to put it off. He wanted to be closer to Pauper Bluff. Jason Miller, who was Colt's chief of homicide, was pretty good at reading a scene, and Colt wanted Yeager to bung things up for a while before Miller arrived. As Colt replayed his scenario in his head, he looked over at Crouch. The man's thick lips were hung open in dumb wonder. Crouch's oily, pimpled face disgusted Fellows. *How does a man past forty get so many zits?* He studied the belly. Colt himself was six feet four inches and weighed 250 pounds. He had a tire, by God, but nothing like Crouch's. He wasn't soft like Crouch either. At fifty-eight, Colt was still plenty man enough. Crouch was nothing of the sort. The guy gave Colt the creeps. *The fucking willies! And good riddance to the little ghoul-fuck.* His eyes flicked toward the mirror. In the back, in the dark, Jack was studying the woods.

"Get a good look at it all, Jack. Talk in the prosecutor's office is you're going to do a lot of time for stalking that little whore-girl you call a stepdaughter."

Jack's eyes met Colt's in the reflected glass. Bland, flat eyes. Convicts get that look. It's the look of hell emptied out, a look so void of expression and meaning it is all the worse for its quiet.

"Things have changed since we were boys, Jack. You can't touch a woman these days without it being some damn thing or another: sexual harassment, rape, *assault*. The way this game goes, see, we get eighty witnesses up in the stand and we say, 'Did you see Jack Hazard grab this little whore?' 'Why, yes we did, sir. He took her by the arm.' 'Well then that proves it; send his sorry ass back to Vienna.' "

"Jack-home-again-in-Vienna," Crouch echoed.

Colt looked at the overgrown piss-ant. "What?"

"Like the song, *Jack-home-again-in-Vienna*." Toby Crouch had a contented look as he explained this.

Idiot. Colt caught Jack's eyes in the mirror. "They give you a private cell over there in Vienna, or give you a fuck-buddy, Jack?"

Nothing.

It was just like shooting a dog, that was a fact. Colt's gut went cold. He stared down the road, watching the edges of his light beam for any kind of movement, foxes, deer, Hazards. Jack had more cousins than a maggot.

Colt looked at his wristwatch. Almost a quarter to ten. The forty miles to Pauper Bluff went slowly on crooked, unpaved roads. A couple of dips took them through a light fog. The rain seemed to pick up a little, and Colt kept the wipers on. Colt checked his watch again.

Jack smiled as he watched the gesture, a look to unnerve Colt. *He knows.* Colt didn't like being read. It especially bothered him that Jack wasn't at least tense about the situation. Knowing and not tense: it just wasn't quite human.

"How many men fucked ol' Josie Fortune after the two of you got divorced, Jack? Could you count that high?"

Talking to a wall.

"I got a question for you. Did Josie Fortune suck as mean a dick as everyone said? I heard a buncha men back after we fished her out of Lues Creek; they were saying after you divorced her, she went wild. Said Josie Fortune sucked that college dry. Liked an educated cock, or so they said."

Jack looked out toward the woods. Colt felt his gut tighten down. A heavy reflux of acid coiled up into his throat.

"How was it, knowing everyone was fucking your wife, Jack? You knew it, didn't you? Those college boys and them professors? She was such a pretty woman; but it just hurts that much more when a pretty one gives it out to them intellectual twerps."

Nothing.

Colt pulled the big car to a stop in the middle of the

road, and set the gear selector in park. He hit his radio and adjusted the bands. He called Yeager, waited a few seconds, then called again. When the county dispatcher answered, Colt identified himself and told the woman he wanted to talk to the sheriff. Cal Yeager came over the radio, more static than usual. "Yeah, Cal," Fellows told him, "we're at Lues Creek Crossing. We'll be in Pauper Bluff in about twenty-five minutes. Officer Crouch has to take a leak so we've stopped for a couple of minutes. I'll call you again when we get started back-up."

Cal answered with an amiable bark of static. *Dumb fuck.* Colt saw Jack's eyes lighting up. *Yeah, well, a little change in the program, Jack. Don't tell me you're surprised? Or is that fear, finally?* Colt tipped his head back a little, "I'm the one that's got to take a leak, Jack, but those transmissions are recorded these days, and I ain't letting it out that I got a weak bladder – not to none of them county boys; I wouldn't hear the end of it."

Crouch seemed to stir himself from his intense stupidity, waking no doubt to the power of suggestion and with it nature's call. "I got to take a leak too, Colt."

"That's great, Tobias!" *A corpse. Key-rye-st!* Colt slung himself around and pulled himself out of the big car, leaving his door open and the engine running. They hadn't seen a car since they had gotten off the highway. Up ahead, just in sight of Colt's headlights was Lues Creek, about a two-hundred-foot spread of water that interrupted the road. A few inches under the water, at least it was a few inches most times of the year, the ground was hunched up to form a mole to drive across; "a disappointed bridge" is what Two-Bit always called it. Folks shied off this road at night, probably because of the ford. The crossing wasn't so bad, but if the water got up too far into your engine and killed the car, you were in deep country, ten miles to the nearest telephone, that at Pauper Bluff. It was plenty quiet here except for the faint sound of water flowing off ahead of them. The night was gray-black, the old moon waning.

Colt slapped the roof of his car, meaning to startle Jack, then walked off the road into the woods a few steps, standing in the shadows and unzipping his pants. Its two front doors open and the headlights still on, the Ford was lit up inside and out. Rain was falling in front of the headlights in a fine mist. Colt could see Jack clearly in the back seat waiting for them. He was seated off on a slant somewhat; he was staring straight ahead. Colt thought about how he had baited Jack. Probably not such a good idea, but it was done now. It had the effect of burning a bridge behind him: there was no going back now. Now it wasn't just a safety measure that he kill Jack; it was suicide not to do it. That made it easier, really. Crotch-sniff still didn't understand. He thought it *was* a piss break.

Colt shook his head. Nobody but his mamma was going to miss him, but dead he had to be. If a cop went down, who would *dare* say Colt had set the thing up? Colt took care of his own; even his enemies gave him that. But it wasn't like Crotch-sniff was a real cop. He was just a deal Colt had made a long time ago. And it wasn't like he could change his mind now. Tobias was here; it wouldn't do to leave a witness to this. That wouldn't do at all. Finishing his leak, Colt zipped up his pants, then reached back and checked his grip on the .44.

If you really thought about going after a man, if you thought about stepping in front of him and leveling a gun on him, then you had no reason to believe killing a man was a hard thing to do. The rest, in fact, was pretty easy, especially in Colt's position. What you don't expect when you think about killing a man in this fashion is exactly what Jack would give him, the fight of his life. Jack was quick and he was mean. If you were within reach of him you were ten feet closer than was safe, and if you thought to take aim on him from maybe ten or fifteen feet away, good luck! Jack was wiry and oily, and one bullet wasn't likely going to stop him, even from a .44. There are men like that; they eat pain like candy; they don't fold up in shock. Dying, they'll snatch your throat out of your neck on their fall to hell. Those men you don't cross without serious purpose and due reservations. If Colt pointed a gun at Jack Hazard, all Jack would see would be a weapon he could use. That was a scary thought, something Hazy Mundy hadn't understood.

Of course, all that had been neutralized with the shackles. Colt had only to get Jack out of the car and a few feet off the road. *Do it quick. You don't know what he'll try.* Afterwards, Colt would shoot Crouch in the heart with the shotgun, then unfasten Jack's hands and put his prints on the stock and trigger of the Remington. Crouch wasn't the problem. Jack was the variable. Even chained up, there was just something about him that left Colt uncertain. He would have liked dearly to simply walk over to the car and finish him as he sat, but that wouldn't do. Crouch was going to have to get him out of the car. Their footprints would look like a scuffle. As soon as Jack was in the clear, Colt would step forward and finish it. But not too close. Who the hell knew what he might try?

Beyond the car maybe ten or fifteen feet, Crouch was on the opposite side of the road still taking a whiz. Colt could see his shadow because of the light of the car. He was finishing now and coming back to the car, his limp pronounced. Colt checked the road in either direction, and walked back to the LTD. Crouch was almost to the car when Colt told him to get Jack out. Crouch asked what Colt had said, and Colt told him again as evenly as he could. "Get him out of the car, and be careful about it."

Colt stood now directly behind his car. His right hand hung to his side, his left hand rested lightly on the trunk. Crouch had some trouble after he opened the door. Jack wasn't coming. He had turned himself into a dead weight, figuring Colt wouldn't shoot him in the car. *Got that right, slew boy. Kind of hard to explain a prisoner breaking loose from you and getting hold of the shotgun if he's shot in the back seat!*

Jack rolled back to the other side of the car, putting his chest to the seat, his hands visible and capable of grabbing anything that brushed up against them. Because his hands were completely restricted, Jack couldn't reach out and take Crouch's gun out of his holster, unless Crouch put his gunbelt next to Jack's hands, but that was precisely Colt's worry: Crouch was slow and stupid. And he didn't understand what Jack Hazard was all about.

"Watch him! God-damn it! He'll get your gun if you're not thinking!" Crouch reached in further, taking the chain and pulling Jack toward him, Jack's face dragging across the seat. Once Jack's legs came out of the car, Crouch leaned forward to take Jack by the shoulders, intending to pull him to a standing position. Colt hollered again, but this time it was too late. Jack bucked back, the force of his body knocking into Crouch's chest. Then, like some kind of eel, Jack wiggled off the seat, and set his feet into Crouch's injured right ankle. Toby screeched out something, and staggered back. Jack sprang up and followed him, hopping quickly, so that when Crouch stopped falling away, he stood directly in front of him. Jack stood chest to chest with Crouch. They were about four feet wide of the opened car doors. The light from the interior of the car shone over both of them. Jack had followed Crouch intending to get his revolver, but had apparently stepped out too far. His back squared up to Colt, he wasn't even close to reaching for Crouch's gun. Crouch was in fact still facing Jack and by now was grabbing for his revolver himself.

Colt had peeled his sports jacket back out of the way and got hold of the .44 as soon as Jack had made his move. It hadn't really surprised him, and other than a slight bump of adrenalin, he was perfectly at ease. He stepped out from behind his car, then brought himself forward two strides as Jack and Crouch scuffled like drunken dancers over the

226

gravel. When Colt saw them stop finally and Crouch reaching for his gun, he leveled his big gun on Hazard's back, cocking it as he did, and fired. Squeezing off the round, Colt saw Jack spin and duck, coming around with his back against Crouch's right hip. Jack grabbed at the revolver and missed the butt of it only because Crouch took the slug of Colt's pistol in the middle of his chest and kicked back under the force. Jack was standing by himself now. Crouch lay on his back, dead or damn near it. Colt brought his thumb over the hammer and cocked the gun without hesitating. He fired the second shot immediately after the first. This time Jack fell to the ground beside Crouch. Hit? Not waiting to be sure, Colt brought the hammer back once more, and stepped one stride closer for his last shot. He saw Jack slide his back beside Crouch's gun, then wiggle slightly as he pulled Crouch's revolver from its holster. Colt leveled his sights on Jack. Jack was still beside Crouch, both men's feet pointing toward Colt. The distance was not even the length of the car; they were only some twelve feet apart. Colt fired his third round at Jack's chest as he lay there looking up at him. He was positive this round got him. He saw Jack's legs kick up and his body twist. At the same time, something hit Colt's shoulder, slamming him back off his feet. The shots were fired simultaneously, or nearly so, causing Colt's .44 to obliterate the sound of Crouch's .38. Colt didn't even understand what had hit him. He thought vaguely a Hazard had picked him off from the woods. He understood dully that Jack had twisted and kicked up in the air because he was hit. He could not seem to take his thoughts beyond that during the next second or two, then found himself focusing only when he realized that he was sitting in a puddle beside the rear bumper of his car, his .44 lying out of reach, close to his feet. He looked across at Crouch's body and expected to see Jack too, but Jack was standing beside the body. Colt looked up and saw the back of Jack's orange uniform. Eighteen feet separated them. Jack

227

held Crouch's .38, his hands still bound tightly to his buttocks by the cuffs and chain. Jack's body was hunched up strangely, and his head was twisted about slightly so he could look at his target. Colt realized he was aiming the gun at him. From eighteen feet, Jack's chances of a kill shot were slim, and Colt reached confidently for his own holstered .38. The action was smooth and quick. Colt was a thirty-three-year veteran. He had been in plenty of fights. Three mule kicks later, Colt was knocked back flat into the puddle, dead.

The Last Man Standing

Jack glanced down at Crouch, dropped the .38, then hopped toward Colt. At the foot of the corpse, he threw himself to his knees and rolled up against Colt's body with his hands close to the man's hips and thighs. He reached up to take the right front trouser pocket and ripped the cloth with two mild jerks, convulsing his body in order to leverage the tear. He felt about in the gravel and mud, touching coins and then the ring with the keys. Handcuffs are not made for a man to release himself, and it took nearly a minute of fumbling before the tiny key fitted into place and the cuffs slipped off. As they did, the chain between his ankle cuffs and wrist cuffs went slack. He reached down and unfastened the ankle cuffs next, leaving the padlock on the chain unopened. Dropping the keys in the gravel, Jack stood up, moving his limbs in odd, pleasant jerks.

He studied Colt Fellows closely now. He lay with his right arm crossed over his chest, his hand gripping his holstered .38. His left arm was stretched out toward the tire of the big Ford. Jack's first shot, fired from a prone position, had gone high and struck Colt above the heart by at least seven inches, a bit under the collarbone. Colt's shot had been a little high, too, and had whizzed by Jack's face. Jack had felt the rocks shooting against his skull, even as he had rolled and kicked up to his feet. He had come to his feet with his back to

228

Fellows, so he could take aim before Colt recovered, which had only taken a second or so. The three shots Jack had then fired had all struck. He saw the wounds now. One slug had hit low in the gut, at about the area of the appendix; another had pierced the arm as Fellows had reached across to grab his .38. That shot was dead center; though broken as it was by the arm, it wouldn't have been fatal. The third had pierced through Colt's nose, at eye level, dead center in the face. The puddle of water he lay in was muddy from the blood of this bullet's exit wound. Jack left him as he lay but checked his coat pockets and found a full box of .38 hollowpoints, which he slipped into his uniform's pants pocket. He pulled the other pocket of Fellows's trousers open with a rip. As the big body stirred slightly, a line of blood tipped out of the left eye and ran over his cheek to his ear. Jack found a wad of bills in this pocket, sixteen dollars. He took the money, then reached under and lifted Colt's wallet.

Next Jack slipped into the front seat of Colt's LTD and retrieved the shotgun, racking a round into the chamber. He turned the engine off and pulled the keys out. Against the console, he saw a large police issue flashlight. It was heavy and cast a good beam. He could use it. In the trunk, Jack found a strand of clothesline, some thirty feet in length, a government issue blanket, a fishing pole and tackle box, with hooks, bobs, extra line and weights, a box of shells for the twelve-gauge, a striking flint, matches, flares, and a first aid kit. Packing the blanket, he made a bedroll, then tied it off and slung it over his shoulder. Pocketing the knife, he grabbed up the flashlight and Remington. Without closing the trunk or looking back at Fellows or Crouch, Jack trotted across the road through the rain.

Inside the forest, he snapped on his flashlight and headed northwest, the direction of Lues.

Part Four

Jason Miller

The silver Bronco beat over the washboard roads relentlessly. Leaping and skidding, it threw its headlights first somersaulting over the treetops, then straight down into the puddles. It rocked and shook; even on the flat the Bronco shivered under the stress; the wipers raced to clear off the water; the engine whined. Chief of Homicide, Lieutenant Jason Miller gripped the wheel tightly, his pale blue eyes searing the darkness. When he had time, he remembered to swear.

Coming to Lues Creek Crossing, Miller passed six county issue sedans and pulled up behind the lone ambulance. The lights of the county cars, the ambulance and his own Bronco illuminated the area. Watching two figures carrying a stretcher, Miller jumped out and hurried forward. He knew the men with the body, and he knew the body they carried. The paramedics stopped when they saw Miller. There is little room for the customary pleasantries at such sites, but Miller spoke each man's name and met their gazes respectfully. They answered in the same fashion. Unzipping the body bag, Miller looked down into Colt Fellows's face. The skin was gray and cool, the muscles slack.

"How long?" Miller asked them.

Kent Guthrie shrugged. "They said a couple of hours."

Colt Fellows looked dead for days. "This the only wound?"

Guthrie shook his head. "Four others: abdomen, chest, left shoulder and right forearm."

As Miller considered Colt's face, he tried not to think about facing Betty or looking at Colt's kids. He heard Charli telling him, *What goes around comes around, Jason*. She had been predicting this night for years.

Nodding, he thanked the men, then stepped past them and squarely into Cal Yeager. Standing here in the rain, Yeager looked the part of a lawman in his yellow slicker and plastic-covered, snow-white stetson. Now past sixty, Yeager hadn't changed much in the twenty years Miller had known him. He still had the vibrant white hair and pale skin, a prominent bulb of a red nose, and a quick smile. It was an affable, intelligent face, all the better in photographs. The eyes possessed a wonderful innocence, as if uncorrupted by a lifetime of law enforcement, and every time Jason Miller confronted the face he had to remember the essential lie of it. Yeager's competencies were limited; his corruption was fundamental; his loyalties extended only as far as his fear.

"He went down fighting," Yeager observed.

Jason ignored this and looked past Yeager to what appeared to be the wrap-up. They were supposed to be gone by the time he arrived, Miller realized. "What's going on!" he shouted.

Yeager was soothing. "Now I know you're upset."

"You're damn straight I'm upset." Miller's blue eyes were dancing in anger. "I get a call twenty-two minutes ago, I get my ass out here, and you're done! How long have you been here?"

"Well, now Jason, we can run things in your absence. We took pictures – "

"I don't want pictures. I want to see what happened." He looked past Yeager to where Colt's big Ford was parked. The doors were shut. One of the deputies had started the car.

"Stop that car, now!"

"Calm down, Jason."

Miller pushed the sheriff out of his way and went to the
232

driver side of Colt's car. "Turn it off, Billy," he told the deputy.

The driver considered Miller briefly, then turned the engine off. Miller looked across at four other deputies, all standing beside the front passenger door.

"Where was the body?" he asked them.

One of them answered. "Colt was around here, some-where, the other . . . I don't know." The speaker was looking at the ground around them. Finally, he looked back at Yeager for some help.

"You had *two* shot?" Jason asked in surprise. His report was that Colt had been shot; Jack Hazard had escaped.

Yeager answered, stepping toward his deputies, "Toby Crouch was assisting in the transfer. He's still alive, but not for long. We got him out first thing, for all the good it will do."

"Was he conscious?"

Yeager shook his head.

Miller looked at the collection of deputies, which now included their sheriff. "Gentlemen, do you suppose it would be too much trouble to move out of the area of the shooting until I look around?"

They glanced at one another. They murmured and shrugged and sauntered away. Only Yeager remained. He was playing tough on this one, no doubt thinking to win a little respect with his own men, and maybe to test the waters against the heir apparent to Colt's crown. If for the moment Jason let it go, he had no intention of letting it go for long. Billy Highsmith got out of Colt's LTD. "Is this the way it sat?" Jason asked him.

"Three of the doors were open, and the trunk was up. Oh, yeah, and the lights were on."

"Where were the keys?"

"In the trunk."

"Like it was, please. Exactly!"

Miller walked around to the other side of the car. Nothing

233

was on the ground, of course. He looked at Yeager angrily. "We don't outline bodies anymore?"

"It's raining, Jason. There's no point in us standing out here in the rain when we know Jack Hazard shot them."

"You're going to take me through what you have, Cal. You're going to lay everything where it was, and you're going to put the outlines as close to perfect as you can, because if you don't, I'll come after you with both fists swinging. I think you know I mean it." Jason Miller was a simple and direct man, purely Lues. When he spoke of fists, he meant fists. Cal Yeager had five armed men with him. It was testimony to Jason Miller's broad shoulders that no one thought to take a head count.

Cal nodded at his men, and Miller shouted a warning to keep out of the area as much as possible. It was too late of course. The road was soft. He could have read every step each man had taken if he had made it to the scene before Yeager. Now the tracks were hopelessly obliterated. While the deputies taped in the outlines, Jason went back to his Bronco and pulled out a slicker and a beat stetson. He changed into a pair of old leather boots that he kept in the vehicle and he fished out a fresh notepad. In the back of the Bronco, Jason reached in for his old Coleman lantern.

Yeager came up to him while he was tying his boots, "We've got the body outlines in. We're taking off. We'll fax a preliminary report to your office tomorrow and get the pictures to you in a few days. I guess you can send someone out for Colt's car when you feel like it."

"You're not going anywhere."

"Now just a minute!"

"You botched this scene up, and you're going to stick around and tell me what you found. I want keys, pennies, shell casings, positions of guns, every last blessed detail."

There was no love lost between the two men. Nineteen and a half years ago Cal Yeager had declared his candidacy against Miller's boss in the early spring of an election year.

234

He had gotten on the ballot with a bribe and had smeared Pat Bitts with lies. It was a dirty campaign, at least from Yeager's camp, and it had left its marks on a blameless man. Miller had stayed on as deputy to Yeager for nearly a year after Yeager had unseated Bitts. Two-Bit had insisted. It had been a hard time in Jason Miller's life, the worst of his career, but at least he was pretty sure he had made it plenty tough for Yeager too.

Yeager tried to stare at Jason threateningly, but failed. In the end, he mumbled that he could spare a *few* minutes. Miller took it as complete acquiescence, because it was. He turned his collar up and tightened down the belt of his slicker. "We'll start at the beginning," he answered.

Brick Walls

On Saturday morning, Josie came up toward consciousness through a series of dense, flashing images. She was driving at night, she realized. The streets were wet. Mansions everywhere. She was driving an old boyfriend's Corvette. She had never been allowed to drive the car. The facts were murky even in her conscious memory – it was nearly ten years ago that she had dated Steve Graham – but Josie always believed she had broken up with him because he wouldn't let her drive his car. She was driving it now and doing it without his permission. Annie was running beside the car, and Josie was explaining to her that in heaven there are no monsters, because we all have tenure. Annie ran ahead of her as Josie said this, her head thrown back, her short gray hair suddenly a floating reddish gold mane. "Yes, there are!" The voice was her mother's. The figure was entirely equine now. When the wall in the middle of the road appeared, Josie realized she was trapped. To either side there were thick trees. They came right to the edge of the pavement. *Where are the houses?* She hit the brakes but nothing happened. The Corvette floated silently toward the wall, as if on ice. *Ask me anything*

235

but don't ask to drive my 'vet. Steve wasn't going to like this. The horse that Annie had become leaped over the wall and flew away in the shape of a dove. Josie was inside her VW. The windows were unbroken, but she was sitting on shards of glass. The tires squalled. She was too close. She was going to hit the wall.

At the moment of impact, Josie saw a canyon of blood red stone. She floated through the air, falling. At the same instant, she sat up in her bed. Her mother's voice shouted something, the words lost as the dream ended. Josie's heart was beating violently. She looked at the room and thought herself a stranger here. She knew nothing of this place.

Confessions

"Annie Wilde." Josie had caught her friend at her office, even though it was Saturday.

"Annie, something's wrong."

"To whom am I speaking, please?"

"It's Josie."

"Josie? I didn't recognize you! What is it?"

Josie hesitated, finally summoning her courage. "I wasn't completely honest about what happened when I went to the police. We have to talk."

The professor's voice sounded a bit more distant, as if this really were a stranger who had called her: "You mean you left something out?"

"Why don't I start over."

Annie thought that might be better. Over the next half-hour, Josie explained what had happened and how she had agreed to level charges against Jack, though in fact she had no idea now if Jack was the man harassing her. She spent a lot of time talking about Jack, especially her feeling that he hadn't meant her any harm. She had spoken to him for only a minute, she said. She hadn't been particularly impressed with the man, and when he had thought she was going to

236

be dancing for Virgil, she had seen a frightening rage in his eyes. " . . . But that's the thing, Annie. He thought Virgil had hired his little girl to dance, and he was going to kill him! I don't think it was an act. I mean he was happy to see me, and when he found out I was teaching at the college – he loved it! He *really* wanted to talk, and then I went to the police and got him arrested. Annie, I betrayed him, and there's nothing I can do to make up for it!"

"It could be a con, Josie. If I were you, I wouldn't try to do anything just yet. Your emotions are betraying you. You can't trust yourself right now."

That could be, she admitted, but there had been something about the man when she had seen him that had brought back her mother's face for her. And there was laughter. *Two* memories and with each the sound of laughter. *The handsomest man in the world!* She wasn't saying he hadn't killed her mother or the black man Colt Fellows had mentioned or his uncle, even. " . . . he's *dangerous*, Annie, don't get me wrong. It's just that I don't think he knew me. He thought I was doing an audition, and that's what he saw, the new girl. And when he was sure it was me, he changed! I don't think the guy is an actor. I think he was excited at seeing me, and I don't think he had any idea I was in the area until I showed up in front of his face."

There was also the matter of the keys for Josie's office and the even stickier problem of Jack's walking into her department office and dropping off an envelope with a university label on it during office hours – without being noticed.

"Annie, around here, slews get noticed, and Jack's definitely a slew. I'm just having trouble believing this guy got office materials, then entered a busy office and left a sympathy card in the faculty boxes."

"He could have friends, Josie, someone to loan him a master key, maybe a friend of a friend to drop the note off, maybe a relative going to school at Lues. Don't keep jumping to conclusions. You're just compounding your problems."

"So what about the folder? Was that just a lucky guess, or did he know I was going to handle *that* folder? I don't think the guy knows what a desk looks like, let alone how to figure out my organization."

"What are you saying, Josie?"

"I'm saying I have a lot of questions about Jack, and suddenly I can't talk to the police. I left a half-dozen messages yesterday – "

"Fellows thought you were going to be screaming about the newspaper report he filed. How was he supposed to know you don't bother reading the local news?"

"Maybe," Josie answered. That made a lot of sense, but still, something about the whole thing bothered her. The thing was, she told Annie, she had gotten the feeling that they were only too happy to have an excuse to arrest Jack. "The first time I mentioned Jack's name to Officer Crouch, I saw something, Annie. He knew the name; I mean it meant something to him."

"Josie, I've said it all along. You don't have enough information."

"I don't know where to start, Annie! I mean this isn't exactly my field. There aren't any good bibliographies, for God's sake!" An academic's joke, and getting no laughs.

"Josie, I was in Women's Studies before there was Women's Studies. If you can't find a good bibliography, kiddo, you make your own. You have some names. That's where you start. Find this Melody Mason and talk to that Sheriff Bitts. Take him a bottle of rye and talk old times in Lues. Read what you can about Jack's other killings. You don't know the truth yet, but it's always there if we're smart enough to coax it out of hiding."

"I guess you're right . . ."

"I know I'm right! You went to Lues to find Josie Fortune – both of them! And ever since you arrived, you've been finding one excuse after another. Kiddo, this is just three-dimensional research. Same steps, same processes."

238

"I guess I've just been afraid of what I was going to find."

"If I were you, Josie, I'd be afraid of what I hadn't found."

Library Hours

"Where is the place of monsters, Annie?" Josie had asked the old professor once. They had been deep in their cups, deep into metaphysics too.

Annie had answered in that strange whisper of hers, strange at least when she was fabulously drunk, a voice from another world, "There are no roads to that place, Josie."

The truth of that day had finally hit. Josie needed to go to the place with no roads. She needed finally to look truth in the eye without blinking or apology or embarrassment. She needed to pretend her life was no different from the literary puzzles she had learned to solve. She would start over. She would start this time with hypotheses, not conclusions. Nothing was an absolute at this point. Everything needed the test of reason, and if a thing were possible she would face it.

She knew she had let Colt Fellows convict Jack for her. She had had no evidence, only faith in a faithless man, and every instinct had been screaming at her to wait, to reflect, to get away from Colt Fellows before she signed anything. She had failed to listen to her own instincts. That would not happen again. If she was to live through this, she had to give up the panic but still hear the inner voice. She had to make this world – history itself – her own private domain and let no one master her. Mastery was information, and when she wanted, no one could amass more information faster. No one. It was her genius, and right now she needed all the genius she possessed. She needed to be conversant with more than a few details here. She needed everything, because eventually everything participates. As Annie had quipped once, "History is rarely finished with us."

Welcome home, Josie.

It *was* home, and she had been a fool to think only her parents and Annie and Dan Scholari knew that Lues was home. A lot of people had known her mother, and anyone knowing her mother could also have known her mother's child. Assumptions were killing her; fear was robbing her of her best weapon.

Oops! was a hell of an epitaph.

She smiled bitterly at the thought. Miss Darling blushed at scandal and blanched at threats. Real life was a little too much for her, and if she didn't change fast she wasn't going to chase the nightmare; she wasn't even going to be able to outrun it. A long time ago there had been a little girl, and when she thought she was going to be killed, she had kicked and screamed, then, caught, she had eyed the man's shotgun. She had known how to use it; she had meant to take it if she had the chance. The thing Josie hadn't understood until now was that the little girl in the grip of the state trooper was not Josie Darling. She had been Josie Fortune. And there *was* a difference. Josie Fortune had been willing to fight.

The Text of Nightmare

Josie took a cab out to the edge of town and rented a black Mustang. Afterwards, she purchased a guest parking tag at the visitors' center, then went to Worley Hall. Inside, Josie moved under the pictures of the honored professors without a thought about them, except perhaps to wonder if any of them might be suspects. She was not to be distracted nor discouraged this time; her very life hung in the balance. She went next to the first floor, the undergraduate area. She needed some telephone numbers. One of these was going to be especially difficult to find, but it was manageable. Afterwards, she scoured the library for sources of Lues's history. There were several books about the area, but the most comprehensive was *The Lues Scrapbook: A Pictorial*

History. There was plenty here to interest her. In the 1950s, for instance, there was the story of a domestic murder. Jack Hazard was pictured, as was his victim. Jack had oily waves of dark hair and a track of freckles over his nose. He had that glum look of schoolboys photographed in black and white. He was nine or ten in the photograph and really, genuinely cute – for a slew. The man he shot was pictured too. Vern Shake, forty-nine, had a violent aspect; if Josie read the eyes correctly he was an alcoholic. She took an hour and found out more about him in the *Rapids*, scanning the arrest reports over a five-year period. His picture hadn't lied. Shake was a man with several vacations spent in the sheriff's jail. He was a man who beat women. Had he beaten children too? Maybe molested them? The pages were silent on that question. They always were in those days. Jack's picture showed a proud boy, but Josie knew that pride is sometimes the biggest lie of all.

Later Josie found warm praise for Sheriff Pat Bitts. He was a tall, beautiful man in those days, and his life read like a hero's saga. Fires, floods, brawls, gunfights, armed robbers, kidnappers, even the occasional speech with a good punchline or two: Two-Bit, as everyone called him, was the man for all seasons. What had Colt Fellows said? *He knew how to get elected; he just didn't know law enforcement.* Interesting.

Josie found her mother's picture in the *Lues State University Yearbook*, and immediately felt a jolt of recognition: it was nearly her own face that she looked at. Just as Jack had said. The hair was longer and thicker than her own. The features were finer, the nose straight, but the essential character, the delicate shape of her forehead and eyes lived in Josie. Even the qualities Josie disliked in herself were there: the bushy eyebrows and round lips, almost like a child's. She had made the dean's list. The dean's list! Virgil had said she wanted to go to school, and so she had – with a passion.

When the lights flickered, Josie looked up and realized the library was closing. Inside the rest-room stalls, she shifted her .357 to the waistband at the back of her jeans, then went out the building through the bag check. There was a faint drizzle, and the lot was busy for a late Saturday afternoon. Josie stayed alert. She could run if she had to; or she could fight. More and more, she felt ready for a fight.

That evening after dinner, Josie checked her notes and dialed a Mrs Grimes, of rural Belleville.

"Hello?" The voice was that of a modestly educated middle-aged, Midwestern white woman.

"I'm trying to reach Melody Grimes."

"This is her." The woman was suspicious, though her tone expressed an unconscious vulnerability. Josie probably sounded like a salesperson; before she said no, she wanted to know what Josie was selling.

"Mrs Grimes, is your maiden name Mason?"

"Who is this?" Real wariness now, as well as panting curiosity.

"My name is Josie Darling; I'm a professor at Lues State."

"Oh, God! You don't want to take my diploma back, do you?"

Josie smiled at the receiver. Melody Grimes was serious.

"I'm doing some research on my mother's death. Her name was Josie Fortune. The police here gave me your name. They said you were the first to find her body."

There was a heavy silence. Josie was sure Melody Grimes was going to hang up. Finally, reluctantly the voice answered, "That was a long time ago."

"Twenty years this April."

"That was your mom?"

"I'd like to talk to you about it. Is there any way you could see me if I came up to Belleville tomorrow afternoon?"

"I don't know what you think I could tell you."

"Anything you remember."

"You're in Lues? That's a long trip. I think you'd just be wasting your time."

"My mother died when I was seven. I don't remember

242

anything about it. I can't even remember much about her. Before I came to Lues this fall, I couldn't remember anything at all. I guess what I'm trying to say is I'm grabbing at straws, and I need your help."

A slight pause. Was she wondering how to get rid of this pest or clearing her schedule? "Sure," Melody answered. "My husband's just watching football tomorrow afternoon. It'll be fun. What do you drink?"

Melody Grimes

Melody Grimes was a heavy-set woman with a reckless teenager's giggle. Josie liked her immediately. Her voice had a certain lilt to it, an engaging inclusiveness about it. Melody might have known that no one ever had a university diploma jerked, but she still believed that kind of thing could happen to her. In fact, it was the sort of thing that could only happen to her.

Josie made one quick assumption about Melody Grimes: she had survived the incident in Lues Creek Canyon without any of it ever affecting her. Her shallowness was rock hard and genial; nothing much got through and so life had never really wrecked her. Neither had it been sweet or thrilling or especially dramatic. Melody saw herself as someone locked inside a situation comedy, maybe as the likeable neighbor to the star. The niche she had carved for herself was a safe place to hide, as long as she kept laughing. Melody's discomfort with Josie, if she had any, was that she wasn't tragic enough about finding a body twenty years ago. It embarrassed her slightly that she had survived it without a legion of nightmares trailing her.

Mr Grimes didn't get off the couch when Josie entered the house. He was a blubbery white man, not even energized enough to bother drinking beer on a Sunday afternoon. When Melody pointed at him, saying "That's my husband, not a pillow," he studied Josie with brief but pointed curiosity, then turned back to the football game. Melody noticed the effect Josie had on him, and made a joke out of it. "It's a real person, honey. See, there's no box around her head, that's how you can tell." She seemed to enjoy her own joke without the bile that usually goes with such marital jousting. As they walked to the kitchen, Melody confided to Josie, "We had a suicide watch for him when the baseball players went on strike."

The place was rundown and shabby, and no apologies for it. The Sunday dinner dishes were still out and crusted. The kitchen table, where they had eaten, was cleared but not cleaned. A couple of kids, one boy, one girl, moved about occasionally but there were no introductions. Melody handed Josie a can of Miller Lite, and they sat across from each other at the kitchen table. In the distance the commentators of the football game were promising a great second half.

"I got your name almost by chance," Josie confessed. "The police didn't show me their file on the case, but they happened to mention that there had been a witness, and they gave me your name when I asked. They said you were with some other kids, but I didn't get the names."

Melody answered with the names of the others. She had forgotten one of the names of the boys; she remembered Bob Tanner, Susie Hill and Cat Sommerville. Smiling, embarrassed, she looked at Josie for a long minute, then explained. "This is tough. I mean she was your mom. I don't feel comfortable talking about it. If someone told me about my mom . . . you know, it would freak me out!"

"I've had twenty years to get used to the idea that someone killed my mother. But you're right. It still freaks me out."

Hearing this, Melody seemed to relax suddenly. She was a girl again, the girl she had been. "We didn't know her. We just found her." She shrugged. "I feel bad about your driving up here just for that. But it's all I know."

"Tell me about the day, why you were out, anything you remember."

Melody confessed that it was all a complete blank, then began telling Josie a series of details with incredible precision. There was no sense of a moving narrative, but there were random images of the day and the forest, the beer they drank, the cigarettes they smoked, even the clothing they wore. Melody's was a mind without order, but it was a mind of brilliant capacity. Josie played like Henry Valentine, and let her go, bumping and urging when necessary, simply watching and listening otherwise. She didn't even take notes.

It was her first time in the woods, Melody said. They were all drunk, " . . . like *that* was something new." She laughed at herself, and launched parenthetically into a description of her life as a debauched college student. It was a long side-trip, but Josie listened and smiled and even probed a little, because she liked the woman and because she saw that memory builds from context, that the more Melody talked, the more she remembered. Melody went back to the canyon now. She told about almost going off the ledge, a rotted board breaking, Bob Tanner pushing her out over the edge as a joke, then losing control of her. That kind of thing just always seemed to happen to Melody, she said. She started to tell about a couple of things more recently to make her point, and Josie nudged her back to the canyon. Melody said when she was safe, she thought she was going to be sick. "That was when I saw her."

About the body, Melody said she remembered nothing. This time it was the truth. She remembered the canyon, the huge boulders, and the high waters; she knew they had telephoned someone afterwards; the rest was gone.

"Listen," she said. "I'm worthless. I don't remember anything." Her eyes grew distant. "I don't know. I know I should, but I don't remember a thing." It bothered her that she couldn't recall the body. Josie had heard the description from Fellows and Crouch. She thought she understood why Melody blanked it out. Melody seemed to give up on her memory, then to laugh at herself in the same gesture. "Must

245

be all the liquor and dope I did back then; *fried* those brain cells! I was always getting trashed. I probably had sex with forty guys in college; I mean who had time to count, right? I couldn't name three of them now. Well, just three . . . but first names only." She looked toward the living room, the direction of her husband. "I forgot his name about twelve years ago and he won't tell me what it is . . . *Hey Honey, you in front of the TV! What's your name?*" There was no answer. She shrugged prettily. "He won't tell me." She giggled, then caught herself and grew solemn. "I wish I could help. We saw her. We called someone. Then we all ran away." Melody considered for a moment, trying once more to remember, then lit a cigarette, Merits, these days, Lucky Strikes in the bad old days. "I wish I could tell you more."

"How did they find you if you ran away?" Josie asked her. Melody frowned, confused. "The police?" Josie asked. "If you ran away, how did they know you had been there?"

"I don't know. Just my luck, I guess. The sheriff came to our sorority house; scared me to death! God! I thought I was going to jail!"

"Why? Because you left?"

"Yeah. He took us into this room and talked to each of us for like two hours apiece. 'Where were you?', 'Why didn't you stick around?', 'Did you kill her?' It was terrible. He was so mean."

"Did he really think you were involved?"

"I don't know. I never understood what it was all about."

Josie wrote a quick note to herself. That had the effect of closing down Melody's concentration, so she went ahead and jotted down several other curiosities. As she finished, Melody got them both another beer.

"Have you been there?" Melody asked her. "Into the canyon?"

Josie shook her head, smiling. She knew she should, but she kept imagining it was there she would die. "The whole thing is a lot tougher than I thought it would be when I started. I've been afraid to go look." Josie gave an amiable shrug, Melody Grimes style. "Not just afraid, but maybe superstitious."

Melody's eyes got large. "Like her ghost?"

"Like it happened to me or it could if I get too close." The truth of her own statement sent a chill into Josie.

"It was your dad who killed her?" Melody was excited. She hadn't thought about this afternoon for years, and the idea of ghosts was positively palpitating.

"My stepfather."

"We thought there was going to be a big trial, but there wasn't. I don't know what happened."

"He confessed to a lesser charge. Accidental homicide, I think it was. That's what the newspaper called it."

"Why did he do it?"

"He says now that he didn't."

"Do you believe him?" Melody was skeptical but kind. She would take what Josie offered at face value. She took all of life at face value.

"I talked with a couple of the cops who were involved. I got a bad feeling that he might have been framed, but I don't know. After all this time, how can anyone know for sure?" This was pure misdirection. Josie believed *she* could know. She wanted to believe it, anyway. Other than running away, it was her only chance.

Josie considered Melody with purpose. "They told me you were one of the witnesses who saw him from inside the canyon."

"Your stepdad? News to me."

Josie's brow knitted furiously. "You didn't pick him out of a line-up?"

"Oh! Right! I saw someone at the falls. I was the only one that did. I thought maybe he was the killer, but I didn't get a good look at him. Some cop brought me some pictures and I couldn't identify anyone, and that was it."

"I just talked with the homicide detective who ran the

247

investigation. He said you identified Jack Hazard in a line-up as the man you saw at the falls."

"I was in the hospital, okay?"

Josie recoiled in confusion. "The hospital?"

"Poison sumac all over my legs and ... up inside. I squatted in it to pee, and oh, *mamma*! Talk about an itch needing to be scratched, let me tell you! I thought I was going to die! I never itched like that in my whole life. It started that evening. It was burning and itching, and I didn't say anything because, you know, I thought I had the clap, and then the sheriff came by, and I was wiggling and almost crying. Anyway, about midnight I finally got a good look at it, and then I showed it to Susie. She thought it was some kind of Asia clap, and man! I was scared to death. Susie took me to the university hospital after that sheriff left. I was there three or four days. Something like that. Oh! it was bad. Anyway, this cop shows up in my room; he's got a handful of pictures. He shows them to me and I say I can't recognize any of them. I think he pointed at one of them and said, 'Could this be him?' and I probably said yes, but I don't remember. I mean I always agree with people. It's easier, you know? But I wasn't certain, and I told him that. I watch these movies, and these witnesses are always saying, 'I'll never forget his face.' Not me, man! My one chance to make a difference in the world, and I blow it. The guy was a slew. That's all I know." She raised her eyebrows ironically. "Waste of time, right? You drove up here for nothing."

"How do you know he was a local?"

Melody shrugged affably, "He looked like a slew. He dressed like one. Look, it's been a long time. The cop probably just doesn't remember it any better than I do." Melody was the kind of person who didn't put blame on other people. She was too easy, too ready to take blame.

"Do you know where any of the others are, the people you were with? I need to talk to all of them."

"Bob was from around there, one of those little towns.

248

Susie was from upstate, Vandalia, I think or Effingham or . . . I don't know. I'd love to see her again. God! We were best friends, and now nothing. I should have gone to the ten-year reunion, but I didn't. I don't even know if she ever got married."

"I've got a best friend from high school like that," Josie admitted. I don't know where she is or what's she's doing. I heard she got married, but I don't know his name or if they stayed in the area."

Agreeing, sad but realistic, "It's a bummer. I've been here, in Belleville, ten years with − " Melody pointed toward the television " − what's-his-name. We have like zero friends. When I was at Lues State I knew everyone." She giggled. "If there was a party, I was there!" This was especially funny, and Melody's eyes danced. She missed those times; even at almost forty she missed them.

"I'm going to find the rest of the people who were there," Josie offered. "I'll get you the information, if you want."

"If you can get Susie's number, that would be great. The little whore still owes me a trip to Florida." Josie asked her what she meant. "When we graduated we were going to go to Florida. We were all set, then one of us didn't get the money or the folks said no way, I don't remember what it was. We were broken up about it, and you know, we went home and that was it. I haven't seen her since."

The boy came into the kitchen. Melody told him to get a shirt on. "It's cold!" she told him. He shrugged, got a can of pop, and left. "Where are your shoes?" she called to him as he left. Nothing.

"Do you have kids?" she asked.

Josie shook her head.

Melody rolled her eyes, "Life's great blessing."

"Did the others graduate?" Josie had found Melody through the alumni association records. Graduation was the way one got on that list.

"Susie and I graduated. Bob stuck around, but I don't

249

know if he ever graduated. The other guy . . ." she shrugged. "He saved my life, right? I can't remember his name. Figure! Oh, and Cat. She dropped out. No. Well, she got pregnant. I mean it's great! She's this virgin till I die, loosen up, bitch, and have some fun, Young Christian League, or whatever, finds this guy, I guess it must have been right after, we found . . . you know . . . and I mean spread them legs right now and give me a baby, *Daddy*!"

Melody's daughter walked into the kitchen on this. She looked to be thirteen, cute and cherubic like her mom and maybe, Josie decided, a girl with a few secrets. "Who spread her legs?"

"Nobody. Go to your room."

"I want to know who you're talking about!"

"A girl I knew in college."

"God! I thought you were talking about someone in *this* century!" She spun on her naked heel and walked away.

"Get some shoes on! It's cold out!"

"You didn't know the guy?" Josie asked.

Melody's face screwed up thoughtfully. "He wasn't a frat. All the frats had already tried. Not so much as a handjob, that's what I heard. Susie and I hated her. Called her everything in the book — whore, slut, you know, because she wouldn't and we always got drunk and did. We said it behind her back, but Cat always heard us. She acted like she didn't, but she did, and she would just smile at us. God I hated her, but she was a boy-magnet, let me tell you! I got the best sex hanging around that bitch. Anyway, he must have been something!" Melody raised her eyebrows expressively: she knew about *something*.

Josie took the offer of a third beer, and heard about the mating habits of another generation. She got nothing now about her mother's murder, but that didn't bother her. She had more than she had anticipated. She had caught Colt Fellows in a lie — a critical one.

Josie stayed simply because she liked the woman and

because she had seen her circle and return, and each time she went back into that canyon, mentally, there was something else. Josie wasn't leaving until they were both exhausted. That seemed to happen just as the football game ended. The husband walked in and got a sandwich. He looked at Josie as he leaned against a kitchen counter and ate. It was a kind of open, raw lust, but he knew better than to think she might see anything in him. Josie might as well have been a beer-commercial babe. He was barefoot like the kids. Melody said something about this, and Josie realized they were done, even a little drunk.

"I better go," she said. "It was close to four hours getting here."

"Good luck," Melody told her at the car. "And I hope you remember . . . you know, what you want to."

Josie thought about the words, *remember . . . what you want to*. That was the memory of Melody Grimes. Josie wanted to remember the rest, the things that weren't so pleasant. According to Annie Wilde, that was the secret to revising the soul.

A Late-Night Interview

That evening a uniformed policeman for the city of Lues stood framed in Josie's peep-hole. Detective Lieutenant Jason Miller of Homicide would like to see her at the Civic Center, he told her. The officer had orders to drive Josie there.

Jason Miller met Josie in a smaller office than Colt Fellows's. The place was all business: folders stacked along one shelf, two file cabinets, twenty-some years of FBI journals, a couple of shelves of true-crime paperbacks, a large chalkboard, a wall full of meritorious service awards, and a coffee pot that was working overtime. Miller was a short, broad man with plenty of gray in his hair and the look of being all cop – one of Colt's own, she decided. He wore a sports jacket and a mismatched tie. His eyes were tired, and she guessed he had been living on short rations of sleep for a day or two. Without so much as an introduction, the man studied her with undisguised suspicion. Josie found herself unable to hold the man's gaze, and looked back at the officer who had brought her there without bothering to answer her questions or explain himself in any way.

"Do you know why I asked you to come in here, Miss Darling?"

Josie focused on Detective Miller again. "I assume it has something to do with the complaint I filed last week."

The detective laughed. It was almost pleasant sounding. "I think you can do better than that."

"I don't understand." Josie was nervous suddenly. There was something in the man's look, the heavy exhaustion in his eyes, which bothered her.

"You mean to say you haven't heard about Jack Hazard's escape?"

Josie felt the blood drain from her face.

Before she could do more than swear a low, frightened oath, Miller explained himself. "Jack was being transferred to the county jail late Friday. Somehow he got free. In the process he killed two of our officers: Captain Colton Fellows and patrolman Toby Crouch."

"Oh, my God." Josie's mind reeled in confusion.

"Since you were the one who made the charges against Jack, I thought we had better talk." He studied her briefly, a skeptical look crossing his face. "You really hadn't heard?"

"No." She thought to compose herself. "I went upstate today. I worked in the library and at home yesterday." Her brain buzzed wildly. *Colt Fellows and Toby Crouch dead?* "How did it happen, exactly?" She meant, how was such a thing possible.

"I don't know what happened, exactly. That's what my investigation is all about."

There was a cold reckoning in the man's pale blue eyes, and Josie looked away again.

"You didn't pick up a newspaper or turn on the TV?" Miller acted as if missing the news for a day or two was incredible.

"I told you I hadn't heard. I've had other things on my mind."

"I want to know how serious Jack's assault on you was, Miss Darling."

Still not looking at him, Josie answered, "The assault charge was Captain Fellows's idea. Colt said it was the only way to get Jack into custody. He said technically what Jack did was an assault and that since there were witnesses to it, it was the best way to get Jack arrested."

"I'm not following you here. Why did you want Jack arrested?"

Josie finally met the man's gaze. "I've had a number of problems since I arrived in Lues: a couple of harassing phone calls, a break-in at my home, another at my office. Whoever's doing it has been leaving threatening messages."

"And you thought Jack was doing it?" There was skepticism in the man's voice but a certain compassion as well.

"When I came here last week, I reported my car vandalized and showed Officer Crouch the note I'd found inside the car. You should have it. It's the only evidence I gave him."

"All I have is a formal charge of assault and your fingerprints."

"You lost the sheet I brought in?" Josie looked at the man's cluttered desk with irritation.

"I didn't lose it; I never had it." A quick smile. Jason Miller wasn't a man to enjoy being accused of things, and underneath all that official business was a boy that could raise some hell if he got pushed.

Josie let it go. She didn't need another lunatic taking aim on her. Her dance card was full.

"The note said, 'Still thinking of you, whore.' Whore was spelled h-o-r. When he saw it, Officer Crouch called in

253

Captain Fellows. Crouch asked if the spelling reminded him of anyone, and Captain Fellows said 'Jack Hazard.' "

"And that was enough to convince you to charge Jack with assault?" This with undisguised contempt.

Josie described Colt Fellows's reasoning, the evidence he had given her, even the witnesses who had identified Jack Hazard at the site of the murder. "It made a lot of sense at the time. He said he could keep Jack away from me at least until December. I'm planning on resigning and leaving the area at the end of the semester, so when he said that, I jumped at the chance."

"How was he going to keep Jack in jail that long?" A sly, curious smile from Miller.

"Set the bail high, make sure the judge and prosecutor knew what Jack had been doing. He said he just wanted to protect me."

"I get the picture."

Josie read a faint irritation in the man's look. She thought it might be for Colt Fellows as much as for herself.

"When I got back to school and found two more messages," she said, "I wasn't so sure Jack was behind any of it. I mean I just didn't know."

"Which is why you called Colt several times on Friday?"

Josie nodded and reached down toward her briefcase. She pulled the envelope with the sympathy card and the computer-generated class roster out and tried to hand them to the detective.

Miller asked her to pull the card out of the envelope for him. He didn't want to touch the evidence. He studied the material earnestly. He was a quiet, thoughtful man, Josie decided, not so eager to help or take sides. For some reason, the man's neutrality appealed to her. In the end, Colt Fellows's sympathy had been self-serving.

Miller pointed at the latest messages: "You found these after Jack was arrested?"

"I found it the same day I filed charges, before the arrest.

254

The handwritten note was inside my office. That bothered me. I keep the office locked. Always."

"You don't think Jack could get a key?"

"I suppose he could, but the sympathy card was left in the main office the morning I was here filing charges."

"You're sure of that?"

"I had some dated material under it. Whoever dropped it off did it after eight and before ten – in full view of the office personnel. A lot of people could do that, but I couldn't quite imagine Jack Hazard blending into the scene. The student helper faces the faculty mailboxes; she knows all the faculty, and we don't have too many students in their fifties."

"Maybe he put it in campus mail." Miller was quick and bright, Josie decided.

She pointed at the envelope, shaking her head. "There's no department listed here, and no one knows me as Josie Fortune. The last time I used that name, I was seven years old."

Miller considered this for nearly a minute before he asked, "So you don't think Jack walked on campus, unlocked your office and planted this message, then went to your department office and dropped off this envelope?"

"Maybe he could have, but I had a problem with it, and I thought Colt might, too. For some reason he wouldn't return my calls."

Seeming to read her dislike of Fellows, Miller answered, "I'll make sure what you've told me goes into my report. It's unusual, but it's not incredible, not given Colt's track record. Colt was the kind of cop who broke rules, sometimes to help people, sometimes just to get a job done."

"I know he lied about one thing."

Miller said he was listening.

"He said Melody Mason saw Jack Hazard in Lues Creek Canyon. I talked to her, and she said she didn't identify anyone."

Miller asked about Melody, and Josie told him what she

knew. He looked up after scribbling the information on a scrap of paper. "If she was really a witness, she signed off on the identification. The prosecutor won't consider any statement solid until he has an affidavit."

"I think she'd sign anything she was told to sign."

"A lot of people do," Miller answered.

"I'd like see the file on my mother's murder, if it's possible. I want to know exactly what went on."

"I can't help you."

"If I don't get some cooperation, I'll be back with more lawyers screaming than you've ever dreamed of!"

"Great. Send all you want, but it's a waste of time; I can't give you what I can't find." Miller smiled sincerely. "I went to look for it yesterday and it was missing. I called the sheriff's office. They don't have their file on the murder either. Ditto with the prosecutor's office. The case might as well have never existed."

"Officer Crouch checked it just last week. I wanted the name of this woman, and he got it from the files."

"I can't help you."

"Why do you think it's gone? Do you think it was destroyed?"

"I don't know the answer, Miss Darling."

"You don't seem very upset about this."

"It's gone. There's nothing I can do about it. I look at that as possibly significant, possibly a coincidence."

"You're not serious! This is unbelievable!"

"It's a twenty-year-old case. Trust me, it's believable."

"I need the information in that file. I want to know if Jack Hazard was set up or if he was the one who killed my mother."

"If you think you can sleuth this thing, I'm afraid you're in over your head."

"Believe me, mister, I'd rather do anything than worry about this. I don't like cops, I don't like guns, and I hate violence. All I'm trying to do here is survive, and right now

256

surviving means getting information. I need to find out what *really* happened to my mother. Somewhere there's a report, and I think you know where it is."

"Did you think about leaving town?"

"What would you do, Lieutenant? I mean if someone was doing this to you?"

Miller smiled. "I guess I'd get pretty mad."

"Not scared?"

"Maybe a little scared."

"And then what?"

Miller seemed to make a decision, his expression softening. "I can't put my hands on the file any more than you can, but for what good it will do you, I know a man you ought to talk to."

"Pat Bitts?"

Mr Scott

Don Scott leaned back in a leather chair, facing Detective Lieutenant Jason Miller as he finished his presentation. It was early Monday, just past eight. The funeral services for Toby Crouch and Colt Fellows were to take place within the hour, and this had been the best time to get Miller's initial report on the double homicide. Miller's version of the shooting was an impressive piece of police work, as usual. Cal Yeager's theories, that the Hazards had sprung Jack during the transfer, was already grist for the newspapers but entirely without evidentiary foundation. Yeager's people had turned up no unexplained footprints in the woods, no bullets or shell casings that were unaccounted for: no signs or evidence of any kind, in fact. Besides Hazard's departing trail, there had been only two other trails into the woods at the scene of the shooting. Both led away and returned to Colt's Ford LTD. Yeager wanted him to believe that Fellows had been stopped by some kind of roadblock, and that once Jack had been released, he had summarily executed Crouch and

Fellows with Crouch's revolver. It was the way of cold-blooded killers like Hazard, Yeager argued; but forensic evidence had already showed the theory's substantial flaws.

Miller held rather a more ingenious opinion about the events but one which accorded perfectly with the facts. It was the sort of narrative of events which could get a man convicted, even executed, and Lues County's long-time prosecutor liked that about the theory.

"Let me get it straight," Scott said. "Fellows stops the car, and he and Crouch walk to the woods. Rest stop." Miller nodded. "They come back, and there's some kind of scuffle at the back passenger door; you're saying they pulled Jack out?"

"Crouch pulled him out. The prints are deep and torn up right there. I've got Colt's footprints from the woods to the back of the car, his fingerprints on the lid of the trunk. So I know where he was. There was a good deal of damage done to the footprints where Jack and Crouch were, but it's still obvious there was a struggle. I found some sharp heel indentations, some clear signs of a foot turning, and I got good plasters of them downstairs. They stumbled back together about eight feet from the body of the car, and there we find another grouping of deep marks. Best estimate, Crouch is standing up pretty square, and Hazard's spinning to get his hands on Crouch's gun. I've got one plaster print that shows a perfect rotation of Jack's shoe. The thing's jail-issue, so there's no doubt it's Jack's heel print."

"It's at that point Colt Fellows puts a .44 slug in Crouch's chest?"

Miller nodded, "Aiming at Jack, he hits Officer Crouch. Jack and Crouch were probably facing each other. Jack's hands were still behind his back, so he needed to spin around to get to Crouch's revolver."

"Now we lose the next two slugs, but you're saying Colt gets two more shots off before Jack plugs him just below the collarbone with Crouch's .38."

258

Miller nodded. "There were a couple of interesting indentations beside Crouch's body. Everything indicates Jack fires one shot from the ground and then gets to his feet before the next three. And I mean that boy can move, Don! I saw him fight the other day. He's *something*. Put you or me in shackles like he was wearing, and we'd still be there. Figure with Jack, about a millisecond."

Scott nodded. He'd been a Lues County resident all his life. There were always plenty of stories about Jack Hazard's quickness. Some of them were even true.

"Why do you think Jack's still in shackles? If he needs a rest stop, they're going to take the shackles off."

"I don't believe he wanted to get out of the car."

"That's not evidence, Jason."

"Okay, I've got marks next to Colt's body. Jack's lying down in the gravel next to the man."

"Meaning?"

"Either he's kissing Colt's corpse, or he's trying to get a grip on Colt's pants pocket. The only explanation is he's still in the chains and needs the key to get free."

Scott accepted this. "Then he gets free and goes to the front seat, gets the car keys, finds a shotgun, goes to the trunk, gets shells, some fishing gear, the flashlight, and heads off in the direction of Lues."

"That's about it," Miller nodded.

"No blood?"

"I don't think Colt got him, no. The way he moved around the car, we'd have found his blood somewhere if he'd been hit with a .44."

Scott nodded. "It sounds perfect. You've done a great job – especially given the sheriff's bunging up the scene."

"A great job but you're not buying the theory?"

"I buy the evidence. I don't like the theory."

"Colt meant to execute him, Don."

"Jason, you have hard evidence for everything you say, except that. We have plaster prints, a detailed picture of the

259

whole scene, and a convincing sequence of action: all of it difficult if not impossible to question. It's just great police work. Then you come in with the part about Colt, and I'm not buying it."

"What's wrong with it?"

"Nothing you've given me puts Colt in the role of executioner. And frankly, I don't want to believe it. It's not good for the department or for that matter anyone in city government."

"I don't care about *good*. I have evidence."

"You have speculations. I don't want to bring the specter of scandal over the department and this office on the basis of speculation. Speculations ruin careers, and nothing brings back a good name once it's lost."

"The arrest is suspect."

"I asked for the arrest myself, Jason. A professor at the university said Jack assaulted her at his brother's bar. Jack had motive, and there were witnesses who saw it. Besides that, Colt informed me there were a number of threats preceding the assault. I wasn't about to have another dead woman show up in Lues County. And my God, we've had our share!"

"She tells me Colt pushed her for the charges. She isn't at all sure now that Jack's behind the threats."

"Right. She's also not sure that Jack killed his ex-wife twenty years ago. The woman's scared. She's got a new theory every day. Who wouldn't? She's jumping at shadows. I feel sorry for her, but that doesn't mean I'm ready to believe every theory she trots out for us! If the woman's a lousy witness last week, she's lousy this week too."

"She has more evidence. She can place her man on the university between eight and ten on the day she made her charges against Jack. Now if Jack has an alibi for that time – "

"Good Christ, Jason! I understand she's a beautiful woman, but give me a break."

"What are you saying?"

Scott studied his man. "I'm saying nothing you've told

me goes to proving that Colt had the intention of executing Jack Hazard."

"The only thing that's going to push Jack to try to go for a gun the way he was chained up is pure necessity. It's an assault charge, Don! What the hell is he looking at? A couple of weeks in jail? He's not going to kill two cops to try to get out of that. The guy's not afraid of a little jail time. He's not going to panic."

"Now you're telling me Jack Hazard is a reasonable man. I don't buy it, Jason. Jack's record tells us what kind of man he is. Jack decides he's got a chance, and takes Crouch's gun. That's how his mind works: if he worried about consequences he wouldn't have spent his whole god-damn life in jail!"

"The whole transfer of the prisoner is suspect," Miller pushed stolidly.

"It's unusual, I'll grant you."

"I've got tapes of Colt's conversation with Yeager: Colt's making a big deal about jurisdiction; the guy's full of apologies. That's not Colt! He had something dirty up his sleeve. His secretary thought so too. She said Crouch and he were suddenly into it thick, and Colt hated Crouch. He was always saying Crotch-sniff gave him the willies."

"Give me a *motive*, Jason."

"Colt sent Jack Hazard to prison nineteen years ago, and Crouch was involved in that case. He was working security for the college and he was the one who identified Jack in a line-up. This whole thing goes back to that murder, and the fact that Jack Hazard didn't kill his ex-wife."

Scott shook his head. "You just gave Jack Hazard a motive. Look, we had our fights about that other murder when we were all younger and handsomer men. That murder's history. There were problems, serious discrepancies, but the truth is you get contradictions in almost every homicide. You know that! Hazard confessed. If he was an innocent man, he wouldn't have confessed."

Miller looked away angrily. "Where's the case file on that murder, Don?"

"Let me give you some advice, Jason. Mr Jack Hazard isn't worth it. You give me a pristine crime scene, every move choreographed, every shot that was fired explained. I mean this is great police work. Then you come up with a decent motive, but you're tagging to the wrong guy. I know you're Two-Bit's friend; I know you want to vindicate him by proving Jack's an innocent man, but that's the past. This is a different homicide. You're just not looking at the evidence *objectively.*"

"The evidence suggests Colt meant to get Jack out in the woods and kill him."

"The evidence indicates that Colt wanted Jack Hazard out of his jail and into county lockup. Given the resistance to arrest, the medical claims we had in one day from half the police force, I can understand *that* motive. Now on the trip Mr Crouch has to make a rest stop. We've got that on tape. Everybody else wants a rest stop suddenly. Can we assume that much?"

"It's a set-up."

"Jack asks to take his turn — just like one of the boys. It's a long drive, and so Colt says, what the hell, get him out!"

"Colt would tell him to piss in his pants."

"What do you really want, Jason? Do you want the Lues police force to look like a bunch of ruthless murderers, and Jack Hazard to be some kind of folk hero? That's what you're giving me, and frankly, I'm not buying it. The guy's a psychopath! Prison tests confirm it. *No* anxiety, Jason. You know what that means? He's got no soul, no fear, and god-damn it, no brains! This is not opinion; this is medical fact."

"I wouldn't trust some test on a guy like that. I mean Jack can hardly read, and you put a doctor in front of him, well he wouldn't take it seriously."

"Jason, Jack Hazard has the moral responsibility of a rattlesnake. Look at the record, for God's sake! He kills brutally, and he kills without the slightest remorse."

"Colt found out that Jack was checking around about his ex-wife's murder. He knew if Jack got enough information he'd put the blame where it belonged — right on Colt's doorstep. You know Colt lied about the time of death."

"*Here we go again!* I had the best medical examiner in five states tell me it was *absolutely impossible* for Josie Fortune to be dead at the time Two-Bit tells us his 'witnesses' spotted her! Come on, Jason. Forget everything else. Do you think Marcel Waldis is going to perjure himself for the likes of Colt Fellows?"

"People saw the body."

"I read all kinds of claims about when they saw what. Nobody I can trust saw that body until well after six."

"I'm just saying the guy behind the confusion is Colt Fellows, and he knew Jack would peg him for it sooner or later."

"The guy behind the confusion was your old boss, but we'll let that go. Your loyalty is commendable. Believe what you want, Jason, but here's how it plays until you give me something as good as the rest you've provided. Crouch and Fellows return to the car. Jack says he has to go too. Colt covers him, while Crouch brings him out of the car. Jack makes a move, and the shooting starts. Two cops dead and a psychopath loose in Lues County. Orders? At the slightest resistance, shoot to kill."

"I'll keep working on it."

"Jason, don't let your emotions get in the way of good police work. This one's finished. Besides, you're going to be too busy to keep working on it. Word is you're about to be named the acting chief of police. I can't think of a better man. And maybe in the big chair, you'll start seeing things with a little different perspective. Everyone I talk to wants the 'acting' part of the title dropped as soon as possible. In other words, you've got a lifetime of good service to this

263

community, and they all want to reward it. Wrecking this department on a hunch can hurt that reputation, Jason; believe me."

"You're not telling me there's a condition to this promotion, are you?"

Scott hesitated. "That's not what I'm saying, Jason. What I'm saying is, ancient history proves nothing. If I don't get hard, irrefutable evidence Colt meant to kill Jack Hazard, I'm going the other way: Jack made the move; Colt reacted. And you'll keep your mouth shut unless you can prove otherwise."

Miller nodded. "I'll get a full report to you by early next week. You don't care if I put my theories in writing, I take it?"

"For my eyes only, I wouldn't expect anything else. Yeager will give me the same report with a different motive. You're not hurting me with your theories. Just see you act responsibly. No news releases. No loose talk in the department or to the public. You want a difference of opinion, fine. You want war, I'm the best there is when it comes to that. If you don't think so, go talk to Two-Bit again."

"I just want the truth, Don."

"Truth's an old soldier that keeps his mouth shut, Jason."

Two-Bit

The phone rang ten times a day, or never at all. Pat Bitts had been up to Lues to Dempsey's Auto Fair to see if maybe he could swap cars: that was three months back, and Dempsey was still calling. Anyone wanted his business that much, he might go back and see what they could do. Then there were the siding people. Didn't want siding, didn't like it, didn't need it. Polly would come up out of her grave if he let Sears near the house. Like Bitts was afraid to get a paintbrush out now and then. Taking it easy was like taking poison. Like that remote control. If he got one of *them*, he'd

264

never get out of the chair. He'd heard there were men who'd died in their recliners and could still channel-surf. A fact! Seventeen no-thank-yous didn't seem to get the message across to Sears. Next time they called, he'd tell them to come on out, then he'd just take a few shots at them while they were coming up the drive. That would stop the calls. Get him Cal Yeager to deal with in the process.

Cal and what army? Wouldn't mind squaring off on that lying sack of horse –

"Hello!"

There was a long silence. Bitts decided he had missed them, whoever they were. He was still plenty fast coming across the yard, but he had been slowing down off the starting blocks for the past forty years. Well, old age beat the alternative.

Someone was on the other end. "Hello!"

A woman's voice: "I'm trying to locate Pat Bitts. He was the county sheriff of Lues from – "

"What are you selling, missy, storm windows?"

"I teach at the university – "

"I'm sorry to hear that; I'm too old to learn anything. Fact is, I'm older than that dog that's too old for anyone to teach."

"Excuse me?"

Give a person two or three doctor degrees and they traded off their common sense every time. "I'm not crazy you know, I'm just mean."

"That's what I hear."

Bitts liked that; he liked the voice suddenly. Youngish, quick. Touch of the east and a little of Lues in it too, if that was possible.

"Where did you hear that, professor?"

"I'm doing research on a murder that happened here twenty years ago. Your name's come up a couple of times."

"You writing a book then?"

"It was my mother who was killed."

265

"Josie Fortune?"

Stunned silence, then: "That's pretty good. I mean, yes. It was."

Bitts smiled. That made this one Josie Fortune, the younger. Polly had fallen in love with the girl. Bitts, too, if truth were told. "Last I saw you, Josie, you were no bigger than a pumpkin seed. You grow up any?"

More than a touch of country now: "I grew up a little. Mr Bitts, may I come out and see you?"

"Everybody calls me Two-Bit; that's twenty-five cents better than nothing. You don't have a jealous husband, do you?"

No answer.

"I'm kidding you. Sure. Come on out. I go to church on Sunday mornings; I get drunk Tuesdays, Wednesdays, and Thursdays from two to five, religiously. The rest of the time it's just me and my fishing pole."

"How about this afternoon? I can be there around three. Is that good?"

And make me miss my Oprah. "Sure that's fine. You been this way lately?"

"No, sir. Why do you ask?"

"They changed the road back about fifteen years ago. Of course in the middle of it, they ran out of money. What we got now is just a disappointed bridge. It's a mess. Just don't be scared when you see the river in the middle of the road. That turns a lot of folks back."

"I don't turn back for much."

"Let me give you directions."

After he hung up, Bitts stretched and ambled back through the house to his office. Back against the corner between his desk and file cabinet, he had a stack of shoe boxes; each box was filled with notepads. Every homicide Bitts or his uncle had ever investigated had a single notepad to describe the investigation; he could hold the whole of a murder case in the palm of his hand. That was the theory, at least. The first box was dated 1921–26; the last ended some nineteen years back, the year Bitts had "retired." Up till then, if you died suspiciously in Lues County, there was a little notebook with your name in one of these boxes. Bitts opened the top box. There were seven notepads. He picked up the one labeled JOSIE FORTUNE and opened it. Almost the entire of it was filled with ruminations, odd marks, cryptic words, times, dates, names, questions.

Bitts turned to the beginning and saw his first estimates. TIME OF DEATH – 2:20–4:15. At the bottom of the second page, the notation clothes! was underlined. Bitts let his chin pump up and down thoughtfully at the entries, flipping the pages as he went. Now he turned back to the first page. He looked at the scratching of a rectangle with two Xs, the time 3:40 beside the drawing. Off to the side 1:30. The phone call from the kids: 4:40.

Bitts flipped back several pages to the medical evidence. Doc Waldis's autopsy. "Here it is," he mumbled, shaking his head. Twenty years and it still made the old man's blood boil: TIME OF DEATH – 6:00–6:20.

Pauper Bluff

Before she left school to meet Lues County's former sheriff, Josie called Virgil Hazard at his home, and got no answer. When she tried the bar, she got no further than giving her name. Virgil hadn't answered earlier that morning nor the night before. She wanted to talk to him, to explain what had happened with her charges against Jack. For all the good it would do. After meeting with Jason Miller, she had gone to Worley Hall and read the newspaper accounts for the last two days. It was immediately apparent to her that Jack was in it too deep to ever find his way out. The worst of it was that if he didn't come in, someone was going to shoot him. One account said that more than a hundred special deputies were combing the woods of Lues County looking

267

for the man, all well armed, with orders to shoot at the first sign of resistance. At last report, law enforcement officials were for making bold predictions about the capture of the "cop killer."

In the parking lot Josie saw Dick Ferrington talking to a pretty girl. At her Mustang, Josie looked back in their direction and saw them both staring at her. She wondered what Ferrington was telling the girl. She suddenly hated the man passionately. The hypocrite. Hated Lues, but she was damned if she would be whispered off the premises. Josie let the engine rumble briefly, then left the lot with a squall.

Pauper Bluff was cross-country through a maze of dirt and gravel roads, forty miles southeast. Josie had thought she had left in plenty of time to make her appointment with Bitts, but by the time she came to Lues Creek Crossing, she was running late and still had ten miles to go. Bitts had been right. There was a lonesome, rusted sign telling you to proceed with caution and a long stretch of nothing but water, telling you to go back. Josie pushed on. She listened to the water rushing across the underside of the Mustang. Realizing that one chuckhole in the middle of all this would sink her, she kept it slow and steady. The water was about eight inches deep, but it felt worse in places, and the current was strong. Sometimes it seemed the car was shifting about. Downstream there were no less than five old rusted vehicles almost entirely submerged. Those were just the ones no one had bothered fishing out. She passed the main body of the creek and rolled on another fifty feet in the creek's shallow overflow before she was safe, that is to say, back in the middle of the primeval forest.

As Josie came into Pauper Bluff, the land turned wildly hilly, but none of it was familiar until she saw the general store in the village. A flagpole out front, the building constructed of dark-stained logs, the place was nothing more than one of those silly tourist traps, but Josie was sure she had been here before. She checked her watch. It was past three already, so she didn't go in. Why did she know it? Josie followed the road out of the village according to Bitts's instructions, slipped for a time along side the big Ohio, watching the barges and boats with a strange sense of nostalgia, and then came to a long quiet lane and a front yard the size of a couple of football fields, perfectly manicured. High up on a hillside at the end of the field she saw a quaint two-storey painted brick farmhouse that looked to be built in the middle of the last century. It was a pale cream color with bright vermilion trim. The view commanded the bend in the river, and looked out toward the Kentucky shore.

Up from the river came a pack of dogs, all shapes and sizes, all of them barking. Behind them came a tall man in a cowboy hat with a tackle box and a fishing pole. He carried no fish. Josie stopped her Mustang in the middle of the drive, brought her purse with her, and walked out toward him.

"Mr Bitts?"

Bitts's stetson was pure poetry, the white felt of it wrinkled and stained into a weathered motley. Bitts's face was the kind to get a man re-elected to the office of sheriff just by posting his picture on a few trees. It was a flinty, intelligent face; and old as he was, the man seemed fully capable of staring down a grizzly.

"Josie Fortune?" His gruff voice was like an accusation.

"It's Darling. Josie Darling," Josie responded.

Bitts shifted the tackle box he carried, and reached his wrinkled hand out toward Josie. "Well, you growed some."

Josie released Bitts's hand, and looked down at the dogs. They were quiet now, eager and friendly. She counted seven.

"Get away from her! Get, now!" Bitts's voice was mean, but the dogs stayed close, sniffing at Josie's jeans and watching her for treats as the two of them started across the rest of the huge lawn toward the old house.

"Is my car okay there?"

"Sure. What is that? A Mustang?" Josie saw a look of genuine interest. "You get that at Dempsey's?"

"No. It's a rental."

"It's a nice one! Dempsey wants me to come swap. I got taken by one of these Japanese tin cans; I never liked it. It don't *fit!* Fifteen years I been complaining about that piece of foreign trash, but it just won't die! Of course now it's not worth more than ten thousand dollars – at least that's what I tell Dempsey – " Bitts winked at her – "and he wants too much for his. How much is that one? You know? That one there looks like it *fits!*"

"It's nice, real fast, but it costs more than what I make in a year."

"For a car that pretty, I'd change jobs."

"Maybe I will," Josie answered, thinking she might have to if Dick Ferrington had a say in matters.

Bitts opened the front door, which was not locked, and kicked at the dogs to keep them out. He made sure not to connect, and the beagle, who seemed to understand his technique better than the rest, got in despite the old man's efforts. Josie stepped into a large kitchen – pure country, right down to a black pot-belly stove and a cord of wood waiting beside it. While Bitts wrestled with the beagle, she walked to the windows. She could see the river stretching below them right on the bend, and she thought it was the prettiest sight she had ever seen. A few barges were floating along and some recreational boats in the last days of the season. The trees were turning some, though it was too early for much color.

"You recognize it?" he asked.

"No, sir. Should I?"

Bitts slipped off his hat and jacket. Inside, he looked like a man close to eighty, his movements tender and careful. "You stayed here a week with Polly and me. Polly wanted to keep you. Well, we both did."

"I don't remember. I'm sorry."

270

"State thought we were too old and sent you to live with some foster home that had about a dozen kids, all from different families. Terrible! Polly raised Cain! Well, we never got you back, but we saw to it you got your chance in life. You get a good family, finally? We tried to see you did."

"Yes, sir. They gave me everything; they're good people."

Bitts took this for what it was, and nodded. Josie wished she remembered the place. She wished she remembered Pat Bitts. She looked around the kitchen and she knew his wife – Polly? – was dead. People like Pat Bitts don't divorce, and he lived here alone. The place was scrubbed clean, it was real clean, but there was nothing here of a woman's touch. The place had a spartan quality. The wallpaper, which a woman had picked out, was years out of date and dingy. The light fixture was a sad piece of the sixties. The stove was perfectly modern, twenty years ago.

"Polly died ten years ago this coming March. I was out . . . ah, you don't want to hear this."

"Tell me."

Bitts studied Josie with a solemn, frightening aspect. He looked around at the kitchen angrily, then walked over, opened a cabinet and retrieved some coffee. As he worked, Josie studied the river. His emotions were too overpowering to contemplate directly.

"She choked to death!"

She looked back at the man. He was busy dumping coffee into a filter. She turned her eyes again to the Kentucky shoreline.

"I was down by the river, cleaning some trash out. These weekend boaters seem to think their trash improves the scenery. Anyway, I come back up, and there she was. I've seen bodies all my life. It comes with the territory, came with it, anyway. I saw Polly right here!" He pointed at the floor between them as Josie answered his volatile hesitation by turning to see where – "and my whole life ended." Bitts finished with the scoops of coffee and put the can back

271

neatly in its place. "You never know," he said finally, and that was it. Nothing more.

She watched him draw some water and pour it into the machine. His gestures were part old habit and part rage. "Come on to the sitting room," he commanded, and set the machine to brewing with a flip of the switch.

Josie took a plush couch that didn't fit with the antiques throughout most of the house. Bitts was a sucker for a good salesperson, she decided. He fell into a recliner that looked to have his signature in its padding. In the kitchen the coffee gurgled. "Now tell me what I can do for you."

"Jason Miller tells me you know more about my mother's murder than anyone in Lues County."

"You know Jason?"

"Not really. I talked to him last night for a while. When I asked about my mother's death, he said the case file on it was missing, but that you'd remember the murder — better than any file."

"I remember it, all right, and I'll tell you something else. It doesn't surprise me a bit they lost that file. *If* they lost it. There wasn't anything about that murder that was done right. The whole thing, everything about your mother's death was . . . off. And I mean off a hundred and eighty degrees!"

"Can you give me an example?"

Bitts studied Josie solemnly. "What do you know about it? What have you found out?"

"I read the newspaper accounts of it."

"Lies."

"I talked to Melody Mason."

"Why is that name familiar?"

"She's one of the kids who found the body."

"Right! She's the one that got the poison ivy! No! Poison sumac, it was. I remember Miss Mason. She squatted in the stuff! Smart as that crooked-tail beagle I got out there, not a lick more."

272

"I talked to Colt Fellows and Tobias Crouch, too."

Bitts grumbled, "What about your stepfather? Did you get his side of things?"

"Do you read the paper, Mr Bitts?"

"I catch the front page now and then," the old man offered. There was a look of accusation and maybe, she thought, a willingness to listen before pronouncing judgment.

"You know what happened, then?"

"I know Colt Fellows. He was a persuasive man, but his tricks finally backfired on him."

"I'd been getting threats against my life and Colt convinced me it was Jack and that he meant to kill me. I had good reason to be scared and about then I was ready to believe anything."

"And I bet now you're worried Jack is looking for you."

"It crossed my mind."

"Let me tell you something about your stepfather, professor. He doesn't make threats, and he doesn't hide in the dark. Everything about Jack Hazard is in your face – the good and the bad. And I'll tell you something else you might not know. He doesn't countenance violence against women. When he was a boy, just after his father was killed, Jack's mother and him and his three brothers moved in with his mother's sister. She was married to a man named Vern Shake. Now that man there was the meanest son-of-a-Missouri-mule that ever lived. That was back when I was the only law in Lues County. I policed the city then and everything else. I knew Vern, and more than once I thought I was going to have to shoot him or he was going to shoot me – if I ever gave him a chance at my back. There was no play in that man. When Jack moved in with him, ol' Vern took to beating the boys regular. He'd come home drunk, and he'd catch one of them, and he'd tan that boy until he bled. No favoritism, he beat his own kids too. The only salvation for any of them was there were so many, they could share the burden.

"Now what I mean to tell you is this: one day a few months after they had all moved in, Vern slapped Jack's mamma. I don't know why he hadn't done it before, but he hadn't. I suppose he'd just been busy with the rest of them. He was married to her sister, see, and she was living with them, and I don't think Vern thought much about it — just a cuff across the cheek. Let me tell you, that was the first and last he ever touched her. The next morning Jack shot him while he was sitting at the breakfast table. Shot him three times, and then he sat down and waited until I showed up to arrest him. That boy was ten, but he knew what's what: nobody was going to touch his mamma."

Josie blinked in wonder. "So it was justified?"

With this, Josie saw a lawman's smile, the careful, and somewhat bitter distinction between law and justice. "It was, in Jack's mind."

"So you don't think he killed my mother either?"

"I know he didn't, and not just for that reason. I know it because I know he was an innocent man. And I could have proved it if I had had a fair call from the coroner's office."

"What do you mean. What happened?"

"Everyone lied about that case — from the start."

"What kind of lies?"

"Everything! Here's the first: I got a call about a *body* at 4:40. I had the call verified by a campus security officer, since I thought it might be a prank. I got a call back at seven o'clock and called the Lues PD to join me. You following this?"

Josie nodded.

"A couple of days later the head of security for Lues State, our sheriff these days, claimed he received my call after 6:30, not 4:45. The security officer he sent in to verify the report was suddenly saying he had started into the canyon only after

274

my call, meaning at 6:45. I got my dispatcher, and Cal Yeager got his, and it was a dead heat of liar's poker."

"That doesn't make sense."

"I'm just getting warmed up, sister! Nothing about that murder made the slightest sense at all! I found the kids that discovered your mother. I figured it six ways to Sunday: they saw your mother's body from the top of the falls at three in the afternoon. They were standing next to her at just after four and called me as soon as they got out of the canyon. When the autopsy came back, the time of death was *after* six o'clock."

"My God!"

"Colt Fellows found the same witnesses I had. I don't know about the rest, but I saw Miss Melody Mason's signature: she was saying it was 6:30 they had called. And one other said the same thing, a boy named Bob Tanner. When I went back to face my witnesses, the university wouldn't let me on campus. Orders from the president of that misbegotten outfit. They said I needed a warrant to step on that campus. And all of a sudden a warrant was a hard thing for me to get hold of."

The coffee finished gurgling, and Bitts went to get two cups. "You take cream?"

"No, sir."

"I put half the cow in mine!"

When he returned with a cup for each of them, Bitts sat down comfortably and continued. "The kids were scared of me; they had instructions not to talk to me by phone or in person, and I didn't see the point of getting them all tied up in the thing — not at that point. I suspect Colt Fellows twisted the times all around and got a couple of the kids to sign statements he'd written. A lawyer could have destroyed the evidence, but it never went to trial, and the county prosecutor's office wanted me to talk to no one. Don Scott liked your stepfather guilty, and no need to get confused with the facts. I told him that, too!"

"There was something about a watch they found . . ."

"Jack Hazard's name on it? I tracked that watch all over Lues County; not a soul ever saw Jack Hazard wearing any kind of watch. It was a plant, whether by the killer or Colt Fellows, I don't know."

"So you're saying Colt Fellows was lying and this director of security – "

"Cal Yeager! Our illustrious sheriff! Yeah, he lied."

"And Toby Crouch, the security officer?"

"And the county medical examiner, Professor Doctor Marcel Waldis! But I didn't tell you the *good* part!"

"There's more?"

"There's more. The kids all told me your mother was on this rock when they found her. There was some bruising on her neck and a rope burn there, too, and something just scratched across her stomach, real fine cuts, and her wrists and ankles were real swollen, but that was it. By the time I got to her, four hours later, the body was in a sink hole and had been ripped open with some kind of knife."

Josie set her coffee on the table, her thoughts struggling to grasp what the old man was telling her.

"Now wait a minute," she said finally. "Her corpse had been moved and cut open?"

The old man nodded his head in slow deliberate agreement. "It takes just under thirty minutes from the base of the falls to the first telephone," he explained, "so I know what time they saw her. Now I had five people describe your mother as she was at four o'clock. They didn't all see the same thing, but it was close enough. What they saw or what they claimed they saw at four o'clock was entirely different from the body I found at 8:20."

Josie struggled to calm herself; she fought for some kind of saving skepticism. An old man's stories; fable and fact can get confused with time, she told herself, and yet she couldn't believe it. Not this old man.

"How do you explain it?" she asked.

276

"Just two reasonable possibilities. The kids were lying, or the killer was still in the canyon when they left and he went back to the body – for whatever reason. I favor the second, but I can't prove it wasn't the kids."

"Why would he return to the body?"

"Maybe they interrupted him. Maybe he got scared and wanted to make sure we wouldn't find any evidence from an examination of the body. I don't know what else to make of it."

"Toby Crouch found the body in the same condition as you did?"

Bitts answered affirmatively.

"Why would he lie about the time he went into the canyon?"

"Simple. His boss Cal Yeager told him to. Then there's the fact that Crouch got a job with the city right after all this. He wanted that real bad, and Colt probably made a deal with him. As long as he happened to see Jack Hazard lurking around the scene, he could become a police officer."

"And the campus security director? Why did he lie?"

"He declared himself a candidate for sheriff within days of your mother's murder; had a lot of people help him get on the ballot. A lot of money got behind him and a lot of prestige at the college was pulling for him. Colt fancied himself something of a kingmaker, and he had his hand in that election too. So did the prosecutor, after he and I crossed on this case. I mean we had words! I can't prove it and I don't know who rigged it, but I've always said Cal carried all the cemeteries in Lues County that election and he only beat me by fifty-two votes."

"So both Yeager and Crouch went along with Colt Fellows because of what he could do for them?"

Bitts nodded.

"What about the medical examiner and the prosecutor?"

"Like I say, I crossed them. They didn't like that, and they went over to Colt's camp."

"And Melody Mason?"

Bitts frowned. "Miss Melody Mason went along with whatever man happened to be talking."

Josie smiled. The old man had quite a memory, she decided. How had Melody put it to her? *I always agree with people . . . it's easier, you know?* Nothing conspiratorial there: Colt asked; she signed.

"And you say the other witness to sign a statement was Bob Tanner?"

"Miss Mason's match, that one!"

"And the coroner's office. They lied too?"

"Ever since they built the university, the coroner has always had the university medical school do the autopsies. In those days, the hospital's director, a man named Marcel Waldis, was a specialist in forensic pathology. This Waldis was good enough to work anywhere, but he had something of a God complex and he liked to fish, so he came to Lues State when they started their medical school. They paid him a lot and no one but yours truly ever questioned a thing he said. He liked it that way."

"He lied?"

"No, he made a mistake, and when I caught him in it, he wouldn't back off and admit it. You see, Colt Fellows had told him some things about the murder. When he did the autopsy, Waldis concluded the time of death could not have been before six o'clock, nor after 6:20. Only way a medical man will put a time of death that close is if he has eyewitness accounts to go by. But of course, once he'd pronounced judgment on the issue, the good doctor wasn't backing down! Now I told him he had based his time of death on *misinformation*; and he said he was all cock-sure of 'the forensic pathology.' He said the misinformation came from *my* office. We almost had a dead medical examiner, now that's the truth. All the good it did me to get mad! Your mother died officially after six o'clock, and I was without the proof or witnesses to do a thing about it."

278

Josie shook her head in disbelief. "What did he say the cause of death was?"

"Strangulation."

"What did you think?"

"She was hanged and strangled both; I saw the marks. I didn't know which killed her, but he sure was cocky about it. No doubt about it, was what he said. Well, that was ol' Doc Waldis. Never had a doubt in his life."

"So how do you know Jack was innocent?"

"Goes back to the time of death. It was a long time later and just an accident I found out he couldn't have done it, but because of the official time of death I couldn't get the case reopened. Plus, by then I wasn't even the sheriff."

"I want to know what happened after you found the body and talked to the kids."

"Well, first thing that happened was I never got to talk to Jack. Colt was out barking about Jack Hazard killing his wife – even though she was his *ex*-wife – and I knew Jack never touched a woman . . . never! So I just let the old blow-hard blow away. Most fools just end up confirming public opinion, but Colt had a way of changing reality, and I guess I didn't speak up soon enough to stop it. I went about my business. I was trying to run an investigation, and Colt Fellows was jumping to conclusions as usual. Before I could get out to his trailer to see him, Jack had already been arrested. I got back to Lues and took care of getting *you* somewhere safe – out here with Polly and me – and then I went to war with the powers of the county. I started off pretty good, professor. I got our prosecutor plenty curious about the *anomalies* of the case. He looked at what I gave him, and then studied Colt's report, and he wanted to get to the bottom of it. That was when he brought in Mr Tobias Crouch for a lie detector test. I thought I had them all, then! Well, I witnessed that test myself, and Mr Crouch passed it without the slightest problem. When he passed a second test, that was it; no one took me seriously after that. A couple of days after that, I

279

was still nosing around, and I heard ol' Jack confessed to it. All I could do then was fold up the tents and go home."

"But you said he was innocent?"

Bitts smiled bitterly. "Seems Colt found out the very night she was found – from Jack himself – Jack had come to the police station at 2:30 that day to report your mother missing."

"You think Colt just made a mistake and wouldn't back down – like this Waldis?"

"I always thought Colt wanted to get Jack. There was bad blood between them – for some reason. Always had been. Of course, it could have been he just made up his mind about who killed your mother and made all the pieces fit. He did that plenty. They say Colt wrecked his kindergarten, putting square pegs into round holes."

"But he knew Jack didn't do it? He let him go to prison *knowing* he was innocent?"

"That's what I'm saying, but Colt wasn't involved in the murder, if that's your next question, not directly anyway. I checked him over before I gave up."

"What about the others? Did all the liars have a good alibi?"

Bitts took a deep, angry breath and exhaled slowly. "Doc Waldis did. He wasn't the sort to get mixed up in the dirt, anyway. He was too excited about himself to bother with the usual motives for a murder. I checked him out twice, anyway. No motive, no connection, real good alibi. He's happily retired these days at the local cemetery, God bless his arrogant soul, so you just have to take my word on it. But believe it, I'd have stuck to him if I thought I had something. *Six o'clock*! I never heard the like of it!

"Now Don Scott was a big problem in that case, too. He was the prosecutor back then and still is today. I checked him over too. He was clean. Out of town the day your mother disappeared and in meetings the afternoon she was killed. I confirmed everything, same as I did with Doc Waldis. Bit of a problem with Cal Yeager. He claims he was talking to K. V. Rogers, the university president. This Rogers was fighting me every step of the way; he said Yeager was with him in a private meeting. The secretary confirmed it, but it was the only proof I could get. And words, my friend, don't make a thing so. It's all the suspicion I could ever muster, though. I can't connect Yeager to any of it, and I spent a little time trying. Then there was Tobias Crouch. He was doing a long lunch – drunk with his buddies; that was until almost three o'clock. The body had already been sighted by that point."

"What about Jack's lawyer? I got the feeling he wasn't exactly doing Jack any favors."

"You got that right! Of course, Jack never did. R. K. Manley. Jack loved him for some reason. Every time he killed someone or was accused of it anyway, he'd bring in Manley and hand himself ten tons of grief. I don't think Manley could have done it. He didn't have the strength for the job; he could lift a shot glass but that was it. Manley died, what? eight or nine years ago."

"Anyone else?"

Bitts blinked in frustration. "That's the list."

"What about Virgil Hazard?"

"Serving drinks."

"So you had no idea who it might have been?"

"I got nothing at all in the way of a lead. People that knew your mother all loved her. I never knew her; I steered clear of Mr Hazard because of our history. He didn't need to see me, and I was just glad he'd finally got his life in order. After it was over, I was sorry I hadn't tried to make amends with Jack. Your mother was something special. She could rough it up with the country boys, but then up at school she was real successful too. Quiet and studious, by all accounts. Near as I could find out, she was a straight-A student."

"Dean's list," Josie said with sudden pride.

"She didn't have many friends on campus; still just a

freshman, and she was a single mother; that took her out of the social life. I take it she and Jack were seeing each other by that spring, too, trying to mend some broken fences. Jack didn't quite fit into the university crowd, so she wouldn't have been involved much with her classmates or any of the professors."

"I have the names of four of the five kids who found the body," Josie said. "When I talked to Melody Mason, she couldn't remember the fifth kid. Is there any chance you have the names?" Josie realized that the fifth *kid* was into ripe middle age by now.

"Everything we gathered went to the homicide investigator, that's Colt Fellows. And of course we know about that! What material we kept in the sheriff's office was all duplicate of what we passed onto Colt, but it belongs to Cal Yeager now. You won't see any of it without a court order."

"It's gone too. Same with the prosecutor's office. At least that's what Jason Miller tells me."

"If Jason said it, it's what they're telling him, true or not. That leaves us with this." He pulled a little notepad from his shirt and smiled like a man with a gold nugget. "My own personal field records, and they're good, professor, the whole of a murder in the palm of my hand. Every homicide I ever investigated I recorded in a little notepad like this, then copied out for the files. It's mostly just names, times, questions, details; in the case of your mother's death I got a lot of question marks. But I've got the names of the kids." Bitts flipped through the first few pages, "Melody Mason, Cat Sommerville, Jim Burkeshire – "

"That's the one! Do you have anything else on them? Parents, home towns? Melody's lost touch with everyone."

Bitts nodded, "Got it all. Got your mother's professors, too."

"Her professors?"

"I thought they might have some information. An older woman sometimes might be more likely to confide in a professor rather than one of her eighteen-year-old classmates. I talked with two of them before I got shut out of things at the college. Whatever I could get about the college, I got through local sources. I even found a couple of local boys that had been in class with her. That's how I found out she was a good student."

"May I have that notebook?"

"It won't mean anything without me decoding it. But I'll copy out that list of professors." Bitts stood. "I'll just go on back to my office, and if you want more about any of it, you can call me or come back out. I don't mind missing a chance to catch a fish or two, not for this, I don't. Tell you the truth, I never quite put this thing to bed. Twenty years I been mulling it over, wondering why so many men were lying, and I just could never figure it."

Josie finished her coffee in a gulp. She wanted another. She was tired and jittery, and the coffee was good. "Do you mind if I get some more coffee?"

"Help yourself." Bitts had risen from his recliner with a couple of strange catches in the effort. Now he hobbled twice, before walking gingerly back toward the hallway.

In the kitchen with a fresh cup of coffee, Josie stood alone and looked out across Bitts's lawn.

She liked the old man and wanted to believe him. But what he said was incredible. Had everyone conspired against Jack Hazard? No. That wasn't what he said. They had lied. There was a difference. A conspiracy would mean they all agreed to an action, then proceeded. This was more like they had just piled on, the way of a feeding frenzy. Guilt by accusation and no room for the facts. But if Bitts was right, Jack was an innocent man, and her mother's killer had gotten away. Had probably stayed in Lues. Had somehow known Josie was coming to Lues – after all these years. *WilcuM HoM jOsie.* Her thoughts drifting in speculation, Josie continued staring out at the river. She was thinking about Fellows and Crouch, Jack Hazard's smile, the notes left for her to find.

283

All the liars. She sipped at her coffee, losing track of time. When Bitts returned, Josie spun around. Before she could stop herself, she had almost reached into her purse. Bitts didn't seem to notice.

"This is about everything. The five witnesses, a list of your mother's professors, then those people who lied. I marked them off if they had a confirmed alibi. Besides the kids – and they were all together up in the woods in the afternoon – Mr Calvin Yeager is the only one I'm not sure about, but I wouldn't make much of that. I pried under that rock as much as I could, and nothing came out."

"They all knew Jack was innocent, didn't they? The prosecutor, the medical examiner, Crouch, Fellows, Yeager. They knew and they didn't care?"

Bitts's smile creased his haggard face. "Jack's an easy man to blame, Josie; he's a hard one to understand."

Lues Creek Crossing

Bitts came out with Josie to her rental car to look at it again. Josie humored him, but soon found herself staring at the late afternoon light reflecting off the river.

"It's pretty here," Josie said. She thought her whole life she had been trying to find this place again and that now she probably wouldn't be coming back.

Bitts looked away from the car and out toward the river. "I was born here seventy-six years ago," he answered. "Right on this hill."

Josie looked at him briefly, wondering what she might have been if this man had adopted her, as he had wanted. Then she looked back at the house. Her home for a week. Something in the shape of the hill and the forest beyond the house reminded Josie of her childhood, but that was all. She couldn't even be sure if this was a real memory or only a happy delusion.

"Pull on up to the house and turn around," Bitts told her

when she had started the Mustang. "The yard's too wet to pull out on." The engine of the Mustang rumbled and Josie nodded. She let the car kick forward with a brief surge of its power, then watched Bitts shake his head and grin. He was a sweet old man, and lonely, she decided. She coasted through the tight circle beside his rusted-out Toyota and a fairly new Ford pickup truck, full size. A moment later she passed Bitts, waved, and headed down the long hill toward the road.

At Lues Creek Crossing, Josie slowed the car and rolled carefully into the water. The mole quickened the current. The heavy rains for nearly a week had swollen the creek, as well, but it had been this bad a couple of hours earlier, and Josie pushed out into the waters with the faith of an old-time Christian. She didn't like the sound of water pushing up under her floorboards. Downstream, she glanced at the abandoned wrecks; none had been added to their number. At the midpoint in her crossing, Josie looked upstream. The water seemed to come right toward the passenger door of the Mustang; it was simply an illusion, but creeks and rivers create powerful illusions, she realized.

After she had crossed the center point and with still some way to go before she was out, something happened. Somewhere back across the broad creek and upstream a bit, Josie thought she heard a faint popping sound. She looked back into the dull light of the woods and saw nothing. The car felt different. Off level? She turned the steering wheel and felt it kick and quarrel in response. The gravel sliding under her wheels? She tried to move the car left. It jumped some, then pulled back right. She turned slightly to the right and felt it pulling hard.

She had a flat tire.

Josie rolled on through the creek, then stopped close to the middle of the gravel road, braking several times before the car slowed. It was just past five o'clock in the evening. There was still plenty of light, but the forest was close around her,

285

and the effect was to make it feel it was almost dark. She looked back down the road and then forward. No one coming. She looked out toward the woods, swore briskly, and got out of the car. She walked around to the front of the vehicle and looked at the tire.

Completely flat. She contemplated the obvious, shaking her head in frustration. What else could go wrong?

She heard rustling behind her. It came quickly. Her hands reached for her purse, left hand rising, right hand crossing – but there was nothing there. The purse was in the car. She turned in time to see the man. He was thin and tall. He had a red beard. He hit her at the waist and carried her back across the hood of the Mustang. Josie curled her leg up and kneed him hard in the ribs. He grunted at the impact. She pushed against him, and felt his weight giving. *Fight!* she screamed to herself, and hit him twice in the face with the heel of her hand. His strength seemed to fade, and she wrestled herself nearly off the car before she saw the others. They were coming toward her on the run. The man who had tackled her grabbed at her again, and Josie hit him once more, with her elbow across his jaw. He fell back, and she tried to crawl across the hood of the car toward the driver side. She wanted to get to her purse. She heard a sickening cry of country glee and felt the next man hit her with the length of his body, knocking the wind out of her. She felt another take her ankles. She pulled back, but the hands stayed on each ankle. She kicked twice with her right leg, vaguely taking her foot into his chest, but not freeing herself, then, lifting her left leg, she took aim at the man's filthy grin. The move took him by surprise, and his smile turned bloody. He fell back out of sight. Josie's first attacker had rolled off the front of the car also, but another of them came scrambling over the hood to take her free arm. Two more of them grabbed for her legs now. Held by four men, Josie jerked with the last spasms of her strength. They had her.

"Tie her up!" the one still in the woods commanded. Her

first attacker, his red beard bloody, stood dumbly looking down at Josie from the front of the car. His nose was bleeding heavily. He reached into deep pockets, bringing out a dangerous-looking pocket knife and several strands of baling twine. Josie ceased fighting as she watched the knife. The man she had kicked came up now, his lips and chin bright red. He swore with a peculiar reverence. The others ignored him.

Seven. Her mind moved quickly. One of them had seen her passing through on the way to Pauper Bluff; he got the others, and they had waited for her to come back. The popping sound was from a rifle. They had shot out her tire. One more of them across the creek, or was that just an echo? The man in the woods held a rifle and one of the others also had a gun. It could have been one of them. As her feet were bound tightly, Josie looked up into their faces.

What they wanted was pretty clear. But not here, apparently. She looked down the road. Still no one coming. *Maybe just the car.* Maybe the car, but that wasn't all. Josie felt the clawing fear of rape deep in her gut. She tried to shut the thought away. She heard something that was not quite a voice telling her to survive, to simply hang on. It was the primal self, there were no words with the thought, it was simply the impassioned scream of life that drowned out even the terrible and sometimes debilitating fear of pain. She studied their faces so she could remember them. Three of them had beards. Two were fat-cheeked, flush, excited, middle-aged. They had light brown hair and flannel shirts with quilted jackets. Muscular, both were average height. The others were physically a mixed bag. Her first attacker was the only one with red hair. He was the tallest and thinnest. The second to come at her was a big, powerful man with dark hair and heavily lidded dark eyes. The one she had kicked was short and wiry, his chin and cheekbones nearly flat against his face. He had had bad teeth to begin with; they were a lot worse after Josie's efforts. The other

287

two were short, powerful men, both with black and gray hair, their eyes dark, intensely disturbing. The leaders. *The killers, when that time comes.*

Her ankles bound, they tied her wrists quickly, taking a length of the twine around her waist to keep her hands close to her body. A bandanna came out now, and was wadded into a ball. A second fluttered and was wrapped into a gag.

"Take it!"

Josie resisted.

"Hold her nose!"

Josie opened her mouth slightly to breathe and tasted the filthy cloth shoved into her mouth. She looked mournfully down the road again. Still nothing. The second bandanna was wrapped tightly across her mouth. She fought with the cloth in her mouth, pushing it forward in a tight knot toward her teeth. She nearly vomited. She breathed desperately through her nose. She felt the cloth softening with saliva. The reflex of nausea passed.

The strongest of them, the one with the dark hair and thoughtful black eyes, slid Josie toward him over the hood of the car now, and heaved her over his shoulder. Josie saw two of them moving toward the car as she was carried into the woods. She saw them open the driver-side door. She saw them getting her keys, then her purse. They found the .357 immediately; one of them stuck the nickel-plated revolver into his pants. A moment afterwards, they opened the Mustang's trunk. She saw nothing else as the heavy brush now obliterated her view of the road. Lying over the man's shoulder and feeling his powerful strides, Josie looked at the legs of the four men. All wore jeans and leather boots. They were clear of the road now. She heard a distant clank of metal and realized they were changing the tire. *Maybe just the car.* This was simply prayer. The forest was covered with leaves, one spot as good as another. Still, they were going deeper into the woods. Josie tried to look back in the direction of the creek. They were angling away from it, taking a small incline. They passed over the ridge finally. Behind them the hills blocked out the road and creek. She twisted around to see to either side – nothing but the October forest and the men. Five of them. Several minutes passed silently. Their feet trampled in the heavy leaves of the forest floor. Josie's stomach rolled against the man's shoulder. Her nerves were merciless.

She forced herself to lift her shoulders and look at the men. Fixing their faces a second and third time in her memory. They were solemn, angry faces, but the men were walking easily. No grins, no winks, no lust. Would they just leave her? Was this to buy some time to get the car out of the county? The next thoughts were so cruelly skeptical they might have been funny in another context. Josie was coming to terms with her own death, slowly, bitterly, sorrowfully.

From the hill that ran between them and Lues Creek, a young man came running to join them. He ran quickly, and the others stopped to wait for him. Six of them now. And the other two with the Mustang. The new arrival carried a rifle with a scope and a wet pair of waders. *The shooter.* He was a kid, twenty-two, maybe as old as twenty-five. He had a beautiful face, a wild, unconscious beauty in his step, and lustrous dark hair. Had she seen him before? she wondered. His teeth were white and square. He was smiling like a boy as he looked expectantly toward the men.

One of them finally rewarded him. "Nice shot, Cy."

"Good work, Cyrus," the oldest added.

"Want me to take her?" another asked.

The man carrying Josie set her down.

"Maybe we can let her walk?" Cy offered. Josie looked at him. His voice was as bashful and country as Lues Creek. Dark eyes, bright. If there was any kindness in any of them, it was here. Josie tried to catch his eye. He didn't notice or didn't react.

"Keep her tied up, she kicked my tooth loose." The speaker moved toward Josie's face, staring at her weirdly. She thought he would hit her, but he only opened his bloodied lips for her to see. When he had, he looked squarely at her: "It hurts."

Did he want some sympathy? *Untie me, you! I'll give you sympathy!* Only the gag kept Josie civil.

One of the shortest men slipped under Josie and took her up on his shoulder. The momentary relief of being able to stand passed quickly, and Josie felt her stomach now pushed into the lump of another man's shoulder. The pressure was slightly different because of the change of position and the shape of him, but soon enough, the ache of being carried simply became more universal. This one walked with different rhythms, his step more pronounced, heavier, shorter. Josie's body flopped painfully so that the wind was knocked out of her in a series of shots just below her diaphragm. She struggled to twist her body away from the same repetitious jolts. She wanted the first man to carry her. Or better, she wanted to walk. She wiggled slightly, managing to take her shoulders and head down some. Her lower stomach hit his shoulder now. For a minute or so, that was some relief, but the discomfort gradually returned, along with the horrible sense of not being able to breathe.

The men moved silently. The shooter, Cy, and another man ran ahead now. Josie tried to drop her shoulders lower still and look forward. The world upside down, she could not quite focus. They were coming to a dirt road. She heard a shout of encouragement, then another. They crossed the road at a trot, then fell back to their original pace. The wet leaves whispered under their boots; the forest swallowed them again.

They meant to keep her, she realized. She looked at their bodies, pulling up to catch the expressions in their faces. She was too weak to hold herself like this long, and fell heavily back so that her focus remained on the back of her carrier's legs and the boots of the men closest to him. They didn't care that she could recognize them. That was bad, real bad.

They started up a hill, and Josie twisted to see off to the side. A cabin. Well here it was. She felt a surge of regret. Maybe an hour or two, maybe a day or two, then one of them takes her out and finishes it. She felt tears. She swore silently, bitterly. At least not that! No tears. *No!* She looked at them again. The shooter might be able to catch her, but if she could get a few seconds' start on him, she'd test him. She could outrun the others, she was sure of it. *Play along, they loosen the ropes for their fun . . . and you go.* She glanced up at the leaders. They probably owned these woods and had claimed their rights in this fashion for years. So it was nothing new for them. Only Josie was new; all else was part of a ritual too macabre to understand. Silently, Josie decided she would have to be patient. And that meant . . . shutting off her mind while they . . .

. . . *not to fight, not to struggle, wait for their mistake, wait your chance. One chance only. If that.*

Nobody was going to come looking for her. Nobody knew where she was; Bitts would never know she had been taken. They had the car: nobody would find it and know she was missing. The first they would know of this would be at eight o'clock tomorrow morning, when she didn't show up for class.

Maybe they'll let you go when they're finished? No, she told herself. It wouldn't do to lie to herself. Her only chance was to face her death, unblinking. If she did that, she had a chance. She was going to have to wait until that moment when they didn't expect her to do anything, and then she was going to have to run. *And keep running. Ten miles back to Pauper Bluff, Thirty to Lues. Thirty miles of woods. Eight of them coming after you, knowing the woods and roads; probably have trucks, cars . . .*

She heard their boots thumping on the boards of the porch. She saw the rough-hewn logs of the cabin. The door opened. She was carried through. Inside, the room was dark and chilly. No light, no fire. There was a damp here like a

291

cave. She lifted herself to look. Two dark, nondescript figures in the shadows under a lone window. *Ten.*

She found herself standing and tried to focus on the two men in front of her. They sat at a small table. One of the men in the shadows said, "Cut her loose." Josie studied the dark face of the speaker. She felt her feet freed; she looked at the knife as it slipped between her wrists and sawed briefly at the twine. The handkerchief was jerked down around her neck, and she reached into her mouth to spit out the wad of cloth they had forced into it.

Clothes next? Cut off, then the men in succession. That's how it goes, isn't it? She looked across the room to a corner, a sole bed, filthy sheets, a couple of blankets.

We all die somewhere, Josie.

"Any trouble?" This time the voice was familiar.

Her eyes adjusting finally, Josie saw it was Jack Hazard. Beside him, still quiet, Virgil Hazard sat contemplating her coldly.

"She kicked my tooth loose. And I think she broke Blake's nose."

Josie stared at the two brothers, ignoring the men around her. Virgil stood up now and walked to her.

"Hello, DJ." His voice was full of bile.

The Cabin

Virgil was standing within range. Josie could take his knee out, for all the good it would do her. If he touched her, she would do it. When he made no move toward her, Josie stared defiantly back at him, an implicit dare. In the dim light of the cabin, Virgil's face seemed peculiarly ugly, as if he were looking at one of his uncooperative girls. Finally he announced, still looking at her eyes, "Come on! Let's go."

They all moved toward the door behind her, and Josie realized they meant to leave her with Jack. She looked at the window just behind the table where he still sat. It provided a small opening high up on the wall. She could crawl out of it once she broke the glass, but to run for it and jump through it was impossible, even if she had the courage to go face first into glass. She looked at Jack's dark features as she watched him stand up. He was in jeans and a flannel shirt. He had on a pair of leather boots and an old baseball cap. A shotgun leaned against the wall behind where he had been sitting, and a revolver was stuck in his belt. As he stepped toward her, she thought maybe to get the revolver from him. With the others outside it didn't promise much, but it was something, better maybe than dying without a fight. *See what he wants. You get one chance. Make it a good one.*

She expected he would hit her before he did anything else.

Like the old days, Josie, she told herself. *"Like that, baby? You want some more?"* And afterwards, hurting too much to complain about the humiliation: *"Philosophical question, baby,"* Dan Scholari's naked body jammed up against her. *"Is it possible to be raped by your own husband?"*

"Hey! it's not McDonald's, but it's going to have to do."

Josie came out of her reverie, recognizing only belatedly what Jack meant: their plans to meet at the Lues McDonald's. He was smiling, joking, his shoulders slanting in a relaxed fashion, his whole body slouching in a posture of feigned ease. In his eyes, though, Jack looked ready to pull the gun and shoot her.

"Colt set me up," she said. "He lied and I fell for it."

Josie announced this as fact, her voice emotionless; she didn't expect it to have any effect, but she wanted it for the record. She wouldn't try to explain herself once the blows came. As much as she could, Josie would turn off when the punches came. No satisfaction, no response at all. If the past was any guide, no fight at all, either. It was how she had always dealt with Dan's rages. She had always wanted to fight him, later, but at the time she never had. Josie Darling who never lifts a finger, not even for a good fight.

"Colt?" Jack was dubious but still putting on a humorous face. "I thought *you* were the one who said let's meet at McDonald's."

Jack was nearly a step from her. Josie thought about trying for his gun now, but she realized Jack knew what she meant to do even as she thought it; his face almost daring her to try now. She looked squarely into his eyes, concentrating on her words not the gun.

"Someone smashed up my car the day I met you. Colt convinced me it was you and that you meant to kill me. He said if I charged you with assault he could protect me from you."

"He didn't do a very good job, did he?" No remorse for killing Colt. And no remorse for this.

"Look, he talked me into something stupid. If anyone could understand that, it ought to be you."

Jack's eyes flashed angrily at the allusion to his confession.

"So are you going to kill me?"

"Did those guys threaten you?" Worried, irritated.

"They didn't say anything at all."

"They hurt you? Any of them hit you?"

"They hurt my pride a little."

"We've been watching you for the past two days," he admitted with a grin, "looking for a chance to get you. You're pretty careful, and I didn't want anyone shot." An appreciative appraisal of her, maybe.

"Who are these people?"

"Family."

"Did you set that up at the creek? Was that your doing?"

He pointed toward the door vaguely. "Louis did. Nice job, huh? Except for what you did to Lincoln and Blake."

"I got a couple of them pretty good," Josie answered, proud of herself suddenly. She *had* fought, hadn't she? Kicked and clawed, so mad she hadn't thought to give in as she always had for Dan.

294

"God, Jack, I'm so sorry for what I did!" she admitted suddenly. She felt the exhaustion that comes of folly. "It was so stupid to trust that bastard! I *knew* you didn't mean to hurt me! I just got pushed around . . ."

"Look, I know I scared you."

"You didn't scare me."

"I just wanted out of the bar. I didn't want you to see me there."

"It wasn't that. Oh, hell, I've ruined it for you, Jack! If I hadn't gone out to find you you'd still be a free man. They're saying, now, when they catch you, they'll ask for the death penalty. And it's my fault."

Jack smiled. Smiled!

"People say a lot of things, Josie. First thing they have to do is catch me, and they're not going to do that."

"So did you kill Colt like they say or was that one of the cousins?"

"I killed him but not the way the newspaper is saying."

"You want to tell me about it?"

"Don't worry about it, okay? I can't prove anything, so it doesn't matter what I say."

"So just tell me the truth. I don't care. I mean it's not like I can turn you in or anything."

"You want the truth? Colt had his man pull me out of the car. They had me chained hand and foot. He meant to shoot me."

"Oh, God! Why? Did he say why?"

"I don't know, Josie. I just know he meant to do it, and I made my move. Colt got a couple rounds off, one of them killed the guy – "

"Officer Crouch – "

" – and I got hold of this Crouch's gun when he went down. I got lucky, Josie. If I hadn't, I'd be dead and Colt would be telling the story."

"You *know* he meant to shoot you? You're sure of it?"

"Forget it. It doesn't matter."

"I'm asking."

"I know what he meant to do."

"I want you to write out what happened. Everything he said, everything you did. I'll take it in to . . . to somebody . . ."

Jack smiled at her. "Somebody? Who are you going to take it to?"

"I'll get a lawyer. We have to try to straighten this out, Jack!"

"Leave it, Josie. I can stay out here forever and they won't find me. Hell, it beats pulling drinks anyway."

"You can't stay out here. They have a hundred special deputies looking for you."

"Those boys answered the sheriff's ad so they could get the beer and hot dogs. It's just a big party in the woods, Josie! But I'll tell you something, there's not a mother's son in Lues County wants to get off the pavement and come in and *look* for me; they're all scared to death they'll find me."

"It's not a joke. Okay? They'll find you eventually. You know they will."

"What are you doing here, Josie? You got out of Lues once. What did you come back for?"

She looked away. She looked to the little window that five minutes before she had thought about trying to dive through. "I didn't like what I'd become, Jack, so I thought I better find out who I'd been."

"Virgil says you don't remember any of it."

"I guess I should have kept it that way." She stared into his eyes – the man who didn't murder her mother – the man she'd betrayed and who didn't care, didn't hit her, didn't yell. The man who made light of an army of men hunting for him. "I've ruined your whole life."

"Hey, if Colt meant to kill me, it was coming down the pike anyway. Don't worry about it. Far as that goes, this here probably saved my life."

Josie shook her head and walked back toward the table
296

and window. Without looking at the man, she asked him, "I want to know what happened between you and my mother. I want to know why you two got a divorce."

She turned now and saw him looking at the planks of the floor. Ashamed, maybe, or maybe just a man with no good answers.

"What's it matter, anyway?"

"It matters," she said, walking toward him, wanting to reach out and touch him the way a girl might her father when they've disappointed each other.

"Josie wanted to be better. Going to the university was just part of it."

Nothing more.

"You were afraid she wanted to get a degree and move away?" Jack tried to look like he didn't understand. "She wanted to leave Lues, and you didn't want to?" Josie asked.

"It's complicated."

"*Complicated* is what you tell a seven-year-old, Jack."

The man growled, turned and walked away. "It was the dumbest thing I ever did."

"Did you cheat on her?"

Jack looked at the floor, "I got real drunk one night." He shook his head. "I was out on my ass before I knew there was an argument."

He still wasn't looking at his stepdaughter; he was a man trapped by his past.

"She filed for divorce, and before we could even talk about it, everything was already settled. We'd ended up selling the place to Virgil on contract, and he tried to bring in dancers."

"You worked for Virgil after you sold him the bar?"

"I end up going to work for him, yeah, but just so he could make his payments to us. They were having fights in the bar, and some of the girls were hustling tricks in the parking lot. I mean Virgil's worth diddle *now* as a manager;

297

back then he was *really* bad. I had to get the place under control or we'd have all lost our shirts."

"Did my mother ever work there after you sold the place?"

"No, Josie wanted nothing to do with that scene. Plus, she was bound and determined to be the best college student anyone ever saw. She started trying to learn everything, even before classes. She was a bright woman, Josie. Your becoming a professor — that would have made her real proud."

Josie let the sentiment fall away without response. She was thinking about the memory of being in an apartment, the feeling that something was wrong, something missing. Jack Hazard had been missing, and they had both wanted him back. *Ahhhh, Josie*, a sad woman, a lonesome ache you share with a child who can't quite understand how things can get wrong so fast.

"Was she seeing anyone, Jack? Did she ever date anyone that you know about?"

"No."

Too quick. Lying or dreaming.

"A friend, someone she studied with?"

"I don't know what she was doing at the college. I stayed out of that part of her life. But there wasn't anyone else."

"How do you know?"

"A man knows those things."

Josie resisted the urge to smile. Jack was serious.

"Was someone writing her threatening notes or calling her?"

A curious twist of his brow. "No."

"You're sure?"

"She would have told me about that."

"Tell me about the day she disappeared. Do you remember it?"

"You called me up at the bar; you said your mom wasn't home. I came to get you. We started looking; I mean everyone in the family, but she wasn't anywhere."

"You went to the police the afternoon they found her?"

"I knew something was wrong by then, and I had to report it. I didn't figure it would do any good, but you never know."

"You were at the police station when she was killed."

"Say it again."

"Colt knew it and he falsified the time of death so he could make sure you'd look guilty."

This was news, and Jack's face cooled like a man who has to make a hard decision. "How do you know that?"

"I know it, okay?"

Jack fished out a Lucky and struck a match. He kicked across the small room and squatted on the corner of the bed. "Colt knew?" Incredulous, bitter, almost laughing at himself, the twenty years he'd lost because of the man's lie. Josie nodded. "I never thought he'd do something like that," Jack said after a time. "I thought it was just bad luck."

Josie remembered the image of Jack in the state police sedan, face bloody, head bent down. Ashamed or just beaten senseless? *"JAAAACK!"*

"You don't want to talk to him, Josie. That man there is the one that killed your mamma." She hadn't wanted to believe it; she had loved him. He was the only father she had ever known.

They were *her* twenty years lost, too.

"You gave up too soon, Jack. They had nothing. It was all bluff."

Jack shook his head. "You don't know the law in Lues County, Josie."

"You just let them bully you, Jack! Pat Bitts told me the whole story. What they had couldn't have ever gone to trial. There were five witnesses who saw the body at three in the afternoon!"

"You weren't there, Josie." Jack's voice was dangerous with calm, and then he caught himself, shaking his head, "I mean you were just a kid. You don't know what these people are like."

299

Authority was his demon, she realized. He had grown up inside the system and never quite escaped its high walls. Except maybe here, deep in his woods, where he was the authority.

"The sheriff was on your side. He was fighting to prove you didn't do it. He says he knows you've never struck a woman."

Bitterly, a man with his life mostly behind him, Jack answered her, "So if Two-Bit knew so much, why didn't he stop them?"

"He tried! Even after you *confessed* he tried. I'd say he fought a lot longer than you did."

"Are you saying everyone knew I didn't do it?" His face had about it a certain aspect of calm which chilled her. His voice was skeptical, as if it were impossible people in authority would lie, but the face was certain: he meant to kill anyone involved in his betrayal.

Carefully, Josie explained what she could, leaving Sheriff Cal Yeager out of it, and hoping he wouldn't think to ask about Yeager's double dealings.

Colt knew it, she said, and the police officer who was with him the other night. "Did you know him? His name was Toby Crouch."

"No."

"This Crouch was a campus cop twenty years ago. He said he saw you at the falls when he went in to check on the kids' report."

"I wasn't there, Josie."

"He lied about that and about what time it was when he was called to go into the canyon."

"What about the rest of them?"

"The medical examiner, a Dr Waldis falsified the time of death, but Colt was behind that. He was behind all of it."

Jack was silent. She could see it was all still before him, but he had no more idea of what had happened than before. It was beyond him. It wasn't quite possible everyone could
300

agree to sacrifice him, despite the evidence. Even knowing the way the law worked in Lues County, it wasn't quite comprehensible – the evil they had done him.

"Did you know Colt? Did he have some kind of grudge?"

Jack hesitated, then answered. "He got drunk one time, and I threw him out of the bar. Another time, your mother put him out."

"That's it?"

Jack shrugged uncomfortably. "That's it."

"He said he didn't drink at your bar; he didn't know my mother."

"He was lying. He knew her." Jack grinned suddenly. "Hell, after the way your mom treated him that one time, he never would have forgot her – I promise you that!" There was a wild, beautiful grin in this, the love of a man for a woman who fought her own fights. Josie felt the pride too.

Cyrus Hazard

Outside, the others were all gone except for Cyrus Hazard. Cy was waiting up the road some, and when he saw them coming out of the cabin, he walked back down the road toward them, a flashlight's bright beam bouncing in front of his steps. Josie turned to say something to Jack, but he was already gone. She was alone suddenly, except for a young man with a rifle.

"I'll take you to your car," he said softly.

As she walked with Cyrus Hazard back toward the Mustang, following the light at their feet, Cyrus was preter-naturally quiet, and Josie thought to say something.

"So you're related to Jack?"

"Nephew." The voice came like a whisper, a boy almost.

"So that means Virgil's your father?"

"My father's dead."

The silence between them returned. Finally, she asked him, "Where do you work, Cy?"

301

"The bar, sometimes."

Josie studied the dark trees, then the light at their feet, the deep carpet of wet leaves.

"Have you ever been out of Lues County, Cy?"

"I was in Vienna a couple of years."

"Austria?" Josie had been twice to Austria and had answered excitedly before she remembered this was a Hazard, this was Lues County. "No," she said, answering herself. "You mean Vienna as in, you robbed a bank?"

"It was a misunderstanding, ma'am."

Ma'am?

A long silence followed with only the sound of their footfalls in the dark leaves. "Tell me about the misunderstanding," Josie said at last.

"Not much to it. This guy was hurting his girlfriend out in Huree at some bar. He was twisting her arm, pushing her face into her beer and calling her names. That kind of thing."

Josie nodded. Nothing new in this. Dan Scholari had done as much to Josie at a faculty party. She still remembered his colleagues – many of them her professors, as well, all of them friends – all watching uncomfortably. Josie had thought they would stop it, but they had only observed the treatment in silence. Cowards.

Cy shrugged, the narrative finished, "I stopped it."

"They sent you to prison for stopping it?"

"Yes, ma'am."

"Did you know the man or the woman?"

"No, ma'am."

Josie thought about this before she remembered the point of his story.

"So what was the misunderstanding, Cy?"

"I said he'd better stop, or I'd kill him. He didn't understand I was serious."

At the Mustang, Cy handed Josie her Smith and Wesson .357, and pointed the way back to Lues Creek Crossing. She could hardly understand the directions for thinking about

Cy's story. Had he really killed a man, or was that just what he had said? She was afraid to ask, afraid she already knew.

After she had started the car and rolled her window down to thank the young man – who would kill or be killed to protect a woman he didn't even know! – Cyrus Hazard told her, "I'm sorry we scared you like that. Virgil was, you know, being an asshole. He's all pissed off about Jack getting arrested."

"Virgil was?"

"Jack wanted to let it go. Virgil wanted, you know, to make a big deal out of it. At least scare you. I think Jack went along with it so he could talk to you. He didn't know how else he could, if we didn't do it that way."

"I guess I deserved it. I brought a lot of trouble on Jack."

"You want to know the truth?" Cy asked her.

"Sure. I'm a great one for the truth."

"Ever since I was little, people talked about Jack like he was something special. Well I saw him in Vienna, and I saw him at the bar, and there wasn't nothing special about him. He was just a guy, you know? Then this weekend he got loose. I got out to help him get things together, and I could see it right away – what everyone used to talk about. It was in his eyes, ma'am, in the way he moved. I don't know how to explain it any better, but he's different. He's got the woods in him or something."

Josie knew what Cyrus meant. She had seen it too without quite realizing it, a kind of animal grace that had been missing in the bar. She had thought of him as an ex-con, just a nice old guy who'd steal a dollar from his last friend, kind of proud his stepdaughter was a professor and real ashamed about pulling drinks at a girly bar. But the man she had met in the cabin was laughing about a hundred special deputies chasing him. Laughing and meant it. These were *his* woods; here even the law hesitated.

"This thing happening to him," Cyrus finished, "it made

303

him a man again. Everybody but Virgil's saying it. Virgil knows it too; he's just too stubborn to admit it."

Josie had no answer for the handsome young man. Their eyes met briefly; she remembered his face now. It was a face like that of the man her mother had loved. With that thought, both terrifying and intriguing, Josie took off in a hurry.

Home

It was dark when Josie pulled into parking spot 27 at her apartment complex on campus. By chance, no one was moving around outside, and only a few windows showed light. The place had an eerie aspect. A wind was kicking in the treetops; clouds were racing over the moon. At the door, her key already into the lock, Josie stopped. She backed away quickly and pulled the revolver from her purse. She looked out at the darkened forms of the automobiles, then back to the door again. A terrible instinct warned her against going inside. She had been giving away too many chances. She knew he could get past a locked door, and yet she was letting herself believe home was safe. Home was anything but safe! Home would be where he was most likely to strike. She might give him the daytime, she might move in the crowds at school, but here, late at night, she could walk right into his hands and no one would know it for days. If not tonight, tomorrow, or the day after. One evening she would return home, tired and thinking about something else, and it would be the last mistake of her life.

Josie hit the Mustang hard as she left. She came off Willow Circle and down the hill quickly. On Willow Drive, she raced through campus at nearly sixty. It was time to think like the hunter, time to settle in a new blind.

That afternoon, Josie had fought two Hazards to a standstill, and if she could have gotten to her gun, she would have stopped them all. She had stared Jack Hazard himself down.

She wasn't the obedient wife anymore, Mrs Scholari cowering before a lunatic husband; nor little Miss Darling hiding from the ex, the fight all kicked out of her. She could claw and kick and shoot a gun. More than that, she knew she could find this man. She needed time; that was all. Nothing said she had to sit and wait and hope he wouldn't strike before she had found him out. No rules at all held her to the whims of a madman. She meant to take the fight to him, and first of all that meant he wasn't going to know where to find her — not after dark, at any rate.

Josie made a fairly lengthy stop at an all-night grocery, getting all she would need for the next day or so, including a stop at a cash machine. Once back in the Mustang, Josie headed west through the hills until she joined with a spur of highway that would take her eventually to Huree. There were a couple of hotels out that way because of the interstate, and that was her destination. A few miles before the town, however, Josie found the perfect motel along a winding stretch of two-lane highway. She turned into the narrow drive on impulse, and dropped down a steep incline so that she was no longer visible from the highway. The Huree Hideaway was a place just made for illicit love affairs: it was cheap, quiet, and relatively clean. Best of all, it was discreet. One registered at the front of the building in a little office, but the motel guests entered their rooms and parked their cars at the back, close up against the woods.

The motel rented rooms for the night and studio apartments by the week, Bea, the old lady at the registration desk, told her. Behind the woman, in a little apartment where she stayed when she wasn't watching the desk, a television was playing. A beer can and pack of cigarettes rested close by on a little table next to the easy chair. Bea was a woman close to sixty, her face a bit bloated, her eyes quick and small and full of an old fire that wasn't quite out. She was the sort to believe people are going to do what they want and no sense worrying about it — though it was kind of fun knowing. She

305

took one look at Josie and thought she was certain of the game: "We don't allow parties, honey, but a quiet friend or two is perfectly okay. Don't worry," she added with a wink, "I keep an eye on things, but I *say* nothing."

Filling out the register, Josie used a fictitious Beacon Hill address as her own, then signed the register, *Josie Fortune*.

Bea looked at the name thoughtfully, then at Josie.

"That's a pretty name you have," the old woman offered.

The apartment itself was small. The bed was cheap, the mattress soft, the cover worn and thin. There was a tiny desk that could barely contain Josie's elbows, a rickety straight-back chair before it, and a broken-down couch pulled up close to an old Philco television set. The flooring was lin-oleum, the paneling dark. The air was tight.

In the kitchenette she found some cookware, and started some water to boil. She tried the phone, but Annie didn't answer. Josie had no one else she could call. She ate the fruit and bread she had picked up at the store, then dropped a couple of tea bags in the boiling water. A couple of minutes later, she began pouring herself small measures of black tea into a tiny yellow cup while she wrote out on motel stationery all that she knew about her mother's death. She had thought to spend only a few minutes on the project, but wrote for nearly three hours. When she had finished, she discovered she knew a good deal more than she might have imagined, and it was with some satisfaction she turned to the thin mattress of her new bed.

That night Josie slept naked. A .357 magnum lay on top of the bedside table, a bible in the drawer.

A Day in the Academy

Josie bribed a mechanic with an awful gee-whiz routine and had her tire patched before eight o'clock the next morning. After her morning classes, she slipped out to Willow Circle and with her revolver drawn, entered the apartment. As quickly as she could, Josie cleared out only the most necessary clothes and files and books, then headed out to see old Bowers for another lesson with the .357. The old man swore to it she'd been practicing. Josie was back to Brand Hall for her office hours with a few minutes to spare. Having missed all of her Monday afternoon office time, Josie was hardly surprised to see so many students waiting for her. They were stacked up outside, and she had to force herself to slow down, to give each of them her full attention. It was easier than she imagined. Here the old routines were comforting; the way was well lit, the answers within easy reach. She read with excitement some new lines in the football epic. The young man was bright and creative, and finding his voice, she told him. She nudged him toward the idea of trying prose, epics being, she said, a little stilted and out of date. The boy wore overalls and carried Homer in his backpack, like some kind of misplaced Alexander, and at her suggestion blinked with a slew's thoughtfulness. Epics, he told her in all sincerity, were bound to make a comeback.

A few minutes later Josie was looking at a sonnet about a young man's eyes and "an older woman's urgent, silent past." Splendid! Beautiful! Josie shouted. She hugged the woman impulsively and saw her eyes fill with proud sad tears. "Now this is poetry, Harriet!" Josie told her, and the smile that answered tore away, if only for the moment, a lot of the woman's aching. A lot of Josie's too.

At three Josie sat down for an unscheduled departmental meeting and what victories the day had given her came crashing down at once. The talk was about hiring standards for the department's lecturers. Scandal lingered in the air, though all the words were about academic credentials. At some point in all this, Josie realized she was sitting utterly alone in the center of the room. She had taken her chair and watched the others file in and had thought nothing of the fact that the sides and back and front had filled with her colleagues and that not even Henry Valentine had gotten within ten feet of her. The meeting culminated when Dick Ferrington finally spoke. He suggested that the department ought "to do away with all the lecturers."

Dr Smith, the chair, cleared his throat nervously. He certainly hoped Dick meant eliminate *the positions* and not the lecturers themselves. There was some laugher at this, and Ferrington answered with good-natured coyness, "Whatever."

The talk turned into a motion, duly seconded, and with no further need for discussion the question was called. Now Henry Valentine stood up. He took his time and looked each professor in the eye. "I should like to remind my learned colleagues of the scholar's enemy . . ." Another long pause with a certain theatrical satisfaction in his cocky grin, then in a stage whisper: "the sin of *haste*, people. The ruin of many, the savior of none!" The professor, having said all that needed saying, sat down again, and with only a little grumbling, the rest decided to kill the lecturers at their next meeting instead.

As they filed out, Josie noticed quite a few furtive looks cast in her direction, and in the hallway outside there were several clutches locked in animated conversation. All grew deathly silent when Josie passed.

Yep. Assassination was on the agenda.

At just past six o'clock, an hour later than she had intended to leave, Josie finished grading a stack of compositions, and checked the halls. Seeing no one, she slung her purse over her shoulder, took up her briefcase and started away. The moment her door shut, Josie heard Henry Valentine, his voice hollow and cold like a stranger's. "I forgot to tell you, Dean Meyers was here yesterday afternoon and again at lunchtime today. He was asking if I had seen you."

Looking back, Josie saw Val nearly thirty feet away, his hands stuffed deeply into his pockets, his shoulder leaning gracefully against Gerty Dowell's office door. He seemed to have appeared out of the very air. All the offices were closed and darkened, and despite the fact that it was only Val, Josie felt a hard punch of adrenalin.

"He didn't leave a message?" Josie hoped her voice was calm, but she couldn't be sure. He had scared her. He was still scaring her.

"I think he wants to bump into you," Val answered pleasantly. There was a faint irony in Valentine's tone and smile, but the eyes belonged to a different man.

"Thanks for the tip, Val." Josie started on. "Wish I could talk, but I'm running late for a meeting."

"Another meeting at this hour?"

Josie scrambled. "I'm meeting some kids at Williams Hall in ten minutes."

"I take it you didn't talk to Dick, as I suggested, Josie?" Valentine's look was nothing so much as an I-told-you-so.

"They can pass all the resolutions they want, Val. I'm under contract to the end of the year. What happened in that meeting was nonsense; we both know it."

The old eyebrows lifted sadly, "I'm hearing rumors, Josie."

"Talk's cheap, Val."

"You're right. It costs you nothing at all to make peace with Ferrington. Just some talk."

"That's not what I meant."

"You're old friends, Josie. All Dick really wants to hear is an apology."

"Would you do it if you were in my shoes? Would you give that arrogant hypocrite the *satisfaction*?"

They were still standing some distance from one another, but there was a kind of intimacy in the narrow hall, the quiet of the place.

Val pursed his big loose lips kindly, "My mother told me once that all of life is perfectly easy to understand. If it feels good, it isn't; if it hurts, it must be the best thing to do."

Josie hesitated.

"Dick has a lot of pull with people around here, Josie. All he really wants is to be your mentor; instead he feels like

309

you've ignored him, that you've plowed around here like some kind of *equal*. This scandal is just an excuse, but if you ask him for his help, he'll give it to you. It's just ego, Josie. Let him know how much you respect him and need him, and all this will be forgotten in a couple of weeks. Swallow your pride, Josie. It won't hurt too much. If you play tough on this, he'll destroy you. He has quite a temper, our Dr Ferrington." The old man shrugged in a kindly manner. "That's my read on the matter, at any rate."

"I'll think about, Val. I really will."

Val made good sense. Dick Ferrington wasn't the man Josie had known in Venice or Madrid, or the half-dozen other conferences where they had spent long hours talking Joyce and the meaning of literature. Here, his reputation was nothing; face was everything, and Dick Ferrington had a lot of face to lose among the faculty. To save it, he was turning into a cheap-shot specialist at the cost of whatever affection they'd had once. Valentine knew it, and he was telling her how to get around her problem. She had gone to him for just such advice, after all.

"I wouldn't wait too long. Rumor is the lynch mob has already formed."

Josie smiled wryly, nodding. That was about right, she said.

In the main hallway Dick Ferrington was coming out of the department office as Josie was coming toward it. The man had a bounce in his step, a crooked little smile. He was carrying an oversized notebook which Josie recognized at once as *The Official University Procedural Document*. One finger was even jammed inside it, as if he'd found some precious page he wanted to study at his leisure. Seeing her, Ferrington's stride caught slightly in surprise. He recovered at once, his face composing into perfect sincerity.

Josie started to speak; she meant to apologize or at least to arrange a meeting where she could, but the man cut her off.

"About what I said in the meeting today, Josie: I want you to know it's nothing personal."

All thoughts of apology fled. *Nothing personal?*

Josie's answer singed the good professor's eyebrows.

Meditations

After a hurried meal and a couple of phone calls, Josie forced herself back to Worley Hall. Once in the library, she forgot about Ferrington's maneuvers against her and Valentine's kindly advice, plunging instead into the past. Josie worked with focus and excitement, convinced she could reach into history and pull her man out of it by his very neck! Gone was the sense of embarrassment about her mother's *slew-ness*. Gone too was any kind of outrage she might have felt about men like Colt Fellows and Cal Yeager using the murder for their own ends. Outrage, numbed shock, even thoughts of revenge were simply emotions that would dilute her vision of things. She was looking for one man. Right now, nothing else counted so much. It was coming, too. She was closing in on some ideas, building the scenes up slowly, each possibility in turn. There were names gathering around the death of her mother; there were motives, passions, payoffs, and still a few enduring enigmas. Josie worked late, worked until her eyes burned, then a bit longer. This wasn't school work or some kind of academic's exercise. This was how she lived or died.

At 10:30, Josie headed back into the dark country. There were cars behind her as she approached her first turn, so she drove until they passed her. Once they were out of sight, she made a quick U-turn and went back. She stepped into the accelerator and the dark woods flashed by. She hit a hundred, then she asked for a little more. At her motel, certain she was alone, Josie emptied her car quickly, and set up her computer and books along the floor just inside the door. After that, she called Bea at the front desk and asked if anyone had been looking for her. "I've got a man trying to sell me a car," she lied, "and I thought he might come by."

Bea told her there had been no one, but she'd keep an eye out for him. "What's he look like?"

"He's a man, Bea. They're all the same, right?"

Bea laughed, the phlegm in her chest crackling like gunshots. God, wasn't that the truth!

When she had made a cup of tea at the tiny stove, Josie called Annie. It was past midnight in Boston, but Annie was up.

Between news about Dan Scholari's imminent return to the classroom and Josie's encounters with the Hazards, Pat Bitts, and Dr Richard Ferrington, it took the better part of an hour for the women to bring each other up to date. What surprised Josie was the calm she felt as she detailed her discoveries. Panic was no longer a luxury she could afford, and she talked about the murder and the threats against her with an academic's detachment. It was the way she worked best; everything a riddle, herself the woman in possession of the facts and piecing together the dark puzzle of history. No longer was there a feeling of overpowering despair or even the frustration of not knowing. She was on the trail of something now, really chasing him. She was no longer the victim of some invisible force. She spoke of details that left her curious. She wondered, for instance, if Colt Fellows's alibi could really hold up under close scrutiny. Now that she understood he might have had a motive against Jack and her mother, she told Annie, all of Colt's actions twenty years ago took on a diabolical aspect. She said she believed he had almost certainly planted the wristwatch with Jack Hazard's name on it, and he had been eager to confuse everyone about the time of death. That argued for his guilt in her mother's death.

On the other hand, there was the issue of character. Colt Fellows had not seemed the kind of man who was really interested in creating the situations Josie had been subjected to since arriving in Lues. She could see it in a deranged ex-husband or some kind of obsessed loner — someone like Toby Crouch for instance, but it wasn't quite what she thought Colt Fellows was about. He was much more the sort to get in your face and growl a bit, she said. Josie had found some things in the Peoria newspaper about police brutality. No names of course, but there had been several meetings of the city council devoted to smoothing out some wrinkles right before Colt bolted for his home town of Lues. In Lues, Josie had found out about three men who were killed after lodging a complaint of police brutality. Annie's interest was piqued. She wanted to know what had happened. Nothing at all, Josie answered. "Colt ran the investigation."

"And you think this guy doesn't fit the profile?" Annie was skeptical. A killer was a killer, after all.

"I'm not just looking for a violent or dangerous man, Annie. My guess is the guy I'm looking for has a peculiar bent toward women; he gets his kicks making women suffer. Colt Fellows was a guy to run the show; he wanted power and prestige; he wanted to be the big dog among *the boys*."

That was the problem with Cal Yeager as well. To all outward appearances, the man's passions were transparent. What he did, the lies he made, were all for the sake of political expediency. Once Colt Fellows had preempted Pat Bitts and had Jack arrested, Yeager had responded. Until then, she couldn't see that he had been involved in the investigation. It wasn't really a matter of caring about the truth or justice. To Yeager it had simply been a matter of taking advantage of Bitts's vulnerability. Yeager's campaign for the office of sheriff that summer and fall verified Josie's theory. He made Bitts look old-fashioned. He talked about an antiquated sheriff's office that hadn't been able to confirm the time of a phone call. "He turned Bitts's accusations against him into the issue of technology, Annie, and he used

Bitts's complaints that the body was moved as proof Bitts was getting old: he said the confusion was Bitts's. The man could no longer recognize the difference between an honest report and lies. It goes on and on like this, Annie. The guy ruined Bitts's credibility, and all of it was an utter fabrication; but that doesn't make him the sort to fit *my man's* profile. He doesn't come close to that kind of monster."

Annie acquiesced. Because a man was a killer, it didn't follow he had killed a certain person. Yes, she could see that. Because a man lied outrageously, it didn't follow that he was involved in the crime either. Indeed, the assumption that a liar has something to hide only misdirected one in this kind of investigation. Everyone was lying, or so it seemed. But that raised an even stickier question. "If you can't catch someone in a lie, Josie, how do you expect to find the real killer? Where do you look next?"

"Napoleon," Josie answered boldly.

"Napoleon did it?"

"Napoleon said it: Geography explains history."

"Okay." Sixteen flavors of irony, this.

"I'm working from the theory that the same man who killed my mother is the one stalking me."

"Josie, you don't have any proof. It could be anyone."

"It's just a theory, Annie, but the theory is this guy has to occupy a given space at a given time. He has to be in Lues twenty years ago and be here now. I was writing out everything I knew about him last night, and realized I can put him in certain places at fairly precise times."

"That's great!"

"Actually it's more of a problem than anything. I've got the perfect killer but he doesn't quite fit into all the boxes."

"Who?"

"Toby Crouch. The guy was a pervert, Annie."

"Three beers and they're all perverts. God bless 'em."

"This one's different. I'm telling you, the guy is perfect. Look at him: he lets Yeager and Fellows trample all over the

314

investigation and cooperates reluctantly. All along, he's got his own motives for lying, and no one really looks at him twice. He was there, Annie. He was close to the canyon on the day of the murder, and he was the first in to see the body. He's also in a position the last twenty years to follow my career. A simple check with no suspicions, he can know everything about me, right down to the fact I've taken a job at Lues State. He was there when I came into town, and he was at the desk when I walked in to file a complaint."

"You think he expected you?"

"I'd just had my car windows broken out. He had to expect I'd go to the police at some point during all this. Maybe he was there some of the other times, too. I mean, who's to say it wouldn't have been Crouch who answered the call if I had phoned the police about the note on my mirror or the one on my balcony door? The guy was a sneak. He could have been out at the Hurry On Up. He could have been watching my mother for a year or so; all of a sudden, she shows up on campus, and maybe he decides to take a chance. He's a campus cop; he wants to talk to her. He wants her to get in his car. What's she going to do?"

"You're right. He's perfect. So what's the problem?"

"Toby Crouch was at the police station when I got the sympathy card in my mailbox. Simple geography: he can't be two places at once."

"You're sure about the time the card was slipped into your mailbox?"

"I can't find any way around it, Annie. Toby Crouch didn't leave that note."

"Napoleon had his problems, Josie!"

Delbert

When Josie entered the department office the next day, she found a handwritten note from Dean Meyers.

See me as son as possible.
del.

Josie assumed Meyers meant *soon* and called his office to arrange a meeting. She made a second call immediately afterwards, then went on about her business, even catching an hour and a half at Worley Hall. She was scanning the intervening years between her mother's death and her own arrival in Lues. If there was no real motive for the murder of her mother, and if the man was still here, as it seemed, Josie thought it possible there could be other murders. The first three years turned up nothing, and before she changed reels to look at the next couple of years, she had to go.

Shortly before noon Josie met Clarissa Holt outside the dean's office, as they had arranged. Clarissa's face was ashen with anger, her dark eyes smoldering. "How are you doing?" she asked.

Her career in a freefall – and that the least of her problems – there didn't seem a reasonable answer to the question, so Josie shrugged and smiled sheepishly. "Nervous. Mad. Numb."

"I'll handle it, Josie. Say as little as possible. Del and I have . . ." she hesitated for emphasis, " . . . a history."

"This whole thing is – "

Clarissa touched her arm. "Don't apologize. Don't even *think* about apologizing. You did nothing wrong. Okay?"

Josie nodded.

"Ready?"

"My gun's loaded, if that's what you mean."

Clarissa smiled. She thought it was a joke.

A man who had come to the university some fifteen years before as a professor of philosophy, Dean Delbert Meyers was in his mid-forties but looked older. He was average height, slightly overweight; his hair was dull and thinning, the eyes narrow, cautious and calculating. Josie knew Meyers solely from the College of Liberal Arts's kick-off meeting in

316

August. He had introduced himself to her briefly, asked a couple of inane questions, then moved onto more interesting quarry. The speech he had given lacked both courage and vision. Whatever else Josie knew about Dean Meyers she had picked up in shop talk. There were contradictory reports about his method. Josie had heard he was capable of any savagery so long as one's back was turned. Others claimed he was confrontational, that he was something of a hot-head, ready to shoot from his hip at the first sign of trouble. That boded ill for the present circumstances. Josie was sure Clarissa meant to antagonize him. Still, Josie had little choice, unless she wanted to crawl to Dick "nothing-personal" Ferrington.

Starting for the door, Clarissa whispered, "We're dealing here with an extremely big dog. Remember, if you let him smell fear, he'll hurt you. On the other hand, if you get him off his own porch, he's just a dog."

Josie saw immediately that Clarissa's presence had somehow gotten Meyers off his porch. The moment Josie and Clarissa entered his outer office, his eyes widened in surprise. "Clarissa?"

Meyers looked like a man with a mouthful of cottage cheese.

"Delbert." Clarissa's tone was something of the school-marm's with the class troublemaker.

Meyers looked at Josie in confusion. "I'm afraid I had a meeting with Ms Darling." This was purely wishful thinking: Dean Meyers read the scenario perfectly.

"We'll have a meeting together," Clarissa told him.

Meyers considered this, his big white face seeming to retract as if from a series of punches, his shoulders wilting. Anything but a happy man, Meyers managed a smile and let his voice boom as he asked rhetorically, "Why not?"

The three of them met in the dean's large conference room, sitting at one corner of the long table. Meyers had probably intended to get right to the point, since meetings before a dean's lunch hour usually lack the amenities of a proper foreplay, but with Clarissa's presence his battle plans were in shambles, and he was forced to start with a query about "things in Communications."

Clarissa gave a detailed answer. After this, the air grew warmer. The two of them seemed to spar with cold smiles and tepid praise, names dropping like so much Lues rainfall. As the conversation continued, Clarissa leaned forward like a big cat on the stalk, while Dean Meyers began crossing and uncrossing his legs, finally tucking his hands between them in a gesture that was entirely unconscious. It seemed to Josie the two had slipped into the time-honored roles of castrating lesbian Mother Goddess and sacrificial old bull.

When the conversation finally turned to Josie's *situation*, Josie readied herself.

"I think you know why I wanted to see Ms Darling," Dean Meyers offered, a patient, nurturing expression coming over his big, plain features.

Neither woman answered him, Josie because she was not addressed, Clarissa because she was waiting, Josie assumed, for the opening salvo.

"This thing in the newspaper," Meyers offered, "is very upsetting."

"The assault on Josie?" Clarissa's voice cooled the room.

"Exactly." Meyers looked suddenly at Josie, almost as if he expected her to sympathize with his position. "My real concern, Josie, is that you're okay. Something like this can be emotionally difficult, and I just wanted to let you know I'm here for you if I can help."

Thunderstruck, Josie stammered her appreciation.

Dean Meyers smiled at Clarissa. "Josie is one of our best teachers, and I'd hate to see the vitality she brings to the classroom damaged in any way."

Clarissa agreed. She spoke briefly about unfeeling systems and insensitive administrators, the implication being that anywhere but Lues State this thing could have turned ugly.

"I'm sorry we couldn't have had more time to talk about

318

it," Meyers said to them as he stood to signal the conference was over, "but unfortunately I have a twelve o'clock meeting with Smith and Ferrington." He looked at Josie with a mock-scolding expression. "That department of yours always wants more money!"

Outside, Clarissa announced, "I think Del got the message."

"What happened in there, Clar?"

Clarissa raised her eyebrows, something of the big cat licking her chops after a good meal. "You remember the reference to Phyllis Morales?"

Josie shook her head. *Phyllis Morales* she had heard. The "reference" she had missed.

"Interesting case. College of Education. She sued these bastards three years ago to the tune of 1.7 mil. Before it was over, her dean found himself scrambling for his golden parachute."

A name among other names, a casual query about what Phyllis was doing, nothing more. Velvet threats, Josie realized. As they stood together, they watched Josie's department chairman and Dick Ferrington approach. Smith, his oily hair falling into his eyes, snuffed and nodded nervously toward Clarissa and Josie, then hurried inside and shook hands with Dean Meyers. Ferrington had a cool smile for the two women. He was still under the impression he was winning. A moment later the three men ensconced themselves in the dean's cubbyhole office.

"That's about me, isn't it?"

"Not anymore. Now it's about how to calm down whoever stirred this mess up in the first place."

"Ferrington."

"Ferrington?" she asked. "That's interesting. In your department I would have guessed Gerty Dowell was behind it."

"Gerty?"

319

"Henry Valentine winds her up and lets her do his dirty work."

"Val's on my side in this, if you can believe it."

Clarissa laughed. It was a dry, spiritless sound. "The only time Henry Valentine ever took sides in something was to get his own way."

"Not this time. Ferrington's the one who's turned me into a cause. Last week, he was waving the newspaper at me and saying how he had backed me with the hiring committee and how this embarrasses him."

Clarissa's mouth twitched.

"Who was on the hiring committee?" she asked.

"Val chaired it, that's all I know."

"So why was Ferrington backing you with the hiring committee?"

"We knew each other from some conferences. Strictly professional."

Clarissa's smile told Josie she wasn't buying the *strictly professional* angle.

"So what happened?"

"When I got in town, we went out for drinks and got in this weird argument. I mean we always used to argue, but suddenly the guy's real condescending."

"He's always been condescending. Maybe you just got old enough to notice it." Clarissa pondered the man's behavior.

"Val said Dick's jealous," Josie offered. "I don't know. I find that hard to swallow. I mean the guy's got four books out and he's on the Board of Directors for the James Joyce Foundation; what's he got to be jealous of?"

"Good teaching, popularity, brains, originality, guts. Do you want me to go on?"

Josie looked back at the dean's office. Clarissa's praise was encouraging, but it was something else. He had had no reason to turn on her and yet he had been different from the start. Hardly the man she had met six years ago in Venice.

"You know Ferrington killed his wife?"

Josie studied Clarissa's expression. She wasn't joking.

"I know he was investigated and that nothing came of it."

"His daughters are terrified of him; they won't even come to Lues anymore. His son hardly talks to him."

"Clar, a lot of people have trouble with their kids. Especially after something like that."

"All I know is that after Cathy filed for divorce, Dick wasn't a very good sport."

"Cathy filed for divorce?"

"I take it this is news to you?"

"Dick made it sound like the perfect marriage."

"It was – for him. He did what he wanted; Cathy did what she was told."

James Burkeshire

Late that afternoon Josie drove north four hours to a suburb on the outskirts of Bloomington. She arrived at the Burkeshires' house shortly after eight. Jim and Mandy Burkeshire lived affluently. They had a large house, nice cars and all the electronic gadgets. The moment Josie saw him, she could see Jim Burkeshire was a serious, reflective man and had probably been the same as a college kid. Her first impression was that he kept his emotions capped. Burkeshire tried to make Josie feel comfortable with her intrusion into his life. He introduced Josie to his wife and two of their three kids, then took her to a well appointed den where they sat down opposite one another over a cup of coffee. He talked about his business and its beginnings. An engineer by training, he owned a small manufacturing company outside of the city and supplied his former employer and a few other customers with packaging products. He seemed satisfied with what he had done with his professional life, but his passions lay elsewhere.

Josie spent some time explaining what had happened to her after her mother's death. She said nothing about Jack

321

Hazard's innocence or the fact that someone was at present stalking her. She wanted to know about the murder, she said. She had never been allowed that knowledge and had come to Lues to face her past, to come to terms with it. Burkeshire seemed to understand. He said he would tell her what he knew. Like Melody Mason, however, he claimed to have forgotten quite a bit. At first, the conversation moved in fits and starts. His entire memory of college was of living through a difficult time. He had forgotten most of it. He had done well in classes. He hadn't particularly gotten on well socially. He was there, the day they had found Josie's mother, because Bob Tanner had talked him into it. Tanner had convinced him that he should get to know Melody Mason. Like most things in his social life back then, nothing had come of it. Melody had ignored him from the start, had in fact seemed more interested in Tanner.

"Can you tell me about Cat?"

"I didn't really know her. We were in a class together – all of us were. She was really pretty. She dated the big men on campus. In those days, I wasn't quite in that league."

"Do you know what happened to her?"

"I don't know that I ever saw her after that day. I mean I know we must have, we were in the same class, I just don't remember."

He said he had forgotten what class it was they had skipped, had forgotten if any of them had had any kind of social contact after that day. What he remembered, he said, was the body of Josie Fortune.

"Truth is, I was in therapy for three years after that."

"I'm sorry to bring it all back."

"It's okay. Part of the therapy was learning to face it."

"Tell me everything you can remember – if you will."

Burkeshire closed his dark brown eyes, two fine, tense lines forming between his eyebrows. "She was on this huge rock just to the side of the falls. It would have been right of the falls as you faced it. The water from the falls hit her

322

indirectly. I don't know, the moisture or something made her seem almost alive. We were all covered in the mist of the falls and standing directly in front of her. We'd waded into the canyon to make sure of what we thought we'd seen from the ledge just under the top of the falls. She was on her back. The rock slanted down toward us so her head was just touching the water. If any of us wanted, we could have reached out and touched her, we were that close."

"Did anyone touch her?"

"No. No one. We just stared at her. Her eyes were open, the pupils rolled back. It was eerie because you could only see the white of her eyes. Her arms were spread to either side. They were about the level of her head. Her left hand and her hair were in the water. The hair was thick and long. A red–gold color. The water in front of the rock was churning and foaming slightly, so the hair was on the surface of the water; it looked liked she had been placed there. Like a sacrifice, I guess."

Burkeshire opened his eyes, blinked several times and then focused on Josie.

"Were there any marks on her?" Josie asked, feeling almost like a hypnotist.

Burkeshire closed his eyes again. His face grew paler. "Her killer had cut the letters *h-o-r* on her abdomen; the *r* was a capital letter. They were thin cuts, no blood, but it was bright red like it had just begun to heal." He opened his eyes. "I found out later she'd been missing for several days. I guess that explains it."

Josie nodded. "Anything else?"

Burkeshire studied Josie with a frightening intensity, then closed his eyes again. "Both her wrists," he answered, "and her ankles had several deep indentations where she had been tied. There was swelling. The same with her face. Around her neck, here – " Burkeshire pointed just under the jaw – "there was a thin, deep mark, about a quarter of an inch wide. It curled up behind her ears. Bright red."

Burkeshire opened his eyes, raising his eyebrows as he said this last part. He stared at Josie now, almost shaking off the trance, but not quite free of it. "I thought at the time she had been hanged, because of the angle of the ligature. I think later they said she was strangled. I suppose they meant garroted. I don't see how from the angle of it, unless maybe the guy didn't know what he was doing and put his hands above her head, you know, like he hanged her with his hands." The man shrugged. He understood nothing any better than Josie.

In the next room Burkeshire's wife moved about, picking up toys and adjusting some pillows. She was checking on Josie, or seeing if her Jim was still okay.

"Do you remember what time it was when you saw her?"

He thought for a moment, then answered simply, "Daylight."

"Do you remember anything about leaving the canyon?"

"Nothing."

"And nothing about going in?" They had covered this point.

He shook his head.

"You talked to someone about it. Do you remember when that was?"

He smiled weakly. He wanted to help, but he had told her all he could remember. "It was a long time ago, Professor Darling."

"You talked to Sheriff Bitts that night, I think?" He shrugged. He wasn't sure. "And to someone else later?"

"I don't know."

Mandy Burkeshire came over and sat next to her husband. It was a consoling, protective gesture.

"One of you said there were bruises from where the killer strangled her. Do you remember the bruises on her neck?"

Burkeshire shook his head, "No bruises, just that ligature."

"You're sure?"

324

James Burkeshire gave a look as much to say, *This is my nightmare, professor; I know what I saw.*

"Positive," he answered.

Library Hours

Tiredly, Josie cranked the handle of the microfilm machine until the next headline came into view: BODY FOUND. She scanned the account. A nude body had been suspended by its feet from a log that stretched over a narrow ravine near Clems Hollow. Police had identified the victim as Shelley Kruger, 24, a Lues State co-ed.

Josie picked up her pen.

The Farm

Josie called Virgil Hazard at his bar in Codswallop Friday afternoon. She wanted to know about her mother's belongings. "Who took them?"

"I did. There wasn't much. We got your stuff out and gave it to the sheriff. Your mom's stuff, I took out to the farm."

"I want you to take me there. I'll be at the bar in an hour. Be in the parking lot."

"I'm working, DJ! I got a hundred lunatics in here. I got to keep things in hand!"

"They'll do fine without you. This is important."

Snidely: "You going to get me arrested if I don't cooperate?"

"Don't make me come inside." Josie hung up and started north through the countryside. Virgil was waiting when she got there, and took her along several twisting back roads toward his farm. A few minutes later they found a long narrow lane and went back along it slowly because of the pot-holes. At the end of the road, they parked next to a couple of antique hearses and got out of their vehicles.

325

Cut out of the forest years before, Virgil Hazard's farm was not much more than a couple of hills and a creek. With a few broken-down outbuildings and a roofless barn, the place was a portrait of Virgil's whole life. Virgil kept a couple of sway-back horses in the field behind his barn and nothing more except a dog, which was something of a roommate, and a couple of outdoor cats, which seemed pretty much to fare for themselves.

The farmhouse was a little shack, essentially two rooms, one set behind the other. Josie stepped into it as far as the front door and then decided she didn't want to go any further. There was a wood stove, a couch and piano in the middle of the room. Beyond that was the dark cave of a bedroom.

"Nice, Virgil!" This with pure sarcasm.

"Yeah, well, it's just me and Buster and the sheriff's phone-tap, DJ."

The dog's name was Buster. He was a big, runny-eyed Labrador male. He moved slowly through the mess of the house and nuzzled Josie with an old slow affection that Josie felt compelled to return.

"So how's Jack doing?" she asked.

"He's still alive. No thanks to you."

"I called a couple of lawyers."

"And?"

"And nothing. If he comes in, they'll work with him."

Virgil smiled. "Jack'll come out of that woods dead; that's the only way."

Josie dropped her eyes. Virgil was probably right, and the blame was hers alone.

"Look, forget it," he said. "I was steamed, but Jack told me what happened. You got conned! Hey! you're not the first sucker Colt tricked. From what Jack was telling me, Colt did him pretty good too. Hell, we always thought Colt was all right, just, you know, wrong about his conclusions.

But if half of what you told Jack is true, you did Jack a favor putting Colt in range." Virgil smiled. He seemed to mean it.

Josie smiled too. Her betrayal of Jack still tore at her. Nothing could appease her for the stupidity of trusting a man every instinct in her had screamed not to trust, but at least there was one happy thought.

"I'm glad he's dead. The bastard deserved it."

Virgil's eyebrows rose appreciatively, "You're all right, DJ."

Embarrassed at his approval, Josie sought to change the subject. "So where are my mother's things?"

Taking a ring of keys from the clutter on his beat piano, Virgil answered gruffly, "Come on! Josie's stuff's out here." As he led her to a paint-peeled shed next to his barn, he told her, "A couple of times I thought about throwing it out, but I figured that was Jack's call, maybe yours if you ever showed up. After a while, you just forget about stuff. You know?" Virgil opened the door to the shed, and they were both overcome with the damp, musty odor of the room. Virgil had forgotten about this stuff at least a decade ago. "The roof went to hell about five years back."

"And you didn't fix it?"

"I meant to. Just . . ."

Virgil left his lie unfinished, and the two of them kicked through the furniture briefly. A brown sofa with the unmistakable traces of mice filled most of the central room. The stuffing was chewed out and exposed, and it was anybody's guess how many warm fuzzies the thing housed. On the bare dirt just next to the couch, there were some boxes of kitchen goods. The cardboard was bowed and waterlogged; what utensils Josie saw were rusted. The whole room stank so badly that Josie was about to tell him she'd seen enough, when he pushed through some tables and chairs in front of the couch and reached bravely back into a pile of clutter.

"The pictures are over here."

Virgil presented three soggy albums, and Josie stepped

327

carefully through the trash to take the top album. The thing was damp, soiled, and broken. Josie opened it with dread.

The first page contained a tiny newspaper clipping centered on a stained sheet of thick paper. Something from the Vital Statistics section of the *Rapids*, the clipping described the stark facts of a civil wedding between John Christian Hazard and Josie Fortune. On the next page she saw Jack and her mother together, his arm around her. They looked like nineteenth-century pioneers on their new homestead.

"That was taken out here on their wedding day."

Virgil seemed almost sentimental. On the next page Josie at about age two stood with Jack; it was apparently taken the same day. Josie felt like she was looking at someone else's memory.

"I don't remember being out here, Virgil."

"I kept it up a little better back then. I mean I had a girlfriend who kept it, you know."

"I think I get the picture, Virgil."

"What?"

"You exploit women. No big deal. You're a pig."

Virgil shook his head. "I'm a businessman. I give women jobs. Around here, people kill for jobs."

"So women love you?"

"Let me tell you something, DJ: not everyone gets to go to Harvard or wherever the fuck you got all your degrees. Some of us have to do things we don't necessarily like."

"Now you're telling me you don't like running your bar."

"It's a lot of work."

Josie nodded, not even bothering to give Virgil mock sympathy. On the next page she saw Josie Fortune holding her daughter, this also on Virgil's farm. She was standing with her hip thrust out so the child could straddle her.

"You were a good kid, DJ."

"You liked her, didn't you?"

He reached down and turned the page. A woman with a shotgun sat on top of a bar. She wore a plaid shirt and jeans.

Her hair was pulled into one long braid and lay over her left shoulder. Her feet were hanging in the air, the shotgun was propped up, so that the butt of it was resting on her thigh and the twin barrels came to about the level of the top of her head. The face was old-world-solemn and country-calm. The gun looked to be a piece of deadly business. The wall behind the bar was made of barn wood, something of the effect of a hillbilly cabin. Out of focus and partially cut off, a sign read: A GOOD PL . . .

"That's the Josie Fortune I remember," Virgil whispered. It was a voice full of awe. "If God made any woman better, He kept her for His-self."

"She looks like a slew, Virgil."

Josie shook her head and started to turn the page, but Virgil put his finger on the paper, stopping her.

"Look at that! Look at it, D.J! That's your *mother*! That's Josie Fortune! Huh? You see that? God-damn, Josie Fortune and her shotgun! You should be *half* the woman she was!"

Josie wanted another image of her mother, something less like a slew, but she was moved by Virgil's passion.

Virgil smiled fondly. "Jack told me one time she put both them barrels right under Colt Fellows's chin and kicked his sorry ass out of the bar. I mean, Colt Fellows!"

"Jack told me about that, but he didn't say anything about the gun."

"Oh yeah, she scared that big boy. Jack said he pissed down his own leg. Now that's the truth! You know, Colt was the guy everyone wanted to do something like that to, but Josie Fortune, your mamma, was the only person in Lues County ever did it to him."

"Kind of gives him a motive, doesn't it?"

Virgil shrugged. "I don't think Colt could have got within fifty yards of Josie without her blowing his fucking head off. Your mother wasn't a woman to cross, DJ."

"So who killed her, Virgil?"

"I told Jack it was someone she trusted, someone she

knew; no one else could have gotten close to her. I saw her in a couple of fights at the bar. Let me tell you something, she was just like Jack: fast and mean and scared of nothing."

"You think someone from the bar might have done it?"

"Someone from the college," he answered. "Yeah, I always thought it was college. You and her are just alike about that. You think those people at the college can't do no wrong. That's what got her killed, trusting some fancy talk; it'll get you killed too. Mark my words."

"Maybe whoever it was just surprised her," Josie answered emptily. She didn't like to think about the destiny that awaited her if she failed.

"The Devil himself couldn't sneak up on Josie Fortune! Listen, Jack married his match! I guarantee it! No, her killer walked up to her face smiling and telling her some line of bullshit, and Josie trusted him because he was college."

"Did you try to find out who it was?"

Virgil smirked. "We went around talking to people, but you know, nobody wanted to deal with us, even if Jack hadn't confessed to it. Hazards at the college would be like you trying to talk to the Queen of England. Right? 'Show the lady the door, Charles . . . '"

Josie looked down at the picture again. Josie Fortune stared into the camera, fearless, beautiful, and something not quite fit for polite society. Then she had changed. She had made the dean's list and lost her edge.

"Do you know where she came from, Virgil? Anything about my father?"

Virgil's fat gray face creased fondly. "She said once she was from Alaska. Other times it was Montana, Texas, Indiana. Truth is she blew in on the wind, you and her together. Now your father was the same thing. One time he was . . . let's see, hell I don't remember; anyone and everyone famous back then. She always had a story, always laughing about it, like the man wasn't that big of a deal. You were *hers*, that's what she said; you didn't belong to anyone else. She let Jack near you, because she God-damn loved Jack even after the divorce. And you loved him too." He shrugged. "Otherwise, you were hers. And spoiled rotten. Still are, as far as I can see."

No use denying it, Josie gave him a lopsided grin. "Was she on the run from something?"

"We're all of us running, DJ; it's just that most of us never get anywhere."

Josie shut the album. "I want the albums. The rest . . . well I don't have the guts to reach in and see what's here. This place is a sty, Virgil."

"Her books are over on this wall." He pointed to a water-logged cardboard box.

"That's it?"

"What do you mean? That's a lot!"

A single box of books. Josie smiled.

"I'll take the books too – " Josie saw the damp box coming off the wall – "I guess."

"Clothes, back there." His arms around the wet cardboard, Virgil rocked his head in the direction of the corner. Under some broken ceiling tiles, a stained pile of cloth answered.

"I'll pass, on the clothes."

"That's it then."

Outside, after they loaded the Mustang's trunk, Josie asked, "What happened to the shotgun?"

"I keep it by my bed. Jack gave it to me. It's illegal as hell, but who gives a fuck? So's cocaine."

"I don't want it, Virgil, but I'd like to see it."

"I'll get it." He started toward the house and stopped. "Speaking of coke, you want to get high?"

"How did you stay out of prison all these years, Virgil?"

Virgil shrugged affably, "Too quick for the law, DJ! Just too damn quick!"

When Virgil returned, he held the shotgun up before him, a well-cared-for prize. The stock was half the length of the full gun. It looked to be a fierce weapon. "I want to

331

fire it," he said. "Come on!" Josie followed him as he carried it out into his yard. There were a couple of metal drums, a fencepost, a piece of plywood, the two hearses, and a suspicious cat. Virgil considered each in turn. Finally, he walked over to the plywood and stood it up against the rusted barbwire fence. The board was four-by-eight. Virgil walked back four paces, then in one motion turned while setting the stock of the gun against his right thigh. Both barrels roared. The fire and smoke and wadding leaped out three of the twelve feet between himself and the plywood. Her pulse quickened as the sound hit Josie deep in her chest and left her momentarily gasping in surprise. The board itself jumped in response, and a gaping hole about fourteen inches in diameter appeared dead center, its edges ragged.

Virgil straightened up and swore fabulously.

"*Oh, mamma!* You want to try it?" he asked. "I got a few more shells in here." Virgil reached into his baggy pants pocket and pulled out two shells. Popping the spent ones, he loaded the twin barrels and closed the gun with a crisp snap. "What do you say?"

Josie took the gun carefully, inhaling the intoxicating cordite and the oily stock. Virgil had taken care of it, even if the rest of his life was in ruin. Josie held the gun with both hands at about waist level, looking for a target. The cat, she noticed, was gone.

"I know this gun, Virgil," she said quietly. "I remember that sound."

"You ought to. Your mother loved that gun. You and her and Jack would come out here all the time. They'd spend half the day shooting different guns, but that one, she was always firing it."

"Did I ever shoot it?"

"She let you dry-fire it, but you were just a kid. You had this little .38 caliber you shot all the time. It was about as big as you were, but I mean you were pretty handy with it!"

"You're kidding me! I don't remember ever shooting a gun when I was a kid."

Josie looked at the gun in her hands, tried to remember the feel.

. . . in the grass, the trooper's shotgun. She had known how to use it . . .

"Go ahead! Fire it! I mean, damn! With that shotgun, you look just like your mother!"

Josie settled on the plywood Virgil had shot. She brought the shotgun down to her thigh as Virgil had done and aimed at the very top portion of the board. The gun kicked hard into her leg as the fire from the twin barrels blew out in wild sparks, but this was nothing to the noise the thing made. Coming as it did up from her thighs, it was the sound of the end of the world.

It was only an afterthought that caused Josie to consider the effect on her target. The board jumped. Across the top of the plywood, the charge cut a crescent of jagged space.

"Nice, huh?" Virgil asked.

"Virgil," she answered, "there's nothing *nice* about it."

The List

When Josie returned to her studio apartment, she called Pat Bitts. She had missed him earlier, but heard him answer now. "I'm sorry to bother you again, Mr Bitts," she began after her introductions, "but I've found some things in the newspaper that I'm curious about, and I thought you might be able to help me."

"I'll do what I can, Josie."

"I need some information on four women. They were all abducted, all murdered."

"From around here?"

"Yes, sir. The first is thirteen years ago. The name's Shelley Kruger." She waited while the old man wrote it down. "Next is Anita Paget. She was found south of Carbine Ridge

333

ten years ago. Two more: Melissa Bates and Cathy Ferrington."

The old man repeated the names as he wrote them out.

"Bates will be seven years this coming April. Ferrington died three years ago last June or July, they aren't sure exactly the date of death."

"I remember both of those last two. The Ferrington woman was the wife of one of your professors up at the college."

"I want to see the police reports on those cases. Everything they have. Can you get that for me?"

There was a long pause, then, "I guess I could talk to Jason about it. He might let *me* have copies. That's the only way he'll agree, if I promised not to loan them out."

"That's what I was thinking too. You up for a partnership?"

"You think these might be tied to your mother's death?"

"The first thing I want to find out is what other people thought."

"Fair enough, I guess. Give me your number, and I'll call you next week."

"Call me at school, and I'll get back to you. I'm kind of hard to catch these days. It's safer that way."

"You need a hide-out, you're welcome out here!"

"If I need another hide-out, Mr Bitts, I'll have a pretty mean man on my tail."

"I'm a pretty mean man, myself, Josie."

Josie smiled. In his day, that had been the truth. "I'll keep it in mind," she answered honestly. "Oh, and something else," Josie added. "I found out my mother put a shotgun in Colt Fellows's face and kicked him out of her bar. Did you know about it?"

"First I ever heard of it."

"Interesting, huh?"

"It explains some things; that it does."

"How good was Colt's alibi?"

"Colt was rousting some boys in West Lues the day they found your mother. There'd been a shooting out there and he arrested them in the middle of the afternoon; you know, Colt could actually do some regular police work now and then! Now that took most of his afternoon that Thursday. He was working with another man, too, and I talked to all of them. Those boys ended up doing serious time over in Vienna, so he hadn't bought them off or anything. Believe me, I pried up all the boards on that one. It was a solid three or four hours in the middle of the afternoon."

"You're not going to let me blame Colt, are you?" Josie felt a pinch of frustration. If it were Colt, her troubles were over, the rest of her research purely academic.

Susan Wallace

Susan Wallace, who had been Susie Hill in college, was a vibrant, thin, attractive middle-aged woman. A manager of a small temporary employment agency, Wallace lived alone in Memphis in an upscale apartment complex. She came across with that kind of southern openness that startles outsiders, a woman proud of her checkered past and amused at the habits which used to hold her hostage: "an ex-bulimic, ex-smoker, ex-drunk, ex-nymphomaniac, ex-druggie, and now a full-time aerobic monster." Her apartment had a certain sterility about it; what Josie could see of Wallace's life she found on a couple of shelves in the living room. There had been a family: three boys and a tall, thin, bald husband; they looked from the clothing and her own age in the photograph to be about ten years behind her. Her hair was longer then, and she was heavier, cherubic, a lot like Melody Mason-Grimes. There was another ex-husband pictured as well. He had the look of a man well acquainted with his vices. Susie Wallace, in that picture, was scarecrow thin, patently dazed. Wallace saw Josie examining this picture and commented: "That's Norman. Norman Wallace. We

335

were doing the group sex thing and Norm ended up finding he liked men better than women." She shrugged, "Last I heard he was in rehab with his lover. I just hope when he gets clean and sober he still likes boys, you know?"

Josie walked away. Something in the easiness of Susan Wallace's manner about her past bothered her. She was certain it was bravado, a simple mask to hide the pain. Behind everything that Wallace admitted to was the fact of losing her children, a fact about which she said nothing.

"How did you get my name?" Wallace asked her when they had settled down to talk.

Josie nodded, smiling, "I talked to Melody Mason – "

Susie screamed like a young girl suddenly. "Oh my God!" she laughed, "I haven't seen that little whore since we graduated! How is she?"

Josie described what she had seen of Melody Mason, happily married, funny, cute. About the relative poverty or at least the sterility of Melody's life, Josie kept her opinions to herself.

"She says the two of you were going to go to Florida when you graduated. I think she would still like to go."

"Florida! Listen, we had the tickets and everything, and Melody comes down with the clap. I mean *serious* stuff. Give that girl a six-pack and she'd do anyone, the little slut!" She considered this with a genial expression then added, "Of course, so would I."

Susie, like Melody, talked for a while about college, her friendships, sorority life, parties and then finally, almost reluctantly, made a feeble sketch of the afternoon they had found Josie Fortune.

" . . . I don't remember very much. What I remember the most is freezing my butt off. It was so cold and we just kept going deeper into this *fucking* canyon! Water up to our asses! Have you been inside there?"

"No. Not yet. I've been kind of busy."

"Froze my ass off!"

"Do you remember the body at all?"

"I could hardly look at her, you know? I think Bill started to touch her – "

"Who's Bill?"

"Uhhh . . . one of the guys . . ."

"Bob Tanner or Jim Burkeshire?"

"Bob Tanner! That's right. Goofy guy! Don't even bother talking to him. Have you talked to him?"

"No."

"Save yourself the trouble. He's the stupidest guy that ever went to college. I mean Melody wanted in his pants so bad and he didn't have a clue! Melody was about as subtle as . . . me! Right? I mean like, 'Hey! You wanna fuck?' But he doesn't catch on. I told Melody, 'You're crazy, the guy's an oaf,' and she goes, 'I don't care, he's cute, and I think he's got a really big one,' so I tell this buffalo, 'I think Melody wants to go out with you.' Subtle, right? The guy spends a month asking *me* out." Susie considered for a moment, before adding. "He wasn't that big, let me tell you."

"You said he started to touch the body . . ."

"Right! The other guy . . ."

"Jim Burkeshire."

"Jim, he screams 'Don't touch her!' So we didn't. We left. That's it."

"Jim said he stayed behind when the rest of you left," Josie lied. "Why did he do that?"

"No. He led us out. Melody thought this slew had followed us in, you know, so we went out in a line. Stupid, right? No, Jim led. And Bill – "

"Bob."

"Why do I call him Bill? Oh, another story, right? I won't get into it, really dumb guy. But *he* had a big one."

"What happened when you left the canyon?"

"God, I'm just going on! Let's see. We left the canyon. We called someone and then uh . . . we went to the room and Cat went off . . . Okay, Cat went off to get a shower

337

and Melody and I talked about running away. She thought this slew she saw — you know about him?"

Josie shook her head.

"Up at the falls, she saw this guy, or said she did. Anyway, she was sure he'd killed this woman . . . I'm sorry." A look of pure embarrassment. *This woman* was Josie's mother.

"Go on. I want to know what happened."

"She'd seen him kind of and she thought he was going to come after us, or her. And I told her, hey, 'Look, maybe you're over-reacting. If it was the killer, he's probably so scared he can't remember what you look like, or any of us, except Cat.' See, like everyone remembers Cat.

"She goes, 'I don't know, Susie!' she's crying and almost laughing, you know, we're all crazy about . . . what we just found . . . Anyway! she goes, 'God-damn slews! I hate slews!'

" 'What if he wasn't the killer?' I go. 'What if he was just some slew walking around?'

" 'He *looked* at me,' she says. Then she goes, 'I think he was trying to remember what I looked like.'

"So then I go something like, 'He thought you were hot. I mean guys think we're hot. Some guys.' You got to remember we had the self-confidence of a couple of slugs. 'He's a slew,' I go. 'He hasn't seen anything but a cow's hind-end for six months and he sees us, and he gets a boner.'

"She goes, 'He killed that lady, Susie.'

"And I go something like, 'Look, he was probably following us to get a look at Cat. Right?' Melody shrugs at this. That's pretty typical, see. 'So anyway,' I go, 'he can't remember us but he remembers Cat and kills the bitch! Our prayers are answered. Party down, God!' "

Susie Wallace sat back, laughing at herself, her narrative finished. "We hated Cat; we had all these jokes about killing her. Not very funny, but you know we were nineteen; it seemed funny. Anyway, Mel didn't run away, and no slew ever came looking for us. And we all lived miserably ever after."

338

"What time of day was this?" Josie asked. "When you got back from the canyon?"

"Dinner was always at 5:15. These days I have lunch at 5:15, but for some reason the sorority served dinner at 5:15, like clockwork. Melody and I didn't go. We didn't have time to get showers. I think we got high and ate cookies or got high on the cookies, and we talked about this slew killing Cat.

"We did that kind of thing in front of her too, but it was dinnertime, and Cat never missed her meal. I don't know how she kept so thin. Her mom paid for it, she said, and she didn't want to cheat her mom, something like that." Susie rolled her eyes. "It wasn't the money. Believe me. She was just *repressed*! She used to get these boys worked up and then walk away. It was wild; she was the queen of tease. Of course she only ended up teasing herself, and her only outlet was food. Food as sex . . . believe me, I've been there!"

Josie asked if Susie knew what had happened to Cat.

"I remember one thing, right? It's Finals Week and she comes up to me all upset and she goes, 'How do you know if you're pregnant?' and I go, 'If you have to ask, it's probably too late, girl!' Anyway, she wasn't back at school the next year and no one ever heard from her again."

"Do you remember anything about what you saw in the canyon? Anything about the body at all, any marks?"

"I wish I could help you. I was so freaked out. I thought she had fallen, you know, but then, you know, someone had . . . you know! I mean god–damn! I'm standing there up to my ass in freezing water and looking down at this naked woman . . . and I'm scared to death."

There was anger in this. Something Josie hadn't seen in her before.

"When you realized she hadn't fallen, how did you think she had died?" Josie asked.

"This fuck did her with a rope . . . you know what I

339

mean? Like up behind her, like that!" Susie Wallace crossed her hands, the gesture of garroting a victim.

Out of Memphis

From Memphis to Cairo, Josie drove toward heavy purple thunderclaps. The rain came in Cairo. The road seemed to empty out as most of the cars pulled over to the shoulder of the road. Josie pushed on stolidly. Sky and countryside were washed in a dull gray.

Josie was tired; she had been tired for weeks now, and she was afraid of her own intuitive leaps, but something was wrong, something at the base of the falls had happened that she wasn't quite seeing. Nor did her interviews with the people who had found her mother quite straighten out the confusion. In fact, no one had reported the same thing as anyone else. Garrotted. Hanged. Strangled. Eviscerated. Dead at three. Dead at six. Cover-ups, lies, elections won and lost, polygraphs, signed statements, lost files . . .

And the worst of it: everyone was sincere, helpful, sympathetic, and so damn nice!

Nothing fit. Nothing worked or made sense.

Well, that wasn't quite right. Josie was beginning to think one scenario made sense. In fact, it was the silence which argued the theory best: it was now just over a week since Colt Fellows and Toby Crouch had been shot. She didn't want to get her hopes up; she could hardly bear to believe it was over, but the silence was arguing profoundly that the man stalking her was dead. The silence whispered to her that her dangers were past.

The theory was that her mother was the victim of some killer who had long ago vanished into history. Finding her mother's corpse, Colt Fellows had sought to have his vengeance on Jack and get him committed to life in prison. That had been spoiled, and ever since Jack's release from prison, Fellows had been worried that Jack might just find out how

340

Colt's enthusiasm for a conviction had actually been a set-up. As it happened, Jack's release from prison had been about the same time that Josie had committed to come teach at Lues State for a year. Colt had seen his opportunity, and immediately began to conspire a rather ingenious trap to get Jack. By leaving a series of threats, Colt could effectively guarantee that Josie would eventually show up at police headquarters. Once that happened, Colt trusted his abilities to persuade her to press charges against Jack. From there, it was simply a matter of executing Jack.

Even the almost silly little detail of a sympathy card addressed to Josie Fortune could be explained if Colt had been behind the break-ins and messages and calls. Colt couldn't have left it, but he had any number of undercover people who could drop a note off. The call for Josie Fortune at the Skyline could also have been set up if the bartender had called him to say Josie had come to the bar. Colt was the man for those kinds of connections. It would have been easy for him to make what had appeared physically impossible contacts with her. And Colt would have had all the information to harass her too. Information, opportunity, motive.

History, so the theory went, was not repeating itself. Colt Fellows had been the source of her problems, and Colt's game had blown up in his face. She was ready almost to believe it. She wanted to believe it was the only reasonable explanation. No one really wanted to kill her. She had not been targeted before she had even arrived in Lues! The threats against her were simply part of an old antagonism: Josie had been the means to another end. It was already over. Her troubles were behind her.

Josie pulled off the interstate at Huree, and ten minutes later she parked her Mustang before her door at the Huree Hideaway, its nose out toward the woods. Regardless of her optimism, she scanned the dark woods, then looked down the well-lit walkway in either direction. The Huree Hideaway, as usual, was blessedly quiet. The place had been a perfect choice. This evening there were three cars down the way, lovers inside. She opened the car door, with her purse in easy reach, the room key ready. Though she wore a jacket, she was drenched in the three quick steps she took before she opened the door to her efficiency. Inside, she saw at once the room had been disturbed. Something – the papers, she thought – was different. She shut the door behind her out of impulse and slid down on the floor. In the same motion, she brought her revolver out and threw aside her purse and briefcase. The door had locked automatically behind her. She could see almost the whole studio apartment. From where she had positioned herself, she could even look under the bed. If he was here, he was in the bathroom. Standing slowly, Josie felt herself shaking, and tried to steady herself with several deep breaths. It did no good at all, and angrily, hoping he was waiting, she marched toward the back where the bathroom door was closed. It was a flimsy piece of wood, and Josie kicked it open with a single blow. Shower, toilet, sink. She could see the entire room was empty at a glance. He was gone, but he had been here.

His words were on the mirror over the sink, written almost certainly in blood:

MIsS mE?

Josie walked back to the front of the apartment quickly, then into the rain. She had her keys and her gun. She checked along the wall and out across the small lot to the trees. She climbed into the car and started the engine. Spraying gravel, she pulled around to the front of the building and stopped. She looked for someone, anyone, then climbed out and went into the registration area, her gun hanging in her hand.

"*Bea!*" she called, walking into the room. Bea kept an eye on things. Maybe she had given Josie's "boyfriend" a key or at least had seen him.

"*Bea!*" Josie saw the woman sitting in her chair watching

television. There was a beer can and her pack of cigarettes set up on the table next to her arm.

"*Bea!*" Josie stepped into the room and could smell it. She came forward now more cautiously, calling Bea's name one last time.

The woman wasn't answering, and never would again.

Coming round to face her, Josie saw the front of Bea's sweater washed in her own dark blood.

Part Five

Midnight

Josie was waiting in the Mustang, her revolver in her lap, when the first deputy's car came off the highway. It was twelve minutes after her call, almost 10:30. Slipping her gun under her seat, she got out of the car to meet the man. Once he had surveyed the crime, the deputy made a call on the motel phone. While he waited for assistance, he took down information from Josie. Who was she? What was she doing here? What did she know about any of this? Josie answered his questions honestly but with care. She was numb, maybe in shock, but hardly ready to trust anyone, especially the law in Lues County. Thankfully, before the interview had gone very far, two more cars arrived, and Josie had time to make a few decisions about how to handle the questions. Both of the new arrivals checked out the apartment where Bea's corpse sat. Afterwards, they interviewed Josie separately. Why was she using an alias? Why had she given a Boston address if she lived on campus in faculty housing? Did she know the woman? Did she see anything? Did she hear gunshots?

Josie explained that she had been in Memphis and had just gotten inside her apartment when she remembered she wanted to tell Bea she would be checking out soon. " . . . I wanted to tell her personally. So I drove around."

"You drove?"

Josie nodded.

The other deputy covered most of the same things, but he wanted to know about the other guests. How long had

345

they been around? What kind of people were they? Josie hadn't seen them, she said. She had come into her room usually late, and she had left early. She was doing research here and hadn't had any interest in seeing the other guests. The place was quiet, she said. "That's why I liked it."

Her answers satisfied them, and both men eventually wandered away, their interest in her finished. A fourth deputy arrived, then the ambulance with two medics pulled into the lot. Finally, two news reporters showed up. They stayed outside, huddled inside their vehicles until the detectives arrived.

As everyone awaited the detectives, Josie stared out into the rain and darkness. Bitterly, she wondered if he was still there. Was he watching them even now? Laughing? *Miss me?* A woman dead so he could leave his threats in blood. Not even threats! It was nothing more than a deadly game of hide and seek. She wondered how long he had known where to find her, if it had humored him to imagine she thought herself safe, knowing he could take her as easily as walking into the front office and grabbing her room key. As easily as shooting a helpless old woman. She wondered how long he would wait before he struck again, and if the next time would be to finish it.

The latest deputy to arrive now came out of Bea's apartment together with the other three. He made for Josie with grim determination. Who was she? What was she doing here? What did she know about any of this? Did she know the victim? Did she hear a car? Gunshots?

As she tried to answer him, Josie heard the deputy in charge say to the medics, " . . . the sheriff won't get out of bed for this old crone. He'll let Lues PD spin their wheels on it, you know what I mean? I mean who cares? Am I right?"

"You don't think . . ."

Josie missed the rest.

"You went to your room?" the man interviewing her asked.

Josie focused on his face and nodded. "Yes. I went to my room, then came here."

"Did you see any strange cars?"

Josie shook her head.

"So you didn't see anyone at all?"

"I didn't see anybody."

"Hear anything?"

"I'm sorry, nothing."

Like the others, this deputy stood up and walked away without thanking her.

"Can I go to my room now?" Josie asked. The deputy looked back at her without responding. "I want to get out of here," she explained. "I don't want to spend another night in this place."

"If you'll wait a bit longer, a detective will be here. He'll want to talk to you."

Josie nodded.

The wait lasted nearly an hour. It was almost midnight. The man who finally showed up was a short, powerfully built man with very little hair and something of a Cupid's bow for lips. Like the deputies before him, he tracked through the office to Bea's apartment with rainwater dripping from his coat, his footsteps sloshing along the same track as the others, the same as Josie's, and probably the same as the killer's. A minute or so later, he came out again.

He huddled for several minutes with two of the deputies. Josie heard the detective ask, "Robbery?" and thought the other said, "She interrupted it." A thumb pointed in the direction of Josie; the men all looked at her. Another deputy volunteered, "The shooter left the money in the till."

"How much?"

Josie missed the answer but heard the words *Darling* and *Fortune*. "Says . . . Boston . . . here."

The detective shook his head and came toward Josie with

347

apparent friendliness. Unlike the officers, Detective Sergeant JP Harpin introduced himself and shook her hand. He was a cherubic man, she decided. He had a thick, raspy voice, eyes with more slyness than intelligence. Josie saw he had two fingers in a splint. The bandages looked a couple of weeks old.

"You're Josie Fortune?"

"It's Josie Darling officially, but I'm in the process of changing my name," Josie lied.

Harpin didn't care about the confusion of names. "You're a writer?"

"A professor."

"I thought you were here writing a book."

"I'm doing some research, but it's not for a book."

"And you've been here, what, a couple of months?"

"A week."

"You got a boyfriend you meet out here?"

"No."

Harpin studied her quizzically.

"You doing some moonlighting?"

Josie felt a flush of real anger. "Just what does that mean?"

"You know what it means." His eyes gave her body the once-over. It was the same assumption Bea had made, but Harpin's attitude — the dirtiness of his expression — irritated Josie.

"I told you what I'm doing," she answered evenly, looking away from the man.

"You know the lady that was shot?"

"Not really."

"You didn't see the guy that did this?"

"I didn't see anybody at all." She was not looking at Detective Harpin, nor giving him any emotion. The insult of his assumptions was still burning.

"How about the last couple of days? Anything unusual? Anyone you thought might be casing the place?"

"No."

348

"Do you know how much money she kept on the premises?"

Josie shook her head.

"She ever tell you she was worried about being out here alone?"

Again, Josie shook her head.

Harpin called to the deputies. "Anyone check on the people in their rooms?"

A sheriff's deputy answered simply, "Tom Hager took some statements. Saw nothing, heard nothing. Asked to keep their names out of the papers."

He shouted, "Did *we* get their names?"

The deputy answered, "I've got them written down."

Harpin looked back at Josie. "How can we get in touch with you if we need to?"

"Lues State, Department of Arts and Letters."

"Thanks for your patience. I know this kind of thing can be pretty rough. If you need any counselling – "

"I'd like to clean my room out and leave. I don't want to stay here any longer. Can I do that?"

"Any objection if our witness leaves?"

The deputies looked at one another, shrugging. One of them called to her, "We got your address in Lues, didn't we?"

Josie answered Harpin, "My home address is on campus, faculty housing: 27 Willow Circle. I'm not there much."

"What's this Boston address you gave the victim?"

"I made it up. I wanted my privacy. I didn't care for her to know I was a lecturer at the college."

"The old lady wasn't too careful about things like that," Harpin told her with a smirk.

Josie's words strained with anger. "She was a good lady. This stinks, what happened."

The detective's delicately curled lips flattened into a world-weary grimace. "I never found a good murder, Miss Fortune."

349

Later, standing in her studio apartment, her car packed up, the place clean except for the bathroom mirror, Josie studied the bloody scrawl one more time. MIsS mE? Bea's blood had dried on the glass. Josie thought there had been some wetness before, but she couldn't have sworn to it. A thin drip had run off the first stem of the capital *M*. Had it been there when she found the words? Had she arrived only a matter of minutes after he had gone? And if the rain hadn't slowed her down, would she have walked into the apartment while he was here? Would she have been ready?

Josie shook her head, looking through the words into her reflected eyes. Angrily, she reached for a wad of tissues, wet them and began wiping the mirror. The glass turned muddy. Meaning faded, then even the smudges.

Sunday Morning

Late Sunday morning from the Huree Motel Six, Josie called Annie, who listened to her narrative impatiently. Shock gave way to anger, anger to fear. Even before Josie had finished, Annie was interrupting her to insist she leave Lues at once.

"Find the nearest airport and come home today!" she blurted.

"Lues *is* home, Annie."

"Josie, listen to me!"

"I've listened to you for years, Annie. Everything you've ever said, I listened to. You're the one who taught me we have to fight if life is going to be worth anything."

"It's too dangerous, Josie. If he found your last hiding place, he'll find the next one."

"Damn it, don't tell me I have to run! I've been running from things all my life, I'm tired of it."

"Josie, we can make it so this semester never happened. I mean it! If you're staying in Lues because of your contract, we can get it worked out. No one's going to blame you for leaving — I promise you!"

350

Josie wondered if Annie recalled saying something to that same effect last fall after Dan had put her in the hospital. *I won't let this semester count against you. We can work this out . . .*

"It's not the contract," she answered coolly. Of all people she had thought Annie would understand her, would know she *must* stay now.

"Then what is it?"

"Annie, I've found my mother."

"What do you mean?"

"I remember things. I know who she was."

"That's all you went there for, Josie."

"Virgil Hazard said she didn't back down from anyone." Josie felt a stirring of pride. She should be *half* the woman, he had said. Her mother, she knew, wouldn't run. And Jack had said if things were different, if it had been her child killed and she had survived, Josie Fortune would have tracked this bastard to the end of the earth. And something in Jack's look as he had said it convinced Josie it was true. As far as was needed, as long as it took.

"Sometimes we just have to be realistic . . ."

"And sometimes we have to be crazy!"

"Josie, I know how you feel."

"You don't," Josie answered. "You have no idea. My whole life I've felt like I ought to apologize for who I am, and suddenly I find out I never had any reason to hang my head. It wasn't just that my mother was killed or even that Jack was set up. It was the rest, the idea that I should be ashamed of my past, that I should forget it. They taught me to shut myself off from what I was!"

"But you found it! You've won, Josie!"

"Annie, my people don't run from things."

Silence. She had said *people*, as in family. Annie wouldn't have missed that, yet she didn't answer it either.

Finally, sadly, the old woman answered, "Josie, I don't want to bury you."

"Don't do this to me, Annie!" Josie raged. "This bastard

351

walked in and shot some lady who never did anyone any harm, and the cops showed up and they called her a *crone*; they said the sheriff wouldn't get out of bed for an old crone like this, that no one would care about her. Well, I care! Annie, I know who did it! It's the same bastard who sliced the womb out of my mother! The same one that walked free while the only family I had left went to prison for the next twenty years!"

"Josie . . ."

"One question, Annie. That stuff you teach – about chasing the monsters and staring down Medusa – is that just bullshit for the undergrads?"

"It's not the same, and you know it! I'm talking about the fears of the psyche, about revising the soul. It's not the same when someone really means to do you physical harm."

"It's got to be the same! To hell with the soul if it isn't! It's all just garbage – everything you ever said – if we can't *live* with it. Is that what it is, just so much garbage to make us all feel better?"

Annie's voice was calm. "You fight smart, Josie. You fight to win. People win against their demons the moment they decide to face them; physical enemies are different. You don't win just because you decide not to run. What happens is you get yourself killed."

"I'm going to find him, Annie."

"How close are you? Realistically, what do you have?"

"I'm working on some things. I've got quite a bit, actually; it just hasn't quite come together."

A fancy way to say nothing.

"Josie – "

"He knows me, Annie. He'll follow me if I go back to Boston."

"He won't follow you, Josie. He'll lose interest."

"I think he means to do it whether it's here or in Boston. There's no running, not unless I disappear – I mean totally change my identity."

352

"You don't know that."

"I know this: I can't find him in Boston."

"Josie, you're all alone there."

"I'm not, though. I've got more here than I've ever had in my whole life."

"Meaning Jack Hazard?" This was pure skepticism. "The man's a fugitive!"

"Annie, all I want is for you to believe in me. Don't tell me I can't do this. Maybe I can't, but I'm going to try, and even if he wins I don't want to go down scared."

"You'll go down scared. The only people who aren't scared when they die are surprised."

"Annie, I have to fight this. I've messed up too much to leave. Jack's an outlaw and Bea's dead because I showed up here. I can't leave like that. I can't live with that."

"You're punishing yourself for what other people have done!"

"I mean to pay this bastard back, Annie. That's what this is all about."

"I'm not going to lie, Josie. I think this is a mistake."

"You don't think I can find him?"

"Josie, in forty-two years of teaching, I've never seen a mind like yours. You're stubborn, flighty, impulsive, and self-destructive, but I've got to tell you, when you decide to do something, you're unbelievable. I'm not going to say you can't. I just don't think it's smart."

"I know it's not smart, Annie. But life's not always about doing the smart thing, is it?"

"One question, Josie." Annie's voice was full of resignation, skepticism, and caution.

"Okay."

"Say you find him, just what do you mean to do then?"

"I'm going to bring all hell down on him, Annie."

Robert Tanner

Before they had finished, Annie asked what she could do to help. Josie answered that she had located her mother's professors and had talked to most of them. Of the witnesses in the canyon, she said she had talked to all but Bob Tanner and Cat Sommerville. Tanner wasn't answering his phone, but she expected to contact him any day. Cat Sommerville was the problem; Cat had vanished from the face of the earth. Josie had the mother's name and address, but she had vanished as well.

"What's the state and county for the mother?" Annie responded.

"It's in-state, Kankakee County. The mother's name is Catherine Johnson. Or it was twenty years ago."

"*Johnson*, yeah, sure, that won't be too hard."

"Johnson is the easy part, Annie; finding the right one is the trick."

"I just dropped out of the midnight basketball program," Annie answered, "so this will give me something to do to keep me from going back to the gang."

"You're a pal, Annie."

When they had finished, Josie made several more calls. Finally, she got through to a Professor Wright, or thought she had when a woman answered. The voice was pleasant and intelligent, the aging wife of a retired professor of business administration. Truth was, Josie had caught the daughter, who was watering plants for her parents. The professor and his wife Joan were sailing in a sloop for Hawaii. Was there a message?

"Wish them luck," Josie answered.

With a feeling of utter futility, Josie tried Bob Tanner for the third time that morning. She had been trying to reach him for so long she was certain he was out of the country, maybe climbing mountains in Peru, but on the seventh ring Josie heard a breathless, "Tanner!"

354

Josie introduced herself and told Mr Tanner she was doing research on the murder of Josie Fortune.

"Wish I could help. I never heard of the lady!" The voice was loud, friendly, and stupid.

Josie told him more, and it came back to him. "Oh! Oh, that!"

"I'd like to set up an appointment to talk with you."

"I'll talk with you anytime, lady."

"Is it possible today? I know it's Sunday, but – "

"Today, sure. I've been on vacation for a couple of weeks, but today's great. I need to get into the office anyway. What time is good for you?"

"I can be there in an hour and a half."

Bob Tanner had a little office that was part of a large rental house in the old downtown of Carbine Ridge. The place was tiny and disorganized. The guy was a slob. The business was run purely on pluck; five minutes with Bob Tanner was enough to convince her of that. The man had no skills and no tack, neither system nor plan, but he was passionate about insurance. Every instinct was tuned so to get the signature, and he talked about his afternoon twenty years ago simply to keep Josie sitting in front of him – a life annuity contract prepared for her to sign, even from the beginning. She was getting older; time to start facing the inevitable: rates go up the older we get!

It was a miserable meeting because Josie was running out of options. A madman was chasing her, and she needed something, some chance to turn the tables. All Bob Tanner could do was remind her she could die anytime. It was a truth too painfully obvious to contemplate, and he forced it on her until she could hardly breathe.

"What did you tell the police, Mr Tanner?"

"To tell you the truth, I don't remember."

"Did you talk to anyone besides Sheriff Bitts?"

"I might have. I think someone came out to the fraternity house."

355

"Did he ask what time you went into the canyon?"

"He said we could get in trouble if we weren't careful."

"What kind of trouble?"

"Perjury. He said if we weren't honest we could go to jail for perjury."

"Anything else? Did you sign anything? Did you give a deposition?"

"Sorry. That's all I remember. I don't even remember who it was I talked to! Well, no, wait . . . no."

So it went. Hope, then nothing, life, death, and good insurance policies. They talked about the condition of the body, its placement on the rock.

"What did you see? What was she like?"

"She was naked."

Nothing else had registered with the man.

Josie tried to walk him into the canyon. She asked who had led the way out, who had trailed. She asked about the people with him. He didn't remember last names. He remembered Susie and Cat and there was another girl, he was pretty sure, but he wouldn't swear to it.

"What about letters cut into her flesh?"

The fat, shiny face of Bob Tanner was screwed into a tight grimace. Nothing.

"Were there bruises on her throat?"

The shoulders hunched up in frustration.

"A rope burn around her neck?"

No idea.

"But you know," he offered, brightening, "it just goes to show you how it can happen anytime, how you need to be ready with a good insurance policy."

The Dead

Monday at midday, Josie pulled up a phone message from her faculty mailbox. No name, no number. Simply the words, "I have the files you requested."

356

The girl at the desk was reading Lucretius' *Origins of the Universe* today. "Marilyn, did you take this?" Josie asked, holding up the pink slip with the girl's initials. She looked up from her text, blinked, then nodded.

"Some old guy. He said you'd understand."

Pat Bitts was waiting when Josie pulled into his drive. "I put the coffee on!" he told her. "It's a cold one!"

He was right about that. Inside, the pot-belly stove was burning wood, the coffee was gurgling. The place felt safe. Bitts had put what looked to be his desk chair, a card table, and a lamp in the kitchen. It was set up so that Josie could work close to the fire and the coffee. The gesture seemed more kind than necessary until she saw the files that Detective Miller had delivered into the hands of his old boss. It was a box stuffed with roughly eight thousand sheets of paper. Four reports in all, the files included detectives' summaries, photos, transcripts of interviews, autopsy reports, and every manner of exchange between the state, FBI and local authorities. Josie, who had been suffering from a dearth of it, had been expecting information, but this was overwhelming. "This could take some time," she told him.

"Well, Josie, my uncle used to say, 'Only trouble comes easy.' "

Josie smiled at the man. "What do you say we find a killer, Mr Bitts?"

"You call me Two-Bit now that we're partners." He gave her a wink. "We called my grandfather *Mister* Bitts!"

Josie sat down to the files at half-past three that Monday afternoon. Bitts joined her. He answered her questions, explained certain terms and talked about procedures when Josie had a question. He stayed with her through dinner without a break; at midnight, he brought out pie and made more coffee. At three, he wandered off to bed. At seven, Bitts came out to the kitchen again, and Josie was still reading. In his robe, the old man padded over to make a fresh pot of coffee and laid out some doughnuts.

"Did you eat?"

Josie grunted impatiently, her eyes never lifting from the page. She hadn't moved for the past four hours, had hardly moved since the previous afternoon. When the coffee came, she thanked the man, and turned another page. She munched a doughnut; she scribbled a note. At eight she asked to use the phone. She was going to have to call in sick, she said. At eleven she closed the last file. Bitts looked at her curiously.

"I'm tired," Josie announced.

"Well, I guess!"

Josie stood up and walked over to her winter coat. "Take a walk?" she asked.

Bitts nodded.

Above the house there was an old shed and barn and some pasture land that Bitts said he rented out to a farmer down the way. At present the cows were in another field. From the peak of the hill, the river twisted beneath them. The only sign of human life was Bitts's house and the near-empty road that was set up a few hundred feet above the river. The air was cold, the sky blue. The old man wore a stetson and an old canvas coat. Josie wore her coat with neither hat nor gloves. She had her revolver in her jeans, nestled against her spine.

For several minutes, Josie said nothing. She had the feeling of coming out of a dream.

Shelley Kruger had been the first. A Lues State co-ed, she had been missing three days when her body was found hanging upside down from a log in a ravine not far from Clems Hollow. The autopsy revealed her captor had neither fed her nor given her water between the time of his abduction and her death. On the night she died, she was bound, gagged and taken naked into the forest. Already weakened from the lack of water and food, unprotected from the elements on a night where the temperature had dipped down into the high forties, Kruger had probably hanged for no more than half an hour before she slipped into unconscious-

358

ness. Death came sometime later, probably between two and five that morning. She was found late the next afternoon by schoolchildren.

Kruger's death had received considerably more attention than that of Josie Fortune. There were probably several reasons for this but the dominant one was that there appeared to be no motive. Nor had a suspect emerged. A TV news account of it had likewise inspired a kind of mass terror in the whole region. It was a murder so bizarre that the local press became obsessed with the possibility that Lues had fallen victim to what appeared to be a serial killer's work. The investigation had made no headway in that direction, however, and detectives soon turned their attention to everyone Shelley Kruger had known. Of the cases before Ferrington's murder, it was the most thoroughly investigated. Two men who had had sexual relations with Kruger were examined repeatedly. Three others who had dated her and had not were under scrutiny as well. One of her professors was looked at. Family also provided alibis or were looked at closely. In the end, the reports began to recycle suspects. Nothing connected. Whole lists of her friends were created; backgrounds for all of them were run. Nothing came of the effort. Eventually the case gathered fewer and fewer reports; finally it was filed. Of the nearly four hundred people listed as friends or acquaintances Anita Moore and Melissa Fry were included.

Moore and Fry were to be victims of violent murders as well, but they would die with different names, and Josie could find nothing in their files which showed that police investigators had connected either of them back to Shelley Kruger. But there was a connection, once you went backwards. They had all started college thirteen years ago; they had all pledged the Kappa Zeta sorority. They were in fact in the same pledge class. Kruger, an older student, had been the president of their class. She had spent five years in the

359

navy and had come back home to Lues to take a degree in mechanical engineering.

Neither Moore nor Fry had been close friends, and there was nothing but coincidence to connect them, but it was coincidence that Josie had spent twenty straight hours looking for.

It was almost precisely three years after Kruger's death that Anita Moore-Paget was found south of Carbine Ridge. A first-year stockbroker in Pilatesburg, living with her husband Wayne in Gallows Hill, Paget had been abducted and held nearly three days. Unlike Kruger, she was given food and water. On the night of her death, she had been stripped naked and set free, apparently to be chased over approximately seven miles of woods. She had been shot a total of thirty-seven times with both a .22 rifle and a pistol of the same caliber. Most of the shots had struck one hand or the other, none at close range. Several had struck her wrist, and fourteen slugs were found or had passed through the fatty part of her thighs and buttocks. None of the shots had been inflicted post-mortem. The woman had died of heart failure, not blood loss.

Like Kruger, Anita Paget had not been touched sexually.

The investigation centered extensively around Wayne Paget. A competitor in national shooting contests, Paget owned, among his collection, three rifles and four pistols, any of which could have fired the .22 slugs which investigators retrieved. Wayne Paget was having affairs with three women at the time of his wife's death, and the interviews of Paget's lovers had read like something from a steamy romance. In the end, no indictment came of the investigation, and like Kruger's death, the murder remained unsolved.

Two years later, in a woods east of Gallows Hill, Melissa Fry-Bates's naked corpse was found nailed to a tree in the fashion of a crucifixion. A schoolteacher in Paducah, Melissa had married two years earlier. It was apparently a good marriage. A woman of remarkable beauty and talent, Bates was loved by her students and genuinely admired by her fellow teachers. Jason Miller, by then head of the Lues Police Department's homicide unit and assisting the sheriff's investigations, had tried to link the death back to Shelley Kruger's and possibly to Paget's. A comparative study showed the bindings might have been from a similar material and the technique of wrapping the wrists and ankles was possibly the same. The detective failed to discover, however, that all three women had pledged the same sorority in the same year. It was the kind of detail that was easy to miss. Names had changed; time had passed. No one was looking into ancient history for a motive.

The last murder was that of Cathy Ferrington, four years after Melissa Bates. Like the others, Ferrington had disappeared probably during the daylight hours. Unlike the others, she had been kept alive for two or three weeks after her abduction. About the time of death there was less certainty. Her corpse remained undiscovered for nearly two months. All that could be concluded was that Ferrington had been bludgeoned to death. The medical examiner felt certain that none of the fractures had begun to heal, so it was likely that the bludgeoning had occurred within a concentrated period, though he could not say if the clubbing had caused death instantly or if it occurred over a period of hours. There was no evidence of rape, no proof that it hadn't occurred.

As with Paget's case, Ferrington's death was suspected to be the work of the husband. No one ever looked at her death as possibly connected to Kruger's, Paget's, and Bates's. The method was different, and there was plenty in the Ferringtons' marriage to suggest problems. From the beginning, however, police investigators had had difficulty implicating him. Certainly there was no physical evidence connecting Ferrington to the body or crime site, and no one had been able to explain how Ferrington could have abducted his wife while he was in Madrid, Spain. Jason Miller had speculated that Cathy Ferrington was not abducted at all but had taken the kids to Dick's parents in Chicago, then drove off to meet her husband for a private rendezvous on his return. Detective Miller had nearly seven days to explain away, and neither the prosecutor nor the FBI had given the theory any credence. Miller himself seemed to abandon the idea finally, but the notes suggested he never quite got rid of his conviction. All proof failing, Cathy Ferrington, like the others, remained an unsolved murder.

The surprise was that Cathy Ferrington was one and the same as Cat Sommerville.

"All night," Josie told Bitts in a quiet, reflective tone, "I was looking for some connection, some link between these women and my mother. Then suddenly I saw the name Sommerville."

"You sure it's the same woman?"

"Positive. As a student she went by the name Cat; she attended Lues State the year my mother was found, then transferred to North Carolina the next fall."

"Where she met Dr Ferrington?"

Josie nodded. For seven years the Ferringtons had lived at Chapel Hill. When Dick took his degree, he had been hired at Lues State. Ten years after that, Cat Sommerville – by then Cathy Ferrington – presumably met Josie Fortune's killer.

"What do you make of it?" Bitts asked.

"I don't know," she answered tiredly. "It's like the whole thing just fell in my lap, and I don't know what to do with it."

Bitts studied the river calmly. "I remember Cat Sommerville best of all of them. Fact is, she threw me off. I kept wanting to blame the kids for moving the body or lying for some crazy reason, and there was Cat Sommerville staring me down, bright, smart, honest. She was a proud one, she was. They'd all taken a vote to call the police anonymously, so she'd gone along with it, but when I went out to find them, it was Cat Sommerville that stood up and said we'd better talk."

"When she was killed, none of the investigators made anything of her going to school at Lues State."

"So none of them noticed that she had been one of the kids who found your mother?"

Josie shook her head.

"Maybe it's nothing more than a coincidence, Josie. A lot of times people leave a place and come back." He shook his head. "It was seventeen years . . ."

"Do you think it's a coincidence she came back to Lues the same year that Shelley Kruger was murdered?"

Bitts stared at Josie in stark wonder.

Josie smiled grimly, "Makes you wonder what we're missing, doesn't it?"

Transcripts

There are parts of a university that have a peculiar life of their own. Here are university personnel that faculty rarely encounter. These are the people moving the mass of paper-work through the system, a whole network devoted to the dark underbelly of intellectualism: the business of business. The woman Josie spoke to was close to fifty. She had a name plate on her desk, NAOMI TEMPLE. A generic certificate on her wall thanked Naomi Temple for twenty years of service; the name and number of years were hand-printed. It was signed by some VP or another. It was Naomi's sole prize, as far as Josie could see, and Josie wondered if Naomi was proud of it, or just kept it on the wall in case her VP happened through. Naomi Temple had two kids, very hand-some boys who were close to maturity, and a husband who looked in his portrait to be a heart attack survivor. A school logo for the Pilatesburg Pirates was stuck next to the larger Lues State Lancer sticker, so Josie figured Mrs Temple to be a longtime local and a sports enthusiast. Her office fronted a large file room. The office was comprised of Mrs Temple's desk and a table her student workers could use. A counter separated the area from public access.

"May I help you?" There was courtesy in this without warmth. Mrs Temple apparently assumed Josie needed to order her transcripts sent to a potential employer.

"I'm Josie Darling, in Liberal Arts, and I wondered if I might look at a few transcripts."

Jaw dropped, eyes stunned, Mrs Temple made the amateur's mistake of overstatement. "You want to look at someone's transcripts?" The voice seemed positively eager for a laugh track to finish her question.

Josie pulled out her faculty ID, flashing it at the woman as if she were allowed any privilege because of it. "Five of them actually. The students are all deceased; so I don't think it's a matter of confidentiality."

"Miss – ?"

"Darling."

"Miss Darling, I can show you *your* transcript, but that's all. Transcripts are entirely confidential."

Josie hesitated. "I just want to see what classes these people took. I don't need the grades. It doesn't even need to be an official transcript."

"Without their express permission I can't do that."

"I told you, they're deceased."

Smiles from both sides of the counter did little to break the ice. Naomi Temple had served twenty-some years in this station, and each year she had guarded her records with the enthusiasm of Cerberus: unless it were officially sanctioned, nothing went out. Naomi was the sort of woman to read the laws of sexual conduct in her state before submitting to her husband. She was a woman who never broke *any* rule. Life had miscast Naomi Temple: she should have taught English.

Josie looked longingly toward the back room with the
364

files. "I need to know what classes and professors five women took. Where do I go to find that information?"

"They're not currently enrolled?"

"I told you, they're dead."

"But not currently enrolled?"

With amazing restraint, "No."

"You come here for that."

"Great. Can you give me the names of their professors, at least that much." Josie had her mother's; she thought if she could run a cross-reference against the others she could find what she needed.

"Our policy has no exceptions; no one can order a transcript without the student's expressed permission" – she tapped a stack of papers – "on one of these forms, filled out by the student or ex-student, as the case may be."

At this point, the boy who had stepped up to defend Josie with her cabbie appeared in the doorway that led to the files, and came into Mrs Temple's office. Thin, studious, alert . . .

. . . what is his name?

"Hey, Miss Darling!"

"*You* work here?"

You. That's good. How could she keep forgetting his name? She was good with names; she knew every student . . . except for *what's his name*, her white knight.

"Ten hours a week. Don't worry; I still have time to write your papers!"

Mrs Temple smiled brilliantly now. "Nelson is a dream. I've worked this office twenty-three years this January, and I've had good workers, don't get me wrong, but Nelson is just the sweetest . . ."

His mother's and *Mrs Temple's pride . . .*

Nelson blushed as Mrs Temple told a rather complicated story about a numeric inversion involving a lost transcript. Josie found herself straining to hold her smile. When Naomi had finished, Josie made her exit as gracefully as her frustration allowed.

A couple of minutes later, Josie was surprised to see Nelson in front of her, opening a steel door that was set flush into the cinder-block wall of the corridor. "There you are," he whispered. He looked back into a darkened file room, and Josie saw that she had come around to the back of the Transcripts and Records without realizing it. "She said you wanted to see some transcripts of people who are deceased."

"It's really important, Nelson," Josie whispered.

"I can get you what you want – if they're dead. I mean, it's not like they'd mind, right?"

In the fashion of a conspirator, Josie looked both ways down the hall and reached into her briefcase. "I need the transcripts for these people," Josie answered.

Nelson looked at the list. "I'll bring them to class tomorrow," he said. "You're going to be there?"

Josie had called in sick for their Tuesday meeting.

She said she'd be there. "You won't get in trouble for this, will you?"

"No. There's no way anyone will know. I just pull the master and copy it and put it back. You don't need it officially stamped, do you?"

Josie imagined Naomi Temple with THE STAMP locked in her desk drawer. "Unofficial transcripts will do."

Nelson's dark eyes flashed wonderfully. "This isn't for a grade. I don't want you to give me a break because I'm doing this."

"I don't give breaks, Nelson."

He smiled, the epitome of average-but-honest and a boy very much smitten with his teacher: "I know; that's what I like about you."

Bookkeeping

It was still daylight, and since she was on campus, Josie drove to her apartment. The mail was overflowing. There were four local billing accounts and two Visa cards boiling over the limits; there was a letter from her adoptive mother. Was Josie coming for Thanksgiving or Christmas? Maybe some weekend while the weather was still nice? Josie groaned. She couldn't deal with the Darlings right now, hadn't been able to deal with them for years. She loved them, but she had long ago learned to turn elsewhere when troubles came. These days Josie's troubles had multiplied, and she just didn't have time for them. She'd call them soon, she told herself. *Call and promise them something. Then hope something comes up.*

Before she left the apartment, Josie decided to drop her mother's books off. She had been hauling them in the trunk of the Mustang, and hadn't even bothered to look through them yet, nor even look at the photographs again. They were taking up trunk space, and the odor had begun to permeate the car. She needed to unpack them and set them out to dry. Josie set the box of books and the albums on the floor of her living room. She considered the pile distastefully. The three albums in ruin, Josie went through them quickly and detached the pictures, laying each photograph out separately. Most of the pictures were in terrible condition, but the images themselves were powerful reminders to Josie that she had lived in a world she no longer understood or even remembered. A part of herself was secret even to her, and now, as she studied her mother in several photographs, she could only hope there was some courage she hadn't yet tapped, some great, hidden strength. Josie Fortune had had courage and strength, with none of the bashfulness of her daughter. She stared brightly into the camera's eye. She had feared nothing, it seemed. Was that what got her killed?

When all the pictures were laid out on the carpet, Josie took the three albums to the trash. That left her with the books. She hadn't really wanted them. She had agreed to take them on impulse, purely the instinct to save books, but they were school books – all outdated – and the water damage was terrible. There was nothing really to save. No one would ever use them again. They were disgusting even to the touch. After she had peeled the cardboard box away, she stacked them on the floor next to the pictures. They were damp, and they stank. They had no value financially or emotionally, but they might have her mother's handwriting, she decided. She had never seen her mother's writing. It would be nice to see that, a treasure to find some old essay she might have written. Josie reached out and took one of the books and pulled it to her. *Macro Economics*. As she flipped through the text she noted certain passages marked with a pen. That was it; the book didn't even contain Josie Fortune's signature or any notes penned to herself. She flipped through two more books, tossing them aside rather quickly. Josie considered quitting; then, resigned to the utter futility of her task, she reached for the next book in the stack, *Marketing in Today's World*. There she struck gold. Three sheets were stuck together in a tight, damp clump. Thinking they might be notes for a test, maybe cheat sheets, or love letters from Jack – or someone – Josie peeled the sheets apart. As the first sheet came free, Josie saw the message: sooon, JOsIe, promiss. On the next was written, stil tHinkING Of u, hoR. The last was: MisS mE? Each was written in red crayon. Numbed, enraged, and certain of her man – certain he could be no other – Josie looked through the rest of the books quickly. She found nothing more, nor did her breathing return to normal. She left the notes on the floor, face up, and went to call Annie. She got nothing but her answering machine.

"I'm at my campus apartment, but not for long. I'll call you tonight. I've got news."

She set the phone back in the cradle and looked at the notes again. Even sitting close to them made her sick. The terror that had cooled as she had chased through history for
368

some sign of this man came throbbing back hotly. He still wore his mask. He still watched her from shadows, but now she was certain he wasn't counterfeit. The man who had killed Bea and who had made Josie's life a living hell was most certainly the killer of Josie Fortune. She knew another thing, too: what he promised he performed.

Records

Josie got a motel room in Carbine Ridge. She ate at the town's one diner; she spent the evening writing out key information from her memory of the files of the murdered women. She called Annie again and got nothing more than the old rant about her Uzi and karate class. When sleep came, it came quickly. Her dreams were vivid. She was bound and waiting in an empty room. There was no door to the room, no give at all to the bindings.

The next morning, pushing to make it to Brand Hall a few minutes before eight, Josie found an envelope taped to her door. There was no name on it, and she was uncertain if the thing was from one of her students or from *him*. She pulled it off the door and inside set her briefcase on her desk as she tore it open. With her heel, she reached back and closed the door. She wanted no surprises at her back. Opening the envelope she saw the obituary of Beatrice Quincy. Nothing but the official marking of Bea's passing. Family upstate, more in Texas, Bea's husband had preceded her in death. They had had no children. There was nothing else in the envelope, no marks, no threats. Resisting the panic edging up in her, Josie tossed the envelope on her desk and reached for her eight o'clock folder and turned to leave. She gasped at what she saw, the blood draining from her face. A bright red happy face had been painted on the inside of her door. The thing was some eighteen inches in diameter, the smile grotesque. For nearly a minute, Josie studied the thing without moving; without thinking, even.

Finally, seeing it was done in an enamel paint and wasn't going to be washed off, Josie taped several memos over the image. He had been in her office again, could enter it at will. She was certain now he had a key and probably one to her campus apartment as well. Was he looking through her family pictures even now? Drawing happy faces everywhere? Josie fought the tears of impotence and ignorance and rage. She cursed the man in the hot silence. She shivered at the end awaiting her. How was she ever going to know who was doing this? How could she see him coming? He was nothing more than a ghost. The truth was, she would never know him until he decided it was time. There was no answer to this riddle. She would not find him among the shadows where he hid. That was only the delusion of an angry young woman. There were no answers in obscure texts; there was no help from the police. How long she would live was his decision and his alone. The more she struggled to find out something, the more he would laugh at her. Laugh as long as he was enjoying himself, then one day come for her.

From the dark? In daylight? Smiling in her face, hidden? And then? She knew the rest. No need to ask that. It was written in all his victims' files. He would bind and gag her. Two, maybe three days. Maybe weeks as he had Cathy Ferrington if she really excited him. And then? What death? What pain? Maybe he would just leave her someplace while he went about his business. As in her dream: the empty room without doors, waiting, hoping. She could almost believe at a certain point you would hope for your killer: anyone would do, so long as it ended the terrible silence of an empty room, the slow death from thirst and hunger. Even now she felt the urge to give over to him. Waiting was so unbearable.

She could still run, she told herself. She had to! She was never going to find the answer. There was no answer. He came and went at his leisure. He was a nobody. These kind always were. Almost always. Oh, God! she thought. For twenty years he had been doing it. For twenty years planning this one? He left messages behind locked doors. He wrote things in mirrors; he called her in places where no one knew she would be; he was full of mock sympathy, utterly indifferent to the death of others. He didn't even seem to have some kind of rage driving him. It was nothing more than play. All of it! Josie could not hide, had been a fool to hide. Was she a fool, then, to run?

No. She *could* run. She could be somewhere new by evening. She could be in Chicago or Atlanta, Cincinnati or Kansas City. She could get on a plane and he would never know where she had ended her flight or what name she took to begin life again. Didn't he care? Or did he know she was going to stay?

That she couldn't leave him?

Josie studied her office. He had been here; had he moved anything? Were there more notes? Had he bugged the place? Installed some kind of camera? Did he know she carried a gun? She closed her eyes and steadied herself. She had some things he couldn't know about. She wasn't fighting in the dark. Not completely. She had the others he had killed; she had the enigma of Cat Sommerville. She had the friendship of Pat Bitts; she had Jack Hazard in her camp. None of this he knew about. If she ever found him, *he* would be the one to know fear. Presently she swore the man to hell and believed it. For the moment at least.

In the hall outside her office, Josie met Val as he was unlocking his door. He was dressed typically, the work shirt buttoned to the collar, a pair of baggy beige pants, a dark sports jacket, a knapsack caught in his big hand. Head in profile, his eye seemed to roll toward her curiously. She said his name; he answered with hers. She pushed on. Her back to him now, she waited for some word or the sound of his door or even his footsteps. She looked down to the floor, expecting his shadow, some motion to explain the silence.

371

Nothing. She turned finally. He was gone, the light of his office shining over his curtain, the door shut.

Josie spent the hour between her classes in Worley Hall. Marcel Waldis, the man who had performed the autopsy on Josie Fortune, had written two books on forensic pathology, the second published at Harvard. In his second volume, *Ascertaining the Time of Death in a Homicide*, the man appended his curriculum vitae. It took over twenty pages to tell all he had done. Waldis had been extraordinary. Arrogant, certainly, but credentials to match the pride. She checked her watch. It was almost ten and she had to leave. She checked the second book out. It was all technical material, but she needed to know something.

Josie stepped into her ten o'clock composition class only a couple of minutes late. She liked this class. She liked the vigor they brought to their studies. So when she entered, having missed their Tuesday class, she stopped with a dramatic gesture. "What? No cheering?"

There was a dumb silence at first.

"Come on, people, I'm as good as Henry Valentine, aren't I?"

Some clapping started, then more. Finally they all began cheering. Josie smiled the polite, embarrassed smile of the deservedly famous, and bowed – Valentine style. When they had finished, she said she felt better. "I thought maybe you didn't miss me on Tuesday." One of the wits in the back row told her to take all the time off she wanted. She was waiting for this and had her answer ready. "I would, Dennis, but I thought you might like to get through this course in *one* semester."

Class was started.

At 10:50, collecting their compositions, Josie noted the large folder Nelson what's-his-name handed her. Josie gave the boy a look. "You've been busy!" she told him.

"Yes, ma'am."

372

Josie took the rest of the papers in hand. She saw Harriet, her sonnet writer, waiting to speak.

"Can you look at some of my stuff?"

"Today's not good. I'm kind of busy with some other things. Next week?"

Nodding, head bent wearily, the rejected poet left her presence as only the rejected poet can. Josie was alone now and felt a surge of guilt. It was crazy, but she thought she owed the woman. Well, of course she did. Annie would have stopped everything to read a poem. Annie would read a poem in the middle of a gunfight! Outside the classroom, Josie looked for the woman and found her. "I have some time late this afternoon. Can you come by after three?"

The woman glowed.

Once in her office, Josie shut the door and left the light off so she wouldn't be disturbed. Over the top of the curtain the light from the hall was sufficient to read. Josie fished out Nelson's folder. *Nelson Rush!* Why couldn't she remember that? His folder was thick, and when she opened it she found the transcripts of five women – including Josie Fortune.

Virgil had said it was college. Maybe it was; maybe here she could find the killer. Clearing her desk, she laid the transcripts out in a single row. Then, in the half-light of the room, she began poring over the material. Though it was simply raw data, probably meaningless to an outsider, she worked through the lists fairly quickly.

Anita Paget, then known as Moore, was a business major and had had three of the same professors as Josie Fortune, though obviously in different years. Cat Sommerville, Melissa Bates, and Shelley Kruger, however, didn't have any discernible relationship with these professors. Bates, then known as Fry, had had a speech class with Clarissa Holt. Kruger had studied in an introductory literature class with Smith, Josie's department chairman. At different times and for different courses, Paget, AKA Moore, and Cat Sommerville had both had composition classes with Gerty Dowell, the resident gossip in sweatpants.

Connecting to none of them, but surprising Josie unduly was the fact that her mother had signed up for Advanced Creative Writing 360 with Henry Valentine. Valentine had not appeared on Bitts's list of Josie Fortune's professors. She saw at once the reason: her mother had dropped the class. Just such missed details had let investigators overlook the fact that Paget, Bates, and Kruger were pledge sisters and that Cathy Ferrington, AKA Cat Sommerville, had been among the five students to find Josie Fortune. What else had been overlooked?

The door shook under a heavy fist, and Josie looked up from the transcripts with a start. Again the door rumbled, and Josie straightened up. Bringing her purse with her, she pulled back her curtain slightly to see who it was. She didn't want to be interrupted, but she wanted to know who was at her door. When she saw it was Clarissa Holt, she smiled and opened the door. Clarissa's tight, dark features brightened with as much enthusiasm as she ever allowed herself, "Your lights are out. I almost didn't knock."

"Come in."

Josie whispered the command and looked back at the opened door of Henry Valentine's office. Val was in and taking confessions from an eighteen-year-old alcoholic. "We were so fucked up, man!" the young man laughed. Clarissa looked toward the door as well, and Josie actually pulled her into her office.

"What's going on?"

Without answering, Josie went back to her desk and retrieved the transcripts. She handed all five of them to Clarissa and asked, "Do you know any of these people?"

"Where did you get . . ." She stopped with the second one. "Melissa Fry." She looked up at Josie, waiting for an explanation.

374

"Her married name was Bates. Did you ever hear what happened to her?"

"Everybody knows what happened. She was crucified. That was years ago." Clarissa's dark eyes burned in curiosity. She shuffled through the others again, considering each in turn. Clarissa shook her head finally. "I don't know these other women."

Josie stepped closer, took the transcripts from her and laid them out so that each student's record could be easily compared to the other four. "All five were murdered." She tapped each in sequence, pronouncing the year of their death: "all found somewhere in Lues County, except this one."

"Who's she?"

"Cat Sommerville. You know her as Cathy Ferrington."

"Oh, Jesus!" Clarissa grabbed the transcript. She scanned it quickly. "Two years. She was here two years! I didn't know that!" Squinting in sudden curiosity, "What's this all about, Josie?"

"I'm looking for a professor they're all connected to."

"Connected? What do you mean?"

"The operating hypothesis is the same man murdered all five women. Abduction, torture, murder. Right now, I just want a name, someone they all might have known."

Holt's eyebrow cocked fiercely. "You think it was a professor?"

Josie shrugged but didn't answer. Clarissa bent over the table, scanning the lists as only someone who has reviewed hundreds of them can. Within a few seconds of starting, her finger fell to the name Henry Valentine on Josie Fortune's transcripts. "Here."

Josie smiled. Clarissa Holt held a low opinion of most of her department, it seemed. Not long ago she had been pushing the theory that Dick Ferrington had murdered his wife; he hadn't been around twenty years ago, so the crime fell now to Henry Valentine.

"I saw it. But none of the others took his class."

Clarissa's face darkened with concentration as she continued examining the transcripts. "Why do you have the lights off?"

"I didn't want to be bothered."

"Did it work?" Josie thought she saw the woman smile.

"Until you came along."

Her eyes never lifting from the papers, "So I wanted you to take me to lunch for saving your ass."

"I don't know, Clar."

"Something greasy and a lot of beer to wash it down — it's been that kind of week."

"Beer's definitely out. I'm living on about two hours' sleep a night lately. One sip and I'd be gone."

"Okay, no beer for you. Just grease and coffee: improve the ulcer." Clarissa still hadn't lifted her eyes from the transcripts. Finally she rapped her knuckles on one of the sheets and straightened up: "Two business majors, a life science major, a mechanical engineer, and a mathematician. Not a one of them taking courses she ought to! Not more than a half-dozen Bs in the whole pack. And look at the two who graduated: Paget takes her degree in two years and a summer. Bates: three years and a summer. Those girls were in overdrive. I took five years for my undergraduate degree and thought I was rushing it."

"Do you remember Melissa Bates?" Josie asked.

"As Melissa Fry, I do. Oh yeah."

"Tell me about her."

"Over lunch?"

Josie looked back at the stack of papers she had meant to try to grade over a missed lunch. They would still be there when she got back, like everything else she had put off. "Sure. To tell you the truth, I'm starved."

In Josie's car, Clarissa told her, "Melissa ended up marrying a slew and got a teaching job somewhere south of here."

"Paducah."

Holt's eyebrow cocked in surprise as she gave Josie a

sideways look. "Right," she answered. "Very aggressive young lady. Physically strong, very bright." She tapped Melissa's transcripts. "I had her in class in the spring of her second year, and of course I tried to recruit her into Communications. I talked about the great combination of a hard science major with a journalism minor. She had a perfect television face, Josie, a real maturity about her. Plus, she had a down-home way about her. She could have had her pick of jobs in any secondary market and moved right into a metro area inside three years."

"You said she was aggressive. Is that aggressive like you and me, or was she a bitch?"

Clarissa did a double-take. She was aware and proud of her reputation as *the bitch* and she wasn't sure if Josie was teasing her about this or not. "Professionally aggressive. In my opinion not quite enough of a bitch in her personal life. I blame the boyfriend on the career choice. He was threatened by her intelligence. He knew if she went into Communications he'd lose her."

Clarissa reached toward Josie's briefcase.

"May I?"

Josie nodded, and watched the woman pull the rest of the transcripts out. As Josie negotiated the snarling lunchtime traffic on campus, Clarissa kept her face in the records. Without looking away, she asked, "Wright, Donaldson, and Lindermann were professors for two of them . . ."

"Paget and Fortune," Josie answered. "Professor Donaldson is dead. Lindermann's in Seattle; I called and asked her about Fortune. She said some nice things but nothing I could connect to the rest of this. I didn't know about Paget at the time. Wright's somewhere in the Pacific Ocean with his wife."

"May I ask you what your interest is in this?"

Josie took a deep breath. "I guess that's fair."

Cokey's

Their lunch and Josie's story finished almost simultaneously, Clarissa lit a cigarette, took a sip of her second beer, and leaned back in her booth. "It's Valentine, Josie."

Josie didn't smile this time. "Why do you think so?"

"Mailbox, key to your office, key to your apartment, anonymous notes: the guy's a sneak. I've heard it for years: he's got all the master keys to every building on campus and he snoops." Josie pondered this, as Holt continued, "You remember your little mess with the dean?"

"That was Ferrington, Clar."

"No, no. Remember what Ferrington said? What was it? 'I backed you with the hiring committee'?"

"Something like that."

She smiled, an old debater who hadn't forgotten how to go for the finish: "And who was the chair of the hiring committee?"

"Valentine. But he said – "

"Forget what he said. He lied. Val yanks Ferrington probably through the good graces of Gerty Dowell and Ferrington comes storming to you. And where do you go?"

Seeing the picture for the first time, Josie answered with some irritation, "I spill my guts to Henry Valentine."

"A nice little departmental circle jerk. Believe me, it's got Valentine's signature all over it."

Josie shook her head, smiling. "Okay, Val saw his chance and decided to have some fun with the new girl. Let's say I buy the whole thing, whether I believe it or not. It doesn't make him a killer. Just the opposite. Clar, I'm looking for a man who's killed six women that I know of. Probably more. This guy crucified a woman! He eviscerated my mother. We're not talking here about someone who gets his jollies yanking people's chain!"

Undaunted, Clarissa answered, "I assume you've heard some of the confessions the kids give Val?"

"They're a bit hard to miss sometimes."

"It's their pain, Josie; that's what he feeds on. Not the games – the misery that comes of games. There's the difference. These notes you're getting – messages, whatever they are: is the guy baiting you to find him or does he just want you to suffer?"

"It's so personal . . ."

"Like he knows you?"

Josie looked at her coffee. "You think Valentine could really do such things?"

"Honestly? I don't know. No. Not really. You say you want a professor. I give you the best candidate. Val gives everyone the creeps. He's strange, but face it, a lot of good teachers are a bit off – it comes with the territory. To give him his due, the guy's a genius with kids. But this?" She shook her head. "Personally, I can't imagine *anyone* doing this stuff. It's just beyond me."

"Someone did it, and he apparently wants to keep on doing it."

Holt's look was thoughtful, angry. "You've got three in a sorority. What about your mother? Was she in a sorority?"

Josie shook her head. "I don't know. I kind of doubt it. She was a single mom; not very likely."

"And I take it you missed that rite of passage?"

Josie nodded.

"How about Cathy Ferrington?"

"Cat Sommerville was in a sorority, but I don't know which one. If it was Kappa Zeta I've got four of his five abductions coming out of a single sorority." Josie flashed an icy smile. "You show me Henry Valentine in the middle of that Kappa Zeta pledge class and he's connected to everyone."

"I'm not so sure he even knew your mother was in his class."

"Val knows all his students. It's his signature, right?"

Clarissa shook her head. "She's a freshman signed up for an advanced course. My guess is she got handed the wrong card, got into the course without knowing it, then found

379

out about it eight weeks later, when she got notice that she was flunking it. She raised a little hell and got an official withdrawal. Never even met the prof. Happens all the time. What's not likely is that she was in the class for eight weeks. She would have been out on her ass the first day if Val found out she hadn't taken the prerequisite. And *he* would."

"So it's just a coincidence?" Josie asked. "Val never met her?"

"I don't know if it's a coincidence or not. I'm just saying your mother doesn't need to be in his class for there to be a connection. In fact, I think it's a lot more likely he's hooked into the Kappa Zetas than with her through this class."

"Why is that?"

"He has his contacts around campus. For one thing, Val's in with all of the frats."

"I didn't know that."

"These guys would offer up a virgin to Val if they could find one."

Josie's face screwed up wryly. "What's the attraction between the frats and Val?"

"Frats in his class take a gentleman's C if they don't want to work for more: they turn in old file papers, and never take a test; just show up and cheer like a maniac. Plus he gives each house a thousand dollars every year."

"He bribes them, you mean?"

"How do you think he gets a standing ovation?"

"Well, *now* I'm disillusioned, Clar."

Clarissa shrugged. "They love him and they love the tradition, but Val knows enough to keep the well primed. And he's got the money to do it, I take it. Val's mommy was a rich heiress back in North Carolina somewhere. He's got a brother who runs the family business, some kind of valve factory. Val wouldn't dirty his hands with commerce, but he doesn't mind the loot. He's got a nice house, some hunting cabins in the area, a nice van; he lives the good life, and he can afford to buy some gratitude."

380

"So if he's connected to the frats, that basically means he knows the sorority girls?"

Clarissa nodded. "They all live out at the north end; they go to each other's parties, they date each other, and yeah, sure, Val knows everything about anyone who interests him. Val has files on his kids, Josie; he knows who his boys date, how often they have sex with their girlfriends, favorite positions, brand of beer, anything and everything. And when they graduate he knows where they go."

"This is creepy, Clar. Maybe the guy just doesn't have a life; that's possible too."

"That's probably all it is, but you never know." She considered for a moment, puffing on her cigarette, "You want to know if it's Valentine?"

Josie laughed; it was a sound without mirth.

"Find where he takes his sabbaticals. If Val's your man, you'll find more bodies. That's the proof."

Office Hour

Josie pulled Henry Valentine's curriculum vitae later that afternoon. A document of prodigious size, it traced Valentine's professional life from his undergraduate days to his latest efforts as chair of a certain hiring committee. Once she had photocopied it, Josie slipped it back into the department files and returned to her office. Three students were waiting in the hall, two for Val and Josie's writer of sonnets. Before she went into her own office, Josie dared to peek into Val's. Val sat as usual facing his student, a young woman on this occasion. "My sister was down on her knees in front of my fiancé . . ." Val held a letter opener in his hands. The handle he had pressed into his palm; its fine point rested poetically against a fingertip. His eyes flashed when he saw Josie looking in. At the same time, the girl's narrative stopped. Caught, Josie waved genially and cursed herself as

381

she ducked into her office. Had he read her mind? It felt that way.

Her poet followed Josie eagerly. Josie tried to get her head into her work. She sat down and read the latest collection while the older woman watched her facial expressions for every twitch. The poetry was getting better even if Harriet's life seemed to be stuck in a holding pattern. Josie spent nearly an hour with the woman, and found herself crossing the line between iambic pentameter and psychology, using the one to talk about the other. She thought herself the last person on earth to be giving a woman almost fifty advice, but once she started, it came easily. Maybe too easily. Harriet's enthusiasm for advice invited it without stint. She said she wanted to be like Josie, " . . . such a take-charge kind of woman!"

Embarrassed, Josie imagined her poet saw what she wanted, but the older woman insisted. "This morning when you asked us to applaud, Miss Darling, that was the greatest! You know, I'm going to do that with my kids sometime. It was wonderful! I don't think you know how important you've been to me these past couple of months . . ."

Josie couldn't remember what good she had done. It seemed to her she had been caught in a running battle for weeks, living without sleep, and now lately moving from one bed to another, night after night. Searching futilely in history for the man who meant to murder her, Josie had hardly been conscious what happened in her classes. The woman's praise reminded her that she could be doing more, that she had so much to offer if she could only survive her present troubles. The woman didn't know someone was trying to kill Josie. Josie wondered if she would have been so certain Josie was a take-charge kind of woman if she knew.

As soon as her student was gone, Josie tried to forget her haunting poems of pain and loneliness, the sense of failure her praise instilled. Josie had other matters to worry about.

She faced another night wondering if it was to be her last or if some detail might give under the terrible scrutiny she gave things, some fact come forward which would bring her man into clear focus. Quickly, not even bothering to close the door, Josie began putting her papers together. As she did, Henry Valentine appeared suddenly. He knocked lightly and pushed the door back, so he was leaning into her office.

"Did you want something, Josie?"

Val's exposed hand took the doorknob. His right hand was outside the room. Through the opening, Josie noticed that the kids in the hallway were gone. She considered the possibility that Val might be holding a weapon in the hand he was concealing, and forced herself not to look at her purse, which was tossed on a stack of papers at arm's length from where she sat.

She tried to smile casually. "I just thought we might get a drink sometime next week, Val."

"What's the occasion?"

"I thought I'd tell you how things went with the dean."

"For that, I'll buy! How about tonight? No time for gossip like the present."

"Tonight, I just don't have any time. I'm sorry."

Josie could hardly breathe with the thought that Valentine was looking at her with the calm of a predator. It was the same look he had had when they had stood facing one another in her bedroom. But it wasn't sex the man was after. Perhaps it never had been. Had she really let him touch her? Every instinct screamed at her to run, to get away from him. And maybe it had even then, only she had let him, had *trusted* when she had felt no trust. Was she doing it again? Letting him slip under her defenses, even knowing the dangers?

"I take it the dean treated you fairly?"

"He just wanted to tell me he was behind me one hundred percent."

383

Val smiled savagely. "Behind you, so he could put a knife in your back, no doubt."

Josie found the expression disconcerting. "Anyway, thanks for the warning. Because of you, I was able to avert trouble. I think I should buy the drinks."

"I know you didn't go to Ferrington as I suggested. Did you face the dean on your own?"

Pure innocence, this.

"No, I asked Clarissa Holt to help. She tells me she has a *history* with Del. She must. She handled him beautifully."

"Yes, Dr Holt. I did see her lurking about in our halls today. I expects she wants her payback."

The man offered a smile full of insinuation and insult. Nothing more.

"I have to go, Val."

As she said this, Val stepped into her office completely, and closed the door entirely. *Romance? Murder?* Josie had not yet finalized her opinion about Dr Valentine, and thought again about the odd trail of facts she and Clarissa Holt had chased almost casually over lunch. Josie had her desk partially between them. Val needed two steps to reach her – unless he came over the desk. Before anything else, he would have to negotiate the desk.

If he steps toward me . . .

If he stepped toward her, Josie had no idea what she would do.

"Have you had any more calls or threats, Josie? That worries me, you know."

Val's voice was low and confidential. His wrinkled face was full of the worry he pronounced.

"I think it's over, Val. The two policemen who were killed a couple of weeks ago were both involved in the investigation of my mother's murder. I think one of them was leaving the notes."

She watched his eyes. Did he know she was lying? Was he thinking about the Huree Hideaway, about Bea? About
384

the obituary he'd left just that morning on her office door? The blood-red happy face? Val tipped his head, his brow wrinkling appreciatively; it was a gesture of mild surprise. It could be innocent or mocking or a man enjoying the game he'd created. She couldn't tell.

"Really?" he said. "The police were behind it?"

Genuine? Sham? How do you know such a thing? What was it Ferrington had said? . . . *we never know what's in the heart of another person.*

"That or it *was* my stepfather. I take it Jack Hazard has more important things to do now than bother me."

Val liked this.

"He hasn't found you since you charged him with assault?"

"Not a chance. I've been hard to find, and Hazards won't come on campus — not even on a dare."

"Afraid they might learn something, I expect!" A joke without humor. Did he know she was lying?

"Exactly," Josie answered. Was this it? Was this the hour she vanished? Standing by the door, his big body lazily coiled up. The sheets of paper covering the latest message from the man who would kill her were posted right behind his bald head. He hadn't turned to look. If he knew it was there, wouldn't he be curious to see if she had covered it?

He could take her, she thought, inside a second or two. She might get to her purse in time. Might not. Josie looked at the pockets of his sports jacket. Maybe a gag, some rope. He could keep her here until late, then take her out to his van.

"Our local paper is very concerned to keep the sheriff's department looking competent — rather a full-time job, and, I might add, a losing proposition — but the Paducah paper has run a couple of columns on your illustrious stepfather, John Christian Hazard, all very praiseworthy of his wood-skills."

"I haven't seen them," Josie answered, taking up her purse and slinging it over her shoulder. Without her coat on, the gesture was odd. She felt the man could see through her. Didn't he know she was scared? Of course he did.

. . . their pain . . . what he feeds on.

"I think the last one was, 'The Legacy of Jesse James Lives On,' or some such nonsense. I dare say you've turned a pathetic old convict into a legend. Deep down, I'm sure he's grateful." This, faintly humored. He was laughing at her; his notion of humor was always at someone's expense, wasn't it?

Does that make him a killer?

"I really have to go, Val."

"I can give you the clippings, if you missed them." This with a bright smile. The genial old professor who collects all manner of trivia. He wasn't leaving. Wasn't budging. He was in fact studying her and wondering, she decided, why the purse before the coat. Maybe she should just pull the revolver and push him out the door. And maybe she would look like a fool, or worse, doubt herself and let him take her gun. She felt perspiration slipping down across her ribs. She looked away. She looked down at her desk. Valentine's vitae was exposed. Josie covered it as smoothly as she could. When she looked up, she knew Val had seen it. His face was placid; he was looking into her eyes. He was contemplating the pain she would know before he killed her.

"I'd like that," she answered coolly, her knees almost giving way. If he came a step closer, she would reach into her purse. Two steps, she would level the gun into his belly, and then they would both have to decide what they did next.

"Why don't you leave them in my department mailbox?" she asked.

Mailbox? Valentine's eyes lost their humor. A heavy silence answered, a reckoning.

Time to play poker: "Or you could put them in an envelope and tape it to my door." She shrugged, tried to smile yet full of terror and rage. "Put a little happy face on it, so I'll know it's from you."

386

Valentine's face went ashen and he answered like a lover who's been told it's over, "I'll do that, Josie. Count on it."

Time Line

Leaving, Valentine checked the door. He pretended to read the memos covering the happy face. He looked back at Josie and gave her a big, loose smile. The eyes were dull with menace, a look so void of passion Josie nearly pulled her revolver. Instead, she stared at him without expression and caught the faint scent of the man, the goatish odor she had once been drawn to. Not now. There was nothing charming about this man; his savagery had no principle. She counted the rhythm she used to reach for her revolver: left hand up, right hand cross, pull the gun, kill the man, one, two, three, four. She was certain the time was now. Certain of her man.

The moment he left, Josie felt a vast disappointment he hadn't made for her over the desk. She had wanted him to, had believed she could do it. Now all certainty was gone. Leaving, she saw several of her colleagues in the hallway. She saw Dick Ferrington and a thin blonde girl talking to him eagerly. It brought back memories of Venice. *Bastard*. Ferrington's eye caught Josie's as she passed them. The girl was all caught up in her frenzy; she saw nothing but her own fantasies unfolding. Ferrington saw the woman he meant to destroy. They were in open warfare now. No matter what else happened, he would see Josie didn't come back the next academic year. Well, that was hardly a worry right now. A year was all she'd come for. She would just go back to Bandolier – assuming she survived. Josie went on. Dick Ferrington wasn't her problem. Valentine was the issue. Valentine the man.

She brought the Mustang out of the lot quickly and got to her apartment in a matter of a minute or so. Her gun drawn, she searched the place to be sure she was safe, then drew the curtains. Her .357 kicked her pulse up. Her heart was pounding. Valentine, Valentine, Valentine!

That look, that . . . that . . . that . . . promise . . .

Count on it.

He was the man she wanted, but the proof! Something more than the gut, something to let her know without the slightest doubt! Wrong so often, leaping to conclusions that had seemed so irrefutable! She couldn't afford to do it again. She had to *know*! And there was just no way, not until the rope tightened over her wrists. She swore angrily at the thought, and went back to the room she used as her office. She laid her revolver on her desk and set out her research. Over two weeks ago Josie had begun a time line, and had periodically redrawn it with ever more detail. Her latest creation stretched over ten sheets of paper and looked like the family tree of Balzac's *Human Comedy*. Presently she tacked it across her office wall as she had its predecessors on motel walls. She studied the names of Shelley Kruger, Melissa Bates, and Anita Paget. They had pledged Kappa Zeta in the fall of their freshman year. She scratched over that same period the names Clarissa Holt, then Dick and Cathy Ferrington. All new arrivals to Lues. She went back to her mother's death, seven years prior. Cat Sommerville at the canyon. She circled the name and wrote, AKA Cathy Ferrington. She checked another sheet. This was an hourly schedule of the day her mother died. Cat Sommerville had gone to dinner alone at five o'clock. Melody Mason and Susan Hill had stayed in their room. Jim Burkeshire and Bob Tanner didn't know what they had done. Toby Crouch was drunk until three. He had been called shortly before five o'clock to go into the canyon. He had been at the mouth of the canyon at ten to eight when Pat Bitts had met him that evening. No one knew when he had gone in, but he had been out by seven. Jack Hazard had been in the police station around two, filing a missing person report. Josie Fortune had been seen dead at three; at the same time the

388

killer – or just a man – had been spotted above the falls, nearly an hour from the body. Dead at two? Waldis said six. She set the man's book out. Light bedtime reading, confessions of a man who had cut open thousands of skulls and dipped out brains from hollow skulls to satisfy his curiosity. All perfectly legal and agreeable. Josie looked at Cat Sommerville, AKA Cathy Ferrington. Why was she was so close to it all? Josie rubbed her hands over her eyes; she was tired like she had never been tired before. She had been living the past week with hardly a meal a day and no more than a couple of hours of sleep, if that. She could still vanish; get the VW, fixed or not, and start over with a new name. She really needed to think about that, because right now nothing made sense.

She fingered Waldis's book, then pushed it aside. She wanted to see Valentine's vitae. First, she thought, she needed to make sure he was on campus or in the area when each of the murders took place.

She hesitated. Could the killer have planned Cat Sommerville's murder on the day of Josie Fortune's death? *Seventeen years later?* No. It was something else. Purely coincidence. Not coincidence. No coincidence in any of this! Something else? Cathy Ferrington hadn't died like the others. Weeks of captivity, then the body hidden away and only found by accident. Not the same, really. The other bodies had been found shortly after death. Spectacular displays of violence. There was a difference, yet Dick Ferrington's wife, like the others, had been abducted, bound, and finally murdered. The other women were all in their twenties; Cathy Ferrington would have been the perfect age when she arrived with Dick on campus thirteen years ago, but she hadn't been killed for another ten years, a woman almost forty at the time of her death. All the others in their mid-twenties. There were other differences. Two of the five women had had children. Four of the five were married or had just finished a marriage. One bludgeoned, one shot, one hanged by her

389

feet, one crucified, and Josie Fortune — no one knew. *Stranged*, according to the newspaper account.

The Devil himself couldn't sneak up on Josie Fortune. That was what Virgil had said. Melissa Bates had been a tough girl. Shelley Kruger, ex-navy. Bates and Paget had had a soft spot in their hearts for a slew. Kruger had dated a local. Josie Fortune had married a slew. Bates, Kruger, and Paget had been locals. Fortune, a transplant. Cat Sommerville, no. Cat Sommerville wasn't the same. For one thing, she had married a professor, a Chicago boy, who was educated . . . in Henry Valentine's neck of the woods. Chapel Hill. Valentine had a degree from Chapel Hill, didn't he?

The phone rang, and Josie resisted the irrational panic it caused. Valentine for a drink? Maybe wants to come over? No one at all, someone she wasn't expecting? Here these twenty years, some old janitor, JP Harpin, the cop. Dan Scholari all along. *Get a grip!* She needed rest. She needed to stop thinking about all this, if only for a few hours; she needed time — and time was the one luxury she didn't have.

Josie picked the phone up cautiously. She said nothing.

"Josie?"

"Annie!" Relief coursed through her, and she tucked the gun she was carrying into her jeans. "Did you get my message?"

"I just got home. We had a little crisis at the rape prevention center, and I logged an all-nighter. I tried at school, then decided to try you here. Are you safe there?"

"As good as anywhere, I guess. You're back to the volunteer work again?"

"Not to worry! I just sleep less. I found Cat Sommerville for you!"

"She's Cathy Ferrington."

"Oh." Annie's voice was pure disappointment.

"I got the police file on Cathy Ferrington's murder. It included her maiden name. I'm sorry. Did it take much time?"

"No! No! I mean I was reading real estate transactions until my eyes swam, Josie, but that's fun stuff!"

"I called you as soon as I found out," Josie apologized.

"Then there were the real estate *agents*. Those kids are *hungry*!"

"So how did you find her, a real estate agent?"

"After a fashion! You want me to tell you about it?"

Annie seemed eager; she was proud of her search. "I'd love to hear it," Josie told her, smiling.

"Okay! Cathy Johnson sold her house to a man named Vic Dubois about a year after your mother's death. Dubois then sells it three years later, but he's a man, so he doesn't keep changing his name every time he thinks he's in love. I followed *him* through four sales, got his number and called to ask him if he remembered the agent who sold him Cathy Johnson's house. He didn't, but he looked it up. I call the agent. She gives me an agent in Phoenix, and he tells me he has to call me back — collect, of course. He's checking with Cathy Johnson, who's now Cathy — get this — *Sommerville*."

"No!"

"Yep. She went back to the first for seconds! How about *that* for a nightmare? You and Dan together again?"

"Don't even joke about it. How is he, anyway?"

"Dan's Dan. He's coming back to class on Monday, or so the rumor goes. Everyone's real excited to see how his new medication mixes with Jack Daniels."

Josie shook her head. Nothing at Bandolier was ever going to change, Dan Scholari least of all. "So did you talk to Mrs Sommerville?"

"A wonderful lady, Josie. I got the story of her daughter's life."

"I'm sorry you went to all that trouble. It's a pure fluke I found her. I mean I was reading about Cathy Ferrington and — "

"Forget it! What's five hours in the life of a scholar? At least I got the scoop on Dick Ferrington."

"What are you talking about?"

"Your Dr Ferrington and Cat Sommerville *had* to get married, not that Mrs Sommerville confessed it, but I got the info from her and then my assistant went into Orange County's record of births and deaths. Their baby was born January twentieth."

"Okay."

"They were married in June. Get your fingers out; it doesn't add up to nine, Josie! By my count, Cat's pregnant two or three weeks after your mother's death, and they're married at the end of June in Kanka-Kanka-Kanka."

"Kankakee."

"Whatever! Seven months later out comes a fully developed premature baby!"

"Wait a minute! Wait a minute!" Josie protested. "The baby wasn't Dick Ferrington's?" Susie and Melody had said as much.

"The baby was Ferrington's, as far as anyone knows, anyway."

"There's something wrong here, Annie. Do you mean to tell me Dick was at Lues State the spring my mother died?"

"That's what I mean to tell you. They were both sophomores at Lues State, met in the spring and fell in love like in the movies. Of course, these days it's all hormones, but back then things were different – "

"Annie, Dick told me they met at Chapel Hill!"

Quietly, with a bit of curiosity, "I guess Dr Ferrington lied to you, didn't he?"

Crazy K-Zs

"Grimes residence."

"Melody! Josie Darling, here. I talked to you – "

"Sure, sure. I remember you. What's up?"

"I got Susie Hill's address for you."

"Oh, great! Let me get a pen!"

A moment later, Josie read off the information. Then, as an afterthought, "One question, Melody. Do you know what sorority Cat Sommerville was in?"

"Sure! We were all in the same one, Susie and Cat and me: Kappa Zeta. The Crazy K-Zs."

Browsing the Time Line

Josie's eye fell to September 1, 4:54 – the call for Josie Fortune while Dick Ferrington sat beside her at the Skyline. AKA the Hurry On Up. Here he was, sitting with her when the phone rang. She followed the line to the next incident. Her first Monday in Lues, Welcome Home, Josie: Ferrington in Zurich. He could have set up the call at the bar, maybe, but he couldn't have slipped back into Lues to leave a message. *Three years ago: Cathy abducted while he's in Spain? Miller's idea: they agreed to meet somewhere. Ditch the kids with his folks and have a very private rendezvous . . .*

Too many problems with it. The reason Miller couldn't get any interest in his theory.

The man just didn't fit. So close! Josie remembered Dick Ferrington the morning he took off from Madrid. Saying goodbye. He hadn't said anything about divorce. In fact, he had been talking about getting home and taking a trip with the family. It had seemed so properly middle class, so typical of a family man, and she had teased him about it – this wonderful scholar who was, after all, pretty much like everyone else. But of course he wasn't. His marriage was falling apart. Josie remembered his letter to her after the murder, the feeling of removal she had gotten from it. Scholarly detachment. Then the speech this fall at the Skyline: again nothing about their problems. Still the wonderful husband of the wonderful wife of the perfect family. Fantasy, denial, or lies? And if lying, why? She thought about the near-tearful recollection of his longing for suicide. Pure bullshit. And the thing about the cop. The agony over a

393

stupid cop who — how was it he had put it? *second-rate detective . . . specious reasoning and confused chronology.*

He had been talking about Detective Jason Miller; she was sure of that now that she had read the file on Cathy Ferrington's murder. Maybe Miller had been closer to the truth than anyone knew. Maybe Ferrington was angry because Miller hadn't taken the bait?

Josie's eye fell to the converging point when Dick and Cathy Ferrington returned to campus and maybe the old sorority house and there met three other future victims. Had he picked them out then? He'd killed Josie Fortune. Now back in Lues, a professor, he decides to stalk three more? Lovers, maybe? Did he get that close to them? Did he make love to them? No. Too dangerous. They had dug up Kruger's lovers. They had looked into Paget's possible relationships, the same as they had her husband's. They had looked at Dick Ferrington's affairs also. They hadn't gotten a comprehensive list on Ferrington, obviously, but the list was extensive; Miller had dug up fifteen women within a three-year period of his wife's death — all with ages that would win most hands of blackjack. The list hadn't included Kruger or Paget or Bates or Josie Darling.

But certainly he hadn't planned to kill his own wife. Not at the start, not if he waited seventeen years. No, that was for another reason, marital discord. The divorce. But how had he done it? There was no answer to that. And there was no explanation of how he had managed to break into Josie's apartment while he was in Zurich.

Josie's attention shifted to Val. The answer was, Dick Ferrington was lying to Josie for his own reasons. He wasn't Cathy's murderer, nor the man stalking Josie. It was Val. It had to be Val. Quietly watching everyone. Tracking his boys *and* his girls. Was Ferrington one of Val's boys? Sure he was. Off to Chapel Hill, then back to Lues State. Ferrington was probably Val's golden boy. Interesting to find Ferrington's transcripts, she told herself. It would give her a better idea

394

if Val got him into Chapel Hill then brought him back to Lues State. Year after year contemplate the man's wife, as he contemplated others. *What did he call it? The thing about haste! The sin of — no! "the scholar's enemy . . . the sin of haste, people . . . the ruin of many, the savior of none!"*

A man who murdered after much contemplation, after years of contemplation! The *sin* of haste. Had he studied Cat Sommerville all those years, knowing he would have her? Had he kept her for weeks, watching Dick Ferrington's confusion, worry, panic? Bringing all the attention to bear on Ferrington, the way Wayne Paget had seemed to be the killer of Anita Paget, and Jack Hazard of Josie Fortune. Playing his games. Quite good at them, really. Every murder a bit different — except in the essence: the capture and delay, the terrible pain he brought his victims before they died. His games and double-crosses, the preternatural fear he inspired in everyone. That look he had given her when she had said the thing about the happy face. *Count on it.* The look of murder. Murder without haste.

Josie walked back to the old metal desk, her throat dry, and flopped down in her chair. She picked up Valentine's vitae. This was the man to look at. UNC-CH, 1961, BA; Duke, 1962, MA; UNC-CH, 1964, Ph.D.; Lues State, 1964, assistant professor; 1966, associate professor; 1974, full professor. First sabbatical, 1970–71, Lawrence, Kansas. From that year he had a grant to study . . .

Hello. "Matricide and the Image of Cultural Ruin," published in *Imago*, 1973. *Matricide? Killing mamma, Val? Is that what this is all about?* Second sabbatical, UNC, Chapel Hill, to work on a book that never came to fruit: a novel. Josie's eyebrows furrowed. Dick Ferrington and Cat Sommerville were still in Chapel Hill at that point in their history. Did he want to have another look at his Cat? Lick his big, loose lips at the thought of her under his power? Had he seen her the day Josie Fortune died? Was he the man in the woods — the slew? Had he followed her for seventeen years?

Josie scanned down the page to Valentine's last sabbatical leave, a year at Indiana State. "Outreach to the Public Schools."

Maybe it was time to take a look for dead bodies . . .

A Man with a Badge

With the knocking at her door, Josie looked up from Valentine's vitae. Her .357 in hand, she walked to the front door and checked in the peep-hole. She didn't recognize the man at first, but once she did, her thoughts raced forward uncontrollably. It was Detective Jason Miller. He had been there to bring her mother's body out of the canyon. He had been in Lues that day, had been a part of the investigation, a part of several of them, in fact, had been here all these years. Had he been Josie Fortune's lover? A friend? The age was right. A slew for a country girl and maybe not scared of Jack Hazard. Never a suspect in the investigation – never a look at all in his direction! Sheriff's friend, Colt Fellows's friend, too?

She swore savagely. She looked at her gun. Finally, she snapped the safety off and opened the door as far as the chain allowed. She held the gun pointed toward the floor, just behind the edge of the door. She peeked out.

"Yes."

Miller flashed his badge. "Remember me?"

"I remember."

"You care if I come in? We need to talk."

Josie stared at the man in confusion. She didn't want him inside. She didn't want to talk to him at all!

"What's this about?" Josie asked.

"Beatrice Quincy."

"Oh, shit."

"I'd like to come inside, if I may."

Keys, no problem. Information, easy. Cover-ups, he could have whispered in Colt's ear. What had happened that sent

396

Miller from a county deputy to the Lues Police Department? What kind of deal? Josie studied him carefully. "I don't think so."

Her bowels churned; breath failed her.

"I don't know you – not really, and I don't like your showing up here without calling."

"I called your office this afternoon, and you didn't get my message, or at least you didn't return my call. I called here tonight, and the line was busy. I thought I'd get out and catch you."

"Well, you caught me."

He nodded. "I just have one question, then I'll leave you alone."

"What's the question?"

They were still talking through a crack in the door. He must have thought she was crazy! *Forget what he thinks! He's the man!*

"What *didn't* you tell Detective Harpin?"

"I don't know what you're talking about."

"That wasn't a robbery that got interrupted. I didn't know what it was, but then I put *Fortune* with *Darling*, and I said to myself the professor knows more than she's telling."

"Fine. So arrest me."

"I might."

They stared each other down. He was smiling a little, but he wasn't happy. She was scared, but she wasn't about to give herself over to this man. Had the badge gotten each woman into his car?

"Do you think I shot Bea?"

"Never crossed my mind. Did you?"

"No, but it crossed my mind that you might have. Where were *you* Saturday night?"

Miller's smile was tense but bright. "Okay. That's fair enough. I was at the football game. The whole family was there. I saw the mayor. He'll remember. Call him if you don't trust me. Call my wife, call my kids."

"I'm not going to call the mayor or your family and you know it!"

Miller shrugged. He didn't care. Was he an innocent man, a good man? She wanted to believe it. Josie Fortune trusted the wrong man. The others too? A cop would be . . .

"It was him, wasn't it? The man stalking you shot Bea Quincy?"

"Maybe it was, maybe not. Look, I'm really busy. If you want to talk, I'll come in tomorrow."

"He leave a note?"

"No."

"It's evidence in a murder if he did. You could get in some serious trouble if you tampered with evidence."

"No note."

"I had a technician examine the mirror in your room. We found traces of blood on the mirror that matched the victim's type. I can have it DNA-tested and prove it was hers. That takes time and costs money. I'd just as soon have the truth from you. Was it Bea Quincy's blood?"

"You just happened to check the mirror in my room?"

"We went over every square inch of your room, actually. What did he write?"

"Nothing."

"I can't help you if you won't let me."

"I didn't ask you for help."

"Oh? What about the files you wanted to look at?"

"That's different."

"You really think I would have given you those files if I was the killer?"

"Why not? They were useless."

"I don't know. I liked the way you connected the victims. We had twenty different detectives going over those files, including FBI; I went over those murders myself. I like to think I'm good. I didn't see it. Sorority sisters." He shook his head.

"Cathy Ferrington was in the same sorority. She showed

398

up on campus with her husband the fall that Kruger, Paget, and Bates pledged Kappa Zeta."

"I'll be damned. That's a little too much of a coincidence, isn't it? What do you make of it?"

"I don't make anything of it. I don't know what anything means. What do you make of it? You're the cop."

The door was still on its chain. They were looking at each other through the crack. Miller seemed innocent enough. But of course he could just be talking his way in. *Praise better than a key.*

"I've already ordered the cases of Paget, Kruger, and Bates reopened. I guess we can add Cathy Ferrington to the list, too."

"Cathy Ferrington was one of the women who found Josie Fortune's corpse."

"Now that's over the top," the man said calmly.

He knows? He's the killer? No? Neutral, never gets excited. God help me!

"Seems to be," Josie answered. Poker face.

"Was it *him* at the Huree Hideaway? That's all I want to know. Tell me and I'll leave."

"I could lie. You wouldn't know."

"I'll know. I want this bastard as much as you do."

"Nobody wants him as much as I do."

"It was him, wasn't it?"

"It was him."

"Bea's blood in the mirror?"

Josie nodded.

"He wrote something?"

"What does it matter?"

"It matters. I can get this bastard, if I have all the evidence."

"You've had all the evidence for years."

"But now I've got a lead."

"I'll tell you this: the man that killed Bea is the same man who killed my mother. You can take it to the bank."

"What about the others?"

"I don't have proof."

"But you believe it?"

"I believe it heart and soul."

"Lady, I'm going to be there when your body shows up. And the rest of my life I'm going to wonder what you knew that you weren't telling me."

"You know everything I know," Josie said.

"Somehow I doubt it."

The letters her mother had received almost twenty years ago were lying on the floor behind her; Josie knew he should have them, but she didn't know that she could trust him. He had been there. She had nothing but his word to trust, and that was as good as nothing at all, right now.

Miller's face twitched when he saw she wasn't going to tell him anything else.

"Look," he said, "when you decide you can trust me, give me a call. If you're not tied up." Dead pan, this, as cold as any look Valentine had ever given. "They say your mother was a scrapper, Josie. They say she handled her share of mean drunks and never lost a fight. And this bastard took her. You think about that. No offense, but I get the feeling you never won a fight in your life."

Browsing

When Miller was gone, Josie hurried to the Mustang and drove back to Liberal Arts. Quickly, she cut through the dark plaza on her way to Worley. She looked in all directions; she half expected Valentine or Miller or Dick Ferrington to be waiting, but the shadows were empty. Her tormentor rested. The victim, never. On the sixth floor, she surveyed the offerings, nearly a thousand newspapers on microfilm, and found the one she wanted. After that it was simply a matter of threading the machine.

Indiana State is in Terre Haute, Indiana. As Josie started through Terre Haute's *Tribune Star* she spotted Val almost at once. Professor Henry Valentine, on a National Endowment for the Humanities grant, had arrived to teach one course in creative writing at the university and to function as a liaison to the public schools. There was a large picture on the front page of the Sunday "Local Newsmakers'" section: Val and select administrative types, Val looking like the cat who ate the canary. Valentine's duties were described in detail. He was bringing his expertise to the secondary schools. Poetry to the cornfields. He was quoted at length. All academic drivel. Josie fast-forwarded the spool. She hit the jackpot soon enough. On January 28, the nude body of Nora Tolley, age thirty-six, of Farmersburg, was pulled out of the Wabash River near Tecumseh, Indiana. A leather thong had been tied around her neck in a hangman's knot; the branch which the thong had been tied to had broken off. Together, the branch and the corpse had floated downriver perhaps a quarter of a mile until they had caught up on a sandbar in the frigid waters. The body lay exposed to the elements four days before it was noticed. Cause of death was ruled to be hypothermia.

Miss Tolley would be greatly missed, Josie read. She was an associate professor of chemistry at Indiana State as well as the Assistant Dean of Arts and Sciences. Josie tracked back to the first entry she had found: Val's grand arrival as he stood among the happy administrative types. One woman alone stood with the old bulls. In the caption Josie found her easily, ASSISTANT DEAN OF ARTS AND SCIENCES, DR NORA TOLLEY.

Josie leaned back in her chair contentedly, whispering now into the light of the microfilm machine, "I've got you, you bastard!"

A Mother's Keepsake

"Josie, here."

"Hey, DJ!"

"I need to borrow my mother's *keepsake*."

"You want to come get it tomorrow morning?" Virgil Hazard asked. It was midnight, and he was slurring slightly, a man at peace with the world.

"I want you to get it now and bring it up to Pilatesburg; I'm at the Sleepy Time, the seven hundred block on South Center Street."

"Jesus, DJ, I work for a living! I don't have time to run all over Lues County delivering your mother's *keepsakes*!"

"Virgil, I want it, and I want it now."

A Late-Night Visitor

Standing just beyond the opened door to Josie's room, his fat figure caught in the light, Virgil Hazard offered Josie a feed sack. "Safety's *off* and it's loaded. Don't kill yourself. Extra shells at the bottom of the sack."

Josie reached quickly to take the sack from him. The stalk of the shotgun was heavy. "Thanks."

"What's going on, DJ?" It was now almost two in the morning, and Virgil's face looked it.

"I need to see Jack."

"Yeah, well, Jack's a little busy playing Jesse James these days."

"Set it up, Virgil. I don't care how you do it; I'll go anywhere you say, but I need to talk to him as soon as possible."

Louis

Josie called in sick Friday, then spent the day reading Waldis's book and looking time and time again at the old yearbook pictures she had photocopied. Outside it was raining. The day dragged interminably.

Virgil called at three. "Same place as before, DJ."

"What? Where?"

"No questions. Take off now. Someone will be waiting."

"I don't understand!"

"Family reunion, hot-shot." Virgil hung up.

Lues Creek Crossing. Josie packed her car quickly. On the highways, she kept to the speed limit, and once she hit the back roads, she watched to be sure she wasn't followed. It was nearly an hour later that she came to Lues Creek Crossing and saw a pickup truck at the side of the road. A middle-aged man was standing in the rain, waiting for her. He wore a rubber poncho and an old stetson. He stood quietly as Josie drove toward him, his hands empty and in plain view.

Josie stopped her car several feet from him and left it running as she stood up beside the car, the driver door open, her mother's shotgun in her hand.

She had ridden the man's shoulder. She remembered the eyes. They were quiet, thoughtful, dangerous.

"Who are you?" she asked.

"I'm Louis. I'm Jack's cousin, Josie. I'm taking you to Jack."

"I'll follow you."

The man studied Josie's face curiously. "You alone, Josie?"

"I'm alone."

"Did anybody follow you?"

"Nobody followed. I was careful."

"What's this about? Virgil didn't know."

"It's about justice, Louis."

Louis considered this for a moment, then he nodded. "Then let's go find Jack!"

The pickup splashed across the creek easily, while Josie nudged the low-slung Mustang through the crossing with more care and difficulty. A few yards beyond the crossing, Louis cut into some brush and took off cross country. Josie gritted her teeth and followed him. For nearly a hundred yards they were driving through branches and over saplings with no sign of a road, but then the truck came to a muddy lane, and ten minutes afterwards, down another long narrow path, they pulled up in front of a primitive cabin. Both vehicles were splattered in black mud. The rain poured down steadily.

Louis stepped out into the rain and whistled. Her windshield wipers humping, Josie watched but could hear nothing until Louis whistled again, this time four crisp notes.

Jack came out from behind the cabin and stopped at the sight of Josie's Mustang. He carried a long-barreled pump shotgun. A revolver was tucked in his belt. Unlike Louis, he wore no rain gear, and despite the cold, he didn't bother closing his coat.

The two men talked briefly, then Louis went inside the cabin.

Jack trotted toward the driver door of Josie's Mustang.

His wet face pushed close as she rolled the window down and felt the rain hitting her. "You find him, did you?"

Josie nodded, "We need to talk, Jack."

The Slew

The knock at his door was heavy, and Nelson Rush looked up from his book in surprise. "Who is it?" he called.

Nelson looked at the clock. It was ten. Friday night, ten o'clock, the dorm rooms were always empty, and someone – who? – was knocking at his door.

"Who is it?!"

The knock came again.

"I'm coming, all right!"

Nelson, I just wanted to come by and thank you for your help . . .

Oh, Miss Darling.

Call me Josie.

Nelson opened the door and felt his heart sink. He saw a man his father's age, a slew. He was average height but built

404

thick; his eyes were clear, piercing, cold. He was dripping rainwater everywhere.

"What do you want?" Nelson asked. Nelson knew karate and he wasn't scared of *any* slew.

The man reached inside his wet poncho, and Nelson was sure he meant to pull out a knife or a gun. His bowels nearly gave out. Then he saw a sheet of paper. It was folded twice, seemingly a letter without an envelope.

"Read this," the man told him, "then give it back to me."

"What is it?"

"Read it."

Giving Notice

As usual, Dr Henry Valentine left his van on the lot northwest of the Liberal Arts complex, and went along a path of his own making toward his office. At five o'clock on a Monday morning, the place was entirely his. The janitors were done, nothing at all was stirring. Val slipped through the halls quietly and approached his office with a feeling of supreme satisfaction. He was thinking of Miss Fortune's Darling – *Little Josie*! Her hour had come. He had hoped for a longer play, but her words on Thursday demonstrated she had become extremely dangerous. It wouldn't do to give her more time. A very suspicious woman, all of a sudden! He had thought Friday to take her, but she hadn't shown, had quite vanished, in fact. Yes. Take her sometime this week and work it slowly. The slowest death the sweetest.

There was still some debate as to the best method for Baby Fortune. One school of thought favored *tradition*. Hang the bitch as her mother had hanged. Another school favored innovation. No ready-made hell for the next generation; each girl her own casket. The innovative school favored a crucifixion. Lues County hadn't had one for years! Nothing had ever quite equaled the scandal of Melissa Bates nailed to a tree. In the Bible Belt a thing like that played mighty big!

Oh, yes. Of course Josie must have her own death, if not her mother's, so the innovative school argued passionately for St Peter's crucifixion. Hasty old Saint Pete, choosing to go at it upside down. Regretting it for hours, one is sure. The exquisite pain of such death! Poor Darling looking at her world all upside down, the blood of her feet dripping into her eyes. Apt. Apt, indeed.

But tradition had its argument. The notes replicated, the same manner of death, the same stone in the same canyon for the body to be laid upon. Henry Valentine pondered the aesthetics of such a death, as he reached for his Brand Hall master key. The trouble with the world was it had lost touch with tradition. Everything always new was indicative of an uneasy spirit. Some things bear repeating. And nice to see if the daughter had the spit of her old *maaaaaa*. Clever of her to find that word. Shame to kill a real scholar. Well, well, another loss to the academy, and who gives a fuck? Give *the word* to Ferrington: he could stand to look clever.

Valentine's contemplative smile froze suddenly. His step caught. Something was on his damn door! He hurried forward and saw it clearly now. Yes! a hangman's noose! A thong of leather twisted into a noose was looped over his doorknob. Tied to the end of it was a piece of wood. Printed boldly in red paint – paint! – on his office door were the words:

Henry VAlentino
mUddered N. Tolley
iN tecum–see–me
ufuk

For a long and terrible moment, Valentine glared at the words. Then he smiled. The little riddle-solver knew a secret. Well, she didn't know them all, did she? And certainly not for long.

Inside his office, Valentine set his backpack on his desk and considered his options. She had been exceedingly hard to track lately, hardly worth the effort, when one considered that she *usually* came to school. On the other hand, this kind of outrage against his property was a matter he knew he had better take seriously. Urgent business, this. He could hardly countenance the idea that someone might see the little whore's graffito. That wouldn't do at all. He was going to have to clean off the mess presently, and take care of Josie Fortune's bastard by and by.

cum-see-me? You don't know what you ask, darling.

Curious, really, that Josie should mention Dr Tolley. The vitae, of course. One of his least favorite girls, really. He had liked Dr Tolley very much at the start of it: her irritating twang, her corn-fed flanks, that tough as nails look, until she had pissed all over herself at the sight of a leather noose. OhGodohGodohGod. Give Josie Fortune her due: noose tight around her neck, she had danced on tiptoe hour after hour, her legs quivering, her body rocking and weaving, the air shut off, never losing her balance, never once the magic *please*. Dr Tolley had been pathetic. She would do *anything*. As if *anything* could equal the perfect bliss of watching her choke to death. Or would have, if the branch hadn't broken.

Valentine took his key and went down to Gerty Dowell's office. Dowell kept paint on her shelves. It went back to the time she had painted her bookshelves, was set on doing the whole department's shelves, until Smith had requisitioned new ones. Simply have to block it out. Maybe Josie imagined he didn't know about her .357? Would she be in her apartment tonight waiting for him to cum-see her? Well, of course she would. Every rat to its corner. And probably very sorry she's made her stepfather her mortal enemy.

Valentine whistled as he took a can of black paint and a clean brush and went back to his office door. Opening the new can with his pocket knife, he considered dreamily the surprise awaiting the woman.

Josie, we have to talk . . .

Why, certainly . . .

When Valentine had finished stirring the can, he splashed huge gobs of the stuff on his door, and considered the effect. He didn't like it. It was obvious he didn't care for the graffito someone had left, so had covered it up. That wouldn't do. Prettily, he added seven swastikas. When he had finished, it appeared the work of a skinhead who mistook a large nose for Semitic blood and some kind of bizarre religious conviction in one MEAN SON OF A BITCH IN THE SKY. That wouldn't do either. Be thought a Jew? Never live it down. Need the random violence effect. Patiently, Val duplicated the effect on three other office doors, including Gerty's; then, impulsive boy that he was, decided to give the nigger a thrill. Now he smashed the window beside Gerty's door so it would look like someone had entered the office by reaching in through the broken glass and turning the doorknob from the inside. Using his key, so as not to risk cutting himself, perish the thought, Val stepped in and decided a bit more might do the trick and spent a minute or so storming the office, dumping books and throwing stacks of papers across the floor and writing Gerty's favorite word on the wall. CockCockCockCock. Enough to keep the withered old virgin hopping and quivering for months. When he had done with it, Valentine went out and broke more windows. He finished the mêlée by throwing the paint can and brush down the hall in the direction of Ferrington's office, a wild wet black spray of it.

Henry checked his hands for paint. Clean as ever. A good boy. He grinned happily. Before going again into his own office, he used his key to enter Josie's office. Nothing out of the ordinary. He checked the drawers, the papers. Rummaging with a light touch, he thought he could smell the woman as he moved about. This morning he would leave no message. No threats, no retribution. Let her wait it out, let her wonder if she's even right. He peeked under the memos on her door. Happy face. Important to keep things light. More chill to it, more the feel of invincibility. Madness is a laughing man, that kind of thing. And the obituary had formed such a nice balance to it. The artist in Henry had resisted the straight journalistic approach, that legal notice *thing*, but he had to admit, in the end, it was just better. The two masks of theater: happy face, legal notice. Fortune's little Darling was going to be sweet to take. Child hastening to her mother's end. And her warm wet had smelt so good. Maybe just once more before she climbs that old rugged cross. Once more for Henry. Act mystified when you talk to her today; if you talk. No implied threats or subtextual messages. Doubt is a terrible demon.

Valentine closed the woman's office door gently, and started for the department office. God! how he loved this place in the mornings. The quiet, the power he felt. A low whistle broke through his lips. The trouble with hanging is it goes rather quickly. Even if one avoids snapping the spine, there's a better than average chance she'll go in a matter of minutes. Assuming one's branch doesn't break! Lord! Lord! Life is absurd; never more so than when your Assistant Dean of Arts and Sciences goes floating downriver, tied and gagged and bobbing like a fisherman's cork! Val laughed outright and shook his head.

Inside the department office, Valentine saw that his mailbox contained a single sheet of paper. Picking it up, he read the childish scrawl:

> Melissa Bates crucified . . .
> Shelley Kruger hanged . . .
> victims of H. vaLenTINY

Valentine looked at the next box and the next. The bitch had copied her scrawl on the Xerox and put a sheet in every box. Every damn box! He began pulling the sheets out rapidly, and this time he forgot to smile.

For the rest of the morning Valentine sat in his office, taking no visitors. Meeting at three. We have called this meeting for the purpose of eliminating all the lecturers. Dick Ferrington. Kill half the girls he fucks, fill a graveyard.

Cathy Ferrington, so surprised. Val! What are you doing here?

I thought since Dick's out of town, we could start an affair, Cathy.

Don't tease a girl if you aren't serious, Val.

Do I look like a tease? Come on, let's take a drive; I'll show you something you haven't seen before.

Oh, you've got me curious.

Curiosity killed the cat . . .

Killed that Cat anyway.

Josie would be a bit more difficult now that she was making accusations. Perhaps work off it somehow. Something, some secret to take to her. Have reasons for approach. Long-held suspicions. Oh yes, for years.

Val kept his head in his stack of papers, sublimely removed from any thoughts other than the occasional fantasy of Josie oh my Darling with a look of surprise all over her face, like a girl who's just stepped in what the dog left behind. So proud of her riddles! Oh but you missed the footnotes, Josie! We live in modern times, child; the riddles nowadays all have footnotes.

Damn it to hell with tradition! Crucify her! She's a beauty, lovely smell she has too, and her tree was already picked out. Palms pierced, feet curled together and spiked, the blood running down her upended legs. Three nails or four? Four for Bates. Val had seen nothing in his life to match the expression of Melissa Bates as she found herself dying the death of Our Little Jesus while the Gospels were read to her. Val had asked her if she could appreciate the different *styles* of the four sainted scribes of God. A shame really to gag her, but a girl's scream once you put a couple of spikes through her feet could carry a long way down the holler.

Eyes so expressive, though. Don't get that in a hanging. All scrunched up. Hadn't really bothered to check religious convictions for Josie Darling. The whole point of Bates's death. Loved her little jew–sus.

Truth was, hangings had never been lucky. Had nearly broken his leg over Shelley Kruger's execution. Dean Tolley, the broken branch. And Josie Fortune getting sucked into a whirlpool! A fortune-ate thing she was ever found! No, hangings were just not lucky. Some things like that. Don't push against karma, Henry.

Shortly before eleven, Val left his office. No sight of Josie today. A very sick girl maybe; stays home lest she catch her death. He walked to Varner Hall in his lazy amble, dreaming lazily. Beautiful day, blue sky, warming after all the cold and rain. When he arrived at his customary time, seven minutes past the hour, Val's tranquility was recovered – at least until he discovered his classroom was empty. There was a standard class cancellation form posted by the door with an explanatory note appended:

Valentine shot to death
Anita Paget and Bea Quincy

Val ripped the notice from the wall and looked about the halls for the bitch. What was she doing? How did she *know*?

Valentine forced himself to stroll back in the direction of his office, calming himself finally with well-reasoned assurances. She did not know. She could not *know*. A minor detail missing: proof! Valentine pushed past two maintenance men painting over his black swastikas. "They got your door, too, sir!"

Filthy slews. Val gave them no answer. He reached to his pocket and pulled out his key-ring. The key slid into place as he heard Gerty Dowell calling out, "They got yours too, Val?"

Val stopped and turned toward Miss Dowell. "Slews, Gerty."

"Did they break into your office?"

"Thankfully, no."

"They did mine! Come look!"

"Oh, Gerty not now."

"They painted my walls with *the c-word*, Val! Come see!"

Valentine indulged himself. Stepping into the office, he studied his handiwork. The word known to all virgins.

"What kind of animals would do such a thing, Gerty?"

"Margaret and Bill had their windows broken, and Our Nigerian had the *n-word* painted all over his door and office."

Gerty's eyes had a kind of spin to them when she got in these moods.

"I wish I had caught the bastards, Gerty."

"I come early sometimes, Val. What if I'd been here alone when they came?"

Val shook his head at the terrible thought. Sleeping with mommy bad enough; gang-banging Gerty, beyond the pale. "None of us are safe anymore, Gerty."

"*She* didn't get it." Gerty pointed to Josie Darling's office door.

"Have you seen her?" Val asked.

"She just came by a couple of minutes ago and left."

"Really? By herself?"

"I didn't see Clarissa Holt with her, if that's what you mean. Those two . . ."

If eyebrows could speak.

"I'm sorry I missed her," Val answered thoughtfully. "Now if you'll excuse me, I need to make some calls."

Valentine looked at his watch.

Perhaps pay a call on Miss Darling, if we can find her.

Inside his office, Val discovered a piece of paper taped to the wall over his desk. It was a photocopy of a photograph. She had been in his office! Stepping closer he recognized the face of Josie Fortune, Miss Darling's sainted mother. She was seated on the counter of the bar inside the Hurry On Up. She held a sawed-off shotgun in her right hand, the stock of it balanced on her thigh, the barrels pointing ceilingward. Behind her was the pathetic little sign, mostly cut off in the

412

photograph: A Good Place to Eat. Across the bottom of the page, written in lipstick, were the words:

MisS mE?

Taking a Message

Valentine reached for the paper with Josie Fortune's image and tore it in half. He was finally out of patience. Did she have one thread of proof? Did she even know the terror of the death that awaited her? He tried to slow his breathing. He sat down and stared at the wall where Josie Fortune's image had taunted him.

Then he heard a knock at his back. It came from across the hall. For Miss Fortune's little Darling.

Val got up and opened his door, only to discover a slender boy seeming in something of a hurry.

"Doctor Valentine?"

"Mr Nelson Rush! And how are you, young man?"

The boy tipped his head toward the door behind him. "Have you seen her?"

"No, I haven't." Val offered an affectionate smile. "Do you have an appointment, Nelson?"

"I was supposed to meet her for lunch at Cokey's. She wanted to talk to me about something, and I can't make it."

"Really? What was it she wanted to see you about?"

The boy looked at his watch. "Something to do with my job, but she didn't say. I thought I could catch her before she left." He looked down the hall nervously.

Val looked at his watch in sympathy. "Did you have a noon date, Nelson?"

"Yes, sir, but I have a lab at noon. I just found out about it, and I can't miss it."

"If she comes by, I'll tell her," Val promised. "And don't worry, if she doesn't show, I can give a call out to Cokey's for you and let her know you can't make it."

Smiling, flush, "You'd do that for me!"

Val's lip were puckered, kindly. He nodded. But of course! What's a favor now and then between friends?

"Great! Hey, thanks!"

Nelson started running. Rush-ing. Valentine smiled. So the little Darling slips. He wandered back to his desk and took up his receiver. "Give me the number for Work Study, please, Marilyn!"

Marilyn gave him the number, and he dialed it. A moment later a voice came across the line, purely Lues. Val answered, "This is Dr Valentine in Arts and Letters: I want to know about the scheduling of one of my students. I think he's lying to me about his Work Study."

"And what is the name, Dr Valentine?"

"Mr Nelson Rush."

"And his student identification?"

"I have that information next door; do I really need it?"

"Just a minute. Here it is: Nelson Rush works in Transcripts and Records, ten hours a week. Do you need the exact times? It's a flex schedule, but — "

"That's quite enough! My mistake entirely. I know Mrs Temple! She's working that boy overtime! I'll take it up with Naomi. Thank you!" Val hung up.

Well, well, Miss Fortune. A little research, I see. Whose grades? Who's who? Who had whom? Where was I when the lights went out? That kind of thing. And dumb luck your *boy* couldn't make it for lunch.

He punched the department number. "This is Valentine! Please cancel my afternoon class."

Such a lovely day, I think I'd like to go hunting.

Valentine set his phone receiver back and looked at his watch again. Probably miss the three o'clock meeting. Phone in the van; call then. He unlocked his file drawer and picked out his S & W 640-1. He picked out six rounds from a slightly depleted box and loaded the gun, then settled the little magnum in his sports jacket pocket. He picked about

414

the cabinet and found some twine. Be prepared, Henry. More in the van. Lovely van, really. A movable feast. Someday kidnap a whole sorority; put them in there. Crime of the century.

Outside, the day was a beauty. Clear warm. Cold tonight, though. Her first night! Valentine headed for his van. As he stepped onto the pavement, he was thinking of the capture. She would be scared and cautious, but perfectly vulnerable for the unexpected. Need a convincing scenario to get close to her, of course. Suspects me, so the best would be a little secret. Know something to tell her. Yes. That would do. She'll be eager. Well, maybe just a gun in her face this afternoon! Straight up and fast. Catch her at Cokey's as she's leaving. Catch her with her panties down. Might be seen, of course. Hate to miss the murder because of that. Could use the phone; call her. Or follow her. See what she does, where she goes. Best is patience. Nothing is lost here. Haste not, Henry.

Preoccupied, Henry Valentine crossed the parking lot, jingling his van keys in his hand. Nearing it, he stopped to consider the thing. The van was off center somehow! He stepped closer. Good Christ! He'd a flat tire! A damned flat tire! Hurriedly he looked at his watch. Worst luck!

A Walk in the Woods

The sky was blue; the colors of the forest at their zenith. Josie waited in Louis Hazard's pickup after her run through Brand Hall with the stolen master key. She kept the engine running. She sat low and wore a baseball cap, so Valentine couldn't pick out her silhouette. She watched Val's black van some thirty yards away and a patch of woods next to the lot. Valentine showed at ten to twelve. She gave him a moment to cross to the van, then started rolling toward him even before he noticed the flat. The flat was on the driver side of his van, and predictably Valentine came to a halt, staring at

415

it dumbly. Josie pushed the accelerator and came up fast on him. By the time he checked his watch, it was too late. He looked around just as Josie brought the truck skidding to a halt beside him. The passenger window was open and when Josie leveled the twin pipes of her shotgun on the man, he looked positively certain she meant to finish it.

His eyebrows were cocked in an expression of confused surprise; his big lips hung open stupidly.

"Drop your keys right there, Val."

There was a pleasant clink as his keys fell to the pavement, an expression in the eyes that seemed to brighten with optimism.

"Now get in!" she told him.

Valentine hesitated, looking around. There were people moving through the lot. Josie kept the shotgun extended out straight, just under the line of the seat back. The twin pipes pointed over the door into Val's face at a distance sufficient to give Josie a two-foot margin of error. "Get in or die now, Val!"

Val's optimism, which had come after a second or so, faded with Josie's voice, but a pleasant bemused expression replaced it. "Certainly, Josie. Certainly. You won't believe this, but I was hoping to find you just now. With this flat tire, I thought I'd miss you."

The big man grinned happily and opened the door. He had the look of a man who's caught his prey. Josie shifted the gun so that it rested in her left hand, both hammers laid back, the twin triggers wrapped in her tense fingers as Valentine came into the truck beside her. "Easy, Val. We don't want any accidents. Keep your hands in view; one bad move, I'm a fugitive, you're a dead man. Are we all right on that?"

The old man settled into the passenger seat and looked down at the weapon which poked into his side. "Very nice, Josie," he whispered. "Very nice, indeed. Perhaps I'll fuck you with it before I kill you."

416

His eyes twinkled with a weird, mad kindness. His odor was overpowering.

"You're on the wrong end of the pipes for that fantasy, Val."

Josie accelerated and pulled out of the parking lot fast. She turned onto a side street, went half a block on, then turned onto another side street, still bordering the lot. This street was empty. She could have finished it here, wiped off her prints and let Louis Hazard explain how his truck had been stolen. It was tempting, and if she had to, she meant to do it.

"It's a beautiful weapon, Josie. Your mother's gun, isn't it? I seem to recall seeing a picture of it." He hesitated thoughtfully. "*Functional*, I expect?"

"We could find out right now, if you want."

"Not necessary, not on my account." Valentine grinned, and looked out the window, his eyes casting about with easy indifference. His amusement was disconcerting. Josie's fingers were wet on the trigger. She could feel the barrels pushing comfortably into Valentine's side, but the truth was she didn't know if she could pull the triggers if she got in trouble. If he moved at all, she knew to give him both barrels at once, but right now, all she could do was pray she wouldn't be put to the test.

A truck rolled up behind her, two country boys riding in it. They followed closely.

"Are we going out for that drink you mentioned last week?"

"We're going for a walk in the woods."

"Splendid, Josie! I've been meaning to take you there since I met you!"

He hardly took her seriously. He took the gun seriously, of course, but once out of the truck he wasn't going to be so easy to manage, and whatever plans she had for him might need quick adjustments.

Josie checked her speed. "I'm glad that makes you happy,"

417

she answered. She turned right onto a gravel road. The truck that had followed her out of town went on. She crossed a covered bridge shortly afterwards. Alone now, she drove a steady twenty miles an hour. She remembered this road. It came straight up the valley toward a ridge, the road bending just before the property where Jack Hazard's trailer had sat twenty years ago. As the road turned left, Josie drove straight over the field. The truck jostled meanly, and Valentine's face paled. He apparently feared an accident.

"Easy, Josie! There's no rush!"

Josie stopped the truck well below the ridge. This was the place she had been looking for on her first day in Lues. She had missed it because the new highway had turned the old into a back road. It was here that she and her mother and Jack had lived for four years. Nestled up against the woods, Lues Creek behind them, West Lues Creek a half mile out in the other direction with its own covered bridge, the site had been a perfect sanctuary, a perfect home. It was beautiful country, especially on a bright October day.

"The old homestead, Josie?"

"Get out, Val."

With some extravagance, Valentine pushed out of the truck cab and stepped clear before Josie followed him.

She slid over the seat, making sure to keep the shotgun pointing at the man. Once standing in the thick leaves and weeds that covered the field, Josie pointed with her left hand to the woods and ridge. "Let's walk that way, Val."

Valentine smiled at her. "Are you sure you're up to this, Josie? You look a bit pale to me. Are you thinking about what I could do to you if I get the gun? Have you thought about things going wrong?"

"All I have to do is pull these triggers. Seems easy enough."

"Hard work, Josie! Hard work! Believe me, all these voices that want you to do the *right* thing, the *good* thing: they can be devils in one's first kill. Maybe you fire too quickly, maybe not quickly enough. Killing's a business like anything else.

418

Experience pays dividends; the novice goes through the school of hard knocks."

"I've had the graduate program of hard knocks, Val."

The old man's brow wrinkled in a cavalier acquiescence.

"Well then I'm sure you'll do fine. Still," Valentine's brow furrowed more deeply as he pretended to be struck by a new thought, "justice is such an abstract thing; hard to get the blood up for old crimes, don't you think?"

He was full of mockery, his big eyes growing calm with the threat of the twin barrels in his gut.

"I owe you the pain of my whole life, Valentine. Nothing abstract about it."

"You owe me your life, Josie. If not for me, you would have grown up in these god-forsaken woods, a well-fucked whore like your mother, and nothing more."

Tucking his hands in his pants pocket, Valentine began to saunter in the direction Josie had indicated. He had the air of a man who's come to see a property he might buy. At the rise, just before the woods, he stopped and looked around at the cinders and weeds where the trailer had sat. Now he looked down the hill toward the big bend in the road.

"All alone, Josie. May I tell you a secret?"

"Just keep going."

His big lips spread in a kindly old man's grin.

"You were marked to die twenty years ago." He pulled his hand from his pocket and pointed it at her forehead as though he actually saw something. "You're still marked. It's your mother's blood: I see it all over you."

Valentine enjoyed the effect he had, then turned and started along the trail through the small grove. Josie imagined the three cars coming down the road behind her. She could see in her memory the dust they threw. As they had in every dream and every fantasy, they came off the road now at the bend and straight across the field until they parked where she had left the truck. Six of them took their positions behind the cars. She saw their guns raised up against the

419

gray sky. They racked their guns at once, as three of the troopers came running toward Jack and her.

"To the right, Val."

Right was the way she had taken as a child. She knew now that Jack could have run once he saw what they meant to do, but that she was on the porch with him, and he was afraid they would just open fire and make their apologies over the dead kid later. So he had stood still. The trooper who had grabbed her hadn't expected her to fight, but she had; she had broken free, and she had run. She had followed this trail back to Lues Creek, and she had run as she had never run before.

As they walked together that same path, Josie followed two steps behind Val and kept the barrels of the gun pointed just above his hips. She knew the power of the gun. At this distance, the blast would sever his spine.

For years, Josie had imagined that she had been running wildly, that she hadn't known where she was going when the trooper had chased her, but that wasn't true. She had only forgotten what she had meant to do. She knew now where she had been going. There were small cave-like niches in the boulders by the falls, and Jack had an old Colt .45 revolver hidden in one of them that she had known about and thought she could reach. She was running for that. Seven years old and running herself right into a gunfight. She had never dreamed the trooper meant her no harm, nor quite imagined her life was already over, that her mother was dead and Jack was gone.

Valentine and Josie came now to the creek.

It was here the state trooper had caught her. He had taken her up by one arm, and she had twisted and kicked at him. It was to be her last fight for years; it was to be the day that she would recall forever, the day when everything fell apart, and to save herself from losing everything again, Josie had let Dan Scholari have any liberty. For that and her lost world, she owed Henry Valentine and meant to see he died for it.

"Is it like you remember, Josie?" he called to her over his shoulder. "I know you have such troubles with your memory, but are these woods the same? Or has it all changed?"

The creek was the same. The water was broad, shallow and slow moving; the October leaves overhanging the water reflected off its surface. In the distance Josie saw the boulders which marked the entrance to Hazard Falls. That too was the same. She remembered it. The trail would end there, and they would have to slip into the current to get onto the falls.

Valentine went on as far as the trail took them, then stopped. His hands in his pants pockets, he turned slowly, and seemed to study Josie's eyes.

"We seem to have run out of trail."

They were no more than a single step apart; the shortened barrels of Josie's mother's shotgun were pointed right into his stomach. Valentine considered the gun casually.

"Afraid to get wet?"

"Do you mean to kill me here, Josie?"

"If you want me to."

Valentine laughed. "And what if I don't *want* you to?" Almost a joking tone, but he was still a man looking dead into the twin bores of his own mortality, and there was just a bit of lonesomeness about his expression.

"If you want to live a bit longer, Val, you'll turn around and get into the creek."

Val hesitated, his eyes almost scolding. "Killing a human being is such a terrible thing, Josie. Have you thought about it? Can you live with it?"

"Letting you live another hour is the worst thing I can imagine."

"Are you scared, Josie? You seem scared."

She nodded, meeting his eye. "Aren't you?"

Henry Valentine gave the barrels of the shotgun a contemplative look.

"You know I sympathize with what you're trying to do,"

421

he said. "I really do, but I have to tell you, your mother would have scared me with that gun. I'm not sure you're quite the old gal's equal. A real tough girl, your mamma. What do you think? Do you think mamma would have let a husband of hers put her in the hospital — twice? Didn't you say something about *freezing* up when you should have fought? A terrible thing, fear. Are you feeling that kind of fear now, Josie? Are you thinking you might not be able to do this?"

"Do you remember the first time you saw her?" Josie asked.

"Josie Fortune?" The thought seemed to startle him, but after a moment, he smiled tightly. "I believe I do, come to think of it. Lovely hair, beautiful figure but such a hopeless slew."

"She was in your class but only for one evening."

"*Very* good, Josie. A real *researcher*. I'm afraid your mother had no talent for research. She was all fight, that one. All fight and no brains. And you're just the opposite. Have you ever even fired a gun like that, Josie? Research, now that's your strength. I should have thought you'd stick with your talents. Call a police detective in with your findings. Aren't you just a little sorry that you didn't?"

"I don't think I'm sorry at all. If I'd called the police, I wouldn't be able to blow your head off, now would I?"

The face went to granite. The game had temporarily lost its charm.

"It was an evening class, Val, and she was late, and when she walked in she asked you if she could talk to you. You said she was talking right now, to go ahead with what she wanted to say. She asked if she should be in an advanced course if she hadn't been in an introductory course. Ring a bell?"

"What's your source, Josie?" He was curious, nothing more.

"She had been on campus for about twenty-four hours

and some adviser stuck her in the wrong class. And of course you let her come in so you could spend the next hour humiliating her. Some academic point for the rest of the class, something about writing as a discipline."

"Yes, yes, of course. But how do you *know* this? I'm really quite fascinated how you've put this all together."

"Once I had you, Val, I knew where to look. I got the class list."

"From Records and Transcripts?"

"I found all the locals in that class and talked to them over the weekend. There were just a handful. One of them remembered it like it was yesterday. He was a friend of my mother's; he knew her from the bar. He said she never would have let anyone treat her like that at the bar, but she took it from you, and not a word of complaint, because she thought she was supposed to. She thought humiliation was part of a college education. And you just piled it on. He said you teased her when she said something about wanting to write stories for her little girl; you mocked her accent; you insulted her intelligence and all because someone else had made a mistake and put her in the wrong class."

"No, Josie. I insulted her because she was an ignorant slew! The woman's voice had all the charm of fingernails on a chalkboard."

"When the break came, she left and didn't come back. A few days later, you got pulled in on the carpet. You got your ass chewed out, and maybe your hand slapped. You thought she had turned you in, but it was the man I talked to who did it. He said he wished he'd kicked the shit out of you; maybe *that* would have done some good."

"What was the name, Josie? I want to know who it was."

"My mother fought her own fights, Val. If she had a quarrel with you, she'd have faced you with it. You were so damn sure of yourself you didn't even think someone else might have found your arrogance offensive."

A small, crooked smile. No shame, no regret.

"My guess is you decided to play one of your patented games and cause her some grief. Only later did you consider killing her. Is that about right?"

"I'm impressed, Josie. You're right, as it turns out. It was months before I decided to kill Miss Fortune. She was an afterthought, really."

This was all a great joke again. He seemed to have reclaimed his courage and was calculating Josie's powers, her willingness to cut him in half, and the proper moment to make his move. Josie could see that much in Valentine's eyes. He was a man who prided himself on waiting his chances, playing things close to the line. The twin triggers felt stiff and unyielding under Josie's grip suddenly, and Valentine seemed to know it too. His eyes had grown steadily duller with the thought of what he meant to do – at the proper time.

"Tell me, Josie," he said with a sudden false charm, the eyes no longer part of the smile, "when exactly did you know you were going to kill me? Do you remember the moment you decided to take blood?"

Josie felt herself giving way to his power. Her strength fading, her anger failing her. Was she afraid to take him off the trail and into the water? Or did she want to talk? She forced herself to look at the man. He killed out of no more compulsion than curiosity. He struck without anger; he struck for no reason at all. He picked his prey and stalked for the sport of it, stalked his prey for years, it seemed.

"Not really a precise moment, is it? Fantasies, then thoughts, then plans, and you never know, looking back, when you crossed the line. Isn't that about the way of it?"

"Not at all. I know why I'm doing this. I promised myself this after Bea. I knew it then. The moment I saw her, I swore you to hell."

Valentine's gaze brightened in a surprising complicity. "You know what it feels like now, don't you? That little tingle you feel, the certainty of murder? Nothing to equal it, is there? Knowing you mean to take blood! The ultimate game, Josie!"

"Tell me how it happened. I want to know how my mother died."

"Do you really want to know, Josie?" The eyes scolded her; he meant to say in his silence she wouldn't like the truth. It was a cocked, questioning look, as much warning as reluctance to confess.

"I know you hanged her; I want the rest."

Henry Valentine shrugged one shoulder, a man recalling a long-ago conquest. "We were in a cabin, not far from here, actually. It was night of course. I tied a leather thong around her neck. I ran it up over a rafter, ripped her gag off of her, then I pulled her up by her neck until she was actually in the air. After a few seconds of this, I cut her feet free and gave her a little three-legged-stool, just enough that she could settle part of one foot or the other on it if she really stretched, then I tied off the leather thong and I watched. I thought she couldn't last more than a few minutes, Josie. She was gasping and spitting, but she quite surprised me. She stood *for hours*. And the whole time, she wasted her air calling down God's own curses – a real Old Testament kind of girl when her blood was up. Oh quite beautiful at first to see such spirit. I have to confess I had very little to compare her against at the time, but later I saw so many beg and cry, so that I've often thought, "None like Miss Fortune, no sir, none at all." But it just went on and on, Josie! She was gasping and choking and *cursing* like an old prophet. I got tired of it, actually, so I gave her a little push. She swung around, pissing all over the floor, gasping, foaming at the mouth, then damned if she didn't get her foot back on that stool and call down God's curse again! Well, fuck it, I thought, and I kicked the stool out from under her and that was it. Your old *ma* took a good twenty minutes going, but she went!"

Valentine's story finished; he smiled at Josie. It was a

curiously quaint, old-man look. He knew the effect he'd had, and when she didn't pull the triggers, he turned and started into the creek. He went forward several steps before Josie followed him. The water was frigid, and soon Josie was into it over her hips. She carried the shotgun off her shoulder now. She thought the man would turn on her here, but he didn't. He moved out at a good pace, going with the current, now several feet in front of her, moving out of range rapidly. There were several heavy boulders to the right of the creek, and while it was possible just before the falls to get out of the water and climb out to a trail, it was far easier to come out of the water to the left, just after the rocky channel widened somewhat. Here there was a broad flat table of rock, maybe fifty by a hundred feet. The rock ran out beside the creek to the very precipice just alongside the falls. Immediately to the left was a huge crag of a rock, then the caves, one of which led down to the ledge just under the falls.

Valentine was nearly thirty feet beyond Josie when he came out of the water and started over the flat rock. If he followed beside the creek, he would go out to the shelf overlooking the canyon, but if he went toward the caves, as he seemed intent on doing now, he could have cover in a small group of rocks midway between the creek and the caves. If he had a gun, that would be his best play. As she watched him stepping more quickly, Josie slipped toward the edge of the creek, ducking in behind a rock ledge. Coming to cover, Valentine drew a small revolver from his sports jacket pocket, and spun down into a near-prone position, using the rocks as cover.

He pointed his revolver at her, and Josie slipped down entirely out of sight. At such a distance, her own gun, practically speaking, was useless. But that was okay. She had done her part. She had taken the man to the edge of the world.

At the Edge of the World

Jack Hazard watched Valentine turn off the trail's end and step into the water. They had stood there a long time, and he wasn't sure the whole thing might not end right there. But then he was in the water. Soon, he was out of Cyrus's view, but was now easily within Jack's range.

Cyrus had had his sights on the man along the creek and coming out of the woods; Blake and Jeremy from the covered bridge to the hilltop; Lincoln and Virgil had followed them from campus through town; and Louis had watched Josie take the man in the parking lot. But this was the tight spot. If Valentine had a gun, he might try her here. Jack didn't like holding a sight, so kept the gun off his shoulder and kept back in the shadows of the small cave he stood within. He didn't want to shoot Valentine; that was the last choice for all of them, but Josie had no cover where she stood, and if he even turned around, he knew he was going to have to pop the old boy. Pop him and bury him where no one would ever find him. And no one ever to know what he had done.

Louis had guessed Valentine knew the area. Once he decided that Josie meant to take him to the falls, Valentine would probably settle in his mind on the defile to make his move. "Either he fights there or he lets the current take him out a little," Louis had told them, "and suddenly he's out of range of Josie's gun without Josie realizing it. He'll play on your inexperience. He'll work your head and either turn on you or slip off a bit. We'll hope he runs. Otherwise Jack and Cyrus are going to have to shoot him." Josie did a good job coming into the water a little slow. She let Valentine pull out the distance between them gradually, so that when he came up out of the creek, she still had a shot if she needed to make it, and he knew it. Now he was up behind the rocks and going to see if he couldn't scare her into blowing off both charges of her mother's gun if he could. If he could do that, he wouldn't care to end it too quick; that was Josie's

427

read on it. The only danger was if he got pushed too far too fast and had to kill to save himself. That was what made this part so tricky. Jack watched patiently. When he pulled some kind of snubnose magnum out of his pocket, Jack set his rifle into a crevice and walked out unarmed toward the man's back.

This one's for Josie, he promised. His Josie, he meant.

Valentine was flattened down close against his rocks, and he held his revolver in one hand pointed up to the sky. Jack was nearly twenty feet behind him and came up softly, quickly. Within four strides he heard the man crowing.

"Josie, I'm afraid you've waited too long!"

Softly, never stopping his advance, Jack answered, "I been waiting twenty years. Is that too long?"

The old boy turned fast. His first shot came just as Jack rolled himself into a ball and somersaulted over the bare rock toward him, coming up face to face against him. Valentine didn't get a second shot off. Jack turned his gun wrist out, nearly snapping it off. Valentine yelled out with the pain, and the gun fell to the rock like a toy. Valentine was a big man, easily six-four, a hundred ninety-some pounds. He was strong, too. Jack felt that at once. He reached over with his free hand to twist Jack away and nearly did it. Jack bumped him once in the ribs, and listened to an animal grunt; then getting his feet under him, he came up with the fellow, taking his hand and thumb up under his wrist as he did. The old boy screeched now, and they started stepping out toward the edge of the world. He moved like a prancing stud on the lead, cussed like a sailor.

Josie came up to them, stepping out of the water and right behind them, making sure to stay off Cyrus's sights, in case Cy needed to make a shot. As Valentine wheeled back toward the creek, he managed to get ahead of Jack finally. The pressure on his wrist freed, he took Jack by his coat and lifted him off his feet. Valentine spun around and threw Jack out toward the ledge. Jack caught Valentine's sleeve as he

428

came down and so kept from skittering off. Then getting his feet placed, he used the man's own force to bring him in turn toward the canyon. Valentine reared up hard to stop himself. His brow went tight. The lips pressed into a long, thin line as they wrestled, and both men grappled for a better hold. When Jack tried to go under the man's arms, Valentine lifted him and spun him toward the precipice again. Jack's foot came down less than a foot from the lip of the canyon. He could feel cool air under him. Beside him the falls rushed out into space. He brought Valentine's arm and wrist around in a tight ball, so the man screamed out again. In the same motion, he pulled himself back in a dancer's pirouette and took Valentine over the edge. As Valentine's back came out over the canyon, he grabbed at Jack's sleeves. Jack slapped his hands away, pushing at the big man's frame. Again and again, Valentine tried to push through Jack's arms and get hold of him. He was determined to crouch down and push his way back to safety; Jack was just as determined to push him over. For a long moment, neither man gained an advantage. Finally Valentine caught Jack's wrist and pulled at him fiercely. Jack came with him too quickly, giving him no resistance at all, and Valentine's own weight tipped him back precariously. Jack put his free hand on Valentine's chest and pushed him the rest of the way. He felt the old boy go back, but he was hanging onto Jack's wrist, and now clutched Jack's coat sleeve with his other hand. It was a grip of desperation. Valentine was already leaning out too far. He was tilting toward his death and Jack Hazard was his only chance of coming back from the brink. The only problem with that was Jack had lost his balance as well.

They could both see straight down into the spewing water of the cataract that roared beside them and fell almost directly below their feet. They could see farther. They could see a thousand feet below to the rocks and creek. Valentine's eyes grew wide, panicked as he leaned out farther, taking Jack along. There was no avoiding it; they were both going over.

Valentine cried out a weird, infantile oath, and now he whimpered. He flung his head from side to side, staring down in to the abyss, the face of a man trapped and looking to die. His eyes watered, his lips quivered, then foamed; his grip on Jack nearly broke Jack's wrist. Jack shoved the man, and kicked his own feet up between Valentine's legs. The recoil kept him from falling too far into space, but it hardly saved him; he was going over. The moment he started to drop under Valentine, the big man let go of him. Jack hit the ledge with the back of his thighs and bounced out into the canyon – right between Valentine's spread legs.

Hooking his left arm around Valentine's right leg, he broke his momentum slightly and swung himself around to face the rock. He was already below the lip when he clawed into the crevices of rock. He slipped twice before he grabbed a solid knob of stone. His feet were still hanging over the canyon, and he kicked up quickly to find some purchase; he scrambled for a better hold, taking a thick vine that was nearly embedded in the rock and pulling himself up. As he did, he saw Valentine directly above him.

The old man was on one leg. He was leaning back almost flat, his arms flailing. As Valentine started to fall, Jack hugged himself tight against the face of the rock. He felt the man's boot strike his head, then he was gone. The scream started well below Jack's position. It was like a bellowing at first. It filled the canyon with its deep reverberations, then came a series of shrieks, sounding all the worse as they echoed back-up to the canyon's rim, echoing even after the fall had ended.

Josie screamed when she saw Jack, her echo picking up off Valentine's last. As he came over the edge and back toward safety, Jack felt the girl take his collar and pull him forward.

"I thought you were dead!" she cried.

She said something else; he didn't really hear the words. Hell, he'd thought he was dead too! For a moment Jack stepped away to be sure of his balance. He looked down to

430

see his fingers bleeding; he'd ripped up both hands, and it hurt. He had done that on the rocks. He looked up-creek and saw Cyrus who had come into the creek. The boy was grinning. The boy always had a grin.

"I thought you were dead, Jack. I thought you'd fallen." This from Josie.

Jack turned to her now. She was looking at him with real fear. He looked back now into the canyon. Some thirty feet straight below he saw the stone ledge he had walked as a boy long before anyone had thought to put up a railing. He looked beyond to the thousands of boulders and what looked to be rivulets of water around them. Directly below them, a tiny dark mass lay over a huge rock just to the side of the falls. It looked to be nothing more than a piece of cloth or some piece of refuse. The mist of the falls drifted over it, swallowing it whole.

Jack looked at Josie again to see how she was taking it. She was close by him and staring down at the mist. She looked scared; she looked like she might go in after the old boy, and Jack put his arm in front of her and nudged her back off the edge. She was shivering with cold, soaked, and crying, but the trance was broken. Jack looked for Cyrus. He was coming up out of the water and starting across the rock toward them. Jack put his other arm around Josie, trying to keep his blood off her. "You did good," he whispered into her ear. "We got him, Josie."

Her eyes still cast into the pit, she nodded dully and then she answered him, her voice crackling with phlegm, gasping some: "He said she cussed him to the end, Jack. She never begged."

Jack stared down into the canyon once more. Bitter and proud, he took the news stoically. "I believe it," he said.

431

The Visitation

In light of certain facts, the memorial service panned
this afternoon for Dr Henry Valentine has been
cancelled.

del.

So read the notice. *Certain facts!* Certain rumors would be
more precise, and Dick Ferrington knew their source. He
was furious, first with Josie Darling, then with Delbert
Meyers, and finally with the university itself.

When he called the VP of Academic Affairs, Rosy Elwood
told him that *the facts* had nothing to do with the police
investigations into charges that Henry Valentine was
somehow involved in a series of local murders. The cancellation of the memorial service, the good woman told him
loftily, was due to a scheduling conflict at the convocation
center. Ferrington didn't believe it, but he knew better than
to cross a VP. The university was moving quickly to distance
itself from scandal, and Henry Valentine's reputation as a
teacher was to be the sacrifice. Dick could throw himself on
the sacrificial fire or he could drop it for the time being and
make his paybacks later. He dropped it.

A memorial service was hardly necessary. He was certain
that the private visitation he had arranged for Val before the
body was shipped back to North Carolina would draw Val's
students. That was what counted; they were the people who
really loved the man. Val would have his hour of respect and
honor, the university willing or not.

Last Rites

When Josie arrived at Lues's Fairview Chapel with Cyrus
Hazard, she was mildly surprised that the place was empty
except for the campus minister and Dick Ferrington. She
nodded toward the back pew and Cy took a seat. Then

going forward past the two men, she came to the closed casket and stared down with a feeling of emptiness at the dark wood which held Val's shattered corpse. She longed to see the ruin of him, but it was a vengeance she was not allowed.

Fondly, she touched the casket, whispering to it, "Burn in hell, Valentine."

"Where have you been, Josie?"

It was Ferrington's voice, cold, calculating, bitter.

Josie turned, giving the man her full attention. "I needed a few days off, Dick, if you need to know."

"A lot of people have been looking for you. I'd say you have some questions to answer."

"I'd say I'm ready to answer them."

Ferrington's handsome face had a pinch of curiosity. "What does that mean?"

"I had Val figured out last Thursday evening when I saw him pictured with Nora Tolley in a Terre Haute newspaper, but there were still a couple of things that didn't quite make sense, so I kept looking around."

Ferrington's brow twisted itself into some kind of an attempt at confusion.

"I found a picture of you and Cathy at the Kappa Zeta sorority. When I saw you two standing next to Shelley Kruger, Anita Paget, and Melissa Bates, I was as certain of you as I had been of Val."

"I'm afraid I'm not following you, Josie."

"I started thinking about their murders, and I realized a man working alone was going to have trouble, a lot of trouble in some cases. I asked myself how one man could get a woman up in a tree and then drive a nail into her hand. I wanted to know how a man could suspend a woman over a ravine or out over a river. I wanted to know why someone would chase a woman through the woods and use two guns to shoot her. I started thinking about the coincidences around your wife's death, how the kids had been

433

taken up north before she was abducted, how you had been in Europe at the time. How everyone knew you had killed her, and no one knew how. I started thinking about my own troubles. A break-in while you were out of the country, a phone call while you were sitting with me in a bar. I started thinking about how easy it would have been for you to start up an old affair and how instead you turned on me. You needed some distance from me if you were going to kill me; a little open department warfare wasn't going to be a motive for murder; a love affair might have been.

"Then I remembered how both you and Val took me to my mother's bar, how you both said it was a good place to eat — with some kind of smirk. She had a sign over her bar that said that. Your own private little joke, I take it, and you thought it was a good joke, that you were giving me these clues and I'd never get it all in time. I started thinking about my mother, how if Val had crossed her, she wasn't going to get trapped by him. From everything I heard, she was the equal of any man. The man who caught her, I decided, had been a friend, maybe someone really close. And with someone threatening her, the way I was being threatened, a phone call to her while you were with her would have been enough to convince her you were okay — proof you were a good guy. Same trick you used on me. And I've got to tell you, I almost let it get by me."

"You're out of your mind, Josie."

"Then I remembered a certain woman found at the side of a road. This was a couple of months before my mother's murder, but suddenly I could see your signature all over it. Nothing special about her, I expect she was a prostitute one of you had kidnapped, except that she had obviously been in trouble when she ran out in front of a car. I checked into it with a phone call to a friend of mine. Neither her clothes nor the car were ever found, but there were footprints and

434

boot-prints in the woods. She had run out of the woods and into the path of an oncoming car.

"Someone had chased her; someone else was waiting and ran her down. It was always a two-man game, wasn't it, Dick? Part of the torture, the way you get close and find out how the torment is working, what they're thinking and feeling. Fear and trust: just like the woman one of you chased out of the woods; you always chased your victims right into a net, physically or psychologically. One of you a friend, the other menacing. I started looking for bodies in North Carolina. I figured if you liked your game so much, you wouldn't sit it out for the seven years you were away from Lues. While you were there, you'd want to have your fun. It wasn't long before I found a murder in the Chapel Hill area. Just so happens, it was the same year Valentine was there on his sabbatical leave. A mother and her fifteen-year-old daughter. Locals – hicks; they watched each other suffocating with plastic bags over their heads. Police were certain two men had been involved. I was certain which men."

Ferrington's eyes look past Josie briefly. He seemed to take Cyrus Hazard's measure then turn his attention back to Josie.

"Is that *boy* supposed to be some kind of bodyguard, Josie?"

"Why don't you touch me and find out?"

"He won't always be there, Josie."

"I think I've got it figured out now, but I have to tell you, it bothered me at first."

"What's that?"

The campus minister stepped toward them.

"Excuse me, Dick, I think I'm going to go on."

Ferrington looked at the minister as if he had betrayed him. Then he seemed to catch himself, his voice picking up the easy modulations of a man who never sweats.

"Sure, Duane. Thanks for coming."

"I thought some kids would come by," the minister offered by way of consolation, "but I guess this is it."

He looked at Josie and Cyrus Hazard, mistaking them for mourners.

"There are a lot of silly rumors on campus; kids don't know what to believe."

The minister had heard the rumors too and hesitated, then he nodded. It was a kindness to Ferrington that hardly included belief.

When he was gone, Ferrington looked murderously into Josie eyes. "Tell me what you figured out, Josie."

"I was trying to decide if Val started it all or if you did."

Ferrington smiled. It had about it neither confession nor denial. It looked to Josie to be the grin of a man beyond someone's reach.

"I know you were in Val's class, and you were both certain my mother had filed a complaint against Val, but I don't think that was what it was all about. Val said it was months before he thought about killing her, and I believe him. I think it was talk. Val had published a paper about matricide, the whole idea of moral freedom and the connection it has to the ritual murder of the mother or mother image. 'Matricide, or the killing of a prominent, powerful woman, whether lover or mother or ruler, is the great transgression, the sin against the holy spirit, as it were, precisely because it takes us outside the moral plane of humanity so that we can never re-enter the old order: and it is because of this that the old order dies away in all the mythic representations of a matricide: it is the beginning of all new and great enterprises . . .' Sound familiar?"

"You're a typical woman, Josìe. Ideas scare you."

"You're a typical man, Ferrington; you can't tell the difference between fact and your own fantasies."

Ferrington's jaw tightened.

"I think Valentine had said it, and that was the end of it as far as he was concerned, but then a certain golden boy reads the essay, and over a beer or two the two of you start talking about murder, a murder, any murder – all in the
436

abstract, of course, and suddenly you find yourselves at the *what if* stage. You talk about *doing* it, maybe about higher moral planes, both of you suddenly anxious to give a woman what you've always wanted to give her, but there's that *practical* consideration you both have: there's getting caught. There's prison. Then one of you decides two great minds working in tandem can do virtually anything with immunity. It's a game, after all. Damn the police, let's kill some bitch!"

Ferrington's eyes revealed a hint of satisfaction. "Proof, Josie. I haven't heard a single thing out of your mouth that is remotely like proof. If Valentine said anything, it won't stand as evidence. You can't prove I was involved in any of this."

"Just one question," Josie answered. "Nothing incriminating, just a curiosity."

"You mean you don't know everything, Josie?" Ferrington brought out the old laugh, the cocky arrogance that was simple habit with him.

"Did Cathy cuckold you, Dick? Is that why you killed her? Your little virgin go off and find someone else? Someone with a soul?"

"Not for long, Josie."

"Did you kill him too? Or do you just hurt women?"

"I'm an innocent man, Josie. I'll swear by God to it."

"You make my skin crawl. At least Henry Valentine had the guts to tell me the truth."

"You want the truth, Josie? I'll tell you the truth. Your mother was as easy to fuck as you were."

"Pray it's quick Ferrington."

Josie stared brightly into the man's confusion, then spun on her heel and started back up the aisle of the chapel toward Cyrus Hazard.

"Just what the hell does that mean, Josie?"

Josie stopped herself and faced the man one last time. "It means you crossed the wrong people."

Bitts and Pieces

Early Saturday morning, Josie drove out to Pauper Bluff in her VW to go fishing with the ex-sheriff of Lues County. She found Bitts waiting with a cup of coffee. When she had taken the cup and after they had talked some about the weather in the solemn way of good country people, Bitts cleared his throat. "I had a call from Jason Miller," he said. There was caution suddenly on both of their faces. "He got the coroner's ruling." Bitts hesitated, letting Josie ready herself. "They were consistent with his own findings."

"Meaning?"

"Meaning, officially, both Dick Ferrington and Henry Valentine committed suicide."

A moment of relief, then carefully, "I see."

Ferrington's car had been found near the mouth of Lues Creek Canyon the morning after Josie had spoken to him. A sheriff's deputy had tracked back into the canyon that afternoon and discovered Ferrington's body in a sink hole just before the falls.

"Jason's already talked with the prosecutor about it," Bitts continued. "Mr Scott seems satisfied with the findings, but he did ask where you were when both men died."

"Where I was?" Josie had talked to Scott the day before, and he hadn't seemed suspicious of her at all. She was genuinely surprised, nearly the picture of innocence.

"He knew you were in trouble. He thought you might have taken the law into your own hands. Plus, they got the campus minister swearing he saw you talking to Dick Ferrington in the chapel the night Ferrington killed himself."

"The night Dick Ferrington died, I went to a bar with Cy Hazard. We went right after we left the chapel. A place called Dion's. Cyrus and I got there at nine o'clock, and we stayed until closing. We made quite a scene, Two-Bit. People are sure to remember us."

"What about Valentine's death? Have you got an alibi for that?"

438

"I was at a family reunion."

"A family reunion?" Bitts was surprised, dubious. But it was the truth, after a fashion.

Josie thought to change the subject. "So has Detective Miller found anything to connect his two suicides to the murders of those women?"

"Valentine's gun, the one they found at Hazard Falls, was used in Bea Quincy's murder. The police are going through everything those two owned. They've already got quite a few of the threads connected. They'll tie it all up before they're finished. I take it Dr Valentine was a careful record-keeper."

"The families of the victims need to know," Josie answered. "They need to know it's finally over."

"They will," Bitts told her. "Jason will take care of it."

"I don't suppose he needs the rest, then."

"What are you talking about?" Bitts asked.

"What happened in the canyon the day my mother died."

"You've got a theory about that?"

"I've got it figured out, Two-Bit. I just don't want the police to have it."

"Did Ferrington tell you something?"

Josie shook her head. "No. It's just that from what we know, the rest falls into place, the only logical explanation."

"The police won't hear from me."

"To start with, the man in the woods was Dick Ferrington."

"Ferrington?"

"He and Valentine had taken my mother into the canyon the night before." Josie held up her hand to stop the old man's protest. "Just listen to me. All morning, no one discovered the body, and I expect that by two o'clock, both Val and Ferrington were afraid no one was going to. That's when Dick went out to take a look from the falls. He had to find out if it was possible to see the body from that distance. I don't know if he had been there and was leaving

439

or if he was just coming to the falls, but sometime before three o'clock Ferrington heard voices and went back into the woods to hide. That's when he saw Melody Mason. Maybe he thought she'd be their next victim; maybe it was something else, but I'm sure he followed the kids back down to the mouth of the canyon so he could find out where Cat lived. That was all he needed to arrange to meet her later, which he did in a matter of days. I don't know what he was thinking at the time, but obviously once things went the way they did and Cat was pregnant, and she was within a matter of weeks, he decided they ought to get married, and she agreed."

"And the move to North Carolina? Was that maybe so he could start over? Get his distance from Valentine?"

"I don't think so. You see, universities don't hire their own, not for tenure jobs. If Dick wanted to teach with Val at Lues State, he had to finish school elsewhere. He went to North Carolina, Val's old stomping ground."

"So you're saying Dick Ferrington was off chasing Cat Sommerville, leaving Henry Valentine inside the canyon to finish what the two of them started the night before?"

"No. That's not what I'm saying. There was no one inside the canyon after the kids left, not until Toby Crouch went in."

"Now wait a minute . . ."

"Patience. It will all make sense."

"I'm listening." Bitts was buying none of it, but he *was* listening.

"I started with Waldis's time of death and what you knew about the time of death. The thing that struck me was the fact that you were both uninvolved in any sort of conspiracy, both completely objective. At the same time, you were each convinced the other one was up to something. Waldis thought you were in a fight with Colt Fellows — some kind of political thing; you thought Waldis had been misled by

Colt and then wouldn't admit a mistake. Neither one of you ever considered the possibility that you could both be right."

"We couldn't both be right, Josie. Waldis said your mother died after six in the evening. I had witnesses see her body at three o'clock!"

"And then there's my theory, that the body was put in the canyon the night before."

With an odd, contemplative expression, "I have to tell you, Josie, I think even Doc Waldis and me could have agreed on that one: you're out of your mind!"

"But all three of us are right. Val and Ferrington took my mother's body to the falls sometime past midnight. Then at three the next afternoon, the kids saw her lying on the rock. At four, they stood within arm's length of her, all of them afraid to touch her. At 4:40, they called your dispatcher. You checked with Yeager, and he sent Toby Crouch in to find out if the call was a prank or legitimate. That puts Crouch at the mouth of the canyon at five o'clock, under the falls at 5:30."

"Both he and Yeager say it was later, that I messed up the times, then got my dispatcher to lie about the calls."

"Some of the kids Colt Fellows talked to went along with the different times, too," Josie answered. "Enough, anyway, that he got signed statements with falsified times. Colt also had two law enforcement officials on his side. Neither Yeager nor Crouch had any apparent motive for lying, so the time of death was pushed to after six o'clock. That's what Colt thought it was to start with, and once he knew Jack was in the police station in mid-afternoon, he forced things to fit. He probably thought he could twist Waldis's times enough, but when Waldis came in with his decision, it was better than he could have hoped. Yeager got what he wanted for playing along, which was to discredit you, and Toby Crouch got to be a policeman, but no one saw those as motives for their lying because by then Jack Hazard had struck his deal with Colt and the prosecutor and made his confession. Waldis

441

was satisfied he was right, and you were convinced everyone was lying – which was *almost* the truth. What no one ever realized was that Crouch had another reason for lying. He wanted time to pass between the sighting by the kids and his own entry into the canyon. It was the only way he could legitimately raise a specter of doubt about what happened to the corpse. He came out at seven, which meant he could have gone in as late as six o'clock if he had some good excuse for losing an hour. He probably had one, but when both Fellows and Yeager insisted he had gone into the canyon well after six, he didn't need to use it."

"So you think he was in the canyon for two hours?"

"I know he was. And under the falls for over an hour."

"I suppose it's possible, Josie, but even if the man in the woods was Ferrington and you proved without a shadow of a doubt that he was following Cat Sommerville, you still have Valentine to explain. What's to say he wasn't waiting in the rocks and just wanted to confuse things? That would be the man's style, wouldn't it? I mean he couldn't have done a better job if he had wanted! And the thing is, it makes sense that Valentine was there. He had just killed your mother, with Dick Ferrington as his lookout. When the kids came in, he could hide in the rocks and not be seen. Then step out and finish what he started."

"They hanged her the night before and took her into the canyon while it was still dark, Two-Bit."

"Josie, there are things that happen when life stops. You can't ignore the signs. I saw your mother's corpse. She couldn't have been dead more than five hours. Fact is, I didn't think – "

"You didn't think she had been dead much more than two hours. That's my guess."

"Well, I thought at the time, but see, I had the witnesses, Josie! They saw your mother's body five hours before I got to her! That's what I could never make Waldis understand!"

"You remember the bruise marks on her neck?"

442

"You know I do."

"Jim Burkeshire said that there were no bruises on the neck when he saw the body."

"But the others saw bruises, Josie! I asked every one of those kids. I remember, I thought they were lying about the condition of the body when they found it. I was furious about it because they'd already lied to me once, and I asked each one what they saw – every detail of it! I got all that in my notepad. I'll get it and show you!"

"Burkeshire didn't see any bruises, but one person did. I know that."

"That's what I'm saying," he answered. He was gruff, determined, not about to give Josie this one.

"Since you saw bruises and one of the kids said she saw bruises, you knew there were bruises."

"That's my point," he answered patiently. "People can miss something, but if *some* of the people see what you know is there, then it was there!"

"I'll bet every last cent I'm ever going to earn, Melody Mason was the one who told you there were bruises on the neck."

"Might have been. Might have been both her and that other girl, Susie Hill. I think it was, actually."

"Melody tells people whatever they want to hear, Two-Bit. Susie Hill wasn't much better."

"So the bruises came after the kids had gone? You're saying Toby Crouch was involved?"

"Crouch stumbled into an opportunity, Two-Bit. He saw a woman's naked body, and he saw that he was alone. No one would ever know if he did something; at least that's what he thought. The victim was dead. From this point of view, it was the perfect crime, because he wasn't going to be found out. But then in the middle of raping the corpse, he realized his mistake. And my mother wasn't just alive; she might have survived if that's all it was. I think she came to. I think she came out of her coma, and she looked at him and understood what was happening to her and who was doing it. Otherwise, Crouch would have felt safe enough to let her live. There wouldn't have been any reason to strangle her."

"My God in heaven, Josie. I never dreamed . . ."

"She had no strength, Two-Bit. She couldn't even resist, and it had to be over in a matter of a few seconds, but I'm certain that's how it happened. I doubt that Crouch even had time to think about what he was doing; I imagine it was just panic. The two of them looking at one another, and then his hands taking her . . ."

Bitts reflected quietly on this a long while. Both of them did, actually, and Josie waited for some objection, some rage, some denial, but Bitts saw that she was right. It was the only way things could have occurred. The only explanation for the lies that worked and the truths that got discarded.

"So why did he move the body, Josie? Did he intend that from the start?"

"I don't think so. Twenty years ago, they would have been able to match his blood type with the blood secretions in the semen – assuming he was what they call a secretor – but they couldn't have printed the DNA. All the blood would show was that Crouch had the same type of blood as the man who raped Josie Fortune's corpse, hardly enough to implicate him, and he knew it. Once he had strangled her, things were different. He was in trouble or thought he could be, and I suppose he was right. He couldn't imagine Colt Fellows and Cal Yeager were going to be so helpful. All he knew was that some kids had seen the body. He didn't know what they would say or what they might remember about its condition. For all he knew, they might have been excellent witnesses, so he had to do something radical. The best thing he could think of was to destroy all physical evidence of the rape. In the process, he mutilated the body so much that everyone was willing to believe the killer had been interrupted and then came back to eviscerate his victim. Crouch's

444

only other problem was to convince people he didn't enter the canyon until after six o'clock. That gave the killer a window of opportunity to return, the reasonable doubt he needed."

"But he passed the lie detector, Josie."

"From the start, he knew he could trick a polygraph."

"You know that?"

"I talked with a couple of criminology professors. They tell me it's routine for crim majors to spend some time with polygraphs in their advanced classes, and they tell me not everyone is proven to be a liar. There are inconclusive tests, and sometimes known lies can pass for the truth. A sociopath for instance can trick a polygraph on virtually any lie; or a multiple, even some psychotics are real good at cheating the machine. Since Crouch had experimented with them, he knew going in that he had nothing to fear from a lie detector, and might even profit by being 'persuaded' to take one. You never looked at him again after he passed the test, did you?"

"Well, you see, once Mr Couch passed that test, *I* was the one everyone thought was lying." Bitterness rolled over the old man's face like a summer thunderstorm.

"I think he might have even told Colt Fellows he could help him with the time of death – and make *you* look like you had some private agenda you were taking care of."

Bitts shook his head. One lie after another, the intricate conspiracies, the petty gains that different men had made by the death of Josie Fortune, the confusion of testimonies from the kids, the quarrel Bitts had had with Marcel Waldis and Don Scott, even the mystery of how the body had come into the canyon without anyone seeing the killer coming or going: all of it fell into place now, just as all of it had been obscured by the simple consequence of a pathetic human being's chance encounter with the scene of the crime.

"She made it through, Two-Bit. She survived those bastards. If it hadn't been for Crouch . . ."

What? How do you describe the childhood you didn't get

445

to live? How do you make sense of a woman surviving a murder only to be raped and killed by her rescuer? How do you undo twenty years of prison or tell a man he might have worked another ten or fifteen years in law enforcement if only one lone sociopath had not happened along *afterwards*. How do you call back all the dead who would not be dead, the string of victims that never would have been, if Josie Fortune had lived to point her finger?

Fishing

"You going to be all right?" Bitts asked her.

Josie knew she would never be "all right," never forget or forgive or see the world in quite the same way again, but she would make it; in the past few weeks, she had found out that much about herself.

"I'd be better," she answered finally, "if we could get the arrest warrant against Jack dropped."

"For the deaths of Colt Fellows and Toby Crouch?"

Josie nodded tiredly. Jack Hazard was still a fugitive from the law, and there seemed no way to save him from it. Crouch's involvement in her mother's death and his conspiracy with Colt Fellows would just be another motive for Jack to murder them.

"Jason can't move the prosecutor, Josie. He's tried. Don Scott won't admit his chief of police meant to execute a prisoner during a transfer. There was plenty of bad blood between Jack and Colt, but that gives Jack as much motive as it does Colt. As long as it's a stalemate, Scott means to get Jack arrested, indict him, and then let a jury decide what happened at Lues Creek Crossing."

"I talked with Scott briefly, then to several lawyers. Scott won't listen, but the lawyers all tell me Jack has a good chance of proving Colt meant to kill him, if he'll just turn himself in."

"I guess he would, especially with the new chief of police

446

ready to testify that the evidence points to Colt Fellows trying to execute his prisoner!"

Josie shook her head. "Jack won't come in. I talked to him about it, but he says he's where he wants to be. 'To hell with cops and lawyers' is the way he put it."

The man was as stubborn as a rock.

"Well, Josie, there's no arguing Jack out of the woods. If he wants to live that way, he's going to do it, and the good Lord help the man that means to pull him out. Maybe it's even for the best. Jack's never had any luck in a courtroom. Even stone-cold innocent, they put him away for nineteen years."

"I just wish . . ."

Josie stopped herself. She wanted to undo things, but wishing it so was never going to change the world.

"I'm not giving up on him," she said finally.

Bitts had no answer, and Josie sipped at her coffee, walking closer now to the kitchen's pot-belly stove. The wood crackled inside and a steady heat spread over her.

After a time, she announced almost sadly, "I'm going north next weekend to see my adoptive parents."

From behind her, Bitts asked, "You haven't been up to see them since you've been here?"

Josie shook her head, looking through the grates at the fire.

"The thing is, I'm afraid I'm going to break their hearts," she offered finally.

"Why is that?"

Josie turned to face the old man. "Because I'm going to change my name back to Fortune. I asked one of the lawyers I talked to to go ahead and start the process. *Josie Fortune* — the name my mother gave me."

"You doing this for Jack or for your mother?"

"I'm doing it because it's my name; it's who I am. I just didn't know that until I came back to Lues."

"I expect they'll understand."

"They wanted me to forget Lues. They thought . . ."

They had thought the worst of Josie Fortune and Jack Hazard. And maybe of her, as well. At least at first.

"They didn't know the truth, Josie. They were like the rest of us, wanting what was best for you and not knowing quite what that was."

"You think I can make them understand — after all these years?"

"Biggest fear they have is losing you. They'll come round. That I promise you."

Josie smiled suddenly. "So what do you say about teaching me to fish?"

At the river's edge, Bitts's dogs sniffing about their feet, Josie watched the old man toss his line out to a small pool beyond the reach of the current, then she walked downstream a way. Leaving the worm Two-Bit had given her off the hook, she tossed her own line in. The weighted line made a quiet plunk. There were small ripples emanating out from it. The river was alive with its own odors. The morning sun was still low in the sky, and the river danced with a thousand sundogs, shifting and scattering with every movement of the water.

Josie had thought she would leave once she had faced down her last nightmare. She had sat inside a pickup truck and watched Dick Ferrington taken into Valentine's van by the Hazards, believing she would resign the next morning and leave shortly thereafter — and no explanations for it. But the next morning, she had not written her resignation, nor on Friday. Now she was certain she wouldn't.

"Are they going to fire you for missing your classes this past week, professor?"

Josie pulled herself from her reveries and looked back toward Bitts. Annie had asked her almost the same thing when she had called her last night, and if she was coming back to Boston right away or in January.

Josie told Bitts what she had told Annie: "I've got a

448

contract until May. I expect they'll let me finish that up, at least."

"Then what?"

The same question Annie had wanted her to answer. And Jack Hazard, too.

"Then, we'll see."

Josie looked back to the river. In the distance a huge white barge beat its way north against the current. On the Kentucky shoreline, a plume of smoke rose up steadily out of the golden leaves of the forest. Bitts seemed to screw down his concentration and play out his fishing line like a man intent on catching a fish, but Josie was sure she saw a deep and abiding satisfaction in the fierce lines of the old man's frown.

In this novel, Henry Miller is purposefully misquoted, though the spirit of the remark was inspired from a phrase in *The Tropic of Cancer*. The reader of *Ulysses* is likely to hear the occasional echo of phrases from that book given without credit. There is finally the matter of James Joyce's juggernaut riddle, *the word known to all men*, which Josie has answered. A puzzle for over seventy years, the riddle has baffled Joyceans no end. A recent publication in *Notes on Modern Irish Fiction*, by M. L. Jockers of Southern Illinois University, Carbondale, however, has presented what I believe is convincing proof that Joyce meant the answer to be found in the infant's primal cry of *maaaaa* at its birth: a sound that in every language has the meaning of *mother*.

C.S.S.

WILLIAM DIEHL

Show of Evil

Lawyer Martin Vail has never lost a case – now he must catch a psychotic killer, or he'll lose his life.

When Linda Balfour, a young mother, is found butchered in small-town southern Illinois, a coded inscription stamped in blood on the back of her head brands her mutilated body.

For Chief Prosecutor Martin Vail, the bloody insignia drags up memories he'd like to forget – memories of Bishop Rushman, slashed and dismembered ten years ago by an altar boy, Aaron Stampler.

But if Stampler's locked away, he can't have murdered Linda. With his career – and even his life – on the line, Vail needs some answers fast before the killer signs someone else's life away.

DAVID RALPH MARTIN

I'm Coming to Get You

Community policing was never meant to be like this.

Two rapes and a dead body in the space of six hours, racial tension exploding into an inner-city drugs war, his job on the line, his marriage out the window and a dumb straight kid like DC Cromer in tow – not just the average Saturday night for Detective Sergeant Vic Hallam. And it looks like it's going to get worse.

Then he meets Ellie – a 26-year-old nurse still bleeding from a sadistic brutal rape. And when things start getting personal, duty turns to revenge. Because Vic can't play by the rules. He hates her attacker as much as the bastard who's now screwing his wife. And whatever happens he's going to bring him down.

And somewhere out there's a maniac called Frank. Good-looking, women-hating, sex-obsessed. And with Ellie's life on the line, the one thing on Vic's mind is: I'M COMING TO GET YOU.

Crackling with tension, brutal and authentic, *I'm Coming to Get You* catapults the British crime thriller into unsettling new territory.

LIONEL DAVIDSON

A Long Way to Shiloh

Winner of the Gold Dagger Award
BEST THRILLER OF THE YEAR

Treasure priceless beyond dreams. The Menorah: seven-branched lamp, true symbol of Judaism – lost for two thousand years.

But now located again – if a Dead Sea scroll has been understood. For the Israelis, no sacrifice is too great to win back this sacred relic. But certain neighbours have different ideas.

Caspar Laing, brilliant young professor of Semitics, with a penchant for some sexy extra-curricular activities, is brought to Israel. His mission: crack a 2000-year-old code and find a piece of the Temple. His problem – staying alive long enough to do so . . .

'Brilliantly entertaining'
Sunday Express

'A very superior thriller indeed'
Daily Mail

'First-class'
Sunday Times

A Selected List of Thrillers available from Mandarin

While every effort is made to keep prices low, it is sometimes necessary to increase prices at short notice. Mandarin Paperbacks reserves the right to show new retail prices on covers which may differ from those previously advertised in the text or elsewhere.

The prices shown below were correct at the time of going to press.

☐ 7493 1972 0	**The Cruelty of Morning**	Hilary Bonner	£4.99
☐ 7493 1528 8	**The Minstrel Boy**	Richard Crawford	£5.99
☐ 7493 1713 2	**Kolymsky Heights**	Lionel Davidson	£5.99
☐ 7493 3665 X	**Primal Fear**	William Diehl	£5.99
☐ 7493 2062 1	**Show of Evil**	William Diehl	£5.99
☐ 7493 1749 3	**Mean High Tide**	James Hall	£4.99
☐ 7493 2112 1	**Gone Wild**	James Hall	£5.99
☐ 7493 0054 X	**The Silence of the Lambs**	Thomas Harris	£5.99
☐ 7493 1400 1	**Carriers**	Patrick Lynch	£5.99
☐ 7493 1964 X	**I'm Coming to Get You**	David Martin	£5.99
☐ 7493 1905 4	**Free to Trade**	Michael Ridpath	£5.99
☐ 7493 1968 2	**The Tick Tock Man**	Terence Strong	£4.99
☐ 7493 2182 2	**The Mortgage**	Sabin Willett	£5.99

All these books are available at your bookshop or newsagent, or can be ordered direct from the address below. Just tick the titles you want and fill in the form below.

Cash Sales Department, PO Box 5, Rushden, Northants NN10 6YX.
Fax: 01933 414047 : Phone: 01933 414000.

Please send cheque, payable to 'Reed Book Services Ltd.', or postal order for purchase price quoted and allow the following for postage and packing:

£1.00 for the first book, 50p for the second; **FREE POSTAGE AND PACKING FOR THREE BOOKS OR MORE PER ORDER.**

NAME (Block letters) ....

ADDRESS ....

....

☐ I enclose my remittance for ....

☐ I wish to pay by Access/Visa Card Number ⬚⬚⬚⬚⬚⬚⬚⬚⬚⬚⬚⬚⬚⬚⬚⬚

Expiry Date ⬚⬚⬚⬚

Signature ....

Please quote our reference: MAND